Liberty's RUN 3

A Time To KALE

WALTER G. ESSELMAN

DARK MYTH

www.darkmythpublications.com

Dark Myth Publications, a division of
The JayZoMon Dark Myth Company, LLC.
145 S Glenoaks Blvd. Unit #3149 Burbank, CA 91502

ISBN: 979-8-9906083-6-8

First Printing November 2024

10 9 8 7 6 5 4 3 2 1

Dedications

Dedicated to my wonderful cousin, Christine Russell, who has been so supportive of my work!
Thank You!

Forward

Still ain't doing these things...

DISCLAIMERS

Please blame me!
I made some stylistic choices with spelling, capitalization, and grammar (ooh, that almost makes me sound like a real writer. Grin!).
So, if anything looks odd, it's totally on me, and *not* the Editor, Steph, 'cause she's awesome.

Love,
~ Walter

Dramatis kinda Persona

Residents of the ship, The Wolf Pack:
- Liberty *"Mija"* Schonhauer
- Uncle Danny Ramirez
- Colin "Cobayo" Boseman
- Dr. Miles "Tagg" McTaggert
- Tessy Ramirez (Danny's niece)
- Brent Smalls, the Navy mechanic.
- Rakduson – an alien-bird

Residents of the Aircraft Carrier Teddy Roosevelt:
- Command
- Antony Cirilo - Rear Admiral
- Crozier - Captain of the *Roosevelt*

Captain Singh's Team
- Captain Deep Singh
- Staff Sergeant Victoria Ruiz
- Sergeant Bath
- Lieutenant Dr. Aaron Washington
- Private Frankline
- Private Jules Cottons – Rookie
- Private Biggs – Rookie
- Private Nguyen - Rookie

Scientists
- Dr. Milton
- Fred

Doctors
- Candleross, SMO Senior Medical Officer
- Radha Patel
- Karrass
- Rodriguez

HairArtiste
- Renoir

Religious Leaders
- Rabbi Spellman
- Father Mark
- Buddhist Priest Teresa

Others
- Farmers
- Jed
- Chloe

Senator
- Butterfett

Captain Singh's Daughter
- Harita

Heaven
- "Abuela" Diana Rivera (Danny's grandmother)
- God

Liberty's Run 3

A Time To Kale

Chapter One

LIBERTY FROZE INSTANTLY.

The librarian-turned-sniper began to move slowly—Carefully!

She didn't dare make a noise. Not yet.

Crouched on the hood of a car, she got off with precise movements and crept towards an alley. Her breath sounded super-loud, so she slowed it down. Taking a deep breath for 4 seconds, she held it and counted to 7. Then she let it out, counting to 8. This forced herself to breathe normally.

The buzzing noise was still a little ways off.

The alley was not that dirty. There was a big green dumpster right near the mouth. This long into the zombie outbreak, the garbage didn't stink anymore, for which she was extremely grateful.

However, there was a zom there; dressed in a fast-food restaurant shirt, which had a Chimichanga on it and urged her to 'Take A Bite'. With jerky movements, the creature turned towards her.

The buzzing was closing fast. She didn't have time to deal with the zom properly.

'Sorry', she said without a sound.

Lashing out with the butt of her rifle, the Librarian hit it right between the eyes. It fell back hitting the ground hard.

Outside the alley, a voice called out. *"Hun kulong."*

Despite her complete discomfort, she knew that there was no time for subtlety. She drove the butt of her rifle down once again, slamming it against the side of the creature's knee.

Something gave a wet pop, and Liberty felt terrible.

The Librarian turned towards the mouth of the alley. On the other side of the street was the open door, into an abandoned pharmacy. She tapped the earpiece.

"Silent running." she whispered.

"*Sí*," came a worried voice through her ear.

The zom she had injured tried to get up, but its knee wouldn't work.

"Ur-ungh!" exclaimed the zom; though not out of pain, but just confusion.

It thrashed around a bit, but its right knee wouldn't cooperate.

Bursting into the alley, two creatures stopped and looked

around. They looked like birds; if the Earth birds were around five feet tall and liked to stomp their prey to death.

The zom flopped like a fish on dry land. Turning onto its stomach, it started to crawl towards Liberty.

Carefully, the Librarian began to back up to the side of the green dumpster.

One of the birds shot forward, drawn by the zom's motion.

The bird had a rust-colored tuft on his head, and there was a definite 'He'-ness about the bird. He stopped just over the thrashing zom.

Out of the back of the large bird's cranium was a device, as if it had been hastily shoved into his head.

Liberty's butt reached the green dumpster. She should have been safe there. Still, trying not to breathe, she quickly climbed up on top of the dumpster. Sweat stained her beret.

The bird made to sniff at the zom.

Suddenly jumping sideways, the bird snapped, right where Liberty's belly had just been.

On top of the dumpster, the Librarian huddled, but not for long. She trained her Steyr sniper rifle on the bird.

Her thoughts boiled.

Liberty did not want to shoot. Really, really did not want to shoot. It wasn't even that she'd have to shoot the other one as well. It just seemed so wasteful. Her finger lay across the trigger though.

'These birds are not the enemy', she reminded herself silently. 'They were dropped by the same aliens that created the zombie virus. They are just as much a victim as that zom.'

Through the open door of the pharmacy, Liberty could not see Uncle Danny, but she knew he was there. He would shoot, if needed. But, after rescuing one of these alien-birds, Rakduson, he would feel even worse than her, spilling their blood.

"*Yi,*" cried the other bird grumpily. She had a lime tuft on her head.

The bird with the rust tuft whipped his head around.

"*Hun!*" growled Rust Tuft.

Liberty's heart leapt. Rakduson had been teaching them her language. '*Hun*' meant 'What?'.

Lime Tuft started to speak swiftly though. Way too fast for her to follow. She wondered if Uncle Danny would know. Her Kids, whom she had adopted, would probably be able to tell her, but—Thankfully!—they were safe on the boat.

"*Klas du ren!*" snarled Rust.

"*REISS!*" snapped Lime, with a literal snap of her beak.

Kicking out, Rust hit the dumpster, and Liberty felt her teeth rattle. With a disgruntled noise, the alien-bird turned and stalked out of the alley, like a child in trouble. Lime stood facing the oncoming bird with her beak pointed down, as if it were a shield. She seemed ready to deflect any attack.

Rust slowed and then came to a stop. A little reluctantly, he lifted his beak in the air. Walking carefully towards Lime, he stopped. Liberty was trying to make sense of it when Lime jerked her beak towards the street.

Lowering his beak, Rust walked back onto the street and was soon followed by Lime.

"*Mija?*" came a soft voice in her earpiece.

"Wait," she replied with a whisper.

Uncle Danny didn't reply.

Liberty waited.

The Lime tufted bird dropped from above into the alley.

The Librarian nearly cried out in surprise.

The zom was still thrashing about.

Suddenly, Lime violently stomped down on it, and it stilled. The alien-bird finally moved, and with an angry noise, left the alley.

Liberty did not know how long she sat on the dumpster. It was probably only 5 minutes tops, but it felt like a hundred years. Keeping her breathing level, she distracted herself by trying to think of what to cook for dinner. But then, happily, she remembered that it was the kids turn to cook.

Her stomach growled, and she glared at it. "Shhh."

"They're gone," said Uncle Danny over her earpiece.

Liberty nodded, even though he couldn't see it.

In the doorway to the pharmacy a Big Mexican man appeared. Shotgun ready, Uncle Danny came out, looking this way and that.

Climbing off the dumpster, Liberty noticed the stomped zom. She had to swiftly look away or lose her breakfast.

'Poor thing' she thought.

Walking out onto the street, Liberty reached Uncle Danny with his barrel chest and handlebar mustache.

The Big Mexican inspected her intently.

"I'm okay," assured the Librarian.

Uncle Danny smiled with relief.

"¡Órale!" His best friend was okay. All was good with the world.

The Alien-birds had gone South.

Liberty pointed North. "I say...we go that way."

"Sí, sí Mija," said Danny with mock annoyance. "If you insist."

Amused, Liberty and Uncle Danny set out. On the street, as normal, zombies congregated in knots of 8 or so. *Dos amigos* easily dodged between the zoms.

"The pharmacy?" asked Liberty.

"Empty," said Uncle Danny with a shake of his head.

"Another one?" hissed Liberty with disbelief. "That's so weird."

"The place got shot up pretty good," said Uncle Danny. "Like Rambo went through there." He made a dissatisfied noise. "Didn't look like they hit much though. Spray-and-Pray."

"You *disapprove?*" asked Liberty.

The Big Mexican shrugged and began to mutter in Spanish, but then he stopped.

Liberty smirked. "Do *You* want to give them a stern

talking to?"

Uncle Danny gave her a pinched Look. "*¿Neta?* You're making fun of me."

With a light, breezy voice, she chirped. "A little teasing. Pequeño."

Rolling his eyes, Danny gave a small smile. "*¡Órale!* Really though, it kinda worries me. Having people like that around."

Liberty's face sobered. "I know. But at least everyone is safe on the…" She whipped towards the Big Mexican. "Mountain Dew!"

"*¡Hijole!*" moaned Danny in annoyance. "I walked right by it, planning to circle back."

They turned around, and dodged around the slow zoms once more, who looked pretty confused. Shortly, they returned to move back around the poor creatures for the last time.

Dos Amigos backpacks were now full.

"I can't believe they shot up the book section," said Liberty angrily.

"I don't think *los mensos* were aiming," said Danny sympathetically. "At least, not much."

"*Qué? Mensos?*" asked Liberty, who was casually learning Mexican Spanish.

"*Idiota*," explained Danny.

"Sí. Cool. Well, at least there were a couple books in the pharmacy," said Liberty.

"True! That's something at…," started Uncle Danny.

Then he said quickly. "*Oye!* If you want books, we could go back to the library that you worked at. It wouldn't be too…". However, he saw the look of horror on her face.

"I…," began the Librarian. But she couldn't find the words.

Swiftly, Uncle Danny said. "It's okay. You don't…"

"No," replied Liberty quickly. She took a deep breath. "I…I'm just not sure that I can go back. Especially if my former co-workers are…" She shook her head. "I really liked the bunch I worked with; like MaryMary and her funny socks. I don't want to be the one who…well if I didn't have to."

Before Uncle Danny could console her, a shout came from up ahead.

Dos Amigos tried to quicken their steps. But, they didn't dare go too quickly, lest the alien-birds noticed them.

"I said, 'Identify Yourself'," demanded an angry voice.

"Are you guys soldiers too?" asked a familiar voice from up ahead.

Liberty and Uncle Danny looked at one another.

"Frankline must be done checking North," said Liberty with a lowered voice.

"Put your Goddamn hands up!" cried the angry voice.

"Hey! Who're you with? We didn't think that there was anyone left on the Coast," called out Private Frankline. He was on the cross-street ahead, around the corner.

"I'm asking the questions here," replied Angry Voice.

"Whoever that is, they're making a real scene," said

Uncle Danny, and he looked worriedly at the sky.

"Yeah. Not smart," said Liberty, nodding her chin up in agreement. She gestured to an abandoned Ford Escort at the intersection.

Uncle Danny nodded. "I'll try and get closer."

Dancing around a zom in golf clothes, Liberty wondered what it was doing in the middle of the City of Angels. Dragging her focus back, she swiftly climbed up on top of the Ford. Staying low, the Librarian aimed her Steyr Sniper Rifle down the way.

There were two men in what looked like regular Army uniforms with their rifles trained on Private Frankline. The Private, who should have been in college, had put his hands up.

"Hey man," smirked Frankline. "We're all on the same team."

"One last warning!" cried Angry Voice. "Identify yourself!"

Liberty zeroed in on soldiers, ready to fire, but she hoped she didn't have to.

"Private Frankline, U.S. Navy," replied the young man, now a little testily.

The other man in uniform scoffed. "Navy! Shoulda known."

Frankline added quickly. "Well, I joined the Army, but then the Captain got sick of all the squabbling between Branches, so he jus' went 'We're All Navy Now', 'cause none of us were Navy soldiers to begin with. An' you might not want to make too much noise."

"Those dumb birds only hunt by movement," said Angry Voice. "What'd you take us for?"

"Well, we captured…or, I guess you could say, saved one of those birds," said Frankline. "Her name's Rak, an' she said…"

"You're in cahoots with the birds?" demanded Angry Voice.

"No, no," said Frankline. "Uncle Danny saved one of the birds that was injured. It was him that explained that the birds aren't dumb. So, I'm jus' saying that we might want…"

In Liberty's scope, a mass of feathers dropped right on top of Angry Voice. She glanced up. As Angry Voice fell out of sight—squealing— the Other Soldier turned his rifle.

Lime Tuft lashed out with her beak and opened up the Other Soldier's neck.

Unable to watch, Liberty looked down.

Danny was already returning with Private Frankline. The three hit asphalt and moved slowly, carefully, away.

When they were out of sight, Uncle Danny looked at Frankline and whispered. "¡Aquas! New *amigos*? I'm not so sure about your taste in friends."

"Hey! I don't know what was up with those guys," said Frankline, quickly, defensively. But he kept his voice soft.

Liberty put a gentle hand on the Private's arm. "It's okay. He's teasing."

Frankline still looked at Uncle Danny, unsure of what was going on.

The Librarian continued. "Can you tell us what

10

happened? Please."

"Oh, sure," said the Private. "I mean, there's not much to say. I went North three blocks, but didn't see any pharmacies, so I came back and while I was waiting, those guys came up thinking they were hot shi..." He blanched and quickly stammered. "I mean, 'Tough guys' ma'am."

Uncle Danny smirked but stayed his tongue.

"And they didn't say who they wer...," started Liberty. "Wait! I guess you were asking that."

"Yeah," shrugged Frankline. "Kinda weird."

"They could've been *loco*," shrugged Uncle Danny kindly.

"I was thinking at first that they were some Gravy Seals militiamen-types," shrugged Frankline. "But they looked trained. But the guy that was shouting only had a patch for the Army's 101st Airborne Division. Not even a name."

Liberty sighed with a heavy voice. "We might have a new player in town."

"It's gonna be okay, *Mija*," said Uncle Danny encouragingly.

Smiling, Liberty looked up. "*Gracias, mi amiga.*"

Uncle Danny cleared his throat meaningfully.

The Librarian blinked and reviewed her words. "Oh Wait! That's right. Because you're a guy, it's *amigo*."

"And I only mentioned it because I don't want the kids learning it wrong," said Uncle Danny—almost apologetically—referring to his biological niece and adopted nephew. "If it were only us, I wouldn't care."

11

"NoNoNo," said Liberty. "It's okay. I want to learn it right the first time."

Frankline asked with a waver. "Um. So, are we headed back?"

Liberty automatically looked at the Big Mexican, but then to the Private.

"That was the plan," she said cautiously. "We gotta be home by dinner."

"Oh," said Frankline.

"*¿Mande?*" asked Uncle Danny. "What's the matter?"

"Well.....," started Frankline. "I don't want to put you out."

"Talk to us," said Liberty.

"Well, I had a crazy thought," said Frankline. "When we're riding around in the tank, the Captain has a strict rule, 'We Don't Stop At Any Stores'."

Liberty shrugged. "Guess that makes sense."

"Well, there's a place nearby that might have something to protect against zom bites...maybe," said Frankline.

After a Quick Look at each other, Liberty and Uncle Danny nodded.

"If it's on the way," smiled Liberty. "Where to?"

Frankline's eyes grew wide. "Oh! Really? Cool. It's just this way."

The Private led them through the streets of the City of Angels. Here and there, nature was trying to reclaim what it could.

"Looks like plants are starting to take back over the

City," said Liberty softly.

"I didn't think that there was enough dirt left," nodded Uncle Danny, when he suddenly stiffened and looked around. He hissed.

"Hide!"

Liberty didn't say a word, she took Frankline's arm and led him into a small alley between some stores.

"Um...," began Frankline.

"Shhhh," replied the Librarian immediately.

The Private gulped as the three slipped down an alley. It was so narrow that Danny had to turn sideways to accommodate his wide shoulders.

Liberty heard the flapping, and they all froze. With only a few quick hand gestures, she and Uncle Danny were covering the way into and out of the alley respectfully. Unsure of what to do, Frankline aimed his M4 Carbine at the strip of blue sky above them. His heart was pounding in his throat.

Frankline almost fired when something shot overheard. It looked like one of the birds. But then, he noticed several alien-birds out on the street. They looked like they were on patrol. Uncle Danny had that part covered, so the Private forced himself to look back up.

Not a moment later, one of the alien-birds looked right over the edge. The buzzing in the back of their head was loud, and the bird had a crazed look. Then it ducked its head back and disappeared.

"Urng," came a soft voice.

Down Liberty's part of the alley, there was a small patch

13

of green, an enclosed space. Out of that came a zom in a tattered "Grateful Dead" t-shirt. It immediately saw them and began to stagger forward the short distance.

Above, Liberty could hear scrabbling about on the rooftops.

"Oh, swearword," bit off the Librarian quietly.

Liberty pulled out her Glock with its suppressor. The sidearm did not come quickly.

The zom was almost on her.

The gun came free of its holster, and Liberty leveled it right between the zom's milky blue eyes.

The creature suddenly came to an abrupt halt.

Brow furrowed; Liberty now noticed the metal collar around its neck. The chain attached to it rattled a little, but softly.

Still, there was a suspicious silence above her.

A second later, the bird with the Lime tuft leaned over the edge of the roof to look down.

"*Garak somme*," muttered the alien-bird.

The Librarian saw a droplet of blood forming on the tip of the beak, right over her. She wanted to move, but didn't dare.

The blood dropped, and Liberty almost flinched hard.

But thankfully the blood missed Liberty.

Slowly, she pointed her Glock towards the bird, but it suddenly pulled away and disappeared. She let out a slow breath and looked around.

Uncle Danny glanced back, saw that she was okay, and

then turned forward with a small smile.

Shortly, the birds moved on.

"That was close," whispered Uncle Danny.

"*¡Mierda!*" said Liberty softly.

Brow furrowed; Uncle Danny looked back. "Hey, who taught you such language." And the two had a little laugh, which relieved some of their stress.

Liberty was going to turn to return to the street when she stiffened.

"Oh no no. That's not good."

The Librarian looked deeper into the alley. The sun lit up a little patch of green behind the chained zom. Holstering her handgun, she used the butt of her sniper rifle to push the chained zom back.

"*¿Mande?*" asked Uncle Danny softly.

The zom, not having much coordination, tripped as it tried to walk backwards. The moment it fell backwards onto a patch of grass, Liberty jumped forward. She didn't step on the zom— too dangerous— but instead stomped on its chain. As much as it tried, the zom couldn't seem to get up. Finally, it gave up and moaned sadly.

"Why didn't you just shoot it?" hissed Frankline with surprise.

Liberty just shrugged. "It wasn't hurting anyone."

"Still, we better be careful," said Uncle Danny wearily.

"*Sí,*" agreed Liberty, but then she pointed to the plants in a small, open space behind some buildings. They had lots of tiny leaves and what looked like a white sprinkle

15

covering it. "I'm more worried about that. Is that alien?" Her tone rose with worry. "If they're starting to plant stuff. Terraform the planet..."

Uncle Danny was staring at the strange plant. "¿Neta? I don't..."

Out of Frankline, a little laugh burst out. "That's funny."

Liberty looked at him in confusion.

Suddenly anxious, the Private's eyes widened. "Oh! You weren't joking. Sorry!"

Some of the tension left Liberty's shoulders.

"It's not alien, is it?" she grimaced with embarrassment.

"Um. No, sorry" said Frankline softly.

"¡Neta! It certainly looks weird," said Uncle Danny. "What is it?"

"Um, it's weed," said Frankline, but both looked at him, puzzled. "It's marijuana."

Liberty gave a little laugh. "Oh Crud! I'm so embarrassed."

The Private shrugged. "I don't think you should be. I only know it because my uncle grew it out behind his house."

Uncle Danny just looked at Frankline with disapproval.

"Hey, we were just kids," said Frankline.

"You're not that old," said Uncle Danny.

Frankline's head hunched.

"It's okay," said Liberty to the Private. "I mean, it's legal here in California, right? Or, at least what's left of it."

"Still." And Uncle Danny's frown was a weapon all in itself. Displeased, he looked down at the pinned zom. "What are we to do with this zom?"

With a little sigh, Liberty began to draw her silenced Glock.

"NO!" cried a voice that made them all jump.

The back door to a store suddenly whipped open and hit the wall beside it with a clang.

"Please!! Don't hurt Bob!!!" cried a young woman. Her hands were outstretched, and her eyes were fearful, but defiant.

Before anyone could say anything, someone grabbed the back of the girl's shirt and pulled her back in.

"What'd you think you're doing?" demanded an older man's voice.

From the darkened hallway came a muffled argument.

Bits floated out.

"They were gonna kill Bob," hissed the young woman.

"But he wouldn't want You to get killed trying to save 'em," replied the older voice. "Especially now!"

Just as Liberty caught Uncle Danny's eye, an older man came to the doorway.

"Ummmmm, Sorry. Please don't be mad at her," said the older man. While still hiding the majority of himself, he put his empty hands through the door. "An' Please don't kill Bob."

"Bob?" asked Liberty, feeling a little confused.

"An' Please Don't kill us too, for that matter," said the

older man.

"What?" asked Liberty in alarm.

Frankline cleared his throat and lowered his M4 rifle, followed by the others. "It's okay Sir. We don't mean you no harm."

"Oh! I'm sorry," said Liberty. "We're a bit on edge."

"¡Órale! What with those big birds trying to eat us," added Uncle Danny with a tired smile.

"The Birds!" said the older man as he stepped further through the door. "Wait!! You've seen them too!"

Liberty nodded. "Oh yes. They're definitely real...if that's what you mean..."

The older man laughed heartily. "I thought they were hallucinations, so I was just trying to ignore them." He said more seriously. "Never talk to hallucinations. You don't want to go down That rabbit hole."

"I tol' you that they were real," came the girl's voice with an annoyed huff behind him.

"Oh! I guess you did," admitted the man.

"Well, yes, they're really out there," said Liberty.

"And they're not friendly either," said Uncle Danny. "Well, most of them."

The older man chuckled. "I believe it. But, where're my manners— *Mama would've given me a sharp word right now*— My name is Jed." He gestured behind himself. "And that's Chloe, who I'm pretty sure is real too."

"And underpaid," came Chloe's voice from behind.

Jed smiled at Liberty. "My new cashier. Not that there's

18

been much business lately."

Liberty introduced them and continued. "Sorry to bother you. I didn't know what these plants were."

"Once everything fell," said the older man, Jed, happily. "I figured I wanted to grow some outside too. Pot's always a little better, coming from direct sunlight. But maybe that's just me."

Liberty saw Uncle Danny's mouth pinch, but he kept quiet.

Jed looked down at that pinned zombie and propped the door open. He went to a small machine attached to the chain and turned it on. The device chugged and started to pull on the chain.

"You can step off his chain now," said the older man.

Stepping swiftly away from the zom, Liberty and the others watched as the zom got up, but he was also being led back to the machine.

"That's Bob," said Jed, jerking a thumb at the zom. "Best worker I ever had."

"Hey!" cried Chloe.

"But you keep 'em chained up?" asked Frankline, but then he winced. "Sorry, that was rude."

"It's okay," said Jed pleasantly. "I guess it does look weird, now that I think of it. But that was all Bob's idea, after he got bitten. Actually, he put the collar on, towards the end."

"Sorry," said Liberty. She wanted to give him a hug, but didn't know him that well.

Jed shrugged. "He figured this might keep the garden

19

free of unwanted visitors." He chuckled a little sadly.

Liberty noticed the sun. "Oh! I'm sorry, we've got to get going soon. My kids are waiting on me."

"And we still have to make a stop," said Frankline. "If that's still possible!"

"Shouldn't be a problem," assured Liberty to the Private.

"Well, you gotta get back to the lil buds," said Jed. "That's important."

Straightening, Liberty asked. "Buds? Do you mean children?"

Jed looked at her in confusion.

It was Chloe that called out. "Buds are the petalless flowers of the plant. Not kids!"

Blushing with embarrassment, Liberty said. "Oh! I'm sorry."

"It's okay," said Jed genuinely. Suddenly, he smacked his head with his hand. "Oh!!! I'm not being neighborly again. Do you want any pot for the road?"

Frankline looked like he was going to say 'Yes', but Liberty and Uncle Danny cut in. "No, thank you."

"No worries," smiled Jed. "Feel free to stop by anytime."

Liberty got the guys back out onto the street and headed the right way.

"He seemed nice," chirped Liberty happily, while they dodged the slow zoms.

Uncle Danny just grunted unhappily.

The Librarian looked at him. "What's wrong Uncle

Grumpy? I thought you were the 'Cool Uncle'."

"*Pollas en vinagre.* I Am the 'Cool Uncle'," replied Uncle Danny hotly. "But 'Cool Uncle's' don't give the kids drugs."

"Um, isn't that the definition of the 'Cool Uncle'," tried Frankline.

"*No,*" retorted Uncle Danny sharply.

Frankline looked like he wanted to say more, but wisely stayed quiet.

Liberty fixed an eye on Danny. "And what did your grandmother have to say about it?"

Uncle Danny sighed softly. "Mi Abuela heard it called the 'Devil's Lettuce', an' from that moment on, that's all she called it. Usually while wielding a flip-flop in her hand. Of course, she always hated the Devil, and Lettuce, so that pretty much summed up her feelings perfectly well."

In no time, they had reached a store called 'Dive Right In' and found the inside abandoned.

"Are you sure it's here?" asked Uncle Danny as he looked around the store.

"Ummm, no," admitted Frankline. "But...I figured it's worth checking."

"As long as we don't stay too long," said Liberty.

After a diligent search, they had almost given up when Uncle Danny called out. Liberty and Frankline rushed over.

"Look at this!" grinned the Big Mexican excitedly.

"I think that's it," grinned Frankline. "I can't believe it!"

Uncle Danny handed over a chainmail suit.

Frankline excitedly spoke. "You can wear this suit to

stop shark bites. And if it'll stop a shark…"

"It should stop a zom," grinned Liberty.

"But…," started Uncle Danny as he looked at the Librarian. "I only found one. *Perdón.*"

Frankline chuckled. "That's okay!! I only needed one."

Liberty and Uncle Danny looked at him questionably.

"I need one to figure out HOW to make more," explained Frankline. "Though…I was going to give it to someone…after I know how to make more."

Amused, Uncle Danny's eyebrows went up. "And whoooo would this be?"

With a sing-song voice, Liberty said. "I think I know."

Frankline's cheeks grew hot with embarrassment. "It's… not really."

"It's okay," said Liberty. "I won't tell…" She saw the Big Mexican frown at her. "Except Uncle Danny."

"If you guys could keep it under your hat," said Frankline anxiously. "I don't want to put her in a bad position. You know, chain of command."

Uncle Danny's eyes grew wide with delight. "*¡Neta, no manches!* No more need be said."

"Okay," said Liberty. "We better get going. We don't want to be late for dinner."

"Yes! Yes! Of course," said Frankline. "Thank You!"

Outside the store, Uncle Danny spoke up. "You should really test that sharkmail before you make anything. Make sure it even works."

"True," said Frankline soberly.

"But not with Your hand in there," said Liberty. "We don't want you getting bit."

"Oh yeah!" nodded Frankline quickly. "I wouldn't."

"Maybe I...," began Uncle Danny, a little reluctantly.

There was gunfire.

Immediately they ducked, looking for a safe place.

"Wait," said Frankline. "It's too far away."

Waiting cautiously, the three looked around.

"We still should head in the opposite direction," said Liberty, listening.

"But...I'm not sure what direction it's coming from," said Frankline.

"Then let's keep heading our way," said Uncle Danny. "And we'll keep an ear out."

"Do you think it's our friends?" asked Liberty thoughtfully.

"I'd rather not find out," replied Uncle Danny.

"Me neither," said Liberty.

The sound of gunfire soon went away.

"No more bullets," commented Uncle Danny with a shake of his head.

As they walked, a voice crackled in their ears. "..ed... and here."

Putting a little pep in their step, they got closer to the signal.

"This is Sergeant Bath," said the voice. "Opened a can of worms here. Sorry." And she gave an address.

***

Up high, Sergeant Bath was *very* perturbed as she carefully climbed across the high metal shelves.

"Sorrryy," whined a voice down the row.

Bath wanted to bite the rookie's head off, but that wouldn't help.

"Let's just get out of here alive," said the Sergeant.

Face scrunched up with embarrassment, the Rookie Private, Jules said. "I just thought there might be some good stuff in the back."

"Later," said Bath. She looked down at the aisles of the big box store and they were filled with zoms. Glancing around, she saw that all her squad was accounted for. "I just wish we'd been in a section with heavy stuff."

"Sooorry," moaned Jules again. Some of her brown wavy hair had escaped from beneath her helmet.

The Sergeant looked at her. "You're a soldier now for the U.S. Arm...I mean, Navy. First, focus on the challenge. Help fix it. It's going to be okay, as long as we work together."

The young woman, Jules, straightened a bit and stiffened her spine.

The Rookie looked around. Thinking furiously.

The Sergeant looked at the rest of the squad. "Everyone — Carefully!!—look around and see if there's anything that could help."

Bath experimentally moved across the top of the metal shelves, but the zoms in the aisle below followed along. Thankfully, she had thought fast, but now they were all stuck.

Right now, Bath was really missing her tank. She had gotten an old M1A2 Abrams moving again. But she had also gotten a battlefield promotion with more duties. Which had led her to this orange metal shelf.

"Grease!" called out Jules behind her.

Carefully, the slim Black woman, Bath, returned to her.

Pointing across the aisle, the Rookie was grinning. "There's a few cases of grease right over there."

"And who's going to get it?" asked Private Biggs sarcastically.

"Well...," started Jules, and her shoulders slumped. "I'm still working on that."

"Great job," grumbled Biggs.

"And what's your idea Private Biggs?" asked Bath loudly.

Biggs' pasty face scrunched up in surprise. "Oh! Um... ah..."

"Why don't we all focus on the problem instead of...," began Bath when Jules jumped.

The Rookie leapt off the shelf that they were on, which wobbled dangerously.

Jules hit the other metal shelf about halfway. Grabbing on for dear life, one boot caught the metal, but the other dangled down. A zom grabbed the boot and pulled hard. Grunting, Jules tried to pull her boot away. The metal shelves began to wobble.

"DamnDamnDamn," she muttered.

Just as Bath drew her Glock, a shot came out of nowhere. One of the front windows shattered to pieces. The zom holding Jules' boot let go and slumped down.

For a moment, Jules was too stunned.

"Climb girl!" barked the Sergeant. "Climb fast."

That snapped Jules out of her surprise.

The Rookie climbed as fast as she dared and reached the top shelf. Once she was safe on the shelf, she tore open a box and pulled out several cans. A grin appeared on her face, and she looked at the Staff Sergeant.

"Follow through with your idea Private," nodded Bath.

Nodding quickly, Jules' face turned grim. She turned over the can. There was a metal lid on top. Pulling out her knife, Jules levered the can open.

Bath had to suppress the instinct to tell Jules to be careful.

The Private poured out the grease. It wasn't very much. She threw the can down, but it just bonked a zom on the noggin harmlessly.

Bath looked down at the front of the store but couldn't see anyone yet. She turned to the Rookie. "Faster Private."

Several of the squad burst out laughing as the zoms began to slip on the grease. At the end of each can, Jules took a moment to whip the can at a zom.

"Good shot," called out another Rookie, Nguyen.

One zom's foot shot out in a comical fashion and they

fell hard on their back. In the middle of the aisle zoms were unable to stand up now.

"Private! Spread the love," said Bath.

Jules looked up in confusion.

"Make sure you're not dumping it all in one spot," said Bath.

Dumping grease up and down the aisle caused a ruckus as zoms were unable to comprehend why they couldn't stand. All the commotion got the attention of other zoms who soon began to fall on their butts as well.

"Last can!" called out Jules as she dumped it out.

"They're sitting ducks," grinned the Rookie Biggs.

"You made out of ammo Biggs?" asked the Sergeant. "Besides, those zom are flopping around a lot."

"Help is on the way!" cried out a voice.

Bath smiled and whispered. "Teamwork."

"*¡Ándele!*" cried Uncle Danny.

Turning, Bath saw one of the oddest sights, ever.

Frankline was pushing an orange HomeLove shopping cart. Seated inside the basket was Uncle Danny waving his dull meat cleaver and...

***

"Wait! Are you serious?" asked Captain Deep Singh. He turned to look at the people around him.

Before Bath could speak, Uncle Danny piped up.

27

"It's true *El Capitán!*" grinned the Big Mexican. "And it was fun too!"

Singh started to turn back to what he was doing, but then looked back. Sergeant Bath just nodded.

"Actually, it was practical as well," she said, a little embarrassed.

Singh opened his mouth, but then—resigned—just said. "Continue your report, Sergeant."

Excitedly, Uncle Danny asked. "*¡Órale!* Actually, if I could...?"

***

"Letting go," said Frankline as he reached the edge of the grease. "Sorry."

As the Private let go and backed up, Uncle Danny did not have time to tell the boy that it was all right.

This was the tricky bit. The cart speeded up in the grease, and Danny needed to keep his balance. One wrong hit and he'd tip over right into a bunch of zoms, which would be annoying, to say the least.

Besides, he could still bleed out if one got an artery.

Reaching out, Uncle Danny grabbed the shelving unit, which stopped him and steadied the cart.

"*¡Órale!*" grinned Uncle Danny. "We did..."

Dried hands grabbed the arm that held the shelving unit. Zom teeth swiftly bit into the side of Danny's hand. However, the zom looked almost puzzled and tried to chew through the sharkmail.

"*¡Ay, pobrecita!*" grinned Uncle Danny as he turned a little bit. His meat cleaver came down with a final blow and the zom sank away.

The cart lurched to the right and Danny barely kept hold of the shelving.

A zom was using the side of the cart to lift itself up. Despite the strain on his arm, the Big Mexican waited.

The zom's head came into full view.

The cleaver dropped down, and then so did the zom.

Uncle Danny had been worried about getting stuck, but the zoms were starting to come to him. He pulled the cart closer to the shelving unit as zom fingers tried to reach through the orange basket.

***

"*Perdón.* Kinda gets boring from that point out," shrugged Uncle Danny.

"I thought he was…," began Liberty, but then she looked at Uncle Danny briefly. "*Loco!* Yep, that's the word for 'crazy', right."

"*Sí,*" replied Uncle Danny with a smile, but then he looked back at Captain Singh. "But it only worked for so long. Soon, I was stuck, and all the zoms immediately around me were dead. That was when these two…" He gestured at Bath and Frankline. "They went to Work!"

As the last zom near him slumped down beside Uncle Danny's cart. The Big Mexican looked around. There were still more outside his reach.

"Um, I think I got all the close ones, but...," called out the Big Mexican. Climbing out might be dangerous. "I now see a drawback in our plan."

"Oh!" began Frankline. "Maybe I..."

"It's okay," said Bath from above. "Both of you. This is good." She held up her Glock and looked at Frankline. "Private?"

With a grin, Frankline drew out two Glocks. "Thank you, Sargent."

"Fire at will, Private!" ordered Bath. She leaned over and fired.

"But not us," grumbled Private Biggs.

The Sergeant pretended not to hear.

Frankline moved quickly, avoiding the grease, and firing his guns. Moving around Bath, the Private went after the zoms that had not gotten stuck in the grease trap. The creatures tried to grab him. He let them get close, just close enough. Then he put a bullet in their head.

Shortly, Frankline called out. "We're clear. I don't see any more." He stopped right beneath Bath's spot. "I can help you down, if you want."

The Sergeant got to the edge of the shelves. "I should be..." But when she started to climb over the edge, it felt pretty high. "Actually, I wouldn't mind."

The Sergeant got down fine, but it did make her feel better to have a little help. As she descended, Frankline put out his hands, but he didn't try any funny business.

"Okay," she said out-loud. "Let's get everyone down and outta here."

***

"And worst yet, the store was empty," reported Sergeant Bath.

Captain Singh did not know what to say, so he fell back on an old standard, he kept quiet.

Turning, his right arm was still in a sling, because an alien-bird had fractured it. He aimed his Glock with his left hand and fired at an empty bottle, which exploded.

Then he took out two more bottles with ease.

"Ha! I tol' you Sir," urged Staff Sergeant Ruiz. "Practice makes perfect."

Singh gave her a smile and then turned to Frankline.

"If this shark chainmail works, that'll help," said the Captain.

"Well, it didn't quite work," admitted Frankline.

Uncle Danny held up his hand to show a tear in the skin.

"BUT it could still work," insisted Frankline. "I just need to experiment with it."

The Captain nodded. "Okay. Go ahead and work on it."

"Yes sir!" saluted Frankline, and he could not help but glance at Ruiz. The Staff Sergeant was smiling too and the

31

Private grinned.

"You'll have to scrounge your own supplies," warned the Captain.

"Already started while we were at the hardware store. Luckily, there were some metal bits left.

"Okay, we need to...," started Singh.

Through an open door, that was propped open to let in the ocean breeze, an alien-bird dove in.

Their wings were pulled in tight to get through the door. The moment that the bird was inside though, the wings snapped open with a whipcrack and slowed the alien's momentum.

Uncle Danny was just turning towards the door when the bird came to a halt right next to him. The alien gently head-butted the Big Mexican's arm.

"¡Oye!" laughed Danny. "You nearly gave me a heart attack!"

"Ha!" cried the alien, Rakduson. with delight. She clacked her beak together, which for her species was like laughing. She stood around five feet tall and looked at Liberty. "Hi!"

"Hello!" chuckled Liberty. "That was a fantastic entrance."

"It was really dangerous," said Captain Singh tartly. He stopped himself from yelling, but it was a close thing. Making a show of putting away his sidearm, Singh went over to the bird. "Please don't do that again, Ms. Rakduson. I nearly shot you, thinking you a threat."

Rak opened her beak to be defensive, but then she

stopped.   Liberty and Uncle Danny were looking thoughtful. The bird dipped her head.

"Sorry," said the alien.

"It's okay," said the Captain sincerely. "Really! And actually, you did show a hole in our defenses..." He turned to Frankline. "Private! Close that door."

The Private ran off to do so.

Singh softened and asked the bird. "Any trouble today?"

Rak shook her head but stiffened. "But Master's ships out there."

Occasionally, they did still see the octagonal ships of the aliens who had started the zombie plague. Then the aliens had dropped Rak's people to hunt for the uninfected.

"Close?" asked Singh.

"No," said Rak. "I could not find my people either."

"Why are you looking for your people?" asked Singh.

"She's trying to free them as well," cut in Uncle Danny. "Her and Smalls are trying to find a way to block the signal to their devices."

"The ones in the back of their head?" asked Singh thoughtfully and looked at Danny. "But didn't you free her." He nodded at Rak.

"*Órale.* I shot it," said Uncle Danny, but then he added quickly. "Accidentally! But it was not good."

"Yes," said the bird with a pained wince. "No shooting please."

"Duly noted," said Singh. "Ms. Rak, can I see the device,

33

just to have a better understanding of what you face. I won't touch it."

Rak almost glanced at Danny, but she realized that it was okay. The Captain would not hurt her, so she turned her head.

Embedded in the back of her cranium were the remains of the device. Not being an engineer, Singh could not determine what was happening. But he could see that the skin around the device was angry and red, probably still healing.

Singh felt a bright flash of anger at the things that did this to Rak and her people. He couldn't call them 'people'. Not anyone who would do this.

Taking a step back, Singh signaled that he was done. When she looked at him, he said, "Thank you."

"Smalls was able to stabilize it," explained Liberty.

"Smalls?" asked Frankline, but then he quickly added. "Oh yeah, the engineer-guy that drives your boat. Sorry."

Liberty smiled kindly at him. "Sometimes, when we're on the carrier, I really wish we had 'Hello, my name is...' stickers for everyone."

"Ain't that the truth," chuckled Staff Sergeant Ruiz.

Uncle Danny continued explaining. "So, Smalls is trying to see if he can even block the alien's signals with a...some type of cage." He looked at Liberty who shrugged.

"A cage?" asked Ruiz.

The bird said. "Faraday cage. Stops signals that make us Crazy. Monsters."

"Oh!" said Ruiz excitedly. "That makes sense."

34

The Captain cleared his throat questionably.

"Rak said it," said the Staff Sergeant. "Basically, you're creating this structure with copper, for instance, and it should block any incoming signals." She looked at the bird. "It might help, but.....if you're not getting any signals anymore, then you're going to have to put one of your people inside it to find out."

"Hard to do," nodded Rakduson thoughtfully. "But I must take care of my people."

Uncle Danny patted the bird companionably on a wing. "You'll do it."

Captain Singh cleared his throat. "Okay. We need to talk about tomorrow before I forget. We're not going to the Coast tomorrow. Admiral Cirilo has called a general meeting tomorrow morning. My team will be there." Singh looked at Rak. "I do know enough that it's not a problem concerning your people."

"Then I keep searching," said Rak. "Will help later if needed."

Singh nodded and looked at Liberty and Danny. "But he did ask if you would be there too."

Dos Amigos glanced at each other, communicating in an instant without words.

Liberty turned back, hopefully. "Will there be breakfast?"

Chapter Two

OUT AT SEA, the Bowrider cut through the ocean waves.

"[¡Oye!] Slow down! You're going to capsize us," called out Uncle Danny, but the wind took away his words.

Not hearing him, Liberty stood at the wheel, leaning slightly forward, with a happy grin.

Having flown, Rakduson was probably already there, but they had to go the slow way.

First, they had seen the aircraft carrier, the [Teddy Roosevelt]. The ship, which was nicknamed 'The Big Stick', towered over the ocean.

But soon, more ships came into view surrounding it. It was a ragtag fleet of vessels including a few more Navy, Coast Guard, fishing boats, and right down to anything that could float. Anything that could get away from the Coast.

This was the Fleet under the command of Rear Admiral Antony Cirilo.

A little ways away was their boat. The find of the century. An-honest-to-God yacht, now called the S.S. *[Wolf Pack]*.

Uncle Danny leaned a little forward. "Is there someone on top of our ship? It doesn't look like Rak."

Liberty peered. "Yeah, it's definitely not her." She pulled in behind the boat.

They had only just gotten out when a little Latina missile shot out and slammed into Liberty. The Librarian had barely enough time to brace herself.

The Latina girl, Tessy, wrapped her arms around and squeezed tight.

"You're back," came the muffled voice of Tessy.

Liberty, for her part, gratefully wrapped her arms around the little girl and felt happy. Tessy might be adopted, but she was Liberty's daughter for sure.

"I missed you so much," murmured Liberty softly.

"[*¡Neta, no manches!*]" called out Uncle with a very melodramatic, hurt tone. "No love for your dear, old Uncle?"

Tessy immediately jumped back.

"Sorry!" she cried and went to hug her biological uncle fiercely. "You know that I love you too!!" Then she added swiftly. "And you're not old!!"

Uncle Danny grinned and assured her. "I'm just teasing."

Tessy noticed the bandage on Uncle Danny's hand.

"What Happened!?!" she asked in alarm.

"I was wearing armor when a zom bit me," explained Danny patiently. "It's only a little cut."

With a vice-like grip, Tessy took his hand and examined the rest of the unbandaged hand thoroughly, turning it this way and that.

Just when Liberty was about to stop her, Tessy let go.

After Tessy had briefly looked them over, to make sure that everyone was okay, she jumped back to face them.

"Hurry!" she cried with joy. "Tagg and I made dinner. Come on!"

As they followed the little girl through the ship, Liberty's brow furrowed in thought.

"Waaaait," said the Librarian slowly. "I thought it was you, Colin and Tagg tonight."

"Ummmm...," started Tessy.

Liberty stepped a little faster so that she walked side by side with the little girl.

However, Tessy looked down.

"I'm no snitch," she replied fiercely to the unspoken question.

Uncle Danny gave an exaggerated cough. "¡Neta! You literally told on Colin yesterday."

"But he was being mean," replied Tessy defensively.

"Still tattling sweetie," said Liberty gently.

Tessy made a disgusted noise. "Well, I'm not gonna tell.

You can't make me."

"That's okay," said Liberty.

They had reached the boat's dining room, but no one else was there yet. It was one of the more spacious rooms on the ship, which is why it had been picked for family dinners. They couldn't all sit in the small booth in the kitchen anymore.

"Tagg is in the kitchen," said Tessy, and she tugged on Liberty's hand.

The Librarian didn't need to be asked twice.

Behind them, Uncle Danny wondered if Liberty knew that she had made a happy, little skip.

It's true that he might have given Tagg a hard time when he and Liberty had first started dating, but really, the Scientist was [*un buen hombre*].

Through the kitchen door, Liberty let go of Tessy's hand and ran up to a man with a barrel chest. The lighter Librarian crashed into Miles McTaggert, and he wrapped one arm around her. In the other, he held a wooden spoon that began to drip marinara on the floor. But neither noticed.

Reaching out, Uncle Danny dragged Tessy back into the dining room.

"Wha...?" asked Tessy, a little annoyed. She pulled away and took a second to pull her shirt back into place.

"Give [*tu Madre e Padre*] a moment," said the Big Mexican, and he steered his 9-year-old niece through the ship.

"Where're we going?" asked Tessy curiously.

"We're going up," was all that Uncle Danny said.

They wound up towards the upper deck and found a large alien-bird sitting with her wings wrapped around her.

"Hola," said Uncle Danny with a subdued voice.

The alien-bird, Rakduson, looked quickly around. "[Hola]."

Rak was about to get up, but Uncle Danny motioned that she did not need to.

In the bird's language, Danny haltingly asked how the alien was doing.

"Good," replied Rakduson. "Colin unhappy. Sorry."

"Was it you he quarreled with?" asked Uncle Danny with surprise.

"Ah...no," admitted Rak.

"[¡No manches!] Then you don't need to apologize," said Danny.

Rakduson nodded towards the Pilot's House.

"Tried to talk," said Rak.

Uncle Danny patted one dark wing. "It's okay." He turned to Tessy. "Can you stay here with Aunt Rak?"

Tessy knelt next to the bird and leaned against her feathers. With her red tuft, Rakduson leaned her head down and despite a razor-sharp beak managed to straighten some of the girl's hair, preening her. Though there was—thankfully—no need to check for ectoparasites in the little girl's hair, thought Rak happily.

Striding forward, Uncle Danny went over to the Pilot's House, which was empty inside.

41

Above came the petulant voice of an 11-year-old boy. "Tessy told on me, didn't she?"

"No," replied Uncle Danny. He tried to look for a way up on top. "She didn't need to. Tu Madre and I saw you as we were coming in."

Jumping up, Uncle Danny managed to grab the edge of the roof. Doing a chin-up, he was just able to look on top.

Colin was sitting cross-legged in an old t-shirt with a gigantic frown.

Unable to keep himself up, Uncle Danny dropped down.

"I don' wanna talk," grumbled Colin from above.

"[Sí], that's okay," said Uncle Danny. He started faking a big yawn, but it quickly morphed into a real one. "Ugh. I'm pooped. We worked hard today." He walked over to grab a small deck chair and made a lot of noise dragging it back, but carefully, so as not to hurt the deck.

Sitting down, the Big Mexican let out an even bigger sigh.

"Oh! There're some new playas in town," said Uncle Danny. There was no reply above, so he kept going. "They dress like military, but anyone can get that. 'Course, the [pendejos] tried to tangle with some birds. It did [not] go well." He chuckled.

It was quiet above.

"Oh! And I took out a zombie in a shopping cart," continued Danny. "As in, I was inside the cart."

There was a little scramble above.

"Wait? What?" asked Colin as he stuck his head over the side.

***

After dinner, Liberty and Uncle Danny stayed behind.

"[_¡Neta!_] I've been to funerals with more life than that dinner," muttered the Big Mexican as he washed the remnants of spaghetti sauce off a dish.

"[_Sí_]," nodded Liberty. "It was pretty somber."

"[_Perdón por pisarte la mano_]," said Uncle Danny.

Liberty's brow furrowed and she looked quickly at him. "Doesn't that mean that you're sorry, and it's your fault."

Danny shrugged. "I tried to talk Colin down, but he was..."

Liberty waved her drying towel menacingly at the Big Mexican. "[_Pollas en vinagre!_]"

Uncle Danny looked at her in shock. "Did you just say, 'dicks in vinegar'?"

Liberty looked uncertain. "It's what you use when you're having a disagreement, right?"

The Big Mexican laughed. "[_Sí_], it is. I just didn't think I taught it to you."

"I overheard you telling Tagg and Smalls about all the naughty words," said Liberty. "And '[_Pollas en vinagre_]' almost gave me away. Nearly broke myself, trying Not to laugh."

"I wasn't trying to keep them from you...," said Uncle Danny quickly, but stumbled. "I just...didn't feel comfortable...you know...Mi Abuela raised me to be very

43

respectful. Or else."

"It's okay," said Liberty sincerely. "That's the only one I remember anyhow." She blinked and her face grew stern once again. "And back to the topic. [*You*] got Colin down from on top of the boat and got him to dinner. That's something."

Uncle Danny sighed. "He didn't talk about whatever happened. Or he didn't talk directly. Sounds like an argument."

"Tagg wasn't ready to talk either," said Liberty. "Oh well, it'll all come out in the wash."

"Sometimes when [*mi amigo*] Pepe and I would fight, we couldn't even remember why at the end," said Uncle Danny as he washed dishes.

***

Liberty was going to knock on the door, but then she checked herself.

"You're allowed," she reminded herself.

A quick rap on the door, she called through. "Hey! It's me. Are you decent?"

There was silence.

It went on too long.

Finally, Liberty decided not to push her luck. "Well, sleep well. Love you."

Just as she started to move away from the door, a sharp voice came through.

"What do you want?" asked Colin.

"I'm opening the door," said Liberty and did so. She saw Colin sitting on his bed, cross-legged in his jeans and playing his Nintendo Switch. He did not look up.

"You don't HAVE to ask if I'm decent EVERY time," huffed the boy.

Liberty froze. "I'm…I just wanted to be polite."

"What's up?" asked Colin.

"Wait! It is important to ask if you're decent," said Liberty quickly and nervously. "You're a growing boy, and…well, you deserve your peace."

Colin looked up at her incredulously. "Are you talking about…" However, his face screwed up. "I already got The Talk from Tagg AND Uncle Danny."

"Good," nodded Liberty. "Still important that I respect your privacy."

"I don't want to talk about this," said Colin hotly.

"Well, I'm not thrilled either," replied Liberty. "But I'm also not going to be a coward and not talk about Sex at all."

Colin blinked at that. "Ummm."

"I did have Tagg, and your Uncle have the initial conversation," said Liberty. "Because they understand guys…and I've never gotten the knack. Sometimes, I feel like I barely understand being a girl."

Liberty shook her head a little to get back on track.

"[*But*] you can still ask me questions. I'd rather that you asked questions than just try and figure it out on your own."

"Oh...okay," said Colin. "My Dad...my old Dad...I mean..."

"Your sperm donor...," suggested Liberty.

Colin's eyes bugged out. "Wait. What? Um..."

"It's just what MaryMary at the library would call her...," started Liberty, but she faltered. "Well, the person who..."

"It's okay," said Colin quickly. "MaryMary had the funny socks, right?"

"Yes she did," nodded Liberty. "And thankfully a really good Stepfather." She shook her head in annoyance again.

"Sorry. We were talking about...that guy," said Liberty, who didn't like Colin's bio-father. He was as close to hate as Liberty really got. "You were saying?"

"Oh. Um...," shrugged Colin. "I was just going to say that...". And he nearly cracked up at the term, sperm donor. But kept it together. "It's just that he never seemed to care about talking about...That Stuff."

Liberty moved forward, stepped over some dirty clothes, and leaned over the boy. She kissed the top of his head and stepped back.

"If you ever want to talk," said the Librarian. "I'm here for you."

Stepping back, Liberty carefully went to the door.

"But I am going to say the old Mom standard." She turned to the boy with a stern tone. "Clean Your Room."

Colin gave a small, but genuine laugh. "But I got everything right where I want it."

46

Liberty melodramatically poked a shirt with her boot. "We talked about this, no pets. Not yet."

"It's just an old shirt," retorted Colin with an amused eyeroll.

"I'm not so sure," said Liberty, peering suspiciously at the shirt. "I swear I saw it move."

In a moment, Colin's face grew serious. "You came to talk about what happened earlier."

"Yes," said Liberty, however she hastily added. "But only if you're ready."

"What...," started Colin. "What if I'm not ready?"

"It's okay," smiled Liberty warmly. "When you're ready. Just don't bottle stuff up forever. It can eat you up from the inside. But for now..." She peered at the floor. "Seriously, I think those pants moved."

"Okay, okay," grumbled Colin as he hopped off the bed. "I'll clean up."

"You don't have to do so this second," said Liberty quickly.

"I'll get it done," sighed Colin unhappily. He pulled clothes quickly off the floor.

"I didn't mean to...," started Liberty.

"JUST...," began Colin loudly, however, he stopped and checked his tone. "Just...I want to go to bed."

Liberty nodded and went to close the door. "Okay...I love you."

Colin didn't respond as he worked on the floor.

Gently, the Librarian closed the door. She quickly went

to Uncle Danny's room, but the door was open, and he was not there. Sighing, she decided it was late, and she wanted to go to bed herself.

Suddenly, feeling completely drained, Liberty stumbled to her room. Tagg was already asleep, so she went to the bathroom for a much-needed shower. It helped a little. After drying herself, she went straight to bed, not even bothering with clothes. She ignored the memory-specter of her Mother complaining that 'Good Girls didn't go to bed naked', and she was soon asleep.

***

Liberty was not sure what woke her. A small noise most likely.

Blinking, she peered into the darkness. To save on gas, they didn't run the engines at night, unless there was an emergency.

Moonlight streamed in through the porthole, or window, or whatever you call it. Her boyfriend, Tagg, was illuminated doing push-ups. Apparently, he hadn't had the energy to dress before going to sleep either.

To hear him tell it, Tagg was grossly fat before they locked down against the zombie outbreak. Before everything fell. But Tagg's former academic advisor, Fred, said that the boy had been a little round when they retreated into the Dyson Science Building. Tagg said that he had taken to daily exercises when he started worrying, and that had helped some.

For that matter, before everything fell, Liberty had had

more than a little puppy fat on her. Something her Mother seemed to relish reminding her about, all the time. However, running around and nearly starving a time or two had helped lean her out.

As Tagg went up and down swiftly, Liberty started to melt.

A little thought reminded her that tomorrow they had some meeting on the carrier.

A smile spread across her face.

'Who needs sleep,' she thought.

Especially if she was staying up for…a good reason.

Slowly, Liberty slithered across the large bed. The soft sheets caused a delicious friction, which tugged at her attention.

So, it wasn't until Liberty's head was nearly off the bed that she saw Tagg's face. His big face was pinched with worry.

Liberty was almost not sure what she was seeing, so she slid off the bed to the carpet.

Tagg suddenly jolted and looked over. "What??"

"It's okay," said Liberty softly. "It's just me."

"I mean…," started Tagg uncertainly. "I'm sorry. I didn't mean to wake you."

"Don't worry about that," she said swiftly. "Are you okay?"

"I was…just working out," he said. His voice was low and shaky, but he didn't seem out of breath from the exercise. "It helps…sometimes. Mostly not."

Liberty sat cross-legged. "Is something wrong?"

After a second, Tagg nodded.

For a second, a stab of fear went through the Librarian, but then she remembered.

"About you and Colin?" she asked.

Tagg looked up so quickly.

Liberty's words tumbled forward. "You don't have to talk about it…if you don't want to. It's okay."

Giving a long sigh, Tagg sat down near her.

"I just wanted to make sure it wasn't me," said Liberty.

"NO," said Tagg quickly. "It's not that." He paused. "I..I screwed up."

Liberty's brow furrowed. "How so?"

Gesturing towards Colin's general location on the ship, Tagg took a moment to find his words, but still, he had trouble. "I don't know how it turned…well, bad. I mean, I know what happened, but…"

"Well," said the Librarian softly. "Why don't we start there?"

Tagg nodded swiftly and said in a small voice. "Okay. I mean, I'm sure you know the basics."

"Nope," said Liberty. "No-one's said anything."

"Colin didn't…," started Tagg, but his words dropped off.

"He wouldn't even come to his door when I knocked on it," said Liberty.

"Which isn't like him," said Tagg worriedly, and he

looked down. "Oh no."

"Why don't we start small," suggested Liberty. "Do we know what started it?"

Tagg nodded. "He said a 'Bad Word'."

Liberty looked a little surprised. "He doesn't normally..."

"Exactly...," said Tagg sadly. "But I felt like I should say something. I don't know. Maybe I should've shut up and not said a thing."

"What word was it?" asked Liberty.

"The F-word," said Tagg.

Liberty's eyebrows rose up. "No, that's a pretty bad word. Especially for an 11-year-old. So, what'd you say?"

Tagg shrugged. "I didn't think anything bad. I mean, That Bad." He sighed. "I told him that that kind of language was not allowed." His voice disappeared and the big man looked at the floor, embarrassed.

"And what happened?" asked Liberty gently.

"He just...exploded," said Tagg. "I don't know. He started yelling, and I raised my voice, but now..."

Liberty got onto her hands and knees and closed the distance. She first head-butted his large shoulder. Big arms wrapped around her, and she slid into his lap.

"It's going to be okay," whispered Liberty. "This happens."

"What happens?" asked Tagg.

"Fights," said Liberty. "You should have heard my Mom and I."

51

"Um...," started Tagg, but not sure what to say.

Liberty chuckled sadly. "She was sure that Satan was going to get me if she let me go too far. So, she kept trying to keep me too close to home."

"And you didn't like that?" asked Tagg. Some of the tension had left his voice.

"I became really good at sneaking out," said Liberty.

Tagg pulled back some and she looked up.

"You! You snuck out?" he asked with exaggerated shock.

"Don't be so surprised," said Liberty with mock annoyance. "Sometimes us librarians can be naughty."

A real smile brightened Tagg's face. "I figured that that was like, shelving a political book under Fiction."

"Tempting," said Liberty. "But that would go against the Code of the Librarian."

"The Code of the Librarian?" asked Tagg.

Liberty gave a mock scowl. "It's a real thing."

"I'm sure it is," said Tagg complacently. His fingers played over her ribs, but not too light to tickle. "It's just..."

Liberty gave a real scowl and turned around a little to see his face, while trying to stay in his warming lap.

"Is this okay?" she asked.

"Yes!" he answered automatically and pulled her closer to say more softly. "Yes. I just...I'm sorry. I just worry. And I can't stop worrying. My parents..." He paused to gather his strength. "They sent me to a doctor who said I have anxiety. Sorry."

"Why are you sorry?" asked Liberty in confusion.

"Well…I don't want to be a burden," said Tagg carefully, embarrassed.

Liberty leaned closer to glare at him. "Who said you were a 'burden'? You are not a 'burden'."

"I woke you in the middle of the night," said Tagg.

"Trying to raise two adopted kids, who aren't related to each other…," said Liberty. "I think we're going to have more than a few conversations in the middle of the night."

Tagg chuckled. "That's true."

"And while I don't know much about anxiety… MaryMary at the Library only talked about hers a little," said Liberty. "But for you, it's worth it." She gave him a huge hug. "Now, why don't you tell me about what happened with Colin. It might help to work out your nerves."

Slowly, with Liberty's patience, Tagg explained as much as he could.

"I don't know why it got so heated," he finished. "He and I always work well as a team."

"Even teammates disagree," said Liberty.

"I don't remember you and Uncle Danny fighting," said Tagg, worriedly.

"We've had a few disagreements," said Liberty soothingly. "And we'll have more, but that's okay, as long as—in the end—we support each other.

"I guess…that's true," he agreed.

Liberty straightened a little. "Wait! Why didn't you tell

me that you needed a certain type of medicine. I could have gotten it for you."

"I thought about it," said Tagg. "But..." He sighed. "Someone out there needs it more than me."

Liberty opened her mouth to argue.

"Besides," continued Tagg. "There's not an endless supply. I'd just run out, again, and that would suck."

"Oh," she nodded. "Without a renewable supply..."

"True," he said, but his voice sounded distracted.

Liberty felt him growing beneath her, and she started to play with his sparse chest hairs.

They kissed deeply.

***

"Got You!" cried Liberty with a loud, booming voice, like a Saturday Morning Cartoon villain. "You thought you could get away, but you were wrong!"

Colin turned his head a little from where he sat. He was hanging over a railing looking out over the water. The boy scowled, and then looked back at the churning water.

Undeterred, Liberty came to sit right beside the boy letting her feet dangle over the ocean. She leaned over and put her head on Colin's shoulder.

The boy squirmed uncomfortably, so she stopped, but kept sitting next to him.

This far from the Coast, there was just open ocean.

"It's kinda pretty," said Liberty.

Colin blinked and glanced her way, before he thought better of it. He quickly looked back out over the water.

"The ocean, I mean," explained Liberty.

"There's nothing out there," grumbled Colin.

"Maybe that's what I like," said Liberty. "No danger…at least beyond the ocean itself." She felt lame at the end, so she gave a huff. "Okay! Enough small talk. You had your time to sulk…"

"I wasn't sulking," shot Colin quickly, but then he paused. "Wait. What's sulking?"

"When you don't want to talk to anyone," said Liberty. "But eventually, you gotta."

"Is this where I get in trouble?" asked the boy, and there was a wince in his voice.

Liberty thought for a moment. "Nope."

Colin blinked. "What?"

"I do agree that you shouldn't swear," said Liberty.

"Why not?" asked the boy defensively.

"Because it's not polite," said Liberty. "You shouldn't swear in front of other people."

"How much of Polite is left?" asked Colin.

"As much as we can," said Liberty. "Let me put it this way, have you ever heard Captain Singh swear?"

Colin straightened a little, deep in thought. The boy had a serious case of hero worship there.

"Or Uncle Danny?" she asked.

"Didn't he swear before, but in Spanish," said Colin.

Liberty was about to give an immediate 'no', but then she thought. "Okay, not the best example." And she gave a chuckle.

Despite himself, Colin gave a little laugh, however, his face grew pinched.

"I don't know why I got so mad," he said in a small voice. She almost couldn't hear it over the wind.

Liberty stood up and gave a little stretch. "Okay, come on."

The boy looked up with surprise.

Nodding towards the ship, the Librarian looked expectantly.

Wearily, Colin stood but hesitated. "What if he doesn't want me to help in the lab?"

Liberty put her arm around his shoulders and led the boy into the ship.

"Come on," she said. "You'd be surprised."

***

"I'm sorry."

Both of the guys said it at the same time, and Liberty had to force herself not to laugh.

Standing behind Colin, she steered him deeper into the room.

Tagg and the boy looked confused about where to go

next.

"Colin," said Liberty. "Why don't you go first?"

So, the boy began, and Tagg soon joined in. A path forward was soon found.

"I was hoping that you two would hug it out," said Liberty.

"Oh no!" said Tagg quickly with mock concern. "We're guys. We're not allowed to hug."

Colin immediately picked up on the joke. "Yeah. We gotta be tough, like Uncle Danny."

"And strong," said Tagg. "With lots of grunting." And he gave a few silly grunts.

The boy quickly joined in.

Chapter Three

"¡*ÓRALE!* THEY'RE NOT wrong," nodded Uncle Danny afterwards.   He pretended to look extremely grave. "*Hombres* are not allowed to hug."

Liberty shot him a concerned look. "That's just silly. It's a new world, guys should be allowed to have feelings."

"¡*Neta, no manches!* *Hombres* can have feelings," replied Uncle Danny.   "We're just supposed to drown them in alcohol."

With heated concern, Liberty began. "Now, don't you say that in front of…" But then she saw Danny's huge grin, so she continued. "Oh, you were joking."

The Big Mexican shrugged. "Well, half-joking. I guess it's true that Pepe and I never hugged, even though, in some ways, he was closer to me than my own hermono." A sad darkness went across his face.

Liberty reached beside her as they walked and patted his arm kindly.

"You really miss them," she said softly.

Uncle Danny just nodded. But then he brought up his chin. "Okay. That's enough moping." He put on a brave face. "I still got the kids and you."

Leaning a little closer, Liberty whispered. "You can show your feelings too."

"I know," said Danny with a small smile. "But not here. Not on the aircraft carrier."

They were being led through the *Teddy Roosevelt*.

"Well, I'm happy to admit that I'm lost once again," said Liberty merrily.

The sailor leading them turned. "Oh! We're almost there Ma'am."

Liberty winced inwardly at the 'Ma'am' but thanked the sailor. She turned to Uncle Danny.

"I wish we knew what this was all about," sage murmured.

"Liberty! Uncle Danny!" called out a voice ahead.

Dos Amigos looked past the sailor to see Captain Singh with part of his squad up ahead. They were waiting outside a door. At the same time, the sailor explained that this was where they were going and asked if they needed anything else. Liberty kindly thanked the sailor who left.

Captain Singh said. "I wish we knew what this was all about."

With a burst of laughter, Liberty snorted and covered

her face. "Sorry, I snorted."

Just as Singh was looking puzzled, Uncle Danny said. "Little Liberty was just asking that."

Shooting a scowl, Liberty asked the Big Mexican. "Who're calling 'little'?"

"Sorry," said Uncle Danny quickly. "I meant *pequeña'*."

Liberty's scowl deepened. "Which just means 'small' in Spanish.

The Big Mexican grinned mischievously.

Turning to Captain Singh, Liberty gave a pleasant smile. "How are you guys doing today?" And she said hello to the others, Lieutenant Washington, Staff Sergeant Ruiz, and Private Frankline.

As they were having small talk, Rear Admiral Antony Cirilo appeared.

"Good to see you all here," said the Rear Admiral with pleasant cheer.

"Trouble?" asked Captain Singh right away.

"Wellllll, he's not frowning like usual," suggested Liberty.

"True," nodded Singh.

"No big fire," said the Rear Admiral immediately, reassuringly, but then he paused and turned to Liberty and Uncle Danny. "When you're leaving the Fleet at night, you do stand guard."

"Sí," said Danny with concern.

"What's wrong?" asked Liberty with steely urgency, ready to fight.

The Real Admiral put up a quelling hand and said quickly. "Nothing immediate. It's more like, a few little events. But have you seen anything?"

"Actually," said Uncle Danny. "Last week and this, there were some ships in the distance. But they never came too close."

Liberty shrugged. "Maybe looky-loos. However, we have a general alarm."

Cirilo looked serious. "And don't wait to call."

"We won't," said Liberty. "Smalls takes his job very seriously." The Rear Admiral nodded at that, mollified.

"And if someone does come on board," grinned Uncle Danny wickedly. "They're in for a few surprises. Not the least of which is Rak."

Captain Singh gave a little laugh. "Finding a five-foot tall bird with a razor-sharp beak…"

"A short, sharp surprise," chuckled Uncle Danny.

"Okay. It's just that radar, and a few of the fishing boats, have spotted some smaller boats further out," nodded the Rear Admiral.

"On reconnaissance?" suggested Singh thoughtfully.

Cirilo gave a little shrug, but then remembered. "Oh. And you should know that one of the ships in the Fleet left."

Liberty's eyes went wide, and she whispered. "¡Mierda!"

"You said it," muttered Uncle Danny.

Captain Singh looked concerned. "And they didn't sink?"

"One of the other refugee ships saw them leave," said the Rear Admiral. "It was the middle of the night, so we decided to wait till dawn."

"And nothing?" asked Singh.

The Rear Admiral just shook his head.

"Did they head for the Coast?" asked Singh.

"No one, but them, knows," said Cirilo. "But truly, we don't give ships that much gas."

Liberty said. "We'll keep an eye out."

"And please be careful too," said the Rear Admiral.

"We will," nodded Uncle Danny seriously.

Captain Singh asked. "Is that what this meeting's about?"

The Rear Admiral smiled more easily. "Totally different topic. All will be explained. I wanted your squad here in case you could help."

"Absolutely," nodded Singh, looking more relaxed.

***

Now seated around a big table, the meeting still had not started. Liberty glanced at her watch and yawned.

"You probably got time for a power nap," said the person next to her. She glanced at Lieutenant Washington, M.D., from Singh's squad.

"Sorry," she said quickly. "I didn't get as much sleep as I wanted."

63

"¡Aquas! I don't want to hear this," said Uncle Danny quickly, and he put his hands over his ears melodramatically.

"No! Not tha...," started Liberty, but then she remembered that 'That' had occurred too. She marched on. "No, it was Tagg."

"Again! I don't want to hear it!" said Danny with a mock whine.

Liberty punched him, a little harder than normal, in the arm.

"Ow," he moaned. "Bony knuckles."

"It's...," started Liberty when she looked at Dr. Washington. "Wait! You're a doctor."

"Last I checked," smiled the clean-shaven black man.

"Oh. I'm sorry," said Liberty quickly. "I just had a question."

"It's okay," assured Washington. "I'm happy to help. But don't you normally go to Dr. Tagg for help?"

"Yes," said Liberty. "But this is..."

"¡Neta! Hopefully, the rabbit hasn't died," said Uncle Danny cheerfully. "I don't want to be an uncle again so soon."

Without looking, Liberty just swiftly punched him in the arm again.

"Bony," muttered Uncle Danny with humor.

Liberty was about to start, but then realized that they were squinched together in the room. She looked at the doctor.

"Can we talk, somewhere a little private?" asked Liberty softly.

"Of course," said Dr. Washington as he got up.

Saying they'd be back, they started to leave, but Liberty turned to Uncle Danny.

"Is it okay…," she said. "If I go alone."

"Oh, sorry *Mija*," nodded Uncle Danny seriously. "Whatever you need. I'll be here."

Liberty flashed a grateful grin. "It's nothing bad."

Then, she followed Dr. Washington out into the passageway.

When they found a place away from the door, Liberty turned to the lieutenant.

"The problem, Dr. Washington," she started, but faltered.

"You can call me Aaron," said Dr. Washington. "If that will make you feel more comfortable."

Smiling, Liberty nodded. "Actually, it kinda would… Aaron."

"I'm just a regular doctor," said Washington. "I put my stethoscope on, one ear at a time."

Liberty snorted with laughter and then apologized. "Okay. The problem is that Tagg has…" She stopped.

"This is also a confidential consultation," said Dr. Washington helpfully.

"Okay," said Liberty, and she took a deep breath to center herself. She began to tell him about Tagg's nervousness the night before, and how she felt powerless to

65

help.

After she had finished completely, Dr. Washington said. "You said that a doctor had told him that he had anxiety, and he had been taking meds for it."

"And I could go to the Coast and get him some," said Liberty. "He said it was Pax-something."

"Maybe Paxil, or it's generic paroxetine," nodded Dr. Washington. "But he's right that we don't have a steady supply of meds. He could *easily* run out again."

"Especially since we found several pharmacies that had been emptied," said Liberty softly.

"Wait! What?" asked Dr. Washington, so she told him about the ransacked pharmacies.

"Is there something else we could use, I guess that's really my question," said Liberty. Before Washington could answer, she asked. "Actually, what's CBD? The pharmacy we just visited had signs all over about it."

"CBD is a derivative of marijuana, without the THC, or mood-altering part," explained Dr. Washington.

Liberty snapped her fingers in joy. "*¡Órale!* That's right! MaryMary!"

Dr. Washington's brow furrowed. "What?"

"Oh!" said Liberty swiftly in embarrassment. "There were two Mary's at my library, so one got nicknamed MaryMary." She shook her head. "But really, that's not important. *Pollas en vinagre.* Sorry. The reason I thought of her was because she used marijuana to help with anxiety."

"Well," said Dr. Washington thoughtfully. "There are definitely people who advocate for it, as a treatment for anxiety."

Liberty's face fell. "Oh, but it's probably addictive, isn't it?"

Dr. Washington shook his head. "Physically? Maybe if you smoke a ton, like a metric ton, all at one time, you could get addicted."

With big eyes, Liberty said. "That's a lot." Then she turned thoughtful. "Soooooo, it's not addictive."

"Well, anything can be mentally addictive," shrugged Dr. Washington. "But it..." He stopped and looked at her. "What're you thinking?"

"We found some marijuana plants when we were wandering around," said Liberty.

"Just like, out in the open?" asked Washington.

"Well, they were a little hidden...but not by much," said Liberty, and she looked embarrassed. "Actually, I didn't know what they were."

Washington frowned though. "I don't know if I've ever seen one IRL."

"Huh?"

"Oh, IRL means 'in real life'," said Dr. Washington quickly.

"Cool. Actually, it was Frankline who recognized it," said Liberty.

With a smirk and a dry, joking voice, Washington said. "What a surprise." His face grew serious. "Though he has been working really hard since we traveled with the tank/bus. Anyhow. Now, you should know that sometimes marijuana makes people's anxiety worse."

67

Liberty looked surprised for a moment. "Good to know. Though I guess it is really legal in California."

"You would not be breaking any laws," said Dr. Washington. "But please consult me if you want to try anything else."

"Oh yeah!" said Liberty quickly. "I don't even know if Tagg would be okay with it."

"Ideally, I'd like to see him on Paxil and/or Wellbutrin for his anxiety," said Dr. Washington.

"Me too," said Liberty quickly.

"But, under the circumstances, it might be worth trying," said Washington. "At least initially, because smoking *anything* long term is *not* a good idea."

"I don't even know how to smoke," shrugged Liberty.

Washington said. "I decided to be a doctor when I was a kid, so I was scared of failing some drug test, so I've never even tried it."

Looking thoughtful, Liberty nodded. "None of my friends were into anything like that." She smiled up at the doctor. "Well, Thank You very much for the help."

"Anytime," said Dr. Washington. "I'll have my office bill you."

Liberty straightened in surprise, but then the doctor gave a huge smile. The Librarian quickly returned it.

More people went into the room, so they hustled back in.

Before she had even sat, Uncle Danny asked. "You good?"

"Yep. I'll tell you everything later. I promise," said

Liberty.

***

The meeting didn't start for another 20 minutes when the Rear Admiral thanked everyone around the large table for coming.

"I'm pretty happy with where our little fleet is going, at least in terms of taking care of people's needs," started Cirilo. "But there are areas that we do…"

The door opened and several people burst into the room. In front was a woman with a big, sheepish grin.

"Sorry," said the woman apologetically. "We didn't mean to be fashionably late."

The woman, wearing a flowing dress with lots of colorful layers, went quickly around the table with some other men.

Uncle Danny leaned towards Liberty.

"Who's that?" asked the Big Mexican with a whisper.

Liberty shook her head. "I don't know."

"But that's definitely a priest's collar on that one fellow," started Uncle Danny.

The Rear Admiral spoke up. "Thank you for coming." Liberty could not tell if Cirilo was happy or upset with the new arrivals. Maybe both. "The reason I called you here was because of a growing concern amongst…well, not only the refugees, but the sailors as well. Now, you're probably wondering who everyone is."

"Yes please!" said the woman. She had a wide, generous smile, and she pointed with a languid finger. "I mean, I can pick out some people." And she looked back at Cirilo with a reproachful pout. "Really, you should have introduced us all earlier."

To Liberty's surprise, the Rear Admiral looked a little flustered, but quick as a wink, he recovered.

"Actually, I'm surprised that I got everyone here today," said Cirilo, trying to sound professional, but sounding a bit petulant. "This hasn't been easy to plan." He heard it in his voice and corrected it to his usual calm and cool demeanor. "But I can—of course—introduce everyone quickly."

The Rear Admiral first introduced the doctors. "This is the SMO, Dr. Candleross, and…"

The lady lifted a hand and twiddle her fingers. When Cirilo looked at her, she said. "Not everyone might know all the alphabet-type titles. I'mjustsayin'." Then she mimed locking her mouth and dropping the key down the front of her shirt. Sitting back, she had a little smile that was contrite, but still mischievous.

With a nod, the Rear Admiral continued, just naming people for now. "With Dr. Candleross are Drs. Patel, Karrass and Rodriguez." Cirilo motioned to the people who had come in late. "And this is Rabbi Spellman, Father Mark, and the boisterous Teresa, who is a Buddhist Priest.

"Boisterous?" asked Teresa and gave Cirilo a mock glare.

The Rear Admiral raised his chin defiantly, but Liberty saw that there was actually a hint of playfulness in his eyes. Which was almost weird because he was always so serious.

70

"Is it me," whispered Uncle Danny. "Or did something just happen?"

Before Liberty could answer, Cirilo quickly continued to introduce Captain Singh, Lt. Washington, Staff Sergeant Ruiz, and Private Frankline. Just as the Rear Admiral was turning, Teresa cried out.

"This MUST be THE Liberty and THE Uncle Danny!"

The woman jumped up to extend her hand partway across the table. Automatically, Liberty reached out and shook the hand. Teresa used her other hand to pat Liberty's, which felt to the Librarian like something an old person might do.

Teresa then shook Uncle Danny's hand.

"I'd give hugs," she said, almost apologetically. "But I figured Antony needs to keep going."

As Teresa pulled herself back across the table, Liberty thought furiously.

Uncle Danny leaned close to her and asked quickly. "Isn't the Rear Admiral's real name Antony?"

Cirilo said. "The Rear Admiral would like to keep going, if that's okay?"

Teresa just smiled unrepentantly and chirped. "Fine and Dandy by Me. But I do have a question for Uncle Danny later."

Liberty and Danny glanced at each other, questionably.

The Rear Admiral gave a little sigh and looked out over the table. "Anyhow. We've managed to get water, food and shelter to the Fleet. And I do want to talk about how hard the Fishermen, and women…" He quickly amended before

Teresa could say anything. "...that they are working."

Rabbi Spellman piped up. "They're even working Saturday and Sundays."

The Rear Admiral looked surprised. "I...didn't know that. They're supposed to be taking off—at least—one day a week."

"They take their duty to feeding the Fleet very seriously," said Rabbi Spellman, and he frowned. "Too seriously."

"They feel that if they stop, people will go hungry," added Father John.

Dr. Patel leaned forward worriedly. "Pushing themselves that hard, makes more room for mistakes. And that's when accidents happen."

Rabbi Spellman nodded. "There have already been a couple of small ones."

"Why haven't I heard about this?" asked the Rear Admiral frostily.

"You work too hard too," countered Rabbi Spellman.

"Hear, hear!" chirped Teresa.

"There's a lot going on," said the Rear Admiral.

"There will *always* be a lot going on," said Spellman.

Cirilo glanced at Teresa, and she gave a small nod.

Then, it looked like the Senior Medical Officer, Dr. Candleross was going to pile on.

The Rear Admiral's face pinched, but then he nodded—as if to himself—and said. "Let's table Me for the moment." He used a voice built out of pure steel and authority.

Even Teresa settled back a little, not that the war was lost, just this battle.

"So," continued Cirilo. "We need to help the Fishermen out. Give them a day off."

"If you want," said Liberty tentatively. "Maybe they could each give a list of a few items they needed, and I and anyone who wants to help…"

"Me," nodded Uncle Danny.

With a small smile, Liberty continued. "We could get a few items from each, If Possible of course…"

Teresa grinned. "That's a brilliant idea."

"Thank you Liberty, Uncle Danny," nodded Cirilo. "I think I'm going to take you up on that. After the meeting, I'd like to look at that more."

"Absolutely!" chirped Liberty.

During the conversation, Uncle Danny noticed several people looking over at Dr. Washington. Sneaking glances with furtive looks, the Big Mexican wondered what was wrong. Washington, for his part, appeared to be trying to ignore them, but he was definitely aware of it.

"*But Next*," said the Rear Admiral. "We have an issue that is growing, which we need to start looking at. Which is why I brought you here." He gestured. "Dr. Candleross?"

Dr. Candleross was an older gentleman, who was constantly trying to keep his eyebrows from becoming bushy caterpillars.

"The issue," said Candleross. "….is that people are not getting enough vegetables, and fruits."

"You know," said Cirilo, cutting in with a small smile.

73

"I'm happy we're at a good enough place that that is an issue."

With a bright smile, Dr. Candleross nodded. "That's true. It does show progress."

The Rear Admiral gave a little wave. "Sorry. Please go ahead."

"It was a fair point," said Dr. Candleross with a friendly voice, but then he grew serious again. "The problem is scurvy."

Liberty and Uncle Danny glanced at each other, but neither quite recognized it.

"British sailors suffered from this when they were at sea," continued Candleross. "Because they were not getting enough vitamin C. It's actually a problem, because—to start with—it can cause your teeth to fall out." The doctor gestured down the table. "It was actually Dr. Washington that brought it to our attention."

A little embarrassed, Washington just looked down. "It was nothing."

Candleross kept going. "A good doctor needs to be observant. You were recently in Med School, did you read about scurvy there?"

"Oh no," said Washington. "It was on an old TV show, *Chance Thompson: Army Medic Lost In Time.*"

Surprised, Dr. Candleross leaned forward. "Really… usually tv shows play fast and loose with medicine."

"*Chance* was different," said Washington, getting a little excited. "They worked really hard not to cheat. The Showrunner was really insistent, and it got a few awards from it."

Uncle Danny saw one of the doctors, Patel, about to speak, but then another voice boomed.

"JOJO THE CAVE BOY!" cried out Rabbi Spellman. Everyone looked his way. He pointed excitedly at Aaron Washington. "He was JoJo the Cave Boy on... *Chance Thompson: Army Medic Lost In Time*." A little embarrassed, he quickly added. "Sorry. My boys LOVED that show when they were little."

Everyone turned back to Dr. Washington in surprise, including Captain Singh.

With a shy smile, Washington said. "It was actually being on *Chance* that got me interested in medicine. I used to pepper Dr. Tanner— who was our medical consultant— with questions ALL the time."

It looked to Uncle Danny like Dr. Patel was thinking of saying something but stopped herself.

Captain Singh spoke up, curiously. "So, you gave up on acting?"

"Actually...I like to think of it more as a break," smiled Washington. He turned to look at Liberty and Uncle Danny. "I'd like to talk with you about finding some plays. I mean, Shakespeare of course, but also Stoppard, Molière, Beckett..." His voice fell off. "Um, sorry. That's off-topic." He looked back to Dr. Candleross. "When we did the episode where me and Chance were trapped on a British ship, I learned all about scurvy."

Candleross gave a happy shrug. "I don't care how you knew. Thank you."

"Just trying to help," smiled Dr. Washington quietly.

75

Turning to the Rear Admiral, Dr. Candleross said. "Once we recognized the scurvy, we began to see other issues. Nothing bad…yet!"

"Fresh vegetables will go a long way towards helping," bounced in Dr. Patel excitedly, but then she stopped and looked at Candleross. "Sorry. I just…"

However, Dr. Candleross smiled encouragingly. "It's okay. Go ahead."

After a moment's hesitation, Dr. Patel leaned forward. Her thick black hair was in a tight ponytail. "You see, if we can get fresh vegetables into our people, that'll help. Like kale, that has a lot of good stuff in it."

"But…," started Captain Singh thoughtfully. "Where can we even get kale?"

Dr. Patel stopped, thoughtfully.

"That's actually why we're here today," said the Rear Admiral, and added heavily. "Because we're not going to start gardening on the deck of this carrier."

That got a small chuckle.

Captain Singh spoke up. "We talking about the islands off the Coast now?"

The Rear Admiral nodded. "Earlier, I was worried about stretching ourselves too thin, but now, we're in a much better place."

Liberty looked at Uncle Danny questioningly, and the Big Mexican immediately nodded.

"Could be fun," he replied to the unspoken question.

Straightening up, Liberty's face lit. "Oh! And we could teach the kids about farming, an' stuff like that."

"*¡Órale!* That could be an important skill to know," said Uncle Danny.

"What?" asked the Rear Admiral curiously.

Liberty whipped her head to look at him with a bright voice. "Oh! We were discussing if we wanted to drive."

"Drive?" asked Dr. Candleross.

Patel whispered to the older doctor.

"Oh! That's right," said Dr. Candleross. "They're the ones with the magnificent boat."

Liberty blushed. "A bit of luck."

The Rear Admiral nodded. "I'll make sure you have a full tank of gas. And I'd like to send Captain Singh and his people too."

Liberty straightened, a little worried. "Oh! Of Course." She looked at her friend.

"*¡Neta, no manches!*" chuckled Uncle Danny. "We just *assumed* that they were coming."

"Yeah!" said Liberty, as if to correct a bad impression. "I mean, we're really just helping them."

Uncle Danny briefly touched her arm and that helped center the Librarian as she settled. She took a deep breath.

"We actually like working with Captain Singh's people," said Liberty, a little gushily.

Singh gave a big grin. "Ditto. They've been a huge help."

Turning back to business, Liberty looked at the Rear Admiral.

"But how many islands are there off the coast of

California?" she asked. She squelched the need to apologize because she didn't know off-hand. Though it *had* been a while since geography class.

"There are 527 named islands in the state," said the Rear Admiral to a chorus of surprise.

"With people fleeing the Coast, there might even be a working farm," said Teresa hopefully.

"That would be the best-case scenario," nodded the Rear Admiral. "My concern is fuel."

"But to find a working farm would solve a lot of problems," insisted Teresa.

"I agree," replied the Rear Admiral. "However, we're going to need a lot of vegetables to maintain even this ship, much less the rest of the Fleet."

Dr. Patel's brow furrowed. "And...it's not like vegetables grow that quickly." Her face turned thoughtful, and she tapped a painted fingernail against her bright teeth.

"First, we need a lay of the land," said Captain Singh. "We pass the Channel Islands when we go to the Coast. But we've never seen any signs of habitation."

"Yeah, just zoms," said Frankline. "Lots and lots of zoms."

The Captain started to fix the Private with a quelling look, but then smiled. He had invited Frankline along after all.

"He's not wrong," said Singh. "The only habitation we've seen is zoms. Not even a campfire."

"The infection came with them," said the Rear Admiral with a heavy voice. He straightened up though. "Start with the Channel Islands, and then branch out from there. How soon can you cast off?"

Liberty first looked at Uncle Danny, who shrugged, and then she turned to Captain Singh.

"We can move as soon as possible," said the Librarian. She thought of the kids and wondered how this trip would be received. Hopefully good! "Do we need to go today?"

"We should make sure *los niños* are good," nodded Uncle Danny.

Captain Singh glanced at the Rear Admiral who gave a minute shrug.

Singh looked back at *Dos Amigos*. "Would tomorrow morning be alright?"

"Definitely," said Liberty.

"The sooner we find a bit of land," said the Rear Admiral. "The sooner that we can get planting."

"I don't know if I can support this," said Uncle Danny.

Everyone looked at him in surprise.

"I mean, *Vegetables*," moaned Uncle Danny with mock sadness. "I liked my world with very little vegetables in it."

And a big chuckle rolled through the group.

***

The meeting might have broken up, but everyone was still walking in the same direction.

Teresa had caught up with Uncle Danny to ask for his

help.

"We have a number of Spanish speakers, but I don't speak Spanish very well, and I wondered if you could help," she asked.

Knowing that her *amigo* was good, Liberty went a little ahead, thinking furiously. She stopped next to Private Frankline, who looked surprised. Before Liberty could start, her attention was caught by the conversation before her.

Two of the doctors were walking ahead.

"You should say 'hi'," said Dr. Karrass with friendly encouragement. "Life's too short."

"I don't know," said Dr. Patel nervously. She started chewing on her nails. "I'm just going to say something stupid."

"He'll probably appreciate it," said Karrass. "Washington seems like a nice guy."

Now, the two doctors had Liberty's undivided attention as Frankline kept pace, still uncertain.

"That's what I heard," said Dr. Patel.

"Then what're you waiting for?" chuckled Karrass. "He's back there right now!"

"You don't understand!" hissed Dr. Patel plaintively. "I had his poster on my wall. I dragged my Mom to the next town because a movie he was in, *The Mist Settled Slowly*. It was ONLY showing at a little art theater there. Like, in the whole state."

"I've heard of *The Mist*," said Dr. Karrass thoughtfully.

"Definitely not that one," said Dr. Patel swiftly.

"So, you were crushing on him," said Dr. Karrass.

"Big time," moaned Dr. Patel. "And...I just..."

Their boss, Dr. Candleross, came to walk with them, and the topic immediately shifted.

Liberty thought furiously. 'Life's too short', she thought. A part of her wanted to grab Dr. Washington right now. But Dr. Patel's boss was there.

"You okay?" asked Private Frankline uncertainly.

Liberty almost jumped. "Oh. I'm so sorry," she said to him. "I didn't mean to ignore you."

"It's okay," said Frankline kindly. "Can I help you with something?"

"Um," started Liberty softly. She wasn't sure how to start, so she just plunged ahead. "How much do you know about marijuana?"

"What?" hissed Frankline. His eyes grew wide with fear. "Have you been talking to the Captain?"

"WHAT?" replied Liberty, quietly. "No! Definitely not. I'm not..." She paused and took a deep breath. "Let's start over. Have you heard of marijuana helping people who are anxious?"

"Um, yeah sure," said Frankline. "That's why my uncle grew it. He had really bad PTSD after Afghanistan, and he didn't think that regular drugs did the job. Though my Dad didn't think he had tried enough."

"In this case it's because we don't have enough medicine," said Liberty, and she thought quickly. "But, if you can keep that under your hat."

"Oh. Sure! Oh course," said Frankline swiftly and

sincerely. "So, you're looking for another method to help with anxiety. Is it Dr. Tagg?"

Liberty looked at him in surprise.

"I just guessed," said Frankline quickly. "I can't see Uncle Danny being afraid of anything."

"Well, he'd say that he was afraid of his *Abuela*, and God, in that order," said Liberty. Then she saw the Private about to ask. "*Abuela* is Spanish for Grandmother."

Frankline nodded. "Ah. That makes sense." His face grew thoughtful. "But you need to go slowly with marijuana and anxiety."

"Why?" asked Liberty.

"My uncle liked to talk about his pet project, like All The Time," said Frankline with a sigh. "And he lived next door, so I was often over at his house, especially with Dad stationed overseas." He shook his head. "Anyways! Sometimes marijuana can make people more nervous, so you might want to have him try it first before you go any further."

Liberty nodded thoughtfully and gave him a big thanks.

***

"Damn! I almost forgot," cried Liberty to herself.

Not too long after, she ran through the group, going in their separate directions, and reached the Rear Admiral. He was talking to Teresa.

"Everything okay?" asked Cirilo.

Surprised, Liberty raised her hands in supplication. "OH! Everything's good! I just had a thought about tomorrow morning. Should that doctor— um, Patel I think her name is— should she come with us? She knows a lot about what we need to do."

"That's a good idea," said Teresa excitedly, and she looked at the Rear Admiral. "They're gonna need all the help they can get."

Cirilo thought for a moment, but as he was doing so, Liberty's eyes went wide with concern.

"Oh wait!" said the Librarian quickly. "Is she Okay?" And she quickly added. "Is she Nice?"

The Rear Admiral looked confused.

"I don't know," he said slowly. "Does that matter?"

And Teresa looked interested as well.

"Wellllllllll," said Liberty, uncertainly. "I mean, for the mission, no. But…" She thought furiously and a face popped into her head. "I don't want a Dr. House."

"From TV…," started Cirilo uncertainly.

Teresa made a happy little noise. "I get it! She doesn't want anyone on the team who's a real jerk."

The Rear Admiral's brow furrowed.

"Don't you see," continued Teresa. "She's bringing a new person onto her boat. Her Home."

"An' the kids *are* going to be there," said Liberty. "So, I didn't want to be a dumb blonde and invite someone I shouldn't have."

Teresa gave her a stern look. "Hey. Being blonde has

nothing to do with it." Turning to Cirilo, she was about to speak.

The Rear Admiral put two fingers in his mouth and let out an ear-splitting whistle. Liberty literally jumped back, and Teresa put her hands over her ears.

"Hey Jim!" called out the Rear Admiral. "You gotta second!"

Dr. James Candleross excused himself from his conversation and trotted over to them.

Before he arrived, Teresa growled. "You Really Need To Warn A Sister Before You Do That!"

The Rear Admiral blinked in confusion.

"Your whistle almost burst my eardrums," said Teresa tartly.

Cirilo looked surprised and glanced at Liberty.

"It was pretty loud," agreed the Librarian.

"Oh, sorry," said Cirilo as the doctor arrived.

"What's happening?" asked Candleross, unsure of whether he should be worried or not.

"Nothing major," said the Rear Admiral. "We had a question about Dr. Patel."

"Is there a problem?" asked Dr. Candleross with immediate concern.

"No!" said Liberty quickly.

"We were wondering if Dr. Patel might be a good fit for the team going out tomorrow," explained the Rear Admiral.

"And more specifically," added Teresa. "Is she an okay person to work with?"

Swiftly and apologetically, Liberty added "It's my fault really," said Liberty shyly. "But my kids will be there, and…"

"Is Dr. Patel a 'jerk'?" asked the Rear Admiral bluntly.

"What?" exclaimed Dr. Candleross. "No! She's actually quite a nice young lady. Just a little green right now but improving by leaps and bounds."

Liberty smiled and her shoulders slumped. "That's a relief."

"The team going out tomorrow could use Dr. Patel," said the Rear Admiral. "I intend to borrow her, because she actually knows what kale is."

Candleross grinned. "I prefer Iceberg lettuce myself."

"Oh no!" said Teresa with a motherly tone. "You don't want Iceberg. It's basically just water."

"Considering how much Blue Cheese I'd put on it…," shrugged Dr. Candleross with a grin.

Turning, Cirilo regarded Liberty. "Actually, will you have enough food for tomorrow?"

Liberty opened her mouth, and then closed it. "I don't…"

"That's okay. I'll send some with Captain Singh," nodded the Rear Admiral.

Teresa gave a long sigh. "It's too bad we don't have hot dogs. That'd be perfect for a day out."

Cirilo gave a wistful smile. "And mustard potato salad."

"Well, veggie dogs for me," said Teresa with a little chuckle.

"I would if I could," said Cirilo with a warm, little sigh.

Chapter Four

LIBERTY FROZE.

Her mind raced. She didn't want to mess this up, not at this early stage of the operation.

The *Wolf Pack* was pulling away from the Fleet, and Liberty saw Dr. Patel on deck, looking around, unsure of what to do.

'What's Dr. Patel's first name?' thought the Librarian furiously.

Shaking her head to help her focus, Liberty looked around and saw her prey. She zipped over.

A small group of people, including Rakduson, were all talking animatedly about science.

"...happy to help make a Faraday Cage," said Staff Sergeant Ruiz with interest.

"That's great," replied Smalls, the Navy Engineer. "I've never tried it, so it'll be real interesting."

"Will it be safe?" asked Dr. Washington with concern.

"Oh yes!" said Ruiz quickly. "It just blocks electronic signals, but it won't hurt anyone inside."

"Actually, it might help them," added Smalls. He nodded at the alien-bird, Rakduson. "If we can dampen the signals that drive her people crazy…"

"They're less likely to hurt themselves," nodded Washington.

"Yes!" said Rak hopefully. "Not fight soldiers. Live happy."

During a tiny lull, Liberty jumped in. "Um. Hey Dr. Washington."

Aaron Washington turned immediately. "Everything okay?"

"Oh! Everything's great," said Liberty quickly. "An' I should actually have said, 'Aaron', because this is more of an 'Aaron' thing."

The Doctor's brow furrowed. "I'm not following."

Liberty took a deep breath. "Okay, let's start again."

"Please do," teased Washington gently.

"Can you help with something?" asked Liberty and she waved him to follow. He ambled along dressed like the rest of Singh's team in their everyday camouflage.

As they neared Dr. Patel, Liberty called out. "Welcome to the *Wolf Pack!*"

Dr. Patel nearly jumped out of her skin and whipped

88

around. "What?"

"Oh! Sorry!" said Liberty quickly with embarrassment. "I didn't mean to startle you, but I realized that I hadn't said, 'hi' yet, and welcomed you aboard."

"Thank you!" said Dr. Patel. "It's actually really nice to get out of the ship and see the sun."

"I know," agreed Dr. Washington with a great big smile. "And the ocean breeze."

"True!" agreed Liberty as she turned to Washington. "Dr. Patel hasn't ever been aboard, so I wondered if you might give her the nickel tour."

Dr. Patel froze. "I don't want to put him out."

"It's not a problem," said Washington. "By the way, my name's Aaron."

"OH!" said Patel with surprise. "I...I'm..."

"This is Radha Patel," said Liberty. "And full disclosure, she knows your work." Then she amended. "Your Work Work."

Washington started happily. "Really? You watched '*Dr. Chance Thompson...*'"

"*...Army Medic Lost In Time*'," finished Dr. Patel.

"And maybe more," slid in Liberty.

Dr. Patel looked at her with cautious concern.

Blushing, Liberty admitted to her. "Okay. I totally heard you talking to your colleague in the hall yesterday. Sorry, not sorry. So, I wanted to introduce you." She turned to Washington. "She saw some movie of yours about '*The Mist*' or something."

89

"Thankfully, it's not *that* movie called *The Mist*," said Washington swiftly, but then he turned to Patel. "I can't believe you saw *The Mist Settles Slowly*. You must be one of the four tickets that sold. My mama was the other three."

Patel looked down embarrassed. "You were really good."

"I really appreciate that," said Washington. "Actually, that was my last work before devoting myself to Med School. Thank you. And what type of medicine do you do? Obviously, nutrition."

"Actually, the Nutrition part was something I was always interested in," said Patel, loosening up.

Liberty backed up. "Okay, I gots to mingle, but you can go anywhere on this deck...well, actually...". She turned and addressed everyone on the deck. "*Hey! Everyone!* Real quick! We just wanted to ask that all guests to stay on this deck and the decks above, but not to go downstairs." She looked embarrassed. "That's where our cabins are...So..."

"What *MS.* Schonhauer is trying to NICELY say," bellowed Captain Singh. "Is that Below Decks is off-limits. Anyone caught down below will be swimming home. Everyone wearing green, I want a 'Yes Sir' like you mean it!"

All the soldiers dutifully shouted a 'Yes Sir', and Dr. Patel did so too.

Captain Singh looked at her, kindly. "That was really just for My People."

Patel grinned though and pulled up her pant leg. "You said, 'anyone wearing green'."

With a smirk, Singh said. "People with green socks are

the exception to the swimming home rule."

"Well, don't worry, I wouldn't wander far," said Patel.

"We weren't worried," assured Liberty quickly. "I just wanted to let everyone know at once." Then she looked at her and Washington. "Well, I'm going to stop meddling."

Holding up her hands in supplication, the Librarian backed off to Washington's amusement. Dr. Patel looked like she didn't know what to say, good or bad.

Liberty walked up behind Colin and Tessy and unabashedly eavesdropped.

The nine-year-old girl, Tessy, was bouncing nervously. "You should ask."

"I'm not asking," replied Colin with a quick dismissal.

"Whyyyyy nooooot?" asked Tessy with a little whine.

"You heard what Uncle Danny said," said Colin. "We're the hosts, so we need to be polite to our guests, which would include *stupid* questions."

"It's not like we can just look it up on the internet," huffed Tessy. She took a little bit of her hair and chewed on it nervously.

"Are you two having fun?" asked Liberty.

The two jumped a little and whipped around.

"Are you *really* asking if we're being good?" asked Colin suspiciously

"My smart man, but I really wanted to know if you were having fun, with a sub-text of checking up on you," admitted Liberty with a warm smile.

"Sub-text?" asked Tessy.

91

With a serious expression at Liberty, Colin said to Tessy. "It's another meaning underneath the words. Mom wants to make sure we're 'good', *and* 'Being Good', at the same time."

"Right," nodded Liberty proudly, which did make Colin feel lighter, even though he'd never admit it. But, then she looked expectantly at Colin.

Finally, he rolled his eyes melodramatically.

"We're being 'Good'." said Colin with a put-upon voice.

Grinning, Liberty grabbed them quickly and pulled both of them into a fierce hug.

"Moooom," complained Colin, but then he noticed Captain Singh and the others starting to look. His voice grew more insistent. "MOM."

Colin started to squirm away. Liberty took a moment to kiss them both on the top of their heads and let them go. This also confirmed that they did indeed wash their hair as asked. 'Nice', she thought.

Stepping further back —so as Not to get snatched again — Colin made a show of fixing his shirt.

"Thank you," said the Librarian. "My Hug Level was getting low." But she wasn't leaving. With narrow eyes, Liberty asked. "Now, what're you two up to?"

The Kids looked down nervously.

"I was just looking," said the Boy swiftly.

Liberty noticed Tessy looking at the boy questioningly, but Colin's eyes started to bug out in warning. Tessy looked up at Liberty and said in a sing-song voice. "Nothing. I think Colin missed you too."

Colin's frown deepened, but he couldn't argue.

While Liberty had worked out that they had been looking at Captain Singh, she instead said to Tessy. "Thank you for not Telling on him."

"What?" asked both Kids at once.

Regarding Colin, Liberty said. "She didn't need to say anything." She pointed at herself. "Secret Mom Powers."

With a squinty look, Colin just murmured incredulously. "Uh-huh."

Smirking mischievously, Liberty clapped her hands together lightly. "We do have some new people who we haven't seen much of, or at all...Oh! You guys are missing your classes today."

Colin groaned.

Tessy looked at him and moaned. "I tol' you she'd remember."

"No, no," said Liberty fast. "Nothing bad. I was thinking that some of our education could come from the people here."

"How so?" asked Tessy curiously.

"One moment," said Liberty. "I'll be right back."

"Oh-oh!" muttered Colin.

Liberty smiled at him. "Don't worry, no 'oh-oh' needed."

"Uh-huh," said the boy suspiciously.

Practically skipping, Liberty zipped across the deck. Captain Singh, who the kids had been looking at, was talking with Uncle Danny.

Liberty stopped beside Singh and gave a big salute. "Permission to speak."

Singh saluted back with a fun smile.   "Permission granted. At ease."

Relaxing, Liberty explained her idea, and Singh was immediately on board. They went to the Staff Sergeant and Private and soon gained their help. She could grab Drs. Washington and Patel, who were talking animatedly, at some later point.

Amused, Uncle Danny followed them back towards the kids.   Before reaching them, he called out melodramatically. *"Perdón por dios!* I tried to stop them, but I have failed you."

Liberty turned and scowled at him. "Don't scare the kids."

However, Uncle Danny just grinned unrepentantly.

Liberty quickly turned to the kids. "Don't worry!"

"Yep," said Colin to Tessy. "We should definitely run now."

The little girl grinned. *"¡Ya te cargó el payaso!"*

"Don't you dare! I will hunt you down," said Liberty with mock sternness, but she could not stop her smile. "And Smother you in hugs."

"Not That!!" cried Colin, over-dramatically.

When Liberty was close enough, she swung around behind them and put her hand on each child's shoulder.

"Trapped like rats," whispered Colin to Tessy with a smirk.

"We don't have official class today, BUT we do have some interesting guests," said Liberty. "And they have graciously offered to field some questions from you."

"Wait, what?" asked Colin.

Captain Singh smiled. "You can ask us any questions that you might have, and we'll answer."

"Within reason of course," interjected Liberty. "They don't have to answer a question if they don't want to."

The Kids looked at each other, eyes wide, and then looked back at the soldiers.

"Really?" they asked as one.

"Really, really," said Liberty because they had found a DVD of *Shrek* recently.

When Captain Singh nodded, Colin took a deep breath. "What's with the turban? Are you a Muslim? Are you a real soldier?"

Tessy broke in. "Hav' you ever killed anyone? Can we see your gun?" She pointed to Singh's empty side holster.

Liberty looked up worriedly, but Deep Singh smiled down at the kids with absolute patience.

"That's a lot of questions," started Singh. "No on the gun, and I'm not a Muslim, I'm a Sikh."

"What's that?" asked Tessy.

Standing back, Liberty listened with interest as they talked.

Chapter Five

LIBERTY, UNCLE DANNY, CAPTAIN SINGH, and Smalls were in the pilot's cabin.

The Navy Engineer said as he steered the ship. "I do have a course that will take us to a number of islands, and conserve fuel, if you want to use that."

"Sounds good," nodded Captain Singh. He noticed the boy, Colin, squatting near the door, listening in, but kept talking. "This is really just reconnaissance. I don't plan on going on any of the islands just yet."

"What if we see any communities?" asked Smalls.

"We'll reach out in that case," replied the Captain. "But...I'm not optimistic."

"Someone has to have survived," said Smalls urgently.

"¡Órale! I agree there must be some," said Uncle Danny.

"But we don't want to pin our hopes on it."

Liberty spoke up. "Even if we find an island with good soil, cleaning it of zoms will be…" Her voice drifted off.

Eyes widening, Uncle Danny whispered. "*Ya te cargó el payaso,*"

"What if we bomb it?" asked Smalls. "Drop a big missile and that should take out a lot of zoms."

Captain Singh nodded. "I wondered about that. But what's that going to do to the soil."

"And if there is someone hiding out in the middle of one of those islands…," said Liberty with a quick worry.

"Yeah. We don't want to drop a bomb on a Friendly," nodded Singh vehemently.

"I was just thinking out loud," said the Navy Engineer quickly, worriedly.

"You're fine," said the Captain immediately. "We're just trying to get ahead of any potential problems."

"And. Even if we can 'Clean' the island," said Uncle Danny. "Then we gotta learn how to farm."

"Oh yeah!" said Liberty with more worry. "Or even if we find a farmer, they might be living day to day as is."

Captain Singh clapped his hands together. "Okay, so what we have here, is too many possibilities to really plan for right now. I recommend that we tour the islands near the Coast and see where we stand…."

***

"...In the poop," sighed Liberty softly.

Singh looked at her. "What?"

The Liberian looked up suddenly. "Oh! I was just..." She gestured futilely at Santa Catalina Island. "That's a lot of zoms."

"*Órale*," agreed Uncle Danny sadly.

Each island had been overrun with survivors, and then soon overrun with zoms.

Slowly, Singh brought up his walkie-talkie. "Mr. Smalls, can you take us to San Clemente?"

"San Clemente! Copy that Sir," said Smalls, up in the pilot's house.

"We can always go up and down the Coast," said Liberty tentatively. "Not every island is going to be covered in zoms."

"True. But...," said the Captain thoughtfully. "If it's too far from the Fleet, then it'll be harder to protect."

"Yeah," muttered Uncle Danny. "We don't want some *cabrónes* coming in, hurting our farmers, and taking our veggies."

Shortly, they could see San Clemente Island growing closer.

"Too bad the Admiral refused to grow food on the deck of the aircraft carrier," said Liberty, and then she chuckled mischievously. "You know. We could sneak aboard and put a garden up there."

Despite his concern, a grin escaped Captain Singh. "I'd love to see his reaction."

"I'd hate to carry up all the soil needed," said Uncle Danny.

"Oooh, good point," said Liberty.

"Yeah," admitted Singh. "That would not be practical. Still, if only we could do something like that."

The boat slowed as it neared the island.

Looking through the detached scope of her sniper rifle, Liberty said excitedly. "I'm not seeing any zoms."

Singh said over the earpieces. "Mr. Smalls, can you move slowly along the coast?"

"Copy that," said Smalls.

The Wolf Pack moved around the island.

"There might be some structures further inland," said Singh as he looked through his binoculars.

"Maybe people," said Liberty. "Like, living ones."

"Captain!" called out Smalls over the earpieces. "We got a boat coming towards us, fast."

As the Captain was looking around, Liberty pointed.

"Over there," she called out. Immediately, she ran to a trunk where they had stored their guns while the kids were around.

Unlocking it, the Librarian sprinted back with her sniper rifle. After snapping her scope back into place, she lifted the rifle.

"They have guns," said Singh, looking through his binoculars and lifted his walkie-talkie. "Mr. Smalls, I need you to start heading for open ocean, but slow enough, so that they can come up next to us. Do Not Stop."

"Copy that. Carefully heading for open water," said Smalls.

"But if you hear one shot…just one," said Singh. "I want you to gun the engine and head straight for the Fleet. Call ahead." He turned quickly to the assembled group. "Rak…I mean, Ms. Rakduson, can you take the kids and Dr. Patel below deck?"

"Trou-ble?" asked Rak with her bird beak.

"Don't know yet," replied Singh thoughtfully.

Uncle Danny added in a hard voice. "But if you see anyone but us, Eat'em!"

"Protect 'dem like my chicks!" said Rak and she opened her wings to herd everyone below.

"Um…," started Dr. Patel looking at the alien-bird's razor-sharp beak.

Colin saw her fear and reached out to tug on Dr. Patel's shirt sleeve. "Come on. It's okay."

Picking up on it, Tessy took Dr. Patel's hand and said in a singsong, little girl voice. "This way."

As they disappeared below, Singh realized he should have told them to hide in the engine room, away from the coming boat, but it was too late now.

Singh looked at Liberty, but before he said anything.

"High ground?" she half-asked/suggested.

"You got your earpiece?" asked Singh.

Liberty tapped hers and checked. A moment later, she had gone to climb up on top of the Pilot's House.

"I want the .50," grinned Uncle Danny.

101

"Keep down though," said Singh. "I want it to be a surprise."

"*Sí*," said Uncle Danny and he went to disappear by the helicopter pad. At the stern of the boat, a .50 cal machine gun had been mounted. Right now, it was pointed down, so he hoped that the boat would not realize what it was.

The oncoming boat blared a siren twice.

"Keep your course Mr. Smalls," said Singh. "But you can slow down a tad more. They might be friendlies."

"Might," said Uncle Danny over earpieces.

The boat was almost here, so the Captain turned his soldiers.

Ruiz was returning with his Beretta, which he took. The rest of his soldiers were there a moment later, fully armed again.

"Washington. Frankline. Keep outta sight until I give a signal. Washington towards the front of the boat and the Private towards the rear."

Frankline was about to correct the Captain about 'bow' and 'stern'. But he wisely kept his big trap shut and ran off.

Someone on the oncoming boat was shouting something through a bullhorn as Singh and Ruiz readied their rifles.

The Captain realized he could have sent Frankline or Washington down with the kids and had Rakduson fly off the opposite side of the boat. Then the alien-bird could have flown up behind the oncoming boat, just in case. If they could get an earpiece, or whatever, for Rak, that would be...

Shaking off the 'Couldas and Shouldas', Singh went

back to the edge of the yacht.

Besides, that could get Rak shot, which would be bad on so many levels.

The oncoming boat was getting closer. With one arm still in a sling, he loosened the gun in its now left-sided holster. The gun he also couldn't shoot well.

"Um, I have an idea," said Ruiz. "A not-direct-approach."

The Bullhorn Man was getting more distinct. "Sto...ow."

"No more time, Staff Sergeant," said the Captain. "Go with your idea."

Ruiz stiffened. "It's a bit unorthodox."

The Captain gave her a calm smile. "You can do this."

Now emboldened, Ruiz straightened. "Yes Sir."

Turning to the oncoming boat, the Staff Sergeant slung her rifle behind her back.

With a boisterous and cheery voice, she cried. "Hey!!! Hi! Hello! It's great to see you."

The Bullhorn Man hesitated.

Backing Ruiz's play, the Captain also waved his uninjured arm enthusiastically.

The oncoming boat started to slow, to come alongside them. Now, they could hear them.

"THIS IS THE UNITED STATES MILITARY!" cried The Bullhorn Man. "STOP YOUR BOAT IMMEDIATELY!!!"

"Like Hell," muttered Singh, without moving his mouth. Loudly, he replied. "Good to see you."

The oncoming boat pulled alongside the slowly moving yacht. Their boat looked civilian. It had a canopy on top, which had a badly drawn figure that looked like a roadkill mermaid.

The Bullhorn Man took a deep breath to speak when Ruiz leaned over the rail towards them.

"Do you got any vegetables?" she asked.

Bullhorn Man froze. "WHAT?"

"Vegetables?" asked Ruiz again. "Kale, cucumbers, tomatoes..." She stopped and looked at Singh. "Actually, tomatoes are a fruit..." She looked back. "Any fresh fruits or veggies?"

Trying to get control of the conversation, Bullhorn Man bellowed. "STOP YOUR BOAT NOW!"

Ruiz reared back from the squall, and then said. "You don't need that. You're close enough now."

"I'LL SAY WHAT I NEED, AND DON'T NEED," snapped Bullhorn Man.

"Oh darn, now he's got to use it the whole time," whispered Ruiz with a grumble. "Possible compensation issues in his pants."

"We're still good," said Singh, and he called out. "How long have you been on the island?"

Bullhorn Man ignored him. "YOU NEED TO STOP THIS BOAT RIGHT FUCKING NOW. WE ARE THE US MARINES."

"Language!" called out Ruiz. "And we're Army." And she added under her breath. "Or, at least we were."

"Close enough," whispered Singh.

"WE'LL DETERMINE WHAT YOU ARE!" said Bullhorn Man.

"No! Seriously! We're U.S. Military too," said Ruiz helpfully.

"WHAT YOU WERE DOING CASING OUR ISLAND," insisted Bullhorn Man. "WE NEED TO DETERMINE IF YOU WERE TRYING TO GET TO THE PRESIDENT."

Singh and Ruiz stopped. They looked at each other in surprise, and then back.

"President Collins is here!!!" cried Ruiz with real excitement. She had liked him.

"WHAT?" Bullhorn Man blinked stupidly for a second, but then he rallied. "PRESIDENT BUTTERFETT!"

Confused, Singh and Ruiz looked at each other again, then back.

"Who?" asked the Staff Sergeant.

"Oh!" said Singh. "I think Butterfett was a senator from Alabama, or Tennessee, or something."

"TEXAS!" snapped Bullhorn Man with irritation. "AND..."

"What happened to President Collins?" asked Ruiz. "Did he get bit? Which would be sad because he seemed like a nice guy."

"WE HAVEN'T HEARD FROM COLLINS IN A LONG TIME," bellowed Bullhorn Man. "SO, THE SENATOR BRAVELY TOOK THE MANTLE."

"Sooooo," started Singh. "We don't actually *know* if he's dead."

105

"WELL, PROBABLY," said Bullhorn Man. One of the other soldiers whispered to him urgently as both boats moved past the island and out into open water.

Pulling himself together, Bullhorn Man tried again, escalating. "IF YOU DON'T STOP, WE WILL BE FORCED TO FIRE."

Singh leaned forward. "My name is Captain Singh, and we're out of the U.S. *Teddy Roosevelt*."

Bullhorn Man's face twisted. "THEY ARE NOT REAL AMERICANS. THEY KICKED THE SENAT...I MEAN, PRESIDENT OFF THEIR SHIP."

"Oh," said Ruiz softly. "When we first got here, I heard about some politician getting booted off. They tried to take control of the ship or something, but no one would join them, except a few."

"I'VE HAD IT!" cried Bullhorn Man, almost petulantly. "STOP, OR WE WILL FIRE." The other soldiers on the other boat eagerly lifted their weapons, ready to fire.

In Singh's ear, Liberty spoke.

"I can't see heads because of the canopy," she said. "But I got their legs."

"Good to know," said the Captain.

Regarding the other boat, Singh spoke up. "We're on the same side. But you're not in my chain of command. We're not going to stop."

"THAT'S IT. WE'RE GOING TO FIRE," screamed Bullhorn Man. "YOUR BOAT IS NOW PROPERTY OF THE UNITED STATES OF..."

Singh sighed. "Mr. Smalls, hit it."

Without replying, and a great big grin, Smalls gunned the engine and began to pull ahead.

One of the other soldiers fired, which was followed by everyone in the small boat firing.

"Everyone Stay Down!" ordered Singh.

"Did they hit our boat?" asked Liberty with a cold voice. "They better not have."

"I'm afraid I heard a few hits," reported Singh, but then he quickly added. "But only a few."

"I think I can get the son of a bitch with the bullhorn," said Liberty.

"Please stand down," said Singh as he hurried up to where she was, just beating Uncle Danny by two seconds. He made it up and then looked back in surprise. "You can really make that shot?"

"Yes," said Liberty with a scary voice. She exhaled slowly.

Singh reached out and touched Uncle Danny's sleeve, who jumped a little.

Liberty's finger began to squeeze the trigger.

"The Kids!" said Uncle Danny as loudly as he dared. "*Mija?* Have you seen the kids?"

The finger stopped, but did not leave the trigger.

"Hey! If they've hurt anyone, it's not like we can't swing back around and finish the job," suggested Uncle Danny. "They aren't going that quick."

Liberty's face contorted. "Shit."

Lowering her rifle, the Librarian scrambled down off the

Pilot's House and bolted downstairs.

The men followed at a slower pace. Singh let out a breath of relief and smiled at Uncle Danny.

"That was so good," said the Captain. "I almost believed it myself."

"¿Qué?" asked Uncle Danny, puzzled.

"The whole, 'finish the job'," said Singh.

Uncle Danny's dark eyes just looked at the Captain.

"We need to check on the kids," said Danny with an icy voice.

Singh slowed for a moment, but then hurried up, even going a little faster to find Liberty. Soon he heard her.

'This must be the Scary Voice that Colin had mentioned,' thought Singh.

"COLIN! TESSY!" cried the Librarian from down below. Both men poured on the speed as she called again.

Singh reached the bottom of some stairs, but he was almost run over by an 11-year-old. The Captain reared back on his tiptoes.

"Sorry!" cried Colin as he ran past. He was holding Tessy's hand, or more likely, she wouldn't let go of him, so he towed her along.

"MOM!" cried the 11-year-old boy.

"COLIN!" replied Liberty. She appeared and dropped to her knees before the kids, putting her rifle down. But they were going too fast.

The Librarian wrapped her arms around the kids as they collided into her. She fell back onto the floor with them.

"Oh no, sorry," cried Colin.

However, Liberty squeezed them tightly and kissed the tops of their heads.

"It'sokayit'sokay!" she burbled.

Kneeling beside them, Uncle Danny rubbed the kid's backs.

"Aunt Rak took us far to the front of the ship," said Tessy breathlessly. "Dr. Patel was pretty worried, but we helped her."

"That's wonderful of you two," said Liberty.

Colin squirmed a bit. "Um, can we get up now."

A little reluctantly, the Librarian let him go, and Tessy followed, a little reluctant herself. Danny started to stand.

"Ergh," grunted Uncle Danny.

"You okay?" asked Liberty with concern as she hopped right up.

"Just having trouble getting up," said Uncle Danny. "My knees don't like getting up."

Liberty offered a hand, but he managed it.

Rakduson appeared with Dr. Patel and the Librarian shot forward.

Wrapping her arms around the alien-bird, Liberty gave her a huge hug.

"Thank you," she said into the warm feathers.

A little stunned, Rak said. "Okay."

With a determined air, Singh stepped away and headed up for the Pilot's House.

Out of view, a memory hit him, and he stopped. Everyone was good. Everyone was safe. So, he let the icy memory creep through him. Sitting beside his wife's hospital bed after the car accident. Dreading the moment when she woke up and asked after their daughter.

Ultimately, Singh never had to tell her that Harita hadn't felt anything.

"You okay?" asked a worried voice behind him. A deep voice trying to be soft.

The Captain straightened up and tucked away the memory. With a brave smile, he turned to look down the stairs where Uncle Danny was standing.

"I'm good," said Singh.

The Big Mexican walked up a few steps to get closer. "Don't keep stuff in. It's like venom. You gotta get it outta you, or things go bad."

Singh nodded. "I tried, but my therapist got eaten."

"I get it," said Danny. "Well, I got a good ear...*dos* in fact."

"For now," said the Captain. "I gotta keep moving."

"Don't fool yourself and walk for too long," said the Big Mexican stridently.

"Yes Uncle Danny," said Singh with a real grin.

Chapter Six

"SOOOOO," SAID LIBERTY thoughtfully.

The Librarian, Uncle Danny, Singh, and Smalls were in the Pilot's House once again.

"It's totally up to you," said the Captain. "As is, I'm going to have to make a full report to the Admiral when I get back, so I'm in no hurry."

Liberty spoke slowly. "Actually, I'm a little fuzzy on just what happened, and who they were."

"It's not just you," said Singh. "It was definitely weird." He shrugged. "But, in the future, if anyone is barreling towards us, we should just go."

"¡Órale!" nodded Danny.

The Librarian looked at the Big Mexican, but he gave a little shrug.

Turning to Singh, Liberty said. "Why don't we look a little more. We'll just be careful. I'm going up on the top of the Pilot's House with my cute umbrella."

"And I'll be watching the radar like a hawk," said Smalls as he drove the boat.

Singh looked at everyone to make sure that everyone was really okay, and then he nodded.

"Thank you," said the Captain. "And we're going to all have our rifles. I don't think the Channel Islands are going to be our best bet, but let's keep going." He looked at the pilot. "Just give us a wide berth Mr. Smalls."

"Yes sir," replied the Navy Engineer.

***

"Hey! How're you doing?" called out a voice.

Atop the Pilot's House, Liberty had been sitting cross-legged with her cute umbrella tucked against her to keep it upright. Moving the rifle across her lap, the Librarian leaned over the edge. Below, Captain Singh was looking up.

"How're the kids?" asked Liberty immediately.

"They're good," said Singh. "We're keeping them entertained."

"So, what're you doing up here? Checking up on me?" asked Liberty with amusement.

"Guard duty is tough, especially alone," said Singh.

"Right!" admitted Liberty with humor. "I thought it

would be a nice sit up here. But the ocean got boring, really fast."

Singh smiled. "The nice thing is that anything is going to show up right away. Much better than having to watch a tree line in the dark, believe me."

"Oh yes," nodded Liberty. "That would suck."

"So, you holding up?" asked Singh.

"It's not too bad," shrugged Liberty.

"If you start feeling like you're going to nod off," said Singh. "I'll send up some relief. I don't want you to sit up here the rest of the day."

"True," replied Liberty.

Singh also placed a bottle of water beside her with an expectant look of 'hydrate'.

"Smalls said that there are some little islands by the Port of the City of Angels. Can't imagine they'd work, but... we're not too far," said the Captain. "What do you think? Do we have time to check it out?"

Liberty looked at the sun which was still well above the horizon.

"I'm good, if Uncle Danny is," she said.

***

Shortly, Liberty looked out at Long Beach, not that she had ever been there. And today would be no exception. She lay atop the Pilot's House looking over at Uncle Danny, Captain Singh and Smalls talking.

113

"I'm sorry," said Smalls, the Navy Engineer. "I thought they might be real islands, and not...well, whatever they are. They look like oil refineries..."

"It's okay," said the Captain quickly. "Not your fault. This whole mission is..."

"Like hunting for a needle in a haystack?" suggested Liberty cheerily.

Singh sighed slowly. "I was hoping that one of the islands would be somewhat deserted."

"*Sí*, but we could try again tomorrow," suggested Uncle Danny.

The Captain shook his head. "The Rear Admiral didn't want to devote too much time to this. In case it's a lost cause. So, tomorrow my team is back on the Coast."

"We could keep looking," said Liberty slowly, uncertainly. She looked at the Big Mexican.

"If the Rear Admiral is okay with giving us that much fuel," added Smalls.

"I wouldn't want to risk the kids," said Uncle Danny.

"Exactly," sighed Liberty. "We'd have to leave them somewhere, preferably with Tagg."

"Maybe there's still room on the medical ship," said Uncle Danny, thoughtfully.

As they came up with a series of plans, Singh looked out and suddenly laughed. Everyone looked at him in case it was a brain-related event.

Pointing, the Captain looked back. "I think that's the *Queen Mary* there. We could always grab that."

This led to a fun conversation about stealing *Queen Mary*.

Finally, they decided to head back to the Fleet, but slowly. If they saw any islands along the way, they'd check them out.

Alone once again, Liberty positioned her cute umbrella against the sun and kept guard. Smalls took them out past the Port of the City of Angels.

Over the earpieces, Singh said. "Actually, if we could secure the Port, think of how many goods are there. Some might be cheap stuff."

"¡*Neta, no manches!* There might even be food that is still good for a year or two more," said Uncle Danny.

"And maybe medical supplies," suggested Dr. Washington.

While they spoke, Liberty kept looking around, stopped, and suddenly lifted her rifle.

"Wait a minute," said Liberty. She dropped and leaned over the edge of the roof. Rapping on a window of the Pilot's House, she called. "Stop! Please stop!"

***

"Okay," said Singh slowly after they had gotten closer. "It looks like a barge."

"Barge *grande*," added Uncle Danny.

"Do you think it would survive out on the open ocean?" asked Liberty.

Smalls leaned over the rail. "There are definitely ocean-going barges, and that one looks big enough to survive out at sea."

"If we can't find a safe island," said Liberty. "What if we bring the island to us?"

Chapter Seven

"WE GOT ONE zom on deck," reported Liberty, looking through the scope of her rifle. "I could take it from here." Her voice trailed off.

Uncle Danny made an unhappy noise. *"No manches*, it seems a bit..." He stopped. "I don't know."

"Unsporting," said Liberty. She sighed. "Well, there's nothing for it..." The Librarian exhaled to still herself.

"Wait!" said Private Frankline. His young face scrunched up. "We could probably just take it."

"Without getting yourself killed?" asked Captain Singh.

"Exactly," added Staff Sergeant Ruiz, and she heard the earnestness in her own voice and felt a little embarrassed.

Frankline turned to them. "Um, should be good." He turned to Liberty and Danny. "I just need one thing."

***

"Here zombie, zombie, zombie!" called out the Captain.

The creature in an orange vest turned on the deck of the barge to face him.

"Ergh," it grunted.   Eat…hunger…eat…bite…, it thought. There was nothing more inside.

"*¡Neta! El Toro!*" cried Uncle Danny. He held his yellow coat to one side like a *Matador de toros*. "*Arriba!* We don't have all day!"

A little ways away on the barge, Liberty let out a snort of laughter.

"Sorry, I snorted," she said with a high-pitched, giggly voice.

"Are you laughing at me?" demanded the Big Mexican, pretending to be insulted.

"Maybe," said Liberty mischievously, but she did keep watch on the piece of wood that lay as a gangway between the barge and the dock. Right now, the other zoms out there had not noticed, but their luck would not hold forever.

"Let's move this along," said Singh, as if reading her mind.

The creature lurched towards Uncle Danny.

A blue tarp fell over the zom. The Big Mexican dropped his coat and ran forward. He grabbed the zom in a bear hug. It bucked a little, making confused noises.

"Okay," said Frankline. "We just need to get them on to the dock and pull out the board after him."

They frog-marched the zom in his tarp. The board to the dock was a little off the ground. Ultimately, Uncle Danny had to lift the zom onto the board.

Suddenly, the zom began thrash about in the tarp.

"*¡Merdes!*" hissed Uncle Danny worriedly, and then he said to the zom. "Stay still."

"Need a hand?" asked Frankline.

The zom twisted and pulled away from Uncle Danny lurching halfway across the board. There was a small gap between the barge and dock.

"Wait!" called Uncle Danny to it. He tried to jump forward in time as Frankline reached them. The Big Mexican grabbed the edge of the tarp, but the zom spun out from under it.

It went right off the board and down into the gap. The zom hit the dock on the way down.

This caused a terrible noise that made Frankline and Uncle Danny flinch in unison. They looked down, crestfallen.

The zom had smacked into the water, but came up, bobbing on the surface.

Uncle Danny called out. "*¡Perdón por pisarte la mano!*"

"Hey guys!" called out Liberty.

They looked up and saw more zoms now coming.

Swiftly they came back onto the barge and pulled the board back for later.

119

Frankline gestured towards the zom in the water. "Sorry about this."

Uncle Danny gave a little smile and patted the young private on the shoulder.

"¡Neta! We tried," said the Big Mexican.

"Okay," said the Captain. "Now that that's done. Let's get Smalls over here and see what he has to say about this thing."

***

"A tugboat?" asked Singh.

"Yeah," said the Navy Engineer slowly. He was looking over the ocean-going barge. "We're going to need one that is okay with being out on the ocean too."

"Well, there must be one in this Port," suggested Liberty.

However, after searching, they couldn't find one.

"The sun's getting low," said Singh. "Let's head back. We can discuss in the morning."

Chapter Eight

"I'M SURPRISED," SAID the Rear Admiral the next morning. "I'd have thought that a Port as big as the City of Angels would have a tugboat."

"Well, there was one," said Liberty from across a round table onboard the carrier. "However, it was too small apparently."

"Maybe if we had two," said Uncle Danny thoughtfully. His face scrunched up. "Probably wouldn't work."

"What about in the Fleet?" asked the Rear Admiral.

"We had Smalls look around this morning," said Captain Singh. "But he couldn't see one."

"Yeah, and it's not like tugs are hard to spot," nodded the Rear Admiral.

Liberty said a little sadly. "So, we figured we'd come

back here and try and think it out."

"Smalls said that there probably were some," said the Captain. "But they were most likely taken."

"And they could be anywhere by now," said the Rear Admiral. "It's like searching for a needle on the bottom of the ocean." He looked closer at the old map in front of him. "But, we have more Ports."

"Really?" asked Liberty excitedly.

"There should be two close to the City of Angels," said the Rear Admiral. "The Port of Hueneme is North of the City of Angels, but then there's the Port of San Diego to the South. San Diego will be a longer trip."

"We could try the Port of Hue...whatever you said," began Singh.

"Hueneme," supplied the Rear Admiral. "It's military and commercial."

"Yes Sir," replied the Captain thoughtfully. "We could try that first, but if it doesn't lead to a barge, we could head South." He turned to Dos Amigos. "But it won't be a day trip."

Liberty and Danny looked at each other and then back.

"¡Órale!" said the Big Mexican. "It could be fun."

"But!" said the Librarian quickly. "We can't bring the kids. Not again."

"Yes, those people in the boat," said Cirilo softly. "I wonder who they were." He looked at Singh. "And they said they were military?"

"Yes Sir," said the Captain. "With Senator Butterfett."

"He's the one you got injured saving," said the Rear Admiral.

"What happened with him?" asked Singh. "No one talks about it."

"Well, only a few people know the truth," said Cirilo. "And I threatened everyone else because I thought it might undermine what we were doing. Actually, everyone was so busy trying to keep the Fleet together, they didn't have time to gossip."

The Captain waited patiently.

The Rear Admiral took a moment before starting. "At first, we thought it was great to have saved a U.S. Senator. Really, we were hoping that this would blow over and that he could reunited with the rest, maybe be able to return to normal." He gave a laugh without any humor in it.

"Did we ever hear from anyone?" asked Singh.

The Rear Admiral shook his head. "Just after the outbreak, everything went dark. I didn't think it was possible to do so."

"Unless *el extraterrestre* did something," suggested Uncle Danny.

"True," nodded Cirilo. "That is possible."

"So, what did Butterfett try and do?" asked Singh. He gave a laugh. "Try to take control of the Fleet?"

The Rear Admiral gave a hard look. "Yes. And he almost managed it."

"Wait! What?" asked Singh. "I was just joking."

"Not sure why," said the Rear Admiral. "Maybe we weren't bowing and scraping enough to him, or even just

123

listening to him."

"What did he want to do?" asked Singh.

"He wanted to go to Washington," said the Rear Admiral.

"D.C.?" said Singh with surprise.

"He was going to take the Fleet down to Panama Canal," said Cirilo. "But, if that didn't work, down past the bottom of Argentina."

"Um. The Whole Fleet? That doesn't sound very safe," ventured Liberty.

"Right off the bat," said Cirilo through gritted teeth. "He figured that we'd lose 30% of the Fleet. Worst case, 50%."

"Why D.C.?" asked Singh.

"He was convinced that that was where the resistance would be formed," said Cirilo, now with a tired voice. "And that we'd be hailed as heroes."

"But…we don't even know if there's anyone in D.C.," said Liberty, however she paused. "Well, alive…you know."

"True. And that was before we had a tanker of fuel," said Cirilo.

"And food," added Uncle Danny.

"But he was selling them on dreams," said Cirilo, and he gave a deep sigh. "I can't believe I voted for the idiot in the last election."

"So, what happened with him?" asked Singh.

The Rear Admiral momentarily closed his eyes, feeling a

headache coming on. "Well, he was getting so brazen about it, he tried to recruit one of our officers, who—of course— let us know." He gave a dry chuckle. "Actually, the officer was quite excited to play spy."

"Oh no!" said Liberty. "What happened to him?"

"She's fine," said the Rear Admiral. "I didn't mean to make it sound like something sinister happened. But she was the one who told me that Butterfett was heading to the Coast to get guns."

"Oh shit!" said Singh in surprise.

"They were planning, with the officer's pretend help, to take the bridge of the carrier," said the Rear Admiral. "We hadn't been letting anyone keep their guns while in the Fleet, or we could have been in trouble."

"What did you do?" asked Uncle Danny, leaning forward with curiosity.

"Actually," said the Rear Admiral. "Butterfett was his own worst enemy. Several ships left in the dead of the night. We saw them, so we tried to call them back because there was a bad storm coming in."

"They didn't listen?" asked Captain Singh.

"Ignored us," said the Rear Admiral. "Maybe they tried to reach the Coast before it hit." He gave a little sigh. "As soon as the storm had passed, we sent out a few ships, found a little debris…but nothing."

"So, now we know that some of them ended up on San Clemente," finished the Captain.

"Which does have a Naval Auxiliary Landing Field," said the Rear Admiral.

"Then this Senator-guy crowned himself emperor," said Uncle Danny.

"This isn't the first time we've run into that," said Liberty.

"Yeah," nodded Singh. "Those weird people on the Coast that kept calling themselves 'President' as well."

Liberty gave a sad, little laugh. "I wonder how many people are out there are thinking that they are 'President'? It's kinda pathetic."

"Well, actually as a Senator," said the Rear Admiral. "It might be that he is in the path of succession to the president, but only if all the others are gone."

"And who knows if there are any out there," said Singh.

"It doesn't matter," said the Rear Admiral. "My plan is to leave Butterfett alone, and Not to engage."

Captain Singh nodded. "Sounds like a good plan to me."

"I wonder though...are they the ones we've been seeing out there," mused the Rear Admiral. "Or, if there is another player out there." He looked over them. "Well, regardless, the kids, and Tagg of course, can stay here on the carrier."

"*Actually*, I need to check with Tagg and make sure he's all right taking care of the kids," said Liberty with a serious expression.

The Rear Admiral's brow furrowed. "I thought he had adopted them."

"He did," explained Liberty quickly. "But I don't want Tagg to feel like we're...well, dumping the kids on him."

"And he might be busy with his work," suggested Uncle

Danny.

A smile forming, Liberty looked at him. "Buuuut... he might like to stay on a real aircraft carrier too."

Uncle Danny grinned. "That would be cool."

With a mock thoughtful expression, the Rear Admiral nodded. "I'm thinking that a tour, or two, could be arranged. If that would sweeten the pot."

"And if we can get some education in...?" suggested/asked Liberty quickly.

"Of course!" assured Cirilo.

"It'd be like a field trip," continued Uncle Danny, excitedly.

"In truth, this crew is really fond of those kids, so they'll be perfectly safe," nodded Cirilo. He shrugged. "A bit spoiled from all the tours and maybe even sweets. I know some people have stuff squirreled away. In case of an emergency."

Muscles deflating, Liberty said with a warm smile. "That makes me feel a lot better leaving them."

"But not Too many sweets," said Uncle Danny.

"I can't promise anything," chuckled the Rear Admiral. It felt like it had been a long time since he last laughed, even a little. "So, just let me know what you decide. And thank you Everyone for working on this problem."

"Sir?" asked Singh with concern. "If Butterfett's people do engage us...?"

"If you are threatened," said the Rear Admiral gravely. "You have permission to use deadly force."

"Understood."

***

They went North a short way, but the ports close by looked like they had been stripped clean, so the *Wolf Pack* headed South.

Watching the beautiful California coast, Liberty rubbed more suntan lotion into her arms. She had her cute umbrella leaning against her front and shading her from above. But since the sun could glint, or bounce, or whatever, off the water and give her a sunburn...she needed to ask Tagg.

Suddenly, she wished that Tagg was here, sitting beside her. Her heart quickened, and she felt this electric warmth grow in her.

'I wish he was here', thought Liberty. 'For sooooooo many reasons'.

But then she remembered that Uncle Danny, Smalls, and the soldiers were all here too. Not exactly a romantic getaway.

And even if it was mostly just her and Tagg, then Smalls would have to drive, and that poured cold water on the idea. Tagg reminded her of the kids, and she found herself missing them terribly.

Glancing over, The Librarian stilled.

Dropping her lotion, she lifted the sniper rifle off her lap and looked through the scope.

An unbidden, and unwanted, thought rose in her head.

Liberty's Mom was saying, "Can't you use binoculars like a regular person. And what kind of young lady uses a sniper rifle. Why can't you be more like sister, Misty? Now, she is always a proper young lady."

In the past, Liberty had tried to stand up for herself. One time, she even went so far as to try to spill what Misty had done with her boyfriend, during church no less.

That wasn't the first time her Mom had slapped her.

Liberty was trying to push the nightmare-memory of her Mother away when she straightened.

Tapping her earpiece, she happily announced. "We got a mighty big bird following us."

Everyone came to greet Rakduson as she landed on the helicopter pad.

"I got bored," explained Rak.

Singh nodded. "Good to have you with us!"

"Will help you look," said Rak.

However, Camp Pendleton and Avalon/Catalina had been a bust, so they followed the Coast down to San Diego.

Near the shore, Liberty saw something curious. Juggling her umbrella and weapon, she leaned over the roof of the pilot's house and tapped gently on a window.

"What's up?" asked Smalls as he came out.

"There's a thin column of smoke, close to shore, but maybe not from the land," said Liberty. "I think we should check it out."

"Will do," said Smalls as he returned to the Pilot's House.

Using her earpiece, Liberty let everyone know about the changed course.

"I'm coming up," said Singh, and he soon arrived with Uncle Danny.

Liberty looked over at the Big Mexican who grinned hugely.

"Hey! I wasn't going to miss out on any fun," he said, a little defensively.

After flashing an amused smile at her best friend, Liberty went back to her scope. Something was definitely coming into view now.

"Looks like a ship," she said. "Not like a little one, but one of those bigger ones for weekend cruises. And...I think it's still on fire."

Singh looked through his binoculars and then got on the earpieces. "I want everyone to have their rifle on them. Just in case of trouble. Frankline, I want you at the back, looking..."

Frankline quickly put down his work on a chainmail suit.

"I want Ruiz on the right side," continued Singh. "And I want Washington up front. Watch for any other boats out there." He went to lean into the Pilot's House. "Mr. Smalls, slow when we get close. I want to look at it before we're right on top of it."

Rak asked. "I fly?"

"Thank you," said Singh. "Just...be careful."

"Yes Mom," chuckled the alien-bird. She took off before he could reply.

130

'When did she get sarcastic?' he wondered, but then he pushed it away.

As everyone got into place, the Captain turned back to the smoke in the distance. He could see the shape of the ship, which was listing starboard. As Smalls got closer, he slowed down, until they were nearly drifting.

"I got a body on the main deck," said Liberty.

"Someone may have set the fire after hitting the ship," said Singh.

"Those military *cabrónes*?" asked Uncle Danny.

"Or another player," said Singh slowly. "We need to start having more than one pair of eyes. I don't want anyone sneaking up on us." He looked up at Liberty. "And you need a break. You've been up there for several hours."

"I'm not gonna say 'no'," chuckled the Librarian as she came down.

Singh turned to *Dos Amigos*. "I say we keep going. There's nothing we can do here." And unconsciously, his eyes went to the charred body on the deck.

***

Not long after, they came into the water outside San Diego. The ship began to slow as it got closer to Point Loma, outside the port.

Liberty was once again perched atop the Pilot's House when Smalls asked for a quick meeting before they arrived.

Drifting aways from the Port of San Diego, Smalls came

131

out of the Pilot's house.

Liberty was perched over the edge of the Pilot's House with her legs up and her chin on one hand.

Smalls began. "I'm a little worried about taking the ship into close quarters. Not that the Bay is that small. But...*If* there is trouble, I'm not sure I could maneuver as easily inside. Plus, there's only one way out."

"And a little caution is never bad in new waters," nodded Singh thoughtfully.

"You thinking we could take the Bowrider?" asked Liberty, about the smaller boat that they towed behind.

'I just don't want to get into a bad situation," said Smalls. "And with that burnt ship..." He stopped nervously.

"No, he's got a point," nodded Singh. "It might be better to take a smaller team into the Port."

"*¡Órale!* And hopefully this port isn't a bust like the others," said Uncle Danny. He looked up. "*Mi Abuela e Dios*, can you give us some help here?"

"Amen," said Ruiz and Washington in chorus.

"What I can do," started Smalls. "...is turn the *Wolf Pack* around, so—if there is trouble—we can start moving, but not so fast that the Bowrider can't catch up."

"We can always go up the coast a little before stopping," suggested Liberty. "And then get back on board."

"If we're going to have a smaller group," said Singh softly. "Mr. Smalls, we are going to need you to come along."

"Wait! What?" asked the Navy Engineer. "But...who's going to drive the boat, in case of an emergency."

"True," admitted the Captain, and he looked at Liberty and Uncle Danny. "You both know how to drive…"

"You're not leaving either one of us here," said the Big Mexican flatly.

"¡*Órale!*" finished Liberty with compounded interest.

The Captain looked like he was going to argue for a second, but then decided—wisely—against it.

"Okay…," he began, thinking quickly.

"Actually Sir," said Dr. Washington. "I should be able to drive the boat."

Singh looked at him, curiously.

With a little embarrassed sigh, Washington said. "In the 4th episode of season 3, my character had to drive a yacht because Chance Thompson had been poisoned by a hairpin because…" He stopped and shook his head. "Never mind. I convinced the owner of the boat to teach me how to drive it for real, and he even let me!"

"Which must have been a thrill for a…," started Liberty. "Well, however old you were."

"I was twelve then," grinned Washington. "And it was super cool."

"I believe it," said Singh. He then looked at Liberty, Uncle Danny, and Smalls. "If you're okay…"

The Navy Engineer also glanced at Liberty and Danny. "It's up to you, but I should be able to teach him pretty quick."

Liberty squinted at Smalls. "You should be in on this decision! You drive her all the time."

133

"Well, it's okay with me," said Smalls with a grateful smile. But then he looked at Washington with a serious look. "As long as you take good care of her."

"Like she were my own child," said Dr. Washington solemnly.

***

The Bowrider shot across the water towards Point Loma.

Liberty had won 'roe sham bo' with rock beating scissors, so she got to drive the smaller boat towards the Port.

Seeing the big grin on the Librarian's face, Uncle Danny couldn't feel bad about losing to her. In back, Smalls and the Captain sat in a bucket-seat. Smalls got to drive the big ship, so he hadn't been eligible.

There were still big cargo ships waiting outside the Port, and Captain Singh wished they had more time.

"What kind of treasures are on those boats," he wondered aloud. He glanced at their path. Before he could say anything more, Liberty started to slow the boat.

They puttered into the Port with Point Loma on the port side of the boat and the North Island Naval Air Station on the starboard.

"Wow," said Liberty as they reached Shelter Island. "This place has been picked pretty clean too."

Standing, Captain Singh walked forward towards the bow, looking around.

"The people who escaped to the islands had to get boats from somewhere," he said.

"¡*Neta, no manches!* This is pretty picked," said Uncle Danny.

Liberty frowned. "And it's kinda eerily quiet. Or is it just me."

"Nope," said Uncle Danny. "Kinda creepy."

As they moved into North San Diego Bay, the Captain tried to ignore such talk. He wouldn't stop them, but he also didn't want to feed into that kind of Campfire stuff. Talk like that can escalate quickly.

"Just follow the water deeper in," said Singh, but then he added. "If you would Liberty."

"Of course," she smiled.

Uncle Danny suddenly jumped up and pointed. "I win!"

They followed his finger to a tug.

"Good eye!" grinned Singh. He held on as Liberty gunned the engine to reach it.

To Liberty's eye, it definitely looked like a tugboat tied up by the USS Midway Museum. Smalls gave the ship a quiet salute.

"I wonder if that ship still runs," said Singh.

"I don't know Sir," said the Navy Engineer. "I don't even know if I could get it going by myself."

"I believe in you," called back Liberty.

In no time, they were aboard the tug. Uncle Danny checked it from bow to stern but found no one. It didn't take Smalls much time before he returned.

"How soon can we take it out?" asked the Captain.

"Welllllll, that's the thing," said the Navy Engineer, looking down. "It does need some repairs."

"But you can do that," asked Singh. "Can't you?"

"I can…yes," started the Navy Engineer.

"What's wrong?" asked Liberty gently.

"It's too small," said Smalls unhappily.

"As in…," began the Captain.

"As in, it can't push that big barge," said Smalls. "Maybe out on the open water, but not very well."

"*Pollas en vinagre,*" grumbled Uncle Danny. "So, we gotta keep looking?"

"Sorry," said Smalls.

The Big Mexican gave a shrug with a smile. "Not you. I just wanted bragging rights for finding it."

"Well, there're more boats here," said Smalls.

"And you're sure?" asked the Captain.

"This is an inland barge, and we need an ocean going one," nodded Smalls.

"Okay," said the Captain. "Let's keep looking."

They were soon back out on the water, going even deeper into the Port of San Diego. They passed a cruise ship with zoms staggering across the deck. In South San Diego Bay, there was another tug, but it was half sunk.

"I'm going to go out on a limb and guess that that one isn't going to cut it," said Liberty.

Cruising a little slower, the Librarian felt their options dwindling.

"We could always go North," suggested Smalls. "But. We'd need to go back to the Fleet to top off on fuel."

The Captain nodded. "Maybe. But the Admiral might just want to cut our losses and look for an alternative plan."

"Cleaning an island...," started Uncle Danny. "*Ye te cargó el payaso*. That's gonna cost us dearly, just in people alone."

"My concern exactly," said Singh gravely.

Liberty turned to look at them. "It's going to be okay! We're going to figure this out."

The Captain could not help but smile. "True. We might just have to get a little creative." Standing a little straighter, he looked around. "Let's finish this pass and then go slowly back out, just in case we missed..."

Smalls bounded up and cried with excitement. "Over there! Look at the size of that one!"

Liberty shot towards a large tug. It was docked at the Marine Group Boat Works Chula Vista. Singh tried calling out, but no one answered.

The Captain looked at Smalls. "Is that big enough?"

"Maybe," said the Navy Engineer. "I'll need to look her over...but yeah, it might be."

As before, the four of them boarded the stern of the tug. Liberty began to turn to the others.

"Okay, roe sham boe to see who...?" she started.

There was the sound of a shotgun and a woman

appeared out a door in the tug.

"Go Away!" snarled the woman. "Hurry! Get out of here!"

Smalls gave a little squeak of terror, and his face immediately turned red with embarrassment.

"We're not here to hurt anyone," said the Captain. "We're..."

"I don't care," said the woman quickly. "Go!" She glanced furtively around, and then focused back on them. "No! You have to go, right now."

"We're part of the Navy," said the Captain.

"Seriously, get out of here. Now!" cried the woman.

The Captain was about to say more, but he stopped and then looked at the others.

"Let's go," he said.

"But...," started Smalls.

"Captain's right," said Liberty, and she looked at the lady. "Sorry to disturb you. We're leaving."

"Quickly," said the woman. "Hurry!"

"Yes, yes. Quickly," said Liberty soothingly.

Moving back to their boat, Smalls wondered. "What was that all about?"

"I don't know, but we better head back to our boat," said Liberty.

"Agreed," said the Captain. "We can talk more when we get there."

Uncle Danny watched the tug as their Bowrider moved

swiftly through the bay, heading for the *Wolf Pack*. The woman with the shotgun watched them for a while, but then disappeared back into the tug. For a second, he wondered if she was crying.

***

Liberty went swiftly out of the Port, but her brow was furrowed.

"You're worried *Mija*," said Uncle Danny. He nodded. "Me too."

"I'm just not sure we can do anything," growled Liberty, but then she stopped. "Not that I'm mad at you."

Uncle Danny waved the concern away and turned to Captain Singh and the Navy Engineer.

Not too far away, the *Wolf Pack* was waiting, and perched on top of the Pilot's House was the alien-bird who stood up. Rakduson let out a happy squawk and took flight.

"*¡Oye!* What do you think?" asked the Big Mexican.

Pensively, Singh was leaning back in the bucket-seat with his legs out in front of him.

"In the past," he said slowly. "I'd say we shouldn't interfere. It's a job for someone else, maybe the police."

"But...there *are* no police left," said Smalls meekly.

Rakduson swooped down above them.

"Took you long enough," joked the alien-bird.

With mock indignation, Uncle Danny shouted up. "Who died and made you boss!?!"

139

"Let's get to the ship and go from there," said the Captain slowly.

***

"You're kidding!" cried Frankline. "We were soooo close! Can't we...I don't know, just take the tug."

The Captain's eyes snapped up. "Stow that talk Private!"

Frankline ducked his head down. "sorry."

Singh's face softened a bit. "I understand your frustration, but we're not pirates."

"We are," chirped Liberty. "But we don't take boats from people."

"*¡Sin duda!*" agreed Uncle Danny with force. "We ain't hijacking nobody."

"Definitely not!" continued Liberty, but she paused and glanced at Danny. "Unless they're bad guys."

Uncle Danny thought for a second, but then nodded. "*Tienes razón.* Agreed. If they're bad guys, then all bets are off."

"Getting back to the problem at hand," said Singh pointedly. "We're not stealing that ship..." He was thoughtful for a moment.

"But. Something was wrong," said Smalls.

"She was almost more worried about us not being seen by someone," said Liberty softly.

"Like she was trying to protect us," said Uncle Danny

They all stood on the deck of *Wolf Pack*, but still near the Port of San Diego.

"Okay," said Singh decisively. "We can't just leave…"

"But we don't want to be creepy either," insisted Ruiz.

"Absolutely," said Singh. "I say we pull back a bit." He looked at the Navy Engineer. "There're all these cargo ships around. Can we hide behind one?"

Smalls nodded enthusiastically. "I can do that. These ships are so big. If I get close, they'd have to be looking for us."

"Let's do that first," said the Captain, though he glanced at Liberty and Danny. "If that's okay."

"If that lady's in trouble…," nodded the Librarian seriously. "She might not be there willingly."

"But, if it turns out that we just read it wrong," said Uncle Danny.

"We gotta back away quick," nodded Singh. "That's why I want to use some stealth."

Uncle Danny chuckled. "That's something we've never really used."

"Not if we could help it," smirked Liberty.

Taking the yacht further from the Port, there were several massive cargo ships anchored there. Smalls brought them behind a big ship.

"Now that we're behind this ship," said Liberty. "How're we going to see the tug? I mean, we could use the Bowrider." Her voice grew uncertain.

"I'm worried that it will be too easily spotted," said

Singh tugging at his short beard. "But...we might have to."

Rakduson shook her feathers a little. "Tug is ship that can push other ships along." She pointed her beak at the huge cargo ship beside them.

"No, smaller," said Uncle Danny. "About as big as this ship."

"What color?" asked the alien.

"It's white with black," said Singh, curiously. "With a tall part in front, and a flatter part behind."

Rakduson clicked her beak, not understanding.

"Oh!" said Frankline suddenly. He got something and knelt near the alien. "It's this shape."

Using the links for making the shark chainmail, Frankline swiftly created a representation of the tug.

"And where is it?" asked Rak.

Singh knelt as well. "This is what the Port looks like." He began to take the link from the picture of the tug.

"Oh! You're ruining my art, Sir," said Frankline with a mock whine.

In no time, Singh had created a map of the Port and then pointed to where the tug was.

"I go," said the alien.

"Rak," said Uncle Danny worriedly. "Be careful. They have guns."

"I will be care-fall," said the alien. "No worry."

"I can't help it," sniffed Uncle Danny.

"Ms. Rak," said the Captain. "We want to try not to be

seen. I don't want them to know we're watching."

"I know," said Rakduson. "I do this 'efore. In past."

Stepping back, the bird took flight. She soared up past the cargo ship and then disappeared above it. Uncle Danny watched her go, berating himself for not telling her 'good luck'.

Private Frankline clapped his hands together. "Well, I'm going to keep working on my chainmail. Holler if you see any zoms that can swim." Singh turned to him, and the young man froze. Quickly he said. "If That's All Right Sir."

"As you were," nodded Singh.

Staff Sergeant Ruiz turned to the Captain. "I'd like to talk to Smalls about that Faraday Cage he's working on."

"Certainly," nodded Singh.

With a happy noise, Ruiz went off quickly with Smalls. Frankline tried not to be a little jealous. But he was a little jealous.

Patting Uncle Danny on the shoulder, as if to say, 'Don't worry', Liberty then went back to her watch aboard the Pilot's House.

On deck, Singh began to sing—a little off-key—Tom Petty's "The Waiting Is The Hardest Part".

...

And they waited.

...

And waited.

***

"There she is!!!" cried Liberty as she jumped to her feet.

Hearing the shout, everyone looked up. Rakduson was coming from the North, but out to sea. Winging in, she landed on the main deck looking a little pooped.

"Do you need *agua?*" asked Uncle Danny.

"Yes, please," said Rak. She nearly collapsed on the deck as Uncle Danny ran off.

Singh marched up, almost barking, 'Report', but then he remembered himself.

"Glad to see you back, Ms. Rakduson," said the Captain instead. "Did you find anything?"

"Know where they are," said Rak, and she pointed North. "They are in danger. We need to help."

While he was tempted to ask more, Singh looked up and saw the Navy Engineer on the way.

"Mr. Smalls?" called out the Captain. "Can you head North right away?"

The Navy Engineer skidded to a halt. "Oh! Yeah, okay."

"We're going to come to you to confer," said Singh. "I promise."

"No...no worries," said Smalls and he ran back.

The Captain looked back at the alien-bird. "Sorry. I wanted to get us underway. Could you tell us what you saw?"

***

144

Rakduson was easily able to find her way thanks to Captain Singh's map. She saw some other birds nearby—Seagulls they were called—and wanted to fly with them, just a bit. Rak missed having someone to fly with.

'The Danny needed wings'; she decided.

It had taken no time to spot the tug, just where they said it was. High up, she circled, but did not see any humans. At least, not the regular kind. In stages, she came down.

Close to the tug was a building with a roof sticking up. Landing on the roof, she found that could just look over the peak of the roof. Nothing moved on the boat, but she soon heard voices.

A big female with a big machine-type gun was leading a group of men. They were all dressed differently, except that each had a purple rag around their neck.

***

"Rag?" asked Frankline.

"If it was tied nicely around their neck, it could have been a bandana," suggested Liberty.

"They were nice," said Rak. "So, bandana. Okay."

"Anyhow," said Singh repressively to everyone, except the bird.

***

145

The big female wearing a purple bandana took a moment to push a zom into the water and almost all of them laughed.

Reaching the tug, the big female called out. "HONEY! I'm home!" And the group, except for the man in the middle, laughed once again.

Out of the tug came the female that The Danny and the others must have met. But now the female was unarmed.

"We had a great haul," cried the big female. "And we lost no one!"

This got another big cheer.

The female on the tug was only looking at the man in the middle. As the group got on the tug, the two embraced.

'Mated?' wondered Rak.

Soon, the two were pulled apart and the male shoved towards the front of the boat. The smaller female tried to protest, but one of the purple men hit her. The male wanted to jump to the female's defense, but the big leader woman put a gun in the man's face. The male reluctantly backed down, looking at the female.

Rak just stopped herself from jumping over the roof.

One of the rag men suddenly looked around. The bird ducked her head just in time. She waited, but no one came.

Soon, the tug was leaving, moving towards the entrance to the Port. When it was far enough away, Rak took off again.

High up, the alien followed the boat as it left the Port and headed North.

'Could go back' thought Rak, but then she'd have to race to catch up.

Resigned, the bird kept with the boat. It was a nice day, so that made her happy.

The tug traveled a while, and Rakduson worried that she had been gone too long. If only there had been another bird with her, she could've sent back a report.

The longer it got, the more she fretted. It was going to take a while just to get back. Looking along the coastline, Rak tried to find something that would be easy to spot from the water. It would mark where she left off.

Coming up, there was a rock sticking out of the water. Rak decided that that would have to do for a marker.

Just as the bird was about to turn around, the boat slowed down.

It turned to the shore.

Dropping down slowly, Rak saw the tug-thing slow to a stop at a small dock. Carefully, the alien came in until the large rock was between her and the boat. She used her wings to slow her descent, but Rakduson still hit the rock a little hard.

***

Is that how you hurt your cheek?" asked Uncle Danny worriedly.

"Not then," said Rak, with a little snap of her beak. "Let me tell story."

"*Perdón*," replied Uncle Danny abashed.

147

Chapter Nine

RAK DIDN'T WANT to try and land on top of the large rock sticking out of the water like a bullet. She was worried that someone might be watching, so she aimed for the side. But Rak was still coming in too fast and smacked into the rock.

"Oof," she exclaimed.

Unharmed, except for her pride and some bruises, Rakduson gripped the rock with the claws on her feet and quickly scrambled up. As she reached the peak, she slowed to carefully peer over the top.

The tugboat had just settled against an old dock and the purple bandana people were throwing ropes around.

Inland, there was a squeal of delight.

A small human child ran across a dirty camp towards

the dock.

Right behind was a big male with a purple bandana chasing them. Just as the human child would have reached the dock, the big male grabbed the child's arm and yanked them to a stop.

The human child let out a squall of pain and Rak had to hold herself still. She ground her beak together in frustration but waited to observe.

On the boat, the Female tried to jump off the ship, but someone knocked her aside. She landed roughly. Despite being in obvious pain, the Female started getting up when one of the Purple Bandanas got ready to hit her.

"Let her go," said the Big Leader Female. They were trying to sound generous, but it came out slimy.

Once free, the Female scrambled to the Human Child and pulled them in close.

The Male had just emerged from inside the tug when the rock next to Rak burst in a small explosion. It was right beside her face, and she felt a hard sting on her face.

The bird heard the sound of the bullet and ducked down as more shots hit the rock.

Leaping off the tall rock, Rak unfurled her wings and swooped down towards the water. Dropping low, she was right above the water keeping the rock between her and the person with a gun.

A big wave grew up to her right, higher than her.

Rak furiously beat the air with her wings, but the water smacked right into her. She was scared as the wave curled over her and dragged her away, tumbling her.

Lungs burning for air, a part of her screamed in panic. Her hurt cheek stung harshly from the salt water. She desperately wanted to start swimming towards the surface. But she stopped herself and took a moment. She remembered her training as a young chick. Soon, she began to float up naturally.

The wave soon spit her out near the shore. Rak scrambled up onto the beach getting covered in sand as well. She took a moment to get air into her lungs. There was some blood from her cheek.

"What're we chasing?" demanded a voice in the distance.

"There was someone on the rock," came an answering cry.

Wings too sodden—and now sand-caked—to fly, Rak forced herself to move towards the tree line. Just as she hit it, another voice came out.

"Didja see that?" cried a voice, getting closer.

Rakduson tucked her wings in and headed deeper into the wood. She wondered if she should just kill the men outright but decided it might be better to wait. The Danny might be unhappy.

Shortly, the voices were now at the beach where she came ashore.

"What's with these tracks?"

"There's blood! I did hit something!"

"It's blue, you idiot," snapped another voice. "Not red! Nothing has blue blood."

Bearing the pain silently, Rak ignored the angry and

151

insistent sting on her cheek. She kept going. Her wings were drying out at a good pace.

The bird jumped when she heard a gunshot to her left.

"What're you shooting at!?!"

"Thought I saw something, but it was just a rabbit. Damn thing got away."

"Stop shooting. You're giving away our position.

"As opposed to you yelling at me?"

This started a louder argument.

Heart racing. Rak wished her wings would dry out a lot faster.

***

Uncle Danny made a worried noise.

Looking at him, Rak said. "As you say—Spoiler Alert—I made it."

Chuckling, Danny rolled his eyes.

***

Rakduson moved closer to the ground and pulled her body inwards to try not to touch any plants and leave a trail. Trying to not leave footprints was hard. The soil was not too soft here, so that helped.

Varying her path, the bird tried to keep the humans guessing. But they were still back there. And not far enough away. A dangerous part of her reminded herself that she could just kill them. Humans can be very fragile.

However, they were not an immediate threat to her. Especially if her wings would dry out sooner, rather than later. Rak made an irritated noise and tried shaking her wings. Unfortunately, the shaking caused some of the blue blood from her cheek to splatter onto a nearby tree.

Rak grumbled inwardly at that, but her wings were dry enough. However, looking up, she couldn't fly yet. The canopy of trees above was too dense.

Holding her cheek once again, the alien-bird shot forward. She tried to look for a good place to take off.

"Over there! I think I see something."

Stupid humans were too close. The trees above were still too dense. She might have to fight, but then her eyes widened with an idea.

Two minutes later, the males wearing Purple Bandanas stopped below a tree.

"I swear I saw something this way," said the first.

"Whatever," grumbled the other one. "Can we go back now?"

"What're you in a hurry for?" demanded the first. "Boss is just going to want us to sit around the campfire reading stories from the Bible."

"At least it's got lots of stories in it," suggested the other one.

Above, head-forward, Rak crouched in the tree. She tried not to even breathe. But, right over the Purple Bandanas below, she noticed blood from her cheek streaming slowly to the end of her beak.

A drop of blue blood shook as more blood reached it.

It started to fall.

Gripping with one foot, she stuck out the other. The droplet smacked right onto the top of her foot.

Not daring to move, Rak perched there awkwardly.

"Come on," said the first Bandana. "Just a little more."

With the other grumbling, they soon went off and disappeared.

Rak waited.

After a minute, the Purple Bandanas stood up from behind some bushes, where they had been hiding.

"What was that for?" complained the other Bandana.

"Shut up," grumbled the first.

Soon, they were truly away.

Dropping down, Rak felt elated until she looked around. She had no idea where she was.

Heading away from those men, the bird looked for a hole in the canopy above.

***

Back at the ship, Liberty cried out happily. "I'm so glad that you're okay!"

She gave the bird a huge hug in relief.

"Definitely," said Singh. "I'm sorry to put you in harm's

way like that."

"It's okay," said Rak. "As long as we help family."

"Most definitely!" said Singh.

"Ms. Rak," said Dr. Washington and he gently moved her beak so that he could look over her wound. "Okay, you're okay."

"*Gracias a dios,*" whispered Uncle Danny.

Washington continued. "Really just a small cut. No need for stitches. I'll clean it up and put some glue on it. Try not to get too active."

"I promise nothing," said Rak with mischief in her eyes.

"I had to say it," smiled Dr. Washington.

Singh cleared his throat. "Can you make a map of their camp...at least what you could see?"

"Can I have metal pieces?" asked Rak as she turned to Frankline.

"Sure!" said the Private, and he ran to get them.

Balancing on one leg, Rak squatted down. With her feathers poofing out, she almost looked silly.

However, with one foot free, Rak delicately picked up the loops metal. Swiftly, she managed to create a map with gentle movements. In no time, the Captain was walking around the makeshift map.

"Okay," he said at last, looking up at the rest. "We're going to need a distraction on the sea, and then I'm going to have to go in by land to get the family out."

Instantly, there was a squall of protest. Singh gave them a moment to get it out of their system.

155

"That's enough," he finally bellowed.

The Captain stared everyone down until there was silence. "I had training before everything fell." He looked at his soldiers. "I haven't taught you that, so No, you can't come." He turned to the civilians. "And you tend not to use stealth."

"We've had to use stealth before," protested Liberty.

Uncle Danny gently touched her arm to get her attention. They had one of their unspoken conversations, which ended with Liberty sighing.

"I know," she finally said to Danny out loud. "I just hate sending him in alone."

"It's okay," said Singh. "I'm not going to take any unnecessary chances. I promise."

"Except for going in alone to enemy territory," grumped Staff Sergeant Ruiz.

Liberty undid her gun belt and handed it to the Captain.

"My gun with a silencer," she said.

Singh nodded seriously. "I'll take good care of it."

"You better," said Liberty with a mock pout.

"Now, we just need a distraction," said Singh.

Everyone grew thoughtful, and Uncle Danny turned to look up at the helipad. Then he gave a hearty chuckle.

"Sometimes, it's hard to see what's right before you," he said.

Confused, the rest turned to look at him.

Grinning, Uncle Danny asked. "Do you think they'd be interested in a luxury yacht?"

***

Smalls let the smaller Bowrider boat drift towards the shore. He turned back.

"I don't know if I can get any closer," he said worriedly. "I don't want to get stuck."

"It's okay," smiled Captain Singh at the back of the boat. He held up a small pack and jumped off the side.

Even with one arm in a sling, he quickly made it to shore and waved for Smalls to head back. The Bowrider didn't move at first, so the Captain waved more insistently.

A little reluctantly, Smalls turned the smaller boat around and drove quietly away until he could race back to the *Wolf Pack*.

Slipping on his pack, Singh made sure that Liberty's silenced Glock was good and then he moved into the forest. As he moved through the woods, he had to admit to himself that it had been a while since that training in stealth. But he had at least had some, so he didn't question his decision.

Singh was supposed to get in place before dawn. Once the sun came over the horizon, that was when the *Wolf Pack* would start to move. He needed to move as fast as he could.

The woods were actually kind of nice right now. Watching the trees, the Captain went along the shore, because he didn't want to lose his way. Today was not the day to get cute and creative.

In the distance, Singh saw the rock jutting out of the water like a bullet.

Suddenly, something made him stop.

"Over here," called a voice, softly.

Turning fast, the Captain started to pull Liberty's gun, but the silencer made it hard to draw quickly.

There was a shape, too close, but it suddenly started to back up calling out, 'Peas, Peas'.

Singh was wondering why they were talking about vegetables when it hit him. He had drawn the silenced gun, but he let it hang by his side.

"Rak?" he asked.

The shape came forward and resolved themself.

"Hi! Hi!" said the alien-bird. "Didn't want to sneak up."

"I appreciate that," said Singh, but then hissed. "Now, What Are You Doing Here?"

"Grew up in woods," said Rak with cheer. She started moving towards the camp and he was forced to follow to catch up.

"I thought I told everyone to stay back," said the Captain with an edge to his voice.

"That's why I didn't ask," said the bird merrily. "Besides, you have a hurt wing."

Singh was going to get heated, but then he noticed how stealthily she moved through the woods. By comparison, he was making a ton of noise.

"Okay," he said quietly. "You know our job."

"When distraction hits," said Rak. "We take family

158

away. Protect them."

"This could get dangerous," said Singh.

Greatly amused, she said. "Danger is my middle name."

Despite himself, the Captain smiled. "Okay, here's the plan."

***

A Purple Bandana saw the smoke before anything else. He'd been on the tug, guarding it because of that weird sighting, and in case the family got any ideas. But they were probably still asleep. He didn't know why the Chief was keeping them alive.

Embarrassed by the Chief's softness, the Bandana turned towards the water. Whatever was burning was still behind that big rock.

Turning to the camp, he wondered if he should tell someone. But he decided to wait.

Shortly, he saw where the smoke was coming from, and his jaw dropped. He was too shocked to even swear.

Running back into the camp, the Bandana roused the Chief out of bed with her guy of the night. Really, she had taken George? He wasn't smart enough to even find his own butt with a map.

"Everyone on me!" roared the Chief in the early morning. The other Bandanas stumbled out of their tent, confused.

Forcing everyone to the water, the Chief yelled for a pair

159

of binoculars. Soon she looked closer, and her breath caught. Her heart raced.

"Is...that a yacht?" asked the Bandana, George.

But the Chief suddenly stilled, and her brow furrowed.

***

Shortly, the Captain and Rak heard the sounds of a boat.

Pausing, Singh murmured. "Wait, was that one boat or two?"

The Captain decided that he could not worry about that right now. He motioned for Rak to follow. It appeared to be an old campground and, while they had waited, he had decided that the family must be in the middle cabin.

Now, they moved around cabin #5 towards the middle one. Stopping, the Captain carefully looked around the side. Inwardly, he swore as he pulled back.

"There's still almost a dozen people still here," whispered Singh. "All between the tug and the camp. I'm worried that if we start shooting, one of the family is going to get hurt."

The Captain thought furiously. He could light a cabin on fire, but the buildings were really close to the woods. He didn't want to start a forest fire if he could help it.

"Got it!" hissed Rak happily. "Wait here."

The bird shot back into the woods before Singh could say a word. Right away, he started thinking some very bad thoughts about a certain bird.

***

On the *Wolf Pack*, Smalls was running back and forth in a Hawaiian shirt that they had found.

"Are they buying it?" he called out.

Hidden in a nook on the yacht, Liberty started. "I don't think they're...Wait! I see a boat leaving. Unless..." She paused. "Darn, it's too far away. There is definitely one big boat heading towards us. It's still too dark to see more."

Over the earpieces, from her own hiding place, Ruiz asked. "The tug?"

"Naw, it's bigger than our bowrider, but smaller than the tug," reported Liberty. "Uncle Danny?"

"*Sí*," he said over the earpieces from where he lay on the helipad by the big gun.

"Did you see anything weird with their boat?" she asked.

"No *Mija*," said Uncle Danny. "But it was so far away, and I wasn't really looking. *Perdón*."

"No, no," said Liberty quickly. "You're good. Thank you."

"Well, let's keep on our toes," said Ruiz. "Smalls, can you relieve Dr. Washington in the Pilot's House?"

"Got it!" cried Smalls and he ran off.

"Okay," said Ruiz. "They're getting close, but this time we'll be ready. Time to nut up!"

***

"Be-rupt."

Singh heard the odd noise and blinked. It was coming from near the tug.

"What the Hell??" called out one of the Purple Bandanas.

"See! SEE! I tol' you!" cried another of the Purple Bandanas.

"Shut up," replied the first.

More 'Bee-rupp' and 'Burp' noises came.

Carefully, Singh peered around the cabin #5. He was a little stunned himself.

By the dock, a large bird stood with a vacant look in their eyes.

"Brupp," chirped the bird and bent over to peck at the ground.

"I tol' you that I shot at a big bird before," cried the Purple Bandana, Caleb. "But you didn't believe me."

"Where'd it come from?" asked another Purple Bandana, George.

"Could be from outer space," hissed another, Leonard.

"Don't be stupid!" grumbled the person in charge, Harve.

The Captain snapped out of his shock and moved towards the cabin with the family, using what cover he could. Opening the door quietly, he slipped inside, and the people looked up in shock. Mom, he assumed the Dad, and a little girl.

"My name is Captain Singh," he began. "And I'm…"

The Mom jumped up and looked at the family. "Okay! This is it! Everyone knows what to do!"

The rest of the family was still a little stunned.

"Hurry! Hurry! Hurry!" ordered the Mom, Cassidy, but without anger. "We might not get another chance."

Immediately, everyone started running around the cabin. Unsure of what to do, Singh guarded the door.

Cassidy stuffed a few things into a pack.

Singh opened the door just a crack and glanced out the door.

***

Making dumb noises, Rak fretted. She didn't know how much longer she could play the dumb bird.

But maybe she could get some, or all, of the Bandanas to follow.

Looking up, as if she had just noticed the men, Rak let out a scream of surprise. She scrambled away as fast as she could.

***

Beside the *Wolf Pack*, the Purple Bandana's smaller boat came aside and threw hooks, catching the rail. With movements born of experience, the two boats were quickly tethered together.

"Be ready to surprise them," whispered Ruiz over the earpieces. "We just need to keep them distracted, we don't need to kill them, unless necessary."

However, no one came from the other boat.

"Liberty?" asked Ruiz softly. "Can you get eyes on the boat?"

Hidden in her nook, Liberty had a clear line of sight into the other boat.

"They got a lot of guns," whispered Liberty worriedly. "Like, big ones."

"Okay you stupid Yuppies!" cried the Chief in charge of the Bandanas. "Give up now and we'll spare your life!" We don't care either way."

"Yuppies?" whispered Uncle Danny over the earpieces. "I'm trying to remember what those are."

"Who uses the word 'Yuppies' anymore?" asked Liberty.

"We can that discuss later," said Ruiz repressively. "Let's stay quiet for now."

"You thought you were so clever," bellowed the Chief smugly. "Probably burning old oily rags. But what really pisses me off is the Pirate flag."

"Shoot," hissed Liberty. "I didn't even think of that."

"How dare you yuppies fly the Jolly Roger!" cried the Chief, suddenly angry.

"We're not yuppies," called back Liberty.

"Lib?" said Ruiz softly.

"Trying to keep them distracted," whispered Liberty back, and then she said loudly from her hiding place. "Actually, we really should be called Privateers, like we were in the service of His Majesty, buuuuuuuuuuuuut it doesn't sound as cool."

"Whose majesty?" asked the Chief in confusion.

They heard a gunshot from the other side of the ship.

The Chief grinned. "It doesn't matter, your time is up."

"I'm checking!" said Uncle Danny over the earpieces.

"Everyone, stay alert," said Ruiz.

***

While people talked on the starboard side, Smalls laid low in the Pilot's House. He just happened to glance to the Port side and did a double take. Brow furrowed, the Navy Engineer hated to leave the ship still going, but there was no other choice.

Taking his M4 Rifle, Smalls carefully stepped out of the Pilot's House and moved to the side of the ship.

His heart started to pound. Grappling hooks clanked onto the rail. Someone was coming aboard. He patted his pocket, but he'd left his walkie- talkie behind.

Nothing for it, Smalls shot forward just as some of the pirates were climbing up and over. And they were armed to the teeth.

"St...stop!" cried Smalls, once he was near.

The bandana froze, but then he started to grin.

165

"Don't move a muscle," said Smalls. "I'm with the U.S. Navy, and I know how to use this weapon."

"Doesn't look like it," sneered the Bandana. And, as he finished climbing over the edge, he reached for his gun.

***

Uncle Danny ran to the left side of the boat, heart in his throat. He stopped as he got close, raising his shotgun.

"That's It!" cried a voice. It was tinged with fear but boiling over in anger. "Untie yourself now."

Glancing around the corner, Uncle Danny took in the tableau.

A man was dead on the deck. But he was only one of the pirates.

Smalls was leaning over the edge of the rail pointing his rifle downward.

"Hurry!" growled Smalls. "I don't have all day."

'Especially since no one's driving the boat right now', he thought to himself with a bit of panic. And he had just killed someone. He'd never even killed a Zom.

"Coming up behind you *mi amigo*," came a familiar voice.

Just as the Bandanas untied their boat, Uncle Danny appeared holding up their dead mate.

"And take your trash with you, You Filthy Animals!" he cried.

The Big Mexican tossed the dead man into the smaller

boat. As the body hit, someone squealed in shock, but then looked embarrassed.

As their boat drifted off, they heard the Bandana's curses.

"I gotta go," said Smalls hastily.

"*Sí*, and I'm done playing," said Uncle Danny, and he turned angry eyes towards the other side.

The Navy Engineer made another stop before he returned to the Pilot's House. Still holding his M4 rifle in one hand, he threw up noisily.

Then he was back to steer the ship. Luckily, it looked like only blue seas ahead and his chest loosened. But he wished he could have grabbed a drink as well.

***

Ruiz saw Uncle Danny first. The Big Mexican emerged quickly with a big knife in his hands heading straight for the other boat.

"Uncle Danny is on the warpath," warmed Ruiz over her earpiece. "Team on me!"

Jumping up, the Staff Sergeant ran to Danny's side with Frankline and Washington close behind.

"Danny?" she called out, as softly as she could.

"*He terminado con esto*," said the Big Mexican and he looked to where Liberty hid.

"Ummm," started Liberty.

"He just said, 'he's done with this'," explained Ruiz.

167

The Librarian saw him closing on the grappling hooks, but the other boat was still too far down to see him.

"I should've attached this knife to a pole," said Uncle Danny apologetically.

Just as the Bandanas saw the Big Mexican, the Librarian made her move.

Liberty fired right past the Chief's nose.

She embarrassingly fell back in surprise.

"Over their heads," called out Ruiz as she dropped to her stomach and moved under the lowest bar on the rail. Frankline and Washington went down next to her and started firing above them.

Uncle Danny jumped forward to cut the ropes, but he couldn't immediately cut through them.

"Stop him!" cried the Chief as she pointed up at Danny.

But most of the Bandanas had hit the ground. One did lift his AR-15.

Liberty's bullet smacked right into it.

Enraged, the Chief pulled her gun and started firing.

Uncle Danny had to drop back.

"I couldn't get the last rope by the stern," he called.

Liberty honed in. Her bullet hit the rope dead-on, but it didn't fully break.

"Damn, that always works in movies," she muttered in annoyance. She tried to focus on the remains of the rope when there was the roar of an engine.

The *Wolf Pack* started to speed up. Still holding by the frayed rope to the back of the Bandana's boat, The front started to veer out. The back turned in and bumped into the *Wolf Pack*.

"Cease fire," called Ruiz. "Pull Back!"

The soldiers quickly scrambled back, out of sight.

The Chief dropped into the helm seat to steer the boat back on course. The rope between the boats gave way. The *Wolf Pack* continued to roar ahead.

The walkie-talkie at Ruiz's side went off.

"Sorry!" called out Smalls. "Another boat was trying to catch up with us, so I had to get ahead of them."

"No! That was perfect," called out Ruiz.

Both the Bandana's boats were coming together as a unit. Ruiz had no illusions that they weren't going to follow hard.

Liberty jumped out of her place and went to Danny.

"You! Mister *Hombre!*" she growled. "What were you thinking?"

"That things were going to get out of hand real fast," he said, a little sheepishly, and turned to the others. "*Gracias!*"

"*Da nada*, dude," replied Washington.

Still standing, Liberty raised her rifle to look through the scope.

"What the heck?" muttered Liberty.

***

Singh stopped and looked out behind cabin #1. He didn't

see Rak anymore, which could be good or bad.

"There's nothing for it," said the Mother, Cassidy, behind him. "We're going to have to run the last part."

The Captain nodded. "If I have to start shooting, keep going and get the boat ready to go."

They moved out.

Across a large swath of dirt was the Bandanas at the tree line arguing.

"I'm Not going into the dark woods after that thing," said the Bandana, George, wisely.

The family didn't mess around. Mother led them swiftly to the tug. Singh moved between them and the Bandanas.

Almost at the dock, one of the Bandanas by the trees screamed.

"Hey! They're getting away!"

"Go! Go! Go!" ordered Singh and the family went onto the wooden dock.

One of the pirates swung around with his AR-15, ready to shoot at the family. Singh fired first, more as a warning, but did catch one in the arm.

The rest turned and started firing wildly. With no cover, the Captain ran towards the tug, hoping not to get shot. Right before his toes, a bullet bounced off the wooden dock but passed harmlessly.

'Darn, darn, darn," he thought.

Suddenly there were cries of surprise from the tree line.

***

With options dwindling, Rak planned the best time to strike. But she had no illusions for her chances.

"Hey! They're getting away!" screamed one of the Bandanas.

Thrilled, the bird saw the family getting away. But the Bandanas started shooting at the Captain as the tug started up.

Zipping towards the back of the Bandanas, Rak plowed into one, which catapulted him into a bunch ahead. She knocked down some others but stopped short of breaking any bones.

Besides, she had already thrown the Bandanas into confusion.

Not wanting to press her God, Du's, good graces, Rakduson darted back into the trees. She heard Captain Singh firing more. A few tried to shoot at her, but the bird was moving way too fast, using the trees as cover. Still a few bullets got close.

Reaching the shoreline, Rakduson burst out and up into the air, she used a few zigzags, just in case. When she felt like she was far enough out, she gently turned.

***

The Bandanas shouldn't have any more boats to follow. Still, Captain Singh crouched in the back of the tug. As they went further out, he could just see the pirates running around the campsite like angry hornets.

171

"Is it safe?" asked a little voice next to him.

Eyes widening, the Captain glanced down. The little girl was wide-eyed with interest, but she was hidden.

"I'd wait a little longer...," said Singh, trying to remember the little girl's name.

"MINDY!" cried a voice inside the tug.

After checking that there were no immediate threats, the Captain called back.

"Ms. Mindy is out here! She's hiding. Safe with me. Best to stay out of sight for now. But we're looking good."

"Mindy and I will talk later," came an ominous voice from inside the tug.

"Oh-oh," murmured Mindy.

"She's just worried," said Singh gently. His heart leapt and he started looking around quickly. Spotting her, he released a breath of relief.

Above them, Rakduson soared, keeping watch.

Singh gave a little chuckle, letting some of the stress go. Turning to the little girl, he asked. "Can you do me a favor? Can you ask your Dad if he can go North, up the coast?"

Mindy was about to say something, but her Mom bellowed for her again. The little girl almost crawled on her belly, but she stayed down.

When the Captain finally felt safe that they were not being followed, he waved up to Rak. It took a try or two, but she finally swooped down and landed gently on the back of the tug.

"I'm going to go talk to the pilot...," started Singh, but

then his face grew serious. "On one hand, I want to yell at you for endangering yourself."

"Distracted," squeaked Rak in protest.

"I know, and it worked," said Singh. "But it was close. And, since it's not proper to hug the people you work with…" The Captain turned to face her and gave a crisp salute.

Rakduson straightened with delight in her eyes.

"But please," said Singh. "Don't Ever do that again."

"Can't promise," said Rak, bobbing her head side to side.

"I'm just glad that you're okay," said the Captain. "Now, can you watch and make sure that no one sneaks up on our butts?"

While Rak watched, Singh headed forward and introduced himself.

"My name's Will Holt," said the guy. Not daring to look up, his eyes darted between the horizon and the radar. "So, your friends lured them away. They headed this way, right?"

"Yeah," said Singh, feeling like he was missing something. "They were going to head straight up the coast, so we may want to go out a bit, so we don't…"

"There!" said Will. He pointed at the radar, and it showed three blips. "We're going to be upon them in a minute. Get everyone to the engine room. It'll be the safest place."

"Um…," started Singh.

"Hurry," said Will. The order was not cruel, but with a

173

worried insistence.

The Captain decided to defer to the Tug's captain. He went and helped the rest of Will's family into the engine room.

With that done, he ran up to Rak.

***

Aboard the *Wolf Pack*, Liberty ran towards the stern of the boat, and the rest followed.

"IS that the tug?" asked Ruiz. "And I'm surprised that those a-holes aren't following us."

"Actually," said Frankline timidly. "That might be because I shot the back of the boat, where I thought the engine was."

Ruiz looked at him in surprise with a warm smile. "Good thinking." And Frankline stood really straight with a grin.

"*¡Fíjate!* Is it just me, or is that tug heading straight for the boats," asked Uncle Danny.

Liberty looked through her scope. "Oh boy!"

The boat with the Chief of the Bandanas tried to get started and move. Then they tried shooting at the bigger ship.

The tug managed to hit the front of the Bandana's boat where no one was. The smaller boat shattered spectacularly and then the tug passed.

"...you...me," came a voice over the earpieces.

Ruiz took the walkie talkie.

"Can you slow down Smalls?" she asked. "The tug is right behind us."

The *Wolf Pack* began to ease up.

"Can you hear me?" called out Singh over the earpieces.

"We read you loud and clear, Sir," said Ruiz. "Good to hear from you."

"Is Rak with you?" asked Uncle Danny worriedly.

"Yes she is," said Singh. "And I'm glad she came along."

Uncle Danny let out a little sigh. "Just wanted to make sure."

"I understand," said the Captain on the tug. He turned to Rak and let her know.

"Good friend," said the bird with delight.

"Now we should...," began Singh when he noticed the little girl by his side, looking up at Rak.

"Tha's a big bird," she said in awe.

Singh smiled down at Mindy. "Her name is Rakduson. You can say 'hi'."

"Hi," squeaked the little girl.

"Hello," replied Rak pleasantly.

But still Mindy jumped a little and grabbed Singh's hand. He looked down in surprise, and then amusement.

"I need to talk to your dad," he said.

Mindy frowned. "My Dad's dead."

Singh paused for a second but rallied. "Um. I need to speak with Mr. Holt then."

175

The Captain started to walk, but Mindy kept holding his hand. He wasn't sure what to say, so he opted for nothing.

Up in the wheelhouse, Will Holt explained. "I'm Cassidy's friend." He looked a little wistful. "About the only friend I've ever had."

"You've had other friends," chided a voice from the door.

Singh turned to see a woman in her early 30's.

With a playful smirk on her face, he looked right at Singh.

"And I see that you made a friend too," she said.

The Captain blinked for a moment. But then he remembered that Mindy was still holding his hand.

"Oh, um…," started Singh nervously.

The Mom's face became completely serious. "Just so you know, You Can't Keep Her. She's mine," said the Mom. "I need her back. Well. Really, mostly, for tax purposes."

"What?" asked the Captain quickly. "I wasn't…"

But the smirk was back on her face. "You are too easy to tease." And she shook her head with a little 'tsk' noise.

Singh decided, for his own sanity, that he needed to get the conversation back on track.

"Okay, we have a plan," he started with.

"But, I don't want to endanger my daughter," said Cassidy seriously.

"Actually," said Singh. "I might know someone who could help with that."

Chapter Ten

TESSY JUMPED FORWARD to immediately embrace Mindy.

"WelcomeIt'sGreatToMeetYou!" said Tessy breathlessly as she let go of the other girl and introduced herself and Colin. Soon the three kids ran off into the yacht.

Liberty gave a smirk.

"What *Mija?*" asked Uncle Danny next to her.

"Didja see Colin," said Liberty. "Trying to act all cool. Like he wasn't thrilled to see a new kid."

Uncle Danny gave a bright grin. "*¡Neta, no manches!* You're kidding. I missed it."

Returning to the Fleet, they had picked up the kids at first, since Tagg couldn't leave just yet.

Cassidy watched the kids disappear. "Um. Are the kids

okay running around?"

"Sí, they are very good *niños*," said Uncle Danny.

"Oh! I didn't mean to say otherwise," said Cassidy quickly.

Liberty leaned forward. "Don't let Uncle Danny fool you, he's a pussycat inside."

"¡Aguas!" said Uncle Danny to the Librarian with a mock scowl. "You tread on thin ice."

Grinning unrepentantly, Liberty looked back at Cassidy and Will Holt, who was standing with Captain Singh.

"If you want," said the Librarian. "You could all stay for dinner. Which is as soon as Tagg gets here."

***

After dinner, the tug returned to the shadow of the aircraft carrier and dropped off Singh's team.

The *Wolf Pack* moved away from the Fleet, in case of hijackers.

The kids reluctantly surrendered to sleep, and Uncle Danny was on first watch with Rak.

The moment the door to their room had closed, Liberty and Tagg embraced fiercely.

"I missed you," whispered Tagg.

"I can tell," she smirked, pressing her stomach forward.

"Oh No!" said Tagg quickly as he pulled back a little. "I didn't mean...I just…"

"It's okay," said Liberty. "Really! It was just a joke."

Tagg relaxed. "Sorry. I...I don't want to be a burden."

Liberty looked up at him. "You're not a burden. Of course not."

"It's just...," started the Scientist. "After I woke you the other night..." And his voice trailed off.

"You were having a bad night," said Liberty softly. "It's okay. I promise. You're allowed to have bad nights, just like me."

Tagg deflated a little. "I suddenly started worrying about it earlier today, and I couldn't stop."

Liberty held him close and worried herself.

***

"So, you're taking our tug?" asked Cassidy with a cold voice.

"What? No, no," replied the Rear Admiral immediately.

Captain Singh jumped in. "We were hoping that you could help us."

"You seriously saved us because of vegetables?" asked Cassidy. She played out the word vegetables into each syllable.

"Who cares Why they saved us," said Will Holt, throwing up his hands.

"It just seems fishy," said Cassidy.

"No, vegetables," replied Will Holt cheekily.

Back on the Carrier the next morning, the introductory meeting was not going well when Liberty and Uncle Danny arrived. They could feel the chill in the air.

"*Ole!*" cried Uncle Danny with cheer.

"How's it going?" asked Liberty with a grimace.

The Rear Admiral looked over as *Dos Amigos* sat.

"Ms. Cassidy is worried about our intentions," he explained.

Liberty blinked. "Um, to get more vitamin C." As Cassidy was beginning to speak, the Librarian leaned forward. "No. See, people are getting sick. I guess they need certain vitamins, which they're not getting. An' we wanted to just garden on an island..."

"They're all filled with zoms," said Cassidy thoughtfully.

"Exactly!" nodded Captain Singh. "Cleaning an island...that just seems too dangerous. Then we saw this ocean-going barge, an' and we thought, maybe that would work."

"How are you going to plant crops on a barge?" asked Cassidy, starting to get curious.

Captain Singh opened his mouth, but then stopped.

"*Nada,*" said Uncle Danny. "We don't have a clue."

"We weren't even sure we'd find a tug," said Singh.

"Lucky me," said Cassidy with a little smirk.

"I'm hoping that this will be lucky for all of us," said the Rear Admiral.

Uncle Danny leaned forward. "I'll admit. This isn't the most macho mission we ever took on."

"But it is important," said Liberty.

"You're going to need to cover the entire top with soil," said Cassidy. "That's a lot of dirt."

"Well, let's get the barge first," said Captain Singh. "I propose..."

"Already?" teased Cassidy. "Isn't it too soon, Mr. Singh."

"Um...I...What?" asked Captain Singh.

Cassidy chuckled mischievously. "Sorry. Keep going."

"Oh...yeah," said Singh as he pulled his thoughts back on course. "No, what I was going to say was that I propo... suggest that we take the tug to the Port of the City of Angels with my squad...". He gestured at Liberty and Danny. "And anyone else who wants to come along."

"Heck Yeah!" cried Liberty. "We didn't come here to kiss spiders."

***

Getting the barge out was terribly uneventful, Liberty had sat atop the tug and watched with a bored expression. Once they had it out, the Captain called a quick meeting.

"The Plan was to go back to the Fleet," said Cassidy wearily.

"Yes, and we'll probably send the tug and barge back," said Singh softly. "However, I'm trying to decide on our next step."

Cassidy waited, impatiently.

"We need a farmer," said Singh thoughtfully. "And/or

books about farming."

Suddenly, Liberty straightened. "I know!"

Chapter Eleven

A SMALL GROUP moved through the streets of the City of Angels, dodging zoms.

Liberty led the way, followed by Uncle Danny and Frankline.

"You sure you can find this place again?" asked Uncle Danny.

"I don't know," said Liberty. "That's why I'm bringing both of you. We can start where those birds attacked that soldier, and then maybe between the three of us..."

"Worth a shot," shrugged Uncle Danny.

As they retraced their path from the other morning, the sun was already heading towards the horizon. Liberty looked at it nervously.

"We were going so fast," said Frankline. "I only

remember bits and pieces."

The sun appeared to drop faster as they walked the streets, looking down alleys. But to no avail.

"Okay," said Liberty. "Maybe we pick back up tomorrow."

As they turned back, Uncle Danny made a small noise. "Should we even try?"

Liberty looked at him. "This is not a 'for sure'. Just a chance."

"I know," said Uncle Danny.

They walked as fast as they dared.

Liberty let out a cry that made him jump.

"[¿*Mande?*]" growled the Big Mexican, leveling his shotgun.

The Librarian took off down a narrow alley, and the other two followed.

"I don't know about...," started Uncle Danny.

"Hi Bob," he heard from ahead.

Reaching her, Liberty made a ta-da noise. "You two wait here."

The Librarian skipped around the plants-that-still-looked-alien to her, and Bob the zom. She rapped on the back door of the store.

"Hellllo!" she called out. "Are you there Mr. Jed?"

Bob was closing, so she jumped back to wait with Danny and Frankline.

After a moment, the door opened cautiously. Bob was

near and reached out, but Jed just swatted the hands away.

"Stop that Bob," said Jed with gentle reproof. And then his eyes lit up as he saw them. "You came back! Well, I'll be damned."

Bob reached out again, and Jed used the metal door to push the zom away. Propping the door open a bit, he ran around Bob and used the machine to pull him in.

Once secure, Private Frankline wandered over to look at the device.

"That's pretty neat," said the Private. "You make that yourself?"

"Got tired of using the hand crank," shrugged Jed. "Mother always said I was lazy."

Frankline turned. "Wasn't it Bill Gates who said he only wants to hire lazy employees, because they find an easier way to do stuff?"

"I dunno," said Jed.

"Anyways, this is a clever device," said Frankline. "As one tinkerer to another."

"Umm," started Chloe from the doorway. "What's going on?"

Liberty cleared her throat. "Pardon me. We need a farmer, and I was wondering how much you knew much about farming." She gestured at the marijuana plants. "Well, obviously you did this…"

"What're you looking to do?" asked Jed.

He was patient as Liberty explained the idea of putting dirt on top of the barge and growing plants. As she finished, the older man turned thoughtfully to Chloe.

185

"What do you think?" he asked the girl.

"I mean...," began Chloe. "It's pretty out there. But, if people are really getting sick..."

"Yeah, that's true," muttered Jed. Looking back at them, Jed beckoned them thoughtfully. "Come into the shop, and mind you, wipe your feet."

They dutifully wiped their feet and entered a small store. To their immediate right was a sleeping bag. It had been made like a bed.

"That's Jed's!" said Chloe. She waved one hand with a flourish. "An' I sleep behind the counter, so I get a little privacy."

"It was for my own privacy," harrumphed Jed. "Man needs his own space."

"Of course," said Chloe sweetly with mock indulgence. She looked back at Liberty. "But what you're really interested in is over here." She gestured to the other side of the store.

"Wow!" said Frankline automatically.

"[¡*Chido!*]" added Uncle Danny.

Across the other side of the store was a complicated rig of hydroponics. Plants that Liberty now recognized as marijuana were under lights.

"Problem is," said Jed softly. "We still got food."

"More or less," grumbled Chloe. "We've pretty much taken everything from the Korean grocer, and the Indian grocer in this strip mall."

"But we're not going to starve this year," said Jed, going back to his original point. "My concern though, is that I don't know how much longer the water and electricity are going to last."

"I'm shocked that they lasted this long," said Liberty.

"I heard a tale that there are still people keeping the water flowing," said Chloe like a storyteller.

Liberty looked at Danny, who shrugged.

"Not heard that," said the Librarian. "But it might be worth checking out some day."

"Can't hold up forever though," said Jed. "An' then we're in trouble without fresh water."

Not saying anything, Liberty let the man put together his thoughts.

"Dirt's heavy," said Jed at last.

Chloe huffed in annoyance. "Everyone who's helped in a garden knows that bro."

"Don't interrupt," said Jed with gentle reproach. "It's not polite."

Chloe rolled her eyes but stayed quiet.

To Liberty, it was like a grandfather talking to his granddaughter, even though they were not bound by blood. She immediately thought of Tagg as a grandfather, and how great he'd be. Flashing across that was the memory of Tagg worrying. All that flashed through her mind in a second. Realizing that her mind had wandered, she pulled her attention back.

"The reason I mentioned the dirt," said Jed patiently. "...is that I grew up on a farm and remember shoveling it. And if you want to cover an entire barge with it..."

Liberty's eyes grew wide. "Oh."

"And then we'd have to put down fertilizer...," continued Jed.

"Shit," said Frankline, but then he said quickly. "Sorry..."

"No, you're right," said Jed. "All in all, that's a lot of heavy lifting."

"An' what if it rained...," said Chloe.

Frankline nodded. "It might just all wash out to sea."

"Damn," said Liberty as her shoulders deflated. She glanced at Uncle Danny who looked similarly downtrodden.

"But that's okay," said Jed quickly. "We're not dead yet."

Everyone looked up in interest, but it was Chloe who got it first. She chirped and pointed at the plants in the store.

"Hydroponics!" she said.

"Exactly," smiled Jed at her, and then he looked at Liberty and company. "You could just build a big hydroponics farm on top of your barge."

"Do you know how to build one?" asked Uncle Danny.

Jed opened his mouth, but then closed it. "Well, no. Not really. I can keep it going, but I've only ever built little ones."

"I could help," said Frankline, but then he looked down. "But I've never made anything like that." He turned to Liberty. "But if you give me a plan, I can follow it."

The Librarian smiled at the Private.

"Good to know," she said, and she glanced at Jed. "It

would be too much to hope that you have any hydroponic books here?"

"Naw," said Jed. "Just a pamphlet. I kinda jury-rigged the rest with spit and baling wire."

"Ewwww," said Chloe with mock disgust.

"You pipe down," replied Jed with a melodramatic glare.

"Don't wanna," said Chloe, keeping up the act.

As they play-bickered, Uncle Danny saw the guarded look on Liberty's face.

"What is it [*Mija?*]" he asked of her.

Liberty looked up in surprise, but then her face became neutral. "Huh? Oh nothing." Before he could ask more, she amended. "Actually, that's not true."

"You thinking about where you can get books?" asked Danny carefully.

"Yeah," admitted the Librarian. She looked at everyone. "I think I know where we can get a bunch of books on the environment. There might be something in there on hydroponics."

"Book store?" asked Jed. "I didn't think they existed anymore."

"Actually... the library," said Liberty slowly, and Uncle Danny looked at her with concern.

"Not sure how we're going to get there," said Jed. "We don't have a car that works anymore."

"Actually, I was thinking of having you two stay here and we're going to get transportation," said Liberty.

"You have something safe to go through these streets?" asked Jed.

"It'll do," smiled Liberty. "We'll collect you two and then go to the library…"

"Actually," said Uncle Danny. "We should hit the library first, and then pick them up. I don't want to make them wait outside while we go through the library."

Liberty nodded. "That could take a minute." Focusing on Jed and Chloe, she continued. "If that's all right?"

"Sure," shrugged Jed, and then he looked at Chloe. "You good?"

"I don't mind it here," she said merrily. "With the windows covered up and a back door, it's safe enough."

"As long as the water lasts," said Jed.

"True," agreed Chloe more soberly.

"I'm hoping we'll be back in a couple days," said Liberty.

"We'll be here," said Jed, and a happy grin spread across his face. "Maybe a little baked, but here."

Uncle Danny's eyes narrowed, but he kept his peace.

"Okay," said Liberty. "We'll be back as soon as we can." She hesitated and looked at Uncle Danny.

Finally, the Librarian gave a little sigh and said to Danny. "I was going to say I forgot something and come back in here." He furrowed his brow in confusion. "But…Rule 1."

"Huh?" asked Frankline.

Liberty glanced at the Private. "Family Rule Number 1 is 'No Lying'." She looked back at Danny for a moment, but then turned.

To Jed, she asked. "I understand that marijuana can help people with their anxieties."

The older man nodded. "I know...well, knew more than a few who used it for that. And CBD, but there was some massive recall for that. And I wasn't big on the idea myself. God knows what they put in there. So, I'm happier with regular old pot that..."

Chloe tugged on his sleeve, and he looked at her.

Understanding, Jed refocused. "Apparently, I'm rambling. And yes, it can help."

"Can I buy some?" asked Liberty. "I know someone who might need it."

Beside her, Uncle Danny made a grunt.

"And I know nothing about it," continued Liberty.

"Well, you can't buy any...," said Jed, and everyone looked at him in surprise. After a dramatic pause, he finished. "What am I going to do with money?" He grinned. "Does the person trying this smoke regularly?"

"Oh God No," said Liberty swiftly, but then she got worried. "Sorry, I didn't mean to be rude."

Jed just waved the concern away and said thoughtfully. "Anxious, you say..."

The older man moved over to the growing plants and Chloe followed.

"What about Heaven's Hello?" she suggested.

"Bit strong," replied Jed.

"That's true," nodded Chloe.

The two went around the store at a lightning pace

gathering stuff.

"Liberty," said Uncle Danny with a dark voice.

"I know," she replied quickly and nervously. "But I don't know what else to do. If we had a steady source of pharmaceuticals…"

"Still…," replied Uncle Danny with a growl.

Returning with Jed, Chloe held out a little paper bag with a bunny face drawn upon it.

As Liberty took it, Jed spoke up.

"In there is Hulu Kush 2: Electric Boogaloo," explained Jed. "Since you don't smoke, I put a vaporizer in there. Less coughing for you."

"Okay…I've never tried one," said Liberty, a little embarrassed.

Before they headed out, Jed gave a quick tutorial.

Soon, they were ready to head out.

"Thanks for your business!" joked Chloe. "Come back anytime!"

***

Out on the street, the three started walking back towards the tank storehouse.

"The Library?" asked Uncle Danny with a growl. "You shouldn't go back there."

Stiffening, Liberty looked at him crossly. "Excuse me."

"It's going to be hard on you," said Uncle Danny. "You

192

should stay with the tank."

"Like Hell!" scoffed Liberty. "Those were my co-workers in there."

"And I don't want You to have to end them," snapped Uncle Danny.

"I'm a big grrl," said Liberty. "I can handle it."

"It's not that you [*can't*] handle it," said Uncle Danny with exasperation and briefly switched to rapid-fire Spanish before continuing. "That's not the point."

Very carefully, Frankline drifted a little away from them as they fought. It was actually weird, and his stomach twisted.

'Like watching your parents fight', he thought.

Watching the sky as well, the Private stayed as far from the argument as possible. Though a part of him wanted to jump in and help make peace. But, as his Daddy always said when Frankline's Mom and Sister were fighting, 'Don't stick your dick in a blender'.

***

That evening, after putting the kids to bed, Liberty took Tagg's hand and led him up onto the upper deck. There, with only the moonlight, they settled onto a built-in sofa.

Tagg looked around a little nervously.

"And what're we doing up here?" he asked with a mischievous and hopeful grin.

"I'm sorry to say that it isn't anything naughty," said

Liberty, but then she stopped in thought. "Okay, maybe... different naughty."

His big brow furrowed. "What?"

Liberty took a deep breath. "We're not finding enough medication to help with your worries."

"My anxiety," said Tagg slowly.

Nodding, Liberty continued. "Even if we did find some..."

"There's no guarantee that it'll be around for long," said Tagg. "We talked about this..." And his voice trailed off.

"One of the librarians I worked with also had anxieties, but she had a little more of an...all-natural way of dealing with it," she said.

"Oh," said Tagg uncertainly.

"An' I wanted something sustainable, and...," said Liberty quickly, but then she stopped herself. "Okay, I'm going to stop rambling. It's marijuana."

"What?" asked Tagg with surprise.

"Well...if we could get some CBD," said Liberty. "Then you can get the good effects without any of the rest...but..." Her voice trailed off.

Tagg looked thoughtful. "I knew people who'd eat it as well...edibles, I think it was called."

"I didn't want to mess around...," began Liberty.

"I don't really like smoking," said Tagg with concern.

"Ah! That's okay," said Liberty. "We got one of those vape-thingies." She took it out of the bag and quickly explained how it was already ready to go.

"Isn't vaping bad for you?" asked Tagg, still exploring the idea.

"Probably," said Liberty. "But—If this works!—we can always make edibles. When we go to my library, I'll see if there's a book."

Tagg stopped and looked at her. "Are you going to be okay going back? To your Library. Uncle Danny seemed really concerned."

"I'm not exactly looking forward to it," admitted Liberty slowly. "And I'd rather not...but I know where everything is. We can find stuff really quick..." She sighed. "...an' I think Uncle Danny is more upset about this." She waggled the vaporizer.

"It...," started Tagg as he looked at it. "Um, I've never tried it. I wasn't very cool in high school."

"I don't know what that has to do with anything," insisted Liberty. "The people I hung out with just weren't into anything like this. Doesn't make me lame." She grinned. "There was so much else about me that made me lame."

"You're not lame!" insisted Tagg.

"It's okay," said Liberty. "I'm okay with my Lameness." She stopped and looked down at the vaporizer. "But this, this might really help you, and we can easily make more."

Tagg's brow furrowed. "I'd worry about the kids getting ahold of it. If it was on the boat."

"Yeah," said Liberty seriously. "That's really important. But we should see if this works first. It might make you more anxious, and a little paranoid."

195

"Paranoid?" asked Tagg.

"That was what Jed at the shop said. And there might be a part of that every time. That's why we're going to try it together and see. And if it doesn't help, I will throw the vape into the ocean myself."

"I guess...," said Tagg. "If it helps..."

"You don't deserve to live in pain," said Liberty, dead serious. "Especially you."

Tagg smiled weakly at that. "I guess that's true. And I am kinda curious."

Liberty explained how to use the vape, and even took the first hit. After she was done, she explained what she did.

"But we don't want to do too much at first," she said seriously.

"I'm okay with that," said Tagg.

"But it has to be enough so that it has some kind of effect," said Liberty quickly and thoughtfully.

"We can try a hit and then try another in fifteen minutes," suggested Tagg.

"And we can cuddle in the meantime," smirked Liberty.

"I'm in," said Tagg, excitedly at that, and he took the vaporizer.

Shortly, he said. "It's not working."

"It's only been two minutes," said Liberty with mock exasperation. The weather was a little cool, so she pulled a blanket over them.

With a happy noise, Tagg cuddled into her, holding out

196

the vape. She glanced around, but it was pretty dark up here. They were alone.

Close, Liberty whispered in his ear. "Well, I'm going to help you relax dammit, one way or another."

As she slid below the blanket, Tagg started to smile, which soon turned into a gigantic grin. And then he returned the favor.

***

"I think I'm feeling it," said Tagg.

A little time had passed, and they were back to cuddling under the blanket.

"Yeah," replied Liberty with a languid voice. "Something's definitely happening. I thought it might just be afterglow…"

"That too," said Tagg. "It feels…good."

***

"Oh My God," said Liberty with surprise.

They had been greatly enjoying each other's company—just cuddling—for awhile, but now she sat straight up.

"What?" asked Tagg with concern.

"No, nothing bad," said Liberty. "I…the munchies are really a thing."

Tagg laughed. "Now that you mention it, I am kinda

197

hungry."

Pocketing the vape and the pot, she grinned.

"Let's go raid the galley!"

"Like pirates!" laughed Tagg.

After a snack, they headed to bed, but they didn't go to sleep right away.

Chapter Twelve

"OH, THAT'S TOO weird," said Liberty with surprise.

"¿*Mande?*" asked Uncle Danny seated next to her.

"Well, we're sitting on a tank, driving through the streets of L.A, but I don't find that odd anymore," said Liberty, bemused.

Uncle Danny gave a hearty laugh. "¡*Fíjate!* You're right *Mija!* It's like another day at the office." He looked at her, but a little frown slipped in. And then his face grew more downcast.

Liberty wanted to say something, but she wasn't sure what.

In the past, her automatic response would have been to apologize and feel bad. But then, she remembered the happy look on Tagg's face last night. No, she wasn't sorry, so apologizing now would be like a lie.

"If you would like to go ahead into the library," said Liberty. "I'd be okay with that."

Uncle Danny looked at her. "If you're sure."

"I did like my co-workers," she said sadly.

The Big Mexican nodded solemnly. "I will treat them with the utmost respect..." But then he paused. "Except for the—you know—."

"It's okay," said Liberty kindly. But then her voice grew hard. "But you better be careful."

"I promise," swore Uncle Danny.

There was a chirp of a bird above them. Most everyone looked up as the tank drove through the streets of the City Of Angels.

Standing astride the tank, Captain Singh waved. "Rak incoming."

Dipping a wing, the alien-bird started down towards them, while Uncle Danny stood up. Thankfully, the tank was not going very fast.

The Captain asked. "Is she going to be able to land on a moving object?"

"She might not need to," said Uncle Danny.

Using her wings to slow her down, Rakduson actually began to land behind them. With her momentum sufficiently dulled, she hopped up onto the back of the tank.

"Ta-da!" cried the alien-bird.

"Nice landing," grinned Singh.

"It was...," began Uncle Danny, and then he gave an exaggerated shrug. "It was okay."

Rak gave the Big Mexican a mock glare. "I will peck you."

"Hey! Let me back up before you do," said Singh, holding up his hands. "I gotta wash my own uniform."

This raised a chorus of laughter from everybody, including Rak.

As it died down, Singh turned to the alien-bird.

"What did you see Ms. Rak?" asked the Captain.

Rakduson tried to salute with a big wing, which caused another chorus of laughs.

"Just zoms at library," said the bird, who was having trouble with the 'm' in zoms, due to not having lips. "No birds. No people. At least living."

"Thank you," said the Captain. He turned to Liberty, who was standing. "Ms. Liberty, can you talk us through the layout of the library again, and where we need to go?"

"All the environment stuff is on the upper level. The stairs are just past the big conference room," said Liberty. "I'm hoping they'll have stuff for hydroponics there, but if not, we might have to go to the other libraries."

"We could have gone to those first," said Uncle Danny, gently.

Liberty shook her head. "I know where everything is here. We can run in and out."

***

201

The front door had been unlocked, so that helped. Uncle Danny had gone first.

The Big Mexican stepped behind the counter to make sure that nothing was back there. Behind the counter, he could not shake the feeling that he was doing something wrong. 'Only librarians are allowed behind the counter', he thought just as the first zom appeared.

The Big Mexican was about to squeeze the trigger when he froze.

"*Madre con Dios!*" he hissed.

***

"It's...taking too long," said Liberty worriedly. "I'm going in."

Singh was about to agree when the front door swung open.

Running out the door, Uncle Danny came up to the tank with a grin.

"The majority of *el morte* will not be bothering us, but there might be some hiding!" he crowed.

Liberty felt a flash of anger that he was so happy. But, he had been right, this was going to be hard. If only she had hated her co-workers.

Danny wouldn't answer any more questions, but just urged them inside.

Liberty steeled herself for the bodies, or at least blood

stains, but there were none. She figured that he had probably moved them to an office, her friends all piled up in…

'Stop' she told herself. Out loud, she reminded herself. "You gotta Cowgrrl Up here."

"*¡Fíjate!* Come!" said Uncle Danny. He waved everyone towards the large conference room.

"What's up?" asked Singh in concern.

"*Perdón!* I took so long in there," said Uncle Danny. "But it was for a good reason."

Liberty saw the chairs piled in front of the conference room.

"You did it!" she cried happily, and her eyes watered up.

"Did what?" asked Private Frankline, confused.

Staff Sergeant Ruiz whispered to him, not unkindly. "He locked all the zoms in the conference room."

Liberty bounced over to Uncle Danny and gave him a bone-creaking hug.

"I got your back *Mija*," he whispered as she pulled back. "Always." His face grew serious. "But there might be more. I wasn't able to find all of them, just the majority."

Looking through the window, she saw a librarian with funny socks.

"It helps," nodded the Librarian quickly, trying not to cry. "It really does."

Liberty left most of them at the Environment section to check for books on hydroponics and gardening. There were a lot of books. As Washington went to raid the theater play section, the Librarian excused herself and kept going.

However, she soon found Rak shadowing her.

"What's u...?" started the Librarian, but then she said. "You keeping an eye on me?"

The bird bobbed her head from side to side, which was the equivalent of a shrug.

"For Uncle Danny?" asked Liberty.

"For kids," said Rak. "Just making sure."

Liberty was about to protest, but then shrugged herself. "I'm happy for the company. We're heading for a storage area where the books that I need are."

"'Kay," replied Rak.

"One person put the books out in the morning, and another hid the books away in the evening," explained Liberty. That fight seemed so far away. And so petty now."

They moved carefully into a back room and found a zom. Rak saw it first and leapt, breaking its leg. Then its neck.

Liberty felt a little chill. She remembered that when they had first met the alien-birds, they killed the soldier with them, Bordeaux.

Rak turned back.

Forcing a smile, the Librarian said. "Thank you."

"Something wrong?" asked Rak, worried.

"No, not necessarily," stammered Liberty. "I'm sorry, I just..."

The earpiece went off.

"We got company," whispered the tank driver, Sergeant Bath. "Birds came sniffing around the tank, and now they're headed into the library."

Over the earpieces, Captain Singh asked. "That means more might be close."

Rak, who didn't have an earpiece, looked curiously.

"Birds in the library," whispered Liberty, and the alien moved close to listen as well.

"How many and are they buzzing?" asked Captain Singh of the tank driver.

"Three," replied Bath. "And I could hear the buzzing from inside the tank.

There was the sound of a rifle being readied. "We're ready for them."

Without a sound, Rak was gone, out the door.

It took Liberty a second. "Shit." Running after the alien, she called over the earpiece. "Rak is on the way."

"What's she doing?" asked Uncle Danny before Singh could.

"I have no idea," said Liberty. Ahead, she saw Rak turn a corner.

"*¡Mierda!*" hissed Danny.

"That's what I said."

There were noises ahead.

"Silent running," said Liberty, who slowed as she reached the bend. Stopping, she glanced around the corner.

Three alien-birds were by the Biography section. The devices in the back of their heads were letting off an irritating sound. The harsh noise bounced off the dark wood walls and got under Liberty's skin.

These new birds were unsure of what to make of Rak, who flapped her wings in front of them.

"*Tass!*" cried Rakduson with a pleading voice. She started to talk fast, too fast for Liberty to follow.

However, the new birds were starting to shift from confused to homicidal. One of them, with a silver-colored tuft, stepped forward, eyes blazing with fury. Lunging, Silver tuft tried to snap at a wing.

Rak hopped away, but kept talking, faster than before.

"Liberty?" whispered Singh through their earpieces.

"Not yet," replied Liberty as soft as she could.

One of the Alien-birds was looking around. Liberty froze. Not daring to move.

"*Hojot Teal!*" cried Rak with a more strident tone.

Silver Tuft shot forward. This time Rak did not make it neatly away and a few of her feathers went flying. The other birds immediately followed as Rakduson scrambled out of view.

Liberty almost moved forward but stopped herself.

Rak and the others reappeared briefly, but then disappeared.

Gritting her teeth, Liberty made herself wait, but with the cold fear that Rak might need her help. But then, Rak didn't ask her to come along.

Just as Liberty was going to slip forward regardless, her earpiece came alive.

"What the hell," said the tank driver. "Rak just flew off with the other three hot on her tail."

"I can help," said Liberty.

"Wait," said Captain Singh. "If Rak has drawn them off, we don't want anyone to come back."

"She is tough," said Uncle Danny, as if trying to convince himself.

Fist clenched hard; Liberty reluctantly nodded. "True. I wouldn't want to meet Rak in a dark alley."

"¡Oye! Wait! Didn't we already do that?" asked Danny.

That drew a chuckle from Liberty. "You're right. Actually, I just saw her take out a zom just now. It was kinda...scary." She grew serious. "But...let's not waste this time. I'm going back to get the books I need."

"We found some boxes, so we're loading up books," said Singh over the earpieces as the Librarian returned to where she had been.

"Meet you by the front door," said Liberty.

"You okay?" asked Uncle Danny.

"I got this covered," said Liberty. Moving through the back rooms, she already had her silenced Glock out. The zom that Rak had stomped was still very dead.

Moving along the outer wall of the room, Liberty remembered right where the box should be. The garbage area came into view and there was a box full of marijuana books labeled 'Trash'. In front of it was Mr. Holbrick, or at least the zombie version.

"Ra-hung?" moaned zombie Mr. Holbrick.

"I just need the box," said Liberty. "I don't want to kill you." Which was a little bit of a lie. A fact that made her feel a little bad. But, then she remembered that he had made Mary-Mary cry.

Zombie Mr. Holbrick lunged.

Shortly, Liberty walked out of the back rooms with a box marked 'Trash' under one arm and her Glock in the other.

By the front doors, Uncle Danny labored under two heavy environment boxes.

"¡Aguas!" he grumped at Liberty as she walked up. "This better work. These books are heavy."

"Hey!" shot back the Librarian with the same grumpy tone. "I'm carrying a heavy one myself. An' you don't hear me whining."

"Whining?" asked Uncle Danny with mock indignation.

"You heard me," sniffed Liberty.

Uncle Danny shook his head. "You shouldn't have put your gun away."

"I figure that, if a zom came at me," said Liberty. "I'd just crush 'em under all these books." Below her beret, she was definitely sweating from having to carry them

Frankline bounded up. "I got you Ms. Liberty." He guarded her with a serious face, and his rifle ready to shoot.

"Thank you," she said sincerely.

Outside there were rifle shots, but with control shots.

"Got some looky-loos here," said the tank driver over the earpieces. "You better hurry."

Standing on the front of the M1A2 Abrams was Sergeant

Bath with her rifle. She fired a second time and a zom on the ground stopped crawling.

"Hurry guys," she called again.

Uncle Danny scanned the skies with grave concern.

"I'm sure she'll be able to find us," said Liberty encouragingly.

With a small smile, Danny nodded. "*¡Tienes razón!*"

***

The nice thing about being back on the carrier is that the Rear Admiral had just sent a large contingent of burly men and women to bring in all the books.

Now that those tomes were all piled up on a table, Liberty had a second of not-wanting-to-deal-with-it. But then, she Cowgrrl'd Up and grabbed a book.

As she was sorting the books, some scientists came in.

"We hear that you have an interesting problem," said Fred, the unofficial leader of the Scientists. His voice was eager and curious.

Behind him, Dr. Milton's pregnant belly moved into the room, quickly followed by the rest of her.

"New books!" she squealed with joy. Since she was in her third trimester, she truly bellied up to the table. Putting her hands out, as if to encompass the table, she jokingly declared. "These are all Mine! I called it first."

Liberty chuckled. "I'm sorry, you do have to share."

Dr. Milton gave a cry of mock despair. "You are SO

MEAN!"

"Besides, I'm a librarian," sniffed Liberty, playfully. "All books are Mine!"

"I'm just happy to see new blood," said Fred happily.

Liberty spotted a ring on Dr. Milton's left hand. Specifically, her Ring Finger! A wave of excitement came over her. Dr. Milton was with Renoir, the hairdresser, though that title did not seem to cover it. HairArtiste was more precise.

In fact, the Librarian looked up at the door expecting Dr. Milton's paramour, Renoir, the hairdresser, but found it empty of the HairArtiste.

Keeping her voice cool, Liberty asked. "No Renoir?"

Dr. Milton looked up, and her face lit up even more. "Oh! He's giving haircuts, you know. But he might try to drop by later. The Admiral wanted every ship to get a chance to get a real haircut. Boost morale and all that."

"His haircut boosted my morale," smiled Liberty. "And I was never that much of a Hair-Girl."

"I was in Middle School," nodded Dr. Milton. "But then I got tired of spending hours on it before school."

"Hours?" asked Liberty in shock. "I can't even conceive."

Dr. Milton leaned forward to whisper. "It's not that hard, and fun too."

"Wha...," began Liberty, but then she got it. "Oh! I meant..."

"You're blushing," grinned Dr. Milton. "I win!"

"Stop that," said Liberty with mock annoyance. "We have work to do."

"Of course, Ms. Librarian-Ma'am," sniffed Dr. Milton, playing along. She took a minute and sat in a chair. "So, what is it that we're helping with?"

Liberty explained the medical need, as best she could, and then what they were thinking.

"These farmer people are right," said Fred as he lazed through one book. "Putting a ton of dirt on top of a barge would be hard work."

"So, the hydroponics thing is interesting," said Dr. Milton, chewing on her lower lip thoughtfully. "I seem to remember reading something about that, before everything fell, but I can't think of what it was." She reached out and took a book.

"We still need to get the...well, they're not...farmers... per se," said Liberty, not sure how they'd react. "They actually grow pot."

Fred looked up in amusement. "Like marijuana pot?"

Liberty nodded, worried that the scientists might be like Uncle Danny.

"Well, hydroponics for pot should transfer to anything else," said Dr. Milton thoughtfully. "After a little experimentation."

"True," nodded Fred, intrigued.

"And hopefully at least one of these books will help," said Liberty as they dug in.

***

211

"Jellyfish!" cried Dr. Milton, holding a book open.

"The...what?" asked Fred in confusion.

Dr. Milton grinned. "I just remembered that article I read. Must've been two or three years now. But it was about sustainable vegetables, and on the water too."

"That sounds like what we're looking for," said Fred encouragingly.

Dr. Milton heaved herself out of her chair and moved over to the dry erase board. After a moment of hunting, she popped the dry erase cap but stopped. She gave a long sniff of the marker, but then looked a little embarrassed.

"Don't judge me," said Dr. Milton.

"Wouldn't dream of it," said Liberty quickly, trying to hide her amusement.

Turning to the board, Dr. Milton began to draw with frantic enthusiasm.

"They're supposed to be like little barges on a river...," started Milton. She drew a dome on a raft.

"But...," began Fred.

"I know, I know," said Milton swiftly. "I don't think it would be a good idea on the open ocean...But, if you put them on the barge, like tents."

Liberty straightened. "That could work."

"An' the design is super simple," continued Milton. "A wood and glass dome and inside, wood racks with PVC pipes and water inside."

"But what do we do with water?" asked Fred

thoughtfully.

"In the original design," said Milton. "There was a way to draw up the river water to use." She looked up for a moment, but then back down. "That's gonna be a problem."

"It's okay," said Liberty as she stood. "One problem at a time. Can you keep fleshing out the design, and I'll be right back."

However, Liberty got lost, twice.

Chastising herself, she said. "You really need to learn how to get around here."

As she went past a door, a voice called out. "*Liberté!*" Immediately recognizing it, the Librarian spun around to a stop.

With his scissors in one hand, Dr. Milton's Renoir came out the door.

"It IS you!" cried the HairArtiste.

"Hi! Sorry! I'm just trying to find my way," said Liberty.

"Oui! It is not easy to navigate a ship this large," replied Renoir.

"But...I'm in the middle of something," said Liberty. "Can we talk later? I'm actually working with Dr. Milton."

"Ah! It was Dr. Milton that I wanted to talk to you about," said Renoir, but then he stopped. "No! I shall not detain you."

Liberty stepped towards him. "Is something wrong? With the baby? Or you two? I thought I saw some new jewelry."

"That is true!" smiled Renoir. "For I have asked her to marry me, hopefully before baby is born."

"That's awesome," grinned Liberty. "I'm so excited."

"I fear that I have already asked too much of you...," said Renoir looking down.

Understanding, Liberty stepped forward. "Would you like to get married on our boat...is that what you were going to ask?"

"*Oui!* I do not want her wedding day to be on a military ship," said Renoir. "Not that it is a bad place, but..."

"It's okay," said Liberty. "Let me check with everyone else." She bounced a few steps backwards. "But I really have to go. Sorry!"

"Of course. Fly *Liberté* Fly!" said Renoir. "And *Merci* for even entertaining the idea."

"I'll get back to you soon," she promised.

"*Merci*, for she is...," started Renoir and he mimed a big belly.

Laughing, Liberty ran off. She reached her destination with an extra frisson of delight.

Inside his bunk, Captain Singh put down his book quickly and stood up.

"Is everything okay?" he asked.

After breathlessly explaining what she needed, Liberty ended with a miserable face. "...and can you help me get back."

Singh was now leading her back with Ruiz, Frankline, and Bath in tow.

214

"Navigating aircraft carriers should be an Olympic sport," said the Captain.

"I need to get the hang of it," said Liberty.

"It's not just you," said Ruiz.

"I've only figured out how to get food," said the tank driver, Bath. "But I still get lost sometimes."

Ruiz turned to Bath. "You're getting lots better!" She jerked a thumb at Frankline. "And He still gets lost."

"Just that one time," said Frankline, a little embarrassed.

"Okay," said Singh, with a calm voice. "Let's get our head in the game."

"Yes sir," replied his people immediately. Even Liberty started to reply.

Returning, Dr. Milton was sitting in a chair again. "You're back! I was starting to get worried."

"I had to find help," said Liberty.

"Hi Dr. Milton," said Frankline excitedly. "I hear that you needed something built."

Chapter Thirteen

THERE WAS A deep rumble that reached through the haze of Jed's mind. He had been sound asleep, but now, his eyes went wide.

"Earthquake?" he asked with concern.

Jumping up from his sleeping bag behind the counter, Jed went to the plants at the other end. They were shaking.

"What's going on?" asked Chloe.

"I don't know," replied Jed. "But whatever it is, it's getting closer."

"Doesn't feel like an earthquake," said Chloe, but then she smirked. "Maybe Godzilla."

"If anything bad happens," said Jed seriously to the girl. "I want you to run out the back, an' don't look back."

Making sure that the plants didn't fall, Jed and Chloe

heard the noise reach a crescendo, right outside their front door.

Jed and Chloe froze.

There was a 'Knock, knock, knock' at the front door.

Both jumped.

"Hello?" came a familiar voice with a happy chirp. "We're back!"

Jed and Chloe looked at each other in surprise and then he went to the front door, but his jaw hit the ground.

"A tank?" he breathed in awe.

"SHIT!" cried Chloe behind him. "Now that's riding in style."

Jed turned back. "Language!"

Chloe's lips pinched. "I'm old enough."

"I'm just sayin'," huffed Jed. He turned back to Liberty, and his face fell. "After you left, I...well, I thought of a problem."

"What's wrong?" asked the Librarian with concern.

"It's about the plants," said Jed, looking down. "I can't just leave'em here to die."

"Oh!" smiled Liberty. "I figured. That's why I brought the tank. Besides, that stuff has Really helped my boyfriend relax."

***

They soon returned to the warehouse that housed the tank

and the school bus.

Captain Singh looked in surprise as the vehicle came to a stop.

"What are those?" he asked with a cold voice.

Confused by his dark look, Liberty followed his gaze, looking from him in surprise and back to the plants.

"oh," she said slowly. She looked back at the Captain. "We should probably talk about that."

"Yes, we should," said Singh.

While he didn't say anything, Uncle Danny also stepped up to listen.

Liberty jumped down and stepped forward to speak quietly.

"This is kinda private, but...," started the Librarian uncertainly. "I..."

Uncle Danny watched her and was torn on what to do.

"I need my plants with me Sir," called out Jed from atop the tank. He set down the one that he was holding and carefully climbed down from the tank, declaring. "Sorry. Didn't want to fall on my ass in front of everyone." Once down, he trotted over. "I'm sorry sir, but I can't just leave my plants. They won't survive long."

"Can't you just plant new ones?" asked Singh skeptically.

"On All my plants?" asked Jed in horror. "I'd rather walk home first."

"No! No!" said Liberty.

"Some of these babies I've been growing for years," said

219

Jed. "An' I'm not leaving Chloe back at the store alone."

"Yeah! We definitely don't want to do that," said Liberty

"Agreed," called out Chloe.

Liberty looked at Singh imploringly.

Uncle Danny sighed. "And—technically—it is legal in California."

Singh looked at him. "It is? I'm never sure which states are or aren't."

"It definitely is," nodded Jed.

"I actually voted for it," said Liberty, a little embarrassed. "Even though I never used it."

'Before' thought Uncle Danny disapprovingly.

"But really," said Liberty. "This is about helping the Fleet. And we need someone who knows hydroponics. Jed is actually the guy who suggested it in the first place."

"You would've broken your back trying to put soil on a barge," said Jed, and he pressed his hand to his back. "I *hurt* just thinking about it."

Liberty looked at Singh. "He's right, that would've sucked. Big time."

Jed's voice turned soft. "And also. Everyone's dead." He took a second, and Singh gave it to him, a little struck by the words. The Farmer continued. "All I got is Chloe, and these planets. Chloe may not be blood, but she's Family. An' some day, she'll probably need to make her own way in the world. Then…"

"I'm not going anywhere," assured Chloe.

"I was just making a point to these men," said Jed.

220

"*¡Mierda!*" growled Uncle Danny harshly.

Jed looked up at the Big Mexican worriedly.

But Danny turned to the Captain.

"We can't take this away from him," said Uncle Danny grudgingly. "An' this is me talking."

"I understand," said Singh. "But it is still considered a Schedule 1 Controlled substance, so…"

"SIR!" said Private Frankline as he marched up from where he had been listening. Back ramrod straight. "Permission to speak freely Sir."

Liberty looked at him in surprise.

"Of course," nodded Singh to his Private.

"It's about what you're discussing," said Frankline.

Realizing what he might talk about, Liberty cut in to say to the Private. "You don't have to…we got this."

Frankline turned to her. "It's okay Ms. Liberty." And he returned back to his commanding officer. "Sir, marijuana is not addictive."

"What?" asked Singh.

"Well, not physically addictive," said Frankline. "Unless you smoke a metric ton at once."

"I would definitely Not recommend that," interjected Jed.

The Captain was about to say more, but the Private kept going.

"Yes, it can be mentally addictive, but you could say that about anything," said Frankline.

"That's true," agreed Jed.

"Books," added Liberty. "I had tons that I hadn't even read, but I kept getting more!"

Frankline pulled the conversation back. "My Uncle Larry was both a soldier and a scholar, as he put it. He fought with the Green Berets, an…"

"Wait!" said Singh suddenly. "There was a legendary soldier, Lawrence Frankline…"

"That's my uncle," said the Private. "An' he went back to college to study this because he found that weed helped with his PTSD. So…"

Singh looked at everyone and sighed. "Well, we should talk to Cassidy on the tugboat at least."

***

Cassidy immediately covered her daughter's ears with her hands.

"Moooooom!" moaned Mindy with a put-upon voice.

Singh braced for anger at the mention of the word 'marijuana.

However, Cassidy whispered. "Oh My God! I'm in. When's the party start Big Guy?"

Mouth opening and closing, Singh tried to form words, until he finally croaked out. "Party?"

Liberty snorted with laughter, and immediately said. "Sorry, I snorted." She looked at the Mom and explained the farmers can't leave their plants behind.

222

The little girl squirmed away from her mother. "What're you talking about?"

To Mindy, the Mom said. "I'll tell you later."

"You *always* say that" huffed the little girl with a pout. "But do you really?"

Looking up at Liberty and Singh, the Mom said in a hushed voice.

"BUT! If it's going to be on the barge," said Cassidy. "We need to keep it away from little ones."

"Absolutely!" said Liberty, resolutely, and the Captain and Uncle Danny looked at her in surprise. She playfully gave a pinched look back at them. "What? It'd probably stunt their growth."

Thoughtfully, Uncle Danny said. "*No manches*, I guess I wasn't sure what you had planned."

Facing him, Liberty spoke. "Apparently the extract from the plant, the CBD...whatever that stands for, is supposed to be okay for everyone...but not the plant itself."

Uncle Danny nodded. "I still have reservations. Especially keeping others away from the plants."

"Actually, let's bring in the Private on that one," said Captain Singh. "He was talking my ear off with ideas this morning."

"So, we're really going to do this?" asked the Mom, Cassidy, hesitantly.

The Captain turned to her. "We really need to give it a chance. Can we continue to have your help?"

Cassidy's face broke out into a grin. "Well, I just can't say 'no' to those puppy dog eyes of yours."

223

"My what?" asked Singh with a start.

And Liberty just managed not to laugh again.

Chapter Fourteen

BACK IN THE City of Angels, Captain Singh walked through an old warehouse that currently housed an M1A2 Abrams Tank and a yellow school bus with flat tires.

And he was trying very hard not to think of Cassidy. He had a job to do. He was a widower. He had a team counting on him. His wife had needed 'space', a year before she and his daughter died.

His daughter, Harita. He wasn't sure whether to smile or cry. His...

Outside the warehouse came a loud voice. "Permission to come aboard?"

Peeking out the back door, Frankline called out. "Hey Rak!" And he turned to the Captain who immediately nodded.

Through the door came the alien-bird.

"You only have to say, 'permission to come aboard' on a ship," said Frankline to her, trying to be helpful.

"What should I say?" asked Rakduson tenuously.

"You were fine," said Singh loudly, so that his voice carried. As he walked over, Liberty and Uncle Danny trotted over as well.

"Hey Rak!" grinned Danny. "You all okay?"

The alien fixed him with a look of mock annoyance. "You are being like Tessy."

Rearing a little in surprise, Uncle Danny blinked. "¿Qué?" He looked at Liberty.

"Pequeño," admitted his amigo.

Reaching Rak, Uncle Danny gave a contrite smile. "Sí, I will try not to be such a madré."

"It's okay," said Rak and she butted her head against his shoulder, and then looked up.

"Ms. Rak," said Singh. "Did you see anything?"

"Yes!" said Rak happily. "Big store. Lots of home-type stuff...but..."

"Here it is," grinned Liberty wryly.

"Lots of zoms," said Rak. She gently shook her feathers in mild annoyance.

"Well, not a huge surprise," said the Captain, and he said to the bird. "Thank you." Starting to turn, he stopped. "Oh, any of your people?"

Rak shook her head. "None I saw."

"Maybe we can fly under their radar," said Singh. He walked over to Ruiz and Bath, who were with the new recruits. But he slowed to a stop, so that he could eavesdrop.

All in Army uniforms, their tank driver, a young African American woman named Bath, stood next to Ruiz.

"Okay!" said Staff Sergeant Ruiz. "What we're doing today is dangerous."

"Even if we only run into zoms," added Sergeant Bath.

"Right," agreed Ruiz. "So, let's concentrate on the problem at hand. As soon as our scout finds..."

One of the privates, Biggs, looked across the warehouse. "Hey! We really do got a tame bird?"

Singh wanted to jump right in, but he held his tongue to see what his sergeants would do.

Ruiz stiffened but didn't respond. Instead, she turned to call out.

"Hey Rak?" she said. "Could you come over here for a moment?"

The alien-bird trotted over.

"What's up?" asked the bird.

"Thank you," said Ruiz, and she gestured to the newest recruits. "I really just wanted to introduce you to our newest rookies."

The alien straightened. She waved one wing as a human wave, which showed the bright feathers underneath. "Hi!"

"Ooooooh," said Private Jules in awe. "You have such pretty feathers under your wing."

Rakduson lifted her wing again.

"And in all different colors," said Jules sincerely. "I'm jealous."

Staff Sergeant Ruiz said. "They use it to distract their prey. The feathers confuse whatever they're trying to kill."

Unsure of where this was going, Rak just looked curiously at the Staff Sergeant.

Ruiz turned fully to the recruits. "Now I brought Ms. Rakduson—And She Only Is *MS*. Rakduson To You. So, I brought her over so that you understand that she is with us! She's not Navy, but she works with us! Commit her face to memory, just like Liberty and Uncle Danny. You Will Treat Them With Respect. All three are helping out of the goodness of their heart." She paused, wondering if the alien had a heart, but immediately kept going. "DO YOU UNDERSTAND?"

There was a half-hearted response.

"WHAT?" bellowed Ruiz. "I CAN'T HEAR YOU?"

"Yes Ma'am," came the response this time.

"WHAT WAS THAT?"

"YES MA'AM!" came the chorus of recruits.

"Damn straight," sniffed Ruiz.

Captain Singh took this moment to step forward. "Sergeants, Staff and otherwise. We found our target." He gestured to the alien. "Actually, thanks to Ms. Rakduson here, we know that we face a big box store with zombies inside."

"Lots," added Rak.

"What if we see other birds?" asked Private Biggs with a snide tone that the Captain noted.

Singh said. "We try not to engage. We're not made out of ammo. And they are really, really dangerous."

"Try not to shoot," said Rak with a pleading voice.

The Captain sighed. "I can't promise that." But he turned to his recruits. "But know this! Those birds have some kind of device in the back of their heads making them attack. Zoms at least don't seem to know what they're doing."

"My people don't want war," said Rak. "Slaves."

"That's why we work to avoid them," said the Captain. He turned to Ruiz. "You'll be leading the team into the store."

"Captain?" asked Bath, and she resisted raising her hand. "Can I have a sidebar?"

Singh nodded, and Bath waved at Ruiz, asking her to follow. Meanwhile Rak started to talk to the recruits.

Once far enough away, Bath said. "Sir, I want permission to clean the store."

The Captain looked at her. "Reason?"

Bath looked down for a moment, but then directly in his eyes. "I didn't have the best experience last time. And I need to do this. A sergeant needs to be able to lead people, or I need to be put in a different rank where I don't command people."

Singh glanced at Ruiz without a word.

"I didn't say anything," replied Ruiz to the unspoken query. "This is all her." She gave a little shrug. "And she's

229

not wrong." Then, she glanced at her friend with a contrite tone. "Sorry sweetie."

Bath put on a brave smile. "It's all good bestie."

Silently, the Captain looked back and then finally nodded. "Okay sergeant. You're in charge. What's your plan?"

Bath had a moment of panic but muscled right through it.

"We'll need the whole tank/bus…"

***

An Abrams tank drove into the Homes and Watson parking lot towing a flat-tired school bus behind it. Angling in, the tank backed the school bus close to the front door.

Sergeant Bath scrambled out of the driver's hatch.

Opening the commander's hatch on top, the Captain stood and said with a hard look. "Okay Sergeant! You are Up! Get those recruits into the bus and clear the store of any zoms."

"I'm gonna try my idea," said Bath.

Reluctantly, the Captain nodded. "Okay, but…be careful. Go slow and methodical if possible. I don't want to lose you. And I did ask Uncle Danny to accompany you, because of his resistance to the virus."

"Thank you Sir! I'll be safe as can be," said Bath. Her eyes bugged out. "Shoot, I gotta get my gun. Sorry."

Singh managed to remain stoic, while Bath scrambled

back into the tank.

The Captain moved aside so Ruiz could exit the tank.

While Singh did not even chuckle at the sergeant, being friends, Ruiz did laugh at her friend as she followed.

***

In the bus, Uncle Danny had his face pressed to a window, looking up.

"I'm sure she's fine," said a voice beside him.

Danny made a quick glance, before returning to the window.

"*Supongo que sí*," admitted the Big Mexican.

"Are you in love with her?" smirked Liberty softly.

Uncle Danny looked at her wide-eyed. "WHAT?"

Chuckling, the Liberian immediately continued. "I was just kidding." Her face grew serious. "But yes, she is important to us."

Looking down, the Big Mexican thought for a moment and then said. "I guess she really is. She's kinda family now."

"Rak Is Family," assured Liberty. However, she said gently. "But, we have to give her her space.

Uncle Danny smiled. "True. I just..."

"Ex...excuse me," called a voice from the front.

Liberty and Uncle Danny looked, but the rest of the soldiers just kept talking deeper in the school bus.

231

Ruiz elbowed her friend lightly with a strong whisper. "Try again." And then she emphasized. "*Sergeant.*"

Bath's eyes widened for a second, but then her face set.

Penetrating right to the back of the bus was an ear-splitting whistle. Everyone jumped except Bath, who started to stalk down the aisle.

As she passed Uncle Danny and Liberty, Bath whispered. "sorry."

Before they had a moment to say anything, the Sergeant had already moved past.

Without even stopping, she bellowed. "BIGGS! JULES! NGUYEN! FRONT AND CENTER."

Ruiz had wandered forward to stand beside Uncle Danny and Liberty.

"I was worried," she admitted to them softly.

Jumping quickly aside, Ruiz climbed onto a seat as Bath returned with her soldiers.

"Um, Mr. Danny," said the Sergeant. "I want to try a plan with the recruits before we bring you in."

"Okay," he shrugged.

Nodding, Bath took her team out of the bus and headed for the glass doors. She glanced back.

"HURRY! WE AIN'T GOT ALL DAY!"

The recruits moved a little faster.

At the doors, they pried them apart swiftly and propped them open.

Stepping inside, Bath froze for a second.

'Shit! That's a lot of zoms' thought Sergeant Bath. Her gut clenched hard. But she gritted her teeth and turned to her team.

"Okay," said Sergeant Bath. She spoke with an authoritative whisper. "This is dangerous…"

"Duh," snapped Biggs.

The Sergeant was about to ignore it, but then realized that she couldn't. Immediately, she stepped into his personal space. He was taller than her.

With a harsh whisper, she said. "Bring your face down here!"

"What?" asked Biggs.

"You will do what I say, when I say it!" growled the Sergeant. "If not, go back to the bus and we'll drive you back to spend the rest of your days on some ship. OR You Will Bring Your Face Down Here Now."

A little shocked, Biggs squatted a little, but she kept him going until they were face-to-face.

"I don't have time for your high school remarks," said the Sergeant. "We are in the shit. And if you can't follow my orders. Get the fuck out!" She gave him a second. "So? Are you IN, or OUT?"

"A…aah," stammered Biggs.

The Sergeant glanced at the zoms, in the store. They were starting to notice them.

"I'm In," said Biggs.

Fixing the private with a hard look, the Sergeant said. "In?"

233

"Yes," said Biggs, but then he remembered himself. "Yes Sir…I mean Ma'am."

After a second, the Sergeant nodded. "Damn Straight." Turning to address the whole squad, she said. "You know the plan. Follow me!"

***

Ruiz assured him. "She's going to be okay."

She had returned to the tank and was waiting with the Captain, who now looked at her in confusion.

"You're playing with your beard. Straightening it," said Ruiz. "You always do that when you're nervous."

"I do?" asked Singh with a little surprise, BUT then he added. "Not that I don't believe you…"

"Attention shoppers!" came a loud voice over the store's P.A. "Due to the world ending, Homes and Watson is closing for…well, forever. Please get the fuck outta here!"

"Oh my," whispered the Captain.

***

Inside the store, Bath grinned. "God! I always wanted to say that when I worked in retail."

Checking that everyone else was in place, she shot down the middle aisle, towards some zoms at the far end of the store.

"Hey, you!" cried the Tank Driver. "We're closing. You don't have to go home, but you can't stay here."

"Ha-rung," grunted a zom without understanding.

"Come on you sorry excuse for monsters," cried Bath, and she now started backing up. Reaching an intersection, she called out to more zoms.

Almost halfway back, a zom moved out of an aisle beside her and grabbed her arm.

"Shit," said Bath. She tried to break its grip, but it was surprisingly strong.

The zoms she had been leading were almost upon her. In the back of her head, she chastised herself for going too slow. Pulling her sidearm, Bath didn't aim for the zoms head, but it's forearm.

The gunshot sounded loud, even in the Big Box store.

Now free, the tank driver ran to the end of the aisle and into the front of the store where she panted a second.

"Sergeant?" came a voice, that was trying to sound calm, over her earpiece.

"I'm okay Captain," replied Bath immediately.

Turning to her people, she called out. "Now!"

Set at varying places at the front of the store, Jules, Biggs, Nguyen started to call out to the zoms.

"Don't take too long getting back," called out Bath.

***

235

"Well, I'll be…," said the Captain happily.

Sergeant Bath and her team led the zoms across the parking lot, while the creatures followed blindly.

The moment they reached the far side of the parking lot, Bath called out.

"Okay, back to the tank," she cried.

The Sergeant and her team moved quicker as they returned.

The moment Bath reached the tank, she instructed her team to go back into the bus. Scrambling up onto the tank, the tank driver gave a quick 'hi' and dropped inside. In short order, the tank pushed the back of the bus right up to the open doors of the store.

"Good job Sergeant Bloodbath," said the Captain into the tank.

The tank driver, beaming, came out of the vehicle.

"Sorry Sir," she said. "The fire alarm didn't work, so I couldn't get all of them."

"It's okay," said the Captain quickly. "You thinned the herd." He looked over at the zoms. "Unfortunately, they're coming back this way…"

Bath opened her mouth.

The Captain cut her off. "Don't you dare apologize! This is good."

"Yes Sir," said Bath shyly.

"Now, take the team inside with Uncle Danny and secure that store," ordered the Captain.

"Yes Sir," grinned Bath and she headed for the bus.

"And don't be a hero!" called Singh after her.

Bath 'Yes Sir'd' again and zipped into the bus.

The Captain made a noise.

"She'll be all right," said Ruiz next to him.

"Yeah," said the Captain softly. He watched through the bus as Bath's whole team moved into the store, now accompanied by Uncle Danny.

Liberty was kneeling on the last seat of the bus with her rifle to provide some cover for the Bath's team.

Turning around, the Captain's eyebrows raised.

"Zoms are moving fast," he said.

Ruiz was looking at him.

Suddenly, she launched herself at him and knocked him over. He bounced on the top of the tank, but luckily fell on his good arm. He skidded to a halt, just at the edge. One of his legs dangled off the side. He pulled it back just before a zom got a grip on his pant leg.

As the Captain was turning over, he realized that something had swooped past when she hit him. 'Ruiz', he thought. She was laying on top of the tank, and there was blood.

Drawing his sidearm, the Captain was immediately at her side, kneeling over her, but watching the sky.

One of the alien-birds was coming in hot towards them. Singh fired a couple rounds, more to get it to veer off, and buy him some time. When it swerved away, he saw that Ruiz was holding her butt, and there was blood dripping between her fingers. Tapping his earpiece, the Captain called out. "We got birds!" He looked down. "Can you move?"

"Damn straight," said Ruiz, but her teeth were gritted.

"I'm here," called out Liberty. She was at the front of the bus. "What can I do?"

"Can you get into the store?" asked the Captain. "Help them!"

"What about you?" asked Liberty. She eyed the bus door, as she wanted to come out and help.

"I'm getting the Staff Sergeant into the tank," said the Captain.

"Like hell," argued the Staff Sergeant.

To Liberty, the Captain basically ordered. "Help those in the store."

The Librarian turned, a little reluctantly, and bolted into the store. Bath's team, and Uncle Danny, were not immediately visible. Running along the cash registers, she spied a small wooden room. It looked like a manager's office with a little window.

"We're in the tank," reported the Captain over the earpieces.

"I was under orders," grumbled Ruiz.

"Try not to kill them, if possible," pleaded Uncle Danny.

Inside, Liberty found that the manager's office didn't have a roof. She immediately jumped up. Catching the edge of the roof, she put her rifle on top and started to haul herself up. 'Once on top...' she thought.

The window high above her exploded.

Instantly, the Librarian let go as shards began to rain

down.

A big piece of glass pierced the desk beside her, not two inches from her hand.

With no time to grab her rifle, Liberty scrambled out of the open office and ducked under a register conveyor belt.

"Yikes," she squealed and tapped her earpiece. "We got birds inside."

"We're trying to get to the backroom," called out Bath over the earpieces.

"Zombie *pendejos*," growled Uncle Danny.

"Sorry," said Bath. "We tried to get them all."

Liberty now heard the gunshots. She was about to climb out from under the conveyor belt when something really heavy dropped on it. There was a terrible buzzing noise.

"*Klas du ren!*" screeched the alien-bird above her.

Carefully, Liberty tried to pull her handgun. But the suppressor on the Glock made it hard to quickdraw.

The alien-bird's head, with a Lime tuft, ducked down and looked right at her.

"Shit," whispered Liberty, handgun only half out, and pointed well away.

By her head, she noticed a foot pedal.

The bird with the Lime Tuft looked like she was ready to snap the Librarian's nose off.

Liberty smacked her head against the pedal and the conveyor belt started. The bird was immediately shifted towards the end of the register.

"*Ik?*" wondered the bird in surprise.

Part of Liberty wanted her to fall on her ass, but Lime Tuft dropped easily onto their feet.

Not bothering to pull her gun, Liberty scrambled beneath another register belt.

Lime Tuft hopped after her.

The Librarian reached the end of the registers and saw something.

The alien-bird was almost there when their prey jumped up. Letting out a screech, Lime Tuft was nearly on top of her, when she lifted up a red cylinder.

White cold blasted out.

Lime couldn't breathe and started to scramble away.

In no time, the bird gulped in some breaths and turned around.

Her prey was gone and the buzzing in Lime's head enraged her.

***

As Liberty ran, she finally pulled her handgun. It sounded like more birds were now inside.

Two zoms were walking towards the back. Two bullets dropped them. Running between, the Librarian slowed at more zom bodies.

***

Earlier, Bath's team had gone into the store silently. Using hand signals, she led them across the front of the store.

"We should split up," hissed Biggs.

Bath just pointed in the direction they were going.

"I'm just saying," grumbled Biggs.

"Shh," said the Sergeant softly. She saw that Jules had her M4 rifle shouldered, and she was ready to go.

Without a word, Uncle Danny took the rear. He shifted his shotgun to one hand, ready to draw his cleaver, if necessary. As Bath led the new recruits through the registers and to the North wall, Danny smiled. Standing over them from behind, he felt a little like a shepherd with his flock.

"*Mi borregos pequeño*," he muttered with amusement.

"What?" asked Nguyen, who was towards the back.

"Nothing. *Perdón*," said Uncle Danny quickly.

The young Vietnamese woman gave him a look filled with mock suspicion.

"If I see you with any mint jelly, I'm outta here," she said softly.

Uncle Danny only just managed to suppress a bark of laughter. But it was a Herculean effort. When he trusted himself to talk, he replied.

"*Perdón. Estás a salvo, te lo prometo*," said Uncle Danny.

Nguyen smiled. "No worries."

"Cut the chatter," hissed Bath from the front.

Uncle Danny mouthed 'sorry', feeling like a schoolkid again. He and Pepe *always* got in trouble for talking in line.

The Big Mexican followed as they moved to the side of the store and started down an empty aisle. They moved quietly. On either side, he could hear occasional groans.

Just as they reached two crossing aisles, Bath signaled that they stop. This was only the first of three such intersections. Uncle Danny watched her carefully look around a corner along a connecting aisle.

The Sergeant jumped back as a zom tried to take off her nose.

Before an order could be given, Biggs jumped forward and shot the zom with his M4 rifle. It made a shocking noise in such a quiet place.

Turning, the Sergeant glared at the private. "I said…"

"Unght," came the voice of a zom. And they all started to move.

"Be. Quiet!" hissed the Sergeant to Biggs. She waved to everyone. "This way! To the back."

As they passed the first intersection, more zoms were appearing.

Their earpieces went off. "We got birds!"

"Shoot. Okay Hurry! I don't want to be caught without a condom," said the Sergeant as they pressed deeper into the store.

Uncle Danny managed not to laugh out loud as they reached the second interaction. Here, the zoms were denser. He suddenly thought of Liberty. His stomach clenched and he hoped she had hid in the tank, though the school bus afforded lots of protection.

"We're in the tank," reported the Captain over the

earpieces.

"I was under orders," grumbled Ruiz.

"Try not to kill them, if possible," pleaded Uncle Danny.

"What're you?" grumbled Biggs. "On Team Bird all of the sudden."

"Biggs," was all the Sergeant said, and he kept quiet.

No one responded, not that he had expected them too.

Private Jules made a noise and pointed forward as zoms poured into the intersection in front.

"Damn," hissed the Sergeant.

Uncle Danny glanced back and saw zoms coming in behind them.

"Getting bad back here," he said.

They were quickly getting surrounded when there was a crash at the front of the store.

"What now?" growled the Sergeant.

"We got birds inside," called out Liberty over the earpieces.

"We're trying to get to the backroom," called out Bath over the earpieces.

"Zombie *pendejos*," growled Uncle Danny.

"Sorry," said Bath. "We tried to get them all."

Two zoms were getting too close behind them. Drawing his cleaver, Danny suddenly leapt towards them. They went down fast, but more were already starting to take their place.

"We're surrounded," whispered Private Jules.

243

Before the Sergeant could ask, Jules jumped forward firing quickly, but only at the zoms on the left. A hole quickly emerged.

"This way," cried the private.

"You heard her!" called out the Sergeant. She led her team into the hole.

Jules kept firing to keep it open.

Sliding along the shelving, they came out the other side. The Sergeant pointed.

"The back room!" she ordered. "Get in and shoot any zom that moves."

Biggs was about to say something when there was a shout behind.

The Sergeant's stomach dropped as Jules fell back.

Private Jules was aiming at another zom when her rifle did not fire. Empty. A hand snatched for her and Jules felt the air of its passing on her nose.

Jumping back, the private's heel hit some zoms that had been dropped. Falling, she dropped onto some of the zoms, some still squirming.

Private Jules gave a cry as several sets of teeth bit into her, including her neck.

Uncle Danny, who had been right behind, was suddenly there. He dragged her up and towards Bath. They were moving her to the back room.

"I got bit, didn't I?" asked Jules quickly. "Oh God, I got bit."

"What were you doing back there?" asked Sergeant

244

Bath, without an accusation.

"Um, we were surrounded, an' I heard that when that happens, you're supposed to concentrate on one point and punch your way through," said Jules. "Oh God. I can feel it."

Uncle Danny could see where she had been bitten on the neck. It already looked extremely infected.

"I saw someone get bit on the neck once," said Jules sadly. "Seemed to go faster. Maybe it gets into the carotid artery through the walls of the vein and just…whoosh."

"Maybe," agreed the Sergeant as they reached the back-room door. Inside, she could hear rifle fire.

"¡Aguas! We might not want to waltz right in there," suggested Uncle Danny.

"Yeah," agreed Bath slowly. "But we also don't want to wait out here too long."

The zoms had been following.

At the swinging back door, Sergeant Bath moved herself and Jules to one side. Uncle Danny stopped before reaching the other side.

Pushing the door open, the Sergeant called out. "It's me! We're coming in."

There was a gunshot, and then a voice.

"Sorry," said Biggs, embarrassed.

Waiting a second more, the Sergeant pushed open the door, but did not go through it immediately. When the door was not perforated with gunfire, she started to go through.

Jules stopped herself by grabbing the side of the door.

"I...need...another clip," she said through gritted teeth. "For my rifle."

The Sergeant looked at her as the rest appeared.

"S...sergeant," asked Biggs with a shaky voice.

"Please," said Jules.

Uncle Danny stepped forward. "Give her the clip. I will walk with the *señorita*. Make sure she gets where she needs to go."

The Sergeant looked at the Big Mexican, her breath caught in her throat. But then she pushed herself to go to Jules, while Uncle Danny helped keep the rookie upright.

Bath took one of her own clips and handed it to Jules.

"Good job Corporal," said the Sergeant.

While Jules was loading her rifle, she blinked and looked up. Her eyes were already a little hazy.

"But" she said. "I'm only a private."

"Not anymore," said Bath softly.

Jules' knees almost buckled, but Danny kept her upright.

"Gotta go," grinned Jules.

As Uncle Danny led her away, Liberty appeared, moving as fast as she dared. She caught the Big Mexican's eye.

"They need help *Mija*," he said.

"At least one bird," she warned, and he nodded in understanding.

Reaching the door, Liberty said as loud as she dared. "Hurry! Back up. We got trouble. Well, more than normal."

Sergeant Bath blinked and shook her head quickly.

"Okay!" called out the Sergeant softly. "You heard the woman. Back up. And make sure that there're no more zoms back here. I don't want one biting my cute lil behind."

As he led Jules away, Uncle Danny smiled despite himself.

"Sorry," said Jules. "Thank you. I just...sorry."

Stopping hard, Danny caused Jules to nearly swing around him, but she ended up looking up at him in surprise.

"*¡Neta, no manches!* You have nothing to apologize for," said Danny. "You showed great courage."

"And look where it got me," chuckled Jules sadly.

"Sometimes that is what we get for doing the right thing," said Danny softly. "It's not fair. But I'm proud to be here with you. To have fought by your side."

Jules' eyes grew wide, shiny with tears ready to fall.

"really?" she asked in a small voice, disbelieving.

Uncle Danny drew himself to his full height and spoke with authority. "*Absoluto!*"

Jules' face lit up, and a crooked smile flew across it.

"Then what are we waiting for?" she said. "Let's get the bastards."

"Whatever you wish," said Uncle Danny.

"Actually, I'd kinda like a Mountain Dew," chuckled Jules.

247

Towards the North Side of the store, Danny heard the unmistakable sound of buzzing. Then his eyes flicked to the front of the store. One of the *extraterrestre-pájaros* was getting closer. He looked down at the recruit, who had been eyeing the zoms with a relish to fight.

"Before *Los Muertos*…," said Uncle Danny. He scooped up Jules in his arms.

"Hey!" she cried, half-heartedly.

"*Perdón*. Save your strength," said Uncle Danny.

Jules was a little grateful to get off her feet. "I don't know you so well that you can carry me like a baby."

"Not as a baby," replied Uncle Danny as he moved down an aisle with her. "A wounded warrior."

Opening her mouth to argue, Jules stopped and shrugged. "And where are we going? I mean, towards the front of the store, obviously."

Danny did not reply because he was fighting for breath. She was heavy enough that he had to concentrate on carrying her. And he realized, a little belatedly, that he wasn't supposed to carry more than 50 pounds, per Dr. Tagg's orders. He decided that he might not tell about this part.

Reaching the front, Uncle Danny set the recruit beside a register.

"Wait here," he said.

Jules almost gave a sarcastic reply, but then decided against it. Instead, she leaned heavily on the register.

The buzzing was very faint now, but still, Uncle Danny didn't move fast, just in case.

248

Waiting, Jules looked around and her eyes settled on something. His mind sparked.

There was the unmistakable sound of a soda pop bottle being opened.

"*Perdón* por pisarte la mano," said Uncle Danny. "I could only find a warm Coke."

Jules' breath caught in her throat, and she gave a shaky smile. When she trusted her voice, she said. "I like Coke too."

Taking the bottle, she drank deeply from it. She stopped and gave a hearty burp. A grin lit up her face.

"Actually, you gave me an idea," said Jules.

"Me?" asked Danny in surprise.

Chapter Fifteen

THE ZOMS TURNED at the sound of the squeaky wheel. A shopping cart full of Jules closed on them. Her rifle set nicely on the front of the cart and started firing. Heads snapped back, and bodies dropped bonelessly.

"Yee-hah!" cried Jules as Danny moved her along. For a second, she almost looked embarrassed by the cry, but then owned it. "Hah! Let's get 'em."

"Whatever you wish," he replied pleasantly. "I have more Coke and clips in the basket waiting."

A zom tried to come up behind him, but Uncle Danny was ready. Taking his shotgun from atop the basket, he fired once.

Backing the cart up, Jules fired as the zoms stupidly followed.

A bullet missed and hit a paint can.

"Damn," muttered Jules.

The next one got the mark, but several after that missed.

Uncle Danny let go of the cart and stepped beside it.

"That was fun," said Jules softly.

Firing his shotgun, Uncle Danny took down a number of zoms.

Jules' rifle tipped forward and out of the cart. It clattered heavily onto the floor.

"Good job, *tu chica valiente*," whispered Uncle Danny.

There was a crash by the front of the store, and he heard several buzzing noises.

"*Mierda*," grunted Danny.

Grabbing the rifle, he dumped it into the basket and moved as fast as he dared towards the North Side of the building.

***

In the back room, Liberty's heart skipped happily when she saw Uncle Danny. He was doing the bird-walk, faster than a zom, but not fast enough to get spotted by a bird. Alone, the Big Mexican returned to the back room.

They moved their makeshift barrier to let him in.

Sergeant Bath was immediately there. "And Jules?"

Uncle Danny's lined face grew sad. "She is safe and won't harm anyone."

The Sergeant stiffened. Her voice was wooden. "Okay."

"I heard more buzzing," said Liberty.

"There are a bunch more at the front," said Uncle Danny, and he smiled wryly. "Came for the Super Sale."

"Rak?"

Uncle Danny shook his head. "Haven't seen her. But those zoms are not far…"

"Contact," cried Biggs from the door.

"Keep your voice down private," hissed Sergeant Bath.

From deep in the store, came the birds talking.

"*Garak du somme,*" cried one of the alien-birds.

"*¡Fíjate!* They are going to find us soon," said Uncle Danny.

"And we still need to get rid of all the zoms," said Nguyen worriedly.

"True, we might…," started the Sergeant, but then her eyes lit up. "I got an idea."

Sergeant Bath handed her M4 rifle to Liberty. "Can you hold this?"

The Librarian took the rifle and the Sergeant was off. She went to the door and slid over the makeshift barricade.

"Sergeant?" asked Biggs, but quietly.

"I'll be back soon," she said.

Liberty, holding the rifle gingerly, looked at Uncle Danny, but he seemed just as perplexed.

"I hope she's all right," said Liberty.

"Let's be ready for when she comes back," said Uncle

253

Danny.

Shouldering their weapons, just in case, Liberty and he went back to the door.

The buzzing was in the distance. Occasionally they saw a bird go past the aisle that they were at the end of. Then came the sounds of moans, unmistakable moans.

Sergeant Bath appeared leading a big group of zoms.

"She's bringing them to us?" asked Biggs with confusion.

The back door was down a short hallway. The moment the Sergeant reached the door, she hopped over the barrier and got her rifle back.

Soon, zoms packed the hallway coming towards them.

"Um....," started Biggs.

"Get ready," said the Sergeant to everyone, and she then leaned a little over the barricade. "HEY! YOU BIG BIRD BRAINS! COME AND GET IT!"

There were more noises from the store. The buzzing got louder.

"Wait," said Uncle Danny. "We're trying to Not shoot the birds."

"We didn't invite them to this party," said the Sergeant, trying not to sound cold. "And we need the lumber in here."

Growing desperate, Danny looked at Liberty. However, she bit her lip, unsure of what to do.

Turning, Uncle Danny went deeper into the back room, stepping over the occasional dead zom. Bath had her people jammed up to the door, ready to fire. The zoms were nearing the barrier.

Liberty followed Uncle Danny who was speaking rapidly in Spanish. Too fast for her to follow. She touched his arm, and he flinched in surprise.

"*¿Mande?*" she asked. "But we gotta switch to English because I'm not that good yet."

Uncle Danny gave a little laugh. "You are Always 'That Good' *Mija*." He sighed though. "I'm just...there *must* be a way to drive off those birds. They don't know what they're doing. That device in the back of their heads is making them crazy."

"I know," she said.

"Maybe some kind of loud noise!" he said desperately. "Or a shrieking noise that will scare them away."

"Getting sprayed with a fire extinguisher throws them off," she replied.

Uncle Danny looked at her for a moment. "I have to hear more about that later." But he turned back to look.

Liberty turned around the partly lit backroom. "My Dad would say that we needed 'the A-Team'."

At the backroom door, the zoms reached the metal barrier, but couldn't get any further. More and more pressed into the hallway when one of the birds looked down their aisle.

"Hey, you!" cried the Sergeant, waving her arms. "Get out of this store. No Pets Allowed!"

"*Klas du ren!*" screeched a bird with an Apricot tuft.

Barreling forward, Apricot Tuft reached the first zoms.

They tried to bite at her, more out of a mindless annoyance than anything else. Slashing with his beak, Apricot Tuft took a big gouge out of the zom, but it didn't go down.

"We're right here!" cried Bath. "Come and get us."

Enraged by the device in his head, Apricot thrust himself forward, tearing through the zoms. He kicked and then stomped, grinding the zoms into the linoleum.

"Be ready," said Bath with a growl in her voice.

Deeper in the back room, Uncle Danny looked around furiously.

"There's gotta be something," he muttered. "Something to scare him off."

Liberty was not seeing anything, but she didn't say that. "It's going to be okay."

"How?" he growled. "We have to…"

Gunshots rang out.

They were loud with a jagged edge that hurt Danny far beyond his ears. He came to a stop, not turning back, not able to go any further.

From the door, they heard Bath.

"Captain, we've neutralized most of the zoms, and a bird," said the Sergeant. "We're just going to do a quick sweep."

"Good job Sergeant Bloodbath," came the Captain's voice over the earpieces, and Danny winced hard.

"It wasn't that good…," started Bath with a heavy voice as Danny took out his earpiece.

Slowly, Liberty came over to her friend and put her hand

on his arm.

"Rak's going to kill me," he whispered.

"One of those birds almost killed me," she said softly.

Uncle Danny turned to her in surprise. Then he looked her over to assure himself that she was okay.

"That's the one that you sprayed with the fire extinguisher?" he asked.

"I managed to slide away," she said. "But, if I didn't have that option…we're not going to go out of our way to hurt the birds. But if we have no other choice…"

***

As they loaded the last of the supplies into the bus, Private Biggs pointed North.

"SERGEANT!" he cried. "Is that…?"

Everyone turned to look. Beside the parking lot, a shopping basket was propped against a tree facing West. They couldn't see the new cans of Diet Coke in the basket.

"This way," said Uncle Danny. "She'll be shielded from the worst of the elements and get to see the setting sun."

Sergeant Bath turned to the Big Mexican.

"Thank you," she said.

***

The tank/bus drove back towards their warehouse with a

257

somber air. Everyone was either too tired, too sad, or both.

Liberty and Uncle Danny had dropped into the first open seat on the bus with bags full of stuff for their ship. Finding herself wanting to fall asleep against Uncle Danny's shoulder, Liberty wished that she had grabbed a Coke before hitting the road.

Their earpieces went off.

"We might have trouble," called the Captain.

Suddenly wide awake, Liberty snapped upright. "Whazit?" She could only see the tank from her vantage point.

"Everyone be ready," continued the Captain.

Liberty and Uncle Danny scrambled to put their big bags down and get out of their seats. However, the aisleway was filled, almost the top of the seats, with pieces of wood. Practically everything that wasn't nailed down.

Liberty took her rifle, which she had retrieved, and climbed over the tops of the seat in front to get access to a window. She managed to slide the top of the window down. There were a few zoms out on the street as they passed.

"No birds," said Uncle Danny with relief as he looked upwards.

"None over here too," reported Private Nguyen from the other side of the bus.

"Then what...," started Liberty. She stuck her body part way out the window.

"Careful," she heard Uncle Danny mutter.

Ahead, before an intersection, were two black SUVs.

They were nose to nose creating a barrier. Liberty ducked back in. "You're not going to believe this, but two blocks down are some SUVs blocking the road."

"Like, not abandoned?" asked Private Nguyen.

"No, more like a police roadblock," said Liberty, perplexed.

Over the earpieces, the Captain asked. "Liberty? Danny? You ever seen anything like this?" They quickly replied in the negative. "Okay, we're going to take a side street. I don't have the patience for fooling around today.

Taking a lumbering right, the tank towed the bus down a side street but had to knock aside a Toyota to do so.

"Sorry," they heard Bath say over the earpieces.

"Hey Captain. When we turned," called out Liberty as well. "The men around the SUVs started scrambling about."

"Like ants," added Uncle Danny.

"Ms. Liberty," said Singh thoughtfully. "Could you go to the back of the bus and watch for anyone trying to follow?"

"*¡Órale!* They looked determined, whoever they are," continued Uncle Danny.

Liberty climbed nimbly over the seats to get to the back. She had been nearly there already. Behind her, Uncle Danny, less ably, climbed behind her.

Reaching the back window, Liberty saw Danny, who didn't say a word. The Big Mexican managed to get to the last row and climbed into the opposite seat.

Liberty watched out the back.

259

"Captain! No convoy of SUVs is pursuing us like in some big dumb action movie," reported Liberty.

"Hey! I like those big dumb action movies," complained Uncle Danny.

Liberty smirked mischievously.

"Which means," suggested Captain Singh thoughtfully. "That they're going to try and get in front of us."

Atop the tank, the Captain watched ahead.

"We're going to need to turn left soon Sir," called out Bath, unseen, from within the tank.

"Okay," replied Singh. "Next street we take. Come hell or high water."

The tank/bus turned another corner messily and pushed a Ford pickup aside.

Bath started to apologize, but then immediately stopped herself.

As they lumbered up the street, a black SUV began to drive across the intersection up in front. It screeched to a halt, almost comically. Backing up swiftly, it went to the top of the street and parked, blocking the left side with its nose at the center. Several men in black military gear jumped out and ran around so the vehicle was between the tank and them.

Singh took all this in pensively.

"I could just shoot it," suggested Bath's voice.

"Let's find out who they are first," suggested the Captain.

"They don't look like Friendlies," muttered Staff

Sergeant Ruiz.

"No, they don't," agreed the Captain.

"Could they be connected to the people Frankline met in the streets," mused Ruiz, and there was a sharp tone in her voice. "Or, to the boat that tried to run us down?"

"Maybe both," shrugged the Captain. "Okay, I'm coming in." He climbed partway into the tank, so that he could duck down easily and close the hatch.

Another SUV screeched to a halt and situated itself so that it was nose to nose with the other.

Singh sighed. "Okay, they really want to do this. Hey Sergeant Bloodbath, stop about ten feet back, but keep the engine running."

"Yes sir," she replied.

Over the earpieces, Singh said. "Let's just sit in our seats, comfortable-like, and smile. Even wave in a friendly manner. Guns down, but Don't open a door for them."

"The back door doesn't have a handle on the outside," said Uncle Danny thoughtfully, but then he looked forward. Immediately, he started moving clumsily to the front of the bus, trying to get over the seats, and the construction supplies in the middle.

"Need a hand?" asked Liberty.

"*Gracias*, but better to have one of us at either end," he said.

Unhappily, she agreed with him, so Liberty stayed put. She did contort her body so that she could remove her Glock with its suppressor, just in case.

Tapping her earpiece, Liberty asked. "Captain? How

many?"

"Four," reported Captain Singh from the tank. "They're in teams of two. Dressed in black, military style. One has an M4 rifle, the rest AR-15s. And handguns it looks like.

"Wonder if they're real, or just Gravy Seals," said Ruiz thoughtfully.

"We'll know soon enough," said Singh. And then he finished over the earpieces. "One is stopping by us, but the other is heading your way, Liberty."

The Captain stood up in the tank.

Using Ruiz's Tactic, he said cheerily. "Hey! How're you doing? I'm Captain Singh of the US Navy and out of the carrier, the *Teddy Roosevelt*. How're you guys today." With one hand, he gave a friendly wave, to distract as he casually laid his hand on the hatch just in case he needed to close it in a hurry.

The closest team stumbled a bit at that but recovered quickly. They came close to the tank as the other team moved towards the bus.

"This is Major Harrid. We're going to need everyone to come out of both vehicles," said the lead man. "That's an order."

The Captain just smiled. "It's good to see some brothers-in-arms." He made a point of peering at them closer. "What branch are you from?"

Harrid growled. "I'm the one asking questions here."

"Umm," started the Captain. "Not to be contrary, but I'm allowed to ask questions too."

"THAT'S WHERE YOU'RE WRONG," barked Harrid.

"I am?" asked the Captain with surprise. "Well then, I better be quiet so that I don't..."

"SHUT UP!" snapped Harrid.

"That's what I was saying," said the Captain with exasperation, and he put on a pleasant, bemused smile.

"AS I was saying," grumbled Harrid.

"Yes! Please go ahead," said the Captain helpfully.

Harrid lost his train of thought for a second, but then plowed on through.

"You are ordered to get out of the vehicles so that they can be inspected."

"For what?" asked the Captain.

"I SAID I was asking the questions," cried Harrid.

"Just curious," said the Captain with a hurt tone. He heard shouting down by the bus, but no shooting. He had to trust them. 'Maybe he should have just let Bath shoot the SUVs', he pondered.

The 'Maybe-Major' was saying something, but Singh was only listening with half an ear. Something about 'looters'.

The Other Team came back from the front of the bus and whispered quickly to the 'Maybe-Major'.

"That's it!" bellowed Harrid. He pointed accusingly. "YOU WILL GET OUT OF THAT VEHICLE!"

"By whose authority?" asked the Captain, genuinely curious now.

"President Butterfett," said Harrid. "He deputized us into the U.S. Military and charged us with bringing law and

263

order back."

Without a word, Captain Singh grabbed the hatch and dropped down into the tank. The moment the hatch was shut and locked, he called out.

"Drive on through Sergeant Bloodbath."

The tank moved forward, pulling the bus.

Harrid and his men jumped back with surprise.

The Captain called over the earpieces. "Everyone get down. Just in case they want to start something."

"Gotcha," said Liberty. She hunkered down as best she could. "Looked like that second team was all scared when they went to their leader-person. Wonder what happened."

Uncle Danny chuckled darkly. "I did. They were trying to lever open the front door, which I expected. So, I came out of hiding and sat on the steps."

"With your shotgun?" asked Bath over the earpieces.

"No. Just my smile," replied Uncle Danny, and Liberty could hear the wicked laughter in his voice.

"Well, that'd scare anybody," said Liberty. She lifted her head. "They're running after us now."

"Nearly at the cars," said Bath.

The Captain grinned. "Ramming speed."

The possibly-soldier left with the cars jumped aside as the tank barreled right between the SUVs. Their fronts crumpled like accordions, and they were easily batted aside, like a cat toy.

"Best not to take the direct route to the warehouse," said the Captain. "If we have the gas."

"We're good," said Bath.

"We got someone following," said Liberty over the earpieces. "Looks like another SUV."

"Hummh," grunted the Captain. "Well, we can't have them following us home."

"Want me to shoot out their tires?" asked Liberty.

"Yes," replied Singh

"Want me to slow down , or stop, Liberty?" asked Bath.

"That's okay," replied the Librarian as she moved over to the emergency exit. "But thank you."

Readying her rifle, she swung open the emergency door and kept it propped with her foot. Aiming, she fired.

The front of the engine began to billow steam.

"Aw shoot," muttered Liberty. "I missed the tire."

"If they're stopping, then you got the job done," said the Captain over the earpieces. "Good job."

"I guess," muttered Liberty, still disappointed in her shot.

***

As they reached the warehouse, Uncle Danny saw Rakduson perched on top.

"¡*Mierda!*" he muttered, now back with Liberty again.

"It's going to be alright," said Liberty soothingly.

When the big doors were opened for the tank/bus, Rak flew in, but stopped a little ways away. She waited until

Uncle Danny and Liberty got out.

"Saw hardware store," said Rak. Her eyes were blazing with anger.

Uncle Danny stepped forward. "I...I'm..." But he couldn't find the words.

"It was on my order," said Bath, jumping off the tank. Despite the sheen of sweat on her head, she lifted her chin and stepped forward. "We were attacked. We had to defend ourselves."

Rak's eyes narrowed, but then they flitted to Liberty.

"Truth?" asked Rak.

Liberty nodded. "Uncle Danny was trying to find some way to avoid it, but..."

The bird lowered her head.

"We didn't pick the fight," said the Captain.

"And you can't let yourself get killed either," said Rak sadly.

Uncle Danny moved forward again and opened his arms. Rak moved forward to lay her head against his chest.

"Did that bird just go in for a hug?" asked Nguyen softly.

"An' we lost Jules," said Biggs with a whisper.

Bath slipped back into Sergeant-mode, but quietly, out of respect. She moved the military people a little ways away.

"Yes, Private Biggs," she said with an icy voice. "We need to talk about why you started shooting when I explicitly told you Not to make any noise."

"But that wasn't my fault," said Biggs. "I was trying to

protect you."

"You looked pretty happy to shoot," said Bath. "Even if it wasn't in your face, I saw the smile in your eyes."

"My...What...?" stammered Biggs.

"And now Jules is dead," said Bath. "Because you couldn't stay quiet."

Biggs reared back, as if struck.

"But we'll talk about that later," said Bath. "In the meantime, I need that bus emptied. So, don't you leave anything in my bus. Now go! Double-time."

The Sergeant pushed the rookies to work.

As she stepped past the Captain, he said. "Good job Sergeant."

And Bath felt a little better.

Singh turned to Ruiz, who he was helping to walk. The backside of her pants were stained with blood, but it had mostly stopped.

"Let's get you to Washington," said the Captain

"WHAT HAPPENED?" cried a voice.

The big warehouse door closed, and Frankline ran over. He screeched to a halt beside Ruiz. "Can you walk? Do you need me to carry you?"

"BELAY THAT Private," said the Captain. "She's okay. They need help emptying the bus."

A part of Ruiz was disappointed to Not get carried, *but* only by Frankline. However, then she felt a pang of guilt because he was a subordinate in her command. But still...

"If I end up with a scar on my butt," grumbled Ruiz for

the hundredth time. "I'm going to be so pissed."

"I'm sure you'll be fine," said the Captain.

Chapter Sixteen

LIBERTY HAD BEEN sleeping.

Between the day, a little smoke, and some invigorating playtime, she'd actually crashed pretty hard. So, she was only just waking up when someone tiny climbed onto her side of the bed. The Librarian was sleeping on her side, with a bed sheet pulled up to her chin. She tried to focus on who it was.

"Baby?" asked Liberty with a muzzy voice. A porthole gave the only light, and there was not that much.

"Sorry," came a small, sad, little voice as they lay right beside her. ""sorry,butUncleDannyisonguardduty," she babbled softly with a sad whine. "An'ColinsaidIcouldn'tstaywithhim'causeI'm brokenan' ,I'msorry."

Liberty immediately freed one arm and wrapped it

around Tessy. The girl snuggled in, her little face almost buried in the bed, but not muffled.

"No, no," said Liberty quickly. "You don't have to be 'sorry'."

"It's just...," she began.

"What?" asked Liberty with authority after the pause had gone on too long.

"nuffin'," said Tessy quickly.

"What did Colin say to you?" asked Liberty, nearing her You-Cheesed-Off-The-Librarian voice.

The little girl looked up in surprise for a moment, but then gave a fleeting smile.

"I guess it wouldn't be anyone else," she admitted.

"If it was Uncle Danny," huffed Liberty. "I'd throw him overboard!"

"If it was Uncle Danny," murmured Tagg sleepily. "He'd throw himself overboard."

Despite herself, Tessy gave a little laugh at that. "He wouldn't be mean."

Tessy shifted for a second to get comfortable and her knee bumped Liberty's hip. A bare hip that only had a bed sheet covering it.

With a little panic, the Librarian realized that both she and Tagg were naked. She knew he was, because he was the big spoon, and someone was definitely poking at the back of her thigh. For a second, she imagined her Mother with a disapproving glare, towering over the foot of the bed.

"Sorry," said Tessy.

The Librarian pulled her attention away from the specter-memory of her Mother.

"Sorry…for what?" asked Liberty.

"Sorry for bumping you," said the little girl.

"Oh! You're fine," said Liberty quickly. She forced herself to focus on the real problem. "So, what happened? I know Uncle Danny's on watch. And you probably tried Colin, which didn't go well."

Tessy turned her face deeper into the bed and said something.

"What was that honey?" asked Liberty.

"I'm not…broken, am I?" asked Tessy.

"What? Of course not," said Liberty quickly. "Who told y…" She stopped and then continued. "Never mind." She uttered a long sigh. "You are definitely not Broken."

"But it's *just* so frustrating," said Tessy. "…I can go to sleep okay by myself. But, if I wake up alone…I gotta come here and bug you."

"Oh sweetie," said Liberty. "You're more than welcome to join us. But it's not your fault that you have trouble sleeping alone."

Tessy's eyes went wide. "It isn't?"

"No sweetie," said Liberty earnestly. "You have Separation Anxiety…"

"Which is not unreasonable," added Dr. Tagg. "So, it's not your fault."

"It…it's not?" asked Tessy.

271

"No," said Dr. Tagg. He moved up and forward behind Liberty, but accidentally poked her hard. Both of them froze for a second, but then swiftly recovered. The Scientist carefully moved behind Liberty to look over her at the girl.

Tagg spoke quickly, trying not to think too hard—he embarrassingly amended that to 'too much'—about anything else.

"I've actually heard about this," he said. "It's a real condition. The problem is that your Mom and I don't know quite how to help you."

"Not That WE Haven't Tried," said Liberty.

"Unfortunately," nodded Tagg. "We need to understand more."

"Oh No!" cried Liberty.

"What?" asked Tessy and Dr. Tagg at once.

"I should've check for a book on it when I was at the library," said Liberty sadly.

"It's okay," said Dr. Tagg.

"Yeah, it's okay," said Tessy.

"I just had so much going on with this project," said Liberty.

"Which is important," said Tessy.

"But not as important as you," said Liberty sincerely, and she gave her a little kiss on the top of her head.

"Even if I'm broken?" asked Tessy tentatively.

Liberty huffed, but not out of anger. "You're Not Broken. Colin was just being mean."

"Colin's starting to go through some changes," said Dr.

Tagg. "In his body. It's called Puberty, and his hormones are going...well, kinda crazy. So, he might act a little odd, kinda like he's sick. One moment happy, the other sad...the other angry."

"But!" said Liberty emphatically. "That doesn't give him the right to be mean."

"Definitely not," agreed Dr. Tagg.

Tessy looked up at him in the dim light. "Colin mentioned that you and Uncle Danny had a talk with him about something like that, but he wouldn't tell me what it was about."

"That's okay," said Liberty. "Maybe you and I should talk too."

"Is that kinda why this separation thing is happening," said Tessy.

"This is different," said Dr. Tagg.

"How?" asked the little girl skeptically.

"Think of it this way," said Dr. Tagg, and he rested his chin on Liberty's arm. "You know that Captain Singh hurt his arm."

"A bird hurt it," said Tessy.

"Right," said Dr. Tagg. "And that caused a fracture in one of his bones."

The little girl just nodded, not sure where this was going. Liberty too was puzzled, but tried not to let it show.

"So, something bad happened, which broke something," said Dr. Tagg. "Well, that can happen in our heads too. We get hurt and it has to heal."

"Soooooo," began the little girl slowly. "I got a fracture in my head?"

"In a way," said Dr. Tagg.

"So, I am broken?" asked the little girl.

Berating himself inwardly, Tagg said quickly. "You're not Broken. Not how he means it. You didn't do anything wrong. Nor did anyone else in this case."

"And we still Love you," said Liberty quickly.

"Without question," nodded Dr. Tagg.

"But" began the Little Girl. "If I got a fracture, or whatever, how do I get better?"

"Well...," started Tagg.

Liberty craned her neck to look back at him.

However, Tagg didn't have the answer.

Looking back, Liberty admitted. "We don't have an answer for you immediately. But. I don't know...we're going to see if we can find something. In the meantime,..." She gave the little girl a giant hug. "We can still give you hugs! Biiiiiig Hugs!"

The little girl laughed, but then gave an involuntary yawn. Tessy started to get up.

"Honey?" asked Liberty, suddenly worried.

The little girl explained in a sleepy voice. "I gotta go potty."

Padding across the room, Tessy disappeared into the suite's bathroom.

Liberty turned and looked at Tagg.

"Hurry!" said the Scientist.

The top sheet flew up into the air. Both scoured across the floor for clothes that had been hastily flung aside.

"Where'sMyBra," hissed Liberty, and she paused. "Wait? Do I need one. I don't normally wear one to bed. Could be conspicuous."

The toilet flushed.

"¡*Mierda!*" she squeaked softly.

Shortly, the bathroom door opened, spilling more light into the room. Tessy tiredly went over to Liberty's side of the bed.

"Gave you more room," said Liberty, patting the bed. She was propped on one arm with one of Tagg's t-shirts on, which read, 'City Of Angels U Football. Go COAU Viruses'.

Tessy climbed in and snuggled down.

Liberty gave a little breath of relief.

"Hope you're feeling more comfortable now," said Tessy. "Now that you got clothes on."

Mouth agape, Liberty was at a loss for words, but Dr. Tagg gave a little chuff of laughter.

Finally, the Librarian leaned over and kissed the girl's forehead.

"Sweet dreams honey," she said.

***

Walking through the aircraft carrier the next morning, Uncle Danny looked at his amiga.

"Oye! Before we get to the meeting, I heard *Cobayo* got a talking to this morning," he said, using his nickname for Colin.

"Sí," replied Liberty, feeling sleepy and wishing she had coffee. Right now, she would argue that that was greatest crisis facing them. "Ugh. He was a jerk to Tess last night, so Tagg and I sat him down."

"Annnnd how did that go?" asked Danny carefully.

"About as well as the voyage of the Titanic," said Liberty after a moment. "Started okay..." She paused, and the Big Mexican waited patiently. "He thinks we're picking on him."

"Would you like me to try talking to him?" asked Danny.

"He got extra chores because of it," said Liberty. "I think we should let it lie for now."

"He's a good boy," insisted Danny.

"I know," said Liberty.

"But we need him to be a good man eventually," said Danny. "We'll think on it , *Mija.* See what we can do, so maybe he won't lash out at Tessy so much."

"We...Tagg and I talked to her last night about her Separation Anxiety," said Liberty.

"Pepe thought about being a psychologist," said Uncle Danny about his friend back in Mexico. "But he couldn't afford college."

At that moment, they reached the meeting. Only Dr. Milton and Private Frankline were there at the dry erase board. On it was a drawing that looked like a jungle gym.

"...that should be steady enough," said Frankline thoughtfully.

"We should build a small-scale model," suggested Dr. Milton. "And make sure it's steady."

"Yeah, what about storms at sea," worried Frankline thoughtfully.

"That's true," replied Dr. Milton. "We're going to not want to put them too close to the edge." rubbed her back unconsciously.

"But that will limit how many we can have," said Frankline.

"*Perdón* Doctor," interrupted Uncle Danny before he got too close. He didn't want to accidentally scare her. Before he reached her, he took a chair and set it behind her.

"Oh! Thank you," she said. "I hate to have to sit like this during a meeting."

"I don't mind," said Frankline immediately, and then she looked back at the board.

"How's it going?" called a voice from the hallway.

Liberty realized that she was still in the doorway. She hastily moved aside. "Sorry."

Rear Admiral Cirilo smiled sleepily himself. "No worries." He turned to the board. "Looking good."

Dr. Milton turned in her chair to look at him. "The Private has been a big help."

Frankline looked down at the floor. "Heck, you had most of it. I jus' helped along the edges."

Milton gave him a Look. "PLEASE! You were a big help."

"Well, we still need to do a mock-up," said Frankline.

"Unfortunately," said Dr. Milton, a little embarrassed, patted her very pregnant belly. "I'm not supposed to travel too much. And Renoir frets if I have to leave the ship. Don't get me wrong, I can leave." She smiled warmly. "He just frets."

"That's okay," said Frankline quickly. "We could draw up the plans, 'cause even I can follow plans…"

"You're too hard on yourself," admonished Milton. "You really have been a big help."

"I was in the neighborhood," said Frankline.

"Private!" said the Rear Admiral Antony Cirilo with authority. He had appeared suddenly in the doorway.

Frankline went stiff as a board and immediately went to attention. He almost saluted.

"Don't diminish yourself like that," said the Rear Admiral. "She gave you a compliment. So, you say 'Thank you'. Or, if she—or anyone—says 'Thank you', You Say 'You're Welcome'. Don't belittle yourself."

"Oh! Um…," stammered Frankline.

In *sotto voce*, Uncle Danny leaned towards the young man. "Say 'Thank you'."

"Hmm? Oh, yeah," said Frankline, and he looked at the Rear Admiral. "Thank You Sir."

"Carry on," nodded Cirilo.

And Frankline smiled.

"Now Private!" continued the Rear Admiral. "I want to see a mock-up of this…" He waved at the board.

"Jungle gym?" asked Liberty.

"Yes, it does look like that," muttered Cirilo.

"It's supposed to be a jellyfish," explained Dr. Milton.

"I see. We'll need to get to full-scale as soon as possible," said the Rear Admiral.

From the passageway behind the Rear Admiral, someone said.

"Are you berating my team?"

The Rear Admiral turned with a smile to Captain Singh.

"And take away all your fun," asked Cirilo.

They immediately got the Captain up to speed.

"I'm worried about supplies," said Singh.

"How so," asked the Rear Admiral.

"What if we need more wood, or glass, or nails," said Singh.

"What're you thinking?"

"That we move the barge near to the Coast," said Singh. "That way it's only a short distance to all the stores we need."

"A bit risky," mused the Rear Admiral.

"They won't be in the shadow of the carrier, yes," admitted Singh. "But if my team was there."

"I volunteer," said Frankline immediately.

Singh chuckled. "Well, you were going anyway. But I appreciate the thought. No, we're going to have to pull construction and guard duty."

"We can come too," said Liberty, then she froze and looked at the Big Mexican. "Well, I shouldn't say, 'We'..."

"It's okay. A few days in the sun, AND not having to worry about zoms," said Uncle Danny. "WE will be there."

***

"Well! Butter my biscuits!" cried Cassidy jovially with a cock of her hip. "If it isn't the eye candy."

Captain Singh almost fell between the *Wolf Pack* and the barge. "Wai......what?"

"Come on aboard," said Cassidy. "*Mi* Barge, *Su* Barge."

"Hurry up there Casanova," smirked Staff Sergeant Ruiz.

Turning briefly, Singh glared at her. "Wanna be a private again?"

Ruiz just grinned unrepentantly. "And get less work? Hell yeah."

With a disgruntled noise, Singh stepped onto the barge.

"Captain!" cried a voice. Little Mindy ran over excitedly. "You'reback!Areyoustaying?Who'reallthesepeople?"

While Singh was trying to parse out the barrage of questions, Cassidy reached out and pulled the girl back.

"Mindy!" called out a voice from the *Wolf Pack*. Tessy climbed on to the temporary bridge between the ship and the barge and pushed past Ruiz.

"Hey, careful," said the Staff Sergeant.

"SorrySorry!" called out Tessy without looking back. She ran over to Mindy and the two immediately started to wander off.

"And don't go too far," called Cassidy.

"Yes!" shouted Liberty from the *Wolf*. "Don't go poking about. It's not safe."

Both girls gave a dismissive wave, almost in chorus.

Colin, who Tessy had towed up on deck, began to turn.

"Oh no you don't," said Liberty as she skipped over to the boy. She grabbed him and hugged him close.

"Moooom," he whined, but without much heat.

"I'm going to miss you," she whispered.

"Yeah, right," grumbled Colin.

Swiftly, Liberty turned him around, just fast enough to be a surprise. She spoke with her You-Cheesed-Off-The-Librarian voice. "I! Will! Miss! You! Don't you dare doubt that for a second."

Colin was surprised, and then a little embarrassed.

"I wish you weren't going for so long," he said quickly, almost forcing out the words.

"The Admiral somehow got ahold of some camping gear," said Liberty. "So, while you all are sleeping all warm and cozy in your bed…"

"With Tessy," he said darkly.

"She can't help how she feels," said Liberty.

"Yeah," said Colin. "Sometimes…it's just so hard. She's

Always there."

"I know," said Liberty and she pulled him in for a last hug and a kiss on the head. Her mouth pinched. "And a shower."

"Mom!" said Colin with more feeling.

"Don't 'Mom' your Mom," said Dr. Tagg as he stepped up. "Lots of people barely have toilets."

Colin rolled his eyes as only an 11-year-old can.

"Just a quick wash of your hair," said Liberty.

Tagg turned to the boy. "Unless you want dreads. Dreads Are pretty cool. Then you don't have to wash your hair much, if ever."

"Really?" asked Colin excitedly.

"But you have to clean the rest of you, because we have to live with you," said Tagg.

"Are you talking dreadlocks?" asked Liberty frostily.

Tagg shrugged, partially apologetic. "Dreads are cool." He stopped and looked at the boy. "But I think you have to use wax, and it gets all over your pillows."

Colin's face scrunched up.

"And as for Tessy…," started Tagg. He stopped, thinking furiously, eyes glazed over for a second. But then he said suddenly. "Zombie bite."

Both Liberty and Colin asked in unison. "What?"

Tagg knelt to look Colin in the eyes. "A zombie bit Uncle Danny, but it didn't kill him."

"Thankfully," muttered Liberty.

"But what...," started Colin.

Tagg kept going. "So, Uncle Danny Is sick. His blood would infect other people. But you just can't see it. Tessy is the same way."

"Wait," muttered Colin. "But she wasn't bit. Was she?"

"There's more than one way to get something," said Tagg. "In this case...think of it as the Fear Monster bit her."

Colin scoffed at that. "The Fear Monster?"

"Hey!" said Tagg, pretending to be hurt. "I'm making this up as I go along."

"I can tell," said Colin sarcastically.

Liberty squeezed one of his shoulders in warning.

"It's just...," started Tagg. "Something happened. Hurt her, and it left something in her. It makes her afraid of being alone. Even if she knows it's not real."

"It's really powerful," said Liberty.

Colin opened his mouth and then closed it. He looked down and quietly walked into the *Wolf*.

"Do you think it helped?" asked Tagg nervously.

"You tried," said Liberty and she got on her tiptoes to kiss his cheek. "You're a good Dad."

***

It took a little while to detach Tessy from her new BFF Mindy.

Actually, Tagg was walking away with Tessy under one

arm, who was complaining bitterly. Liberty felt the urge to help him, but she knew he had this.

"IT'S NOT FAIR!" cried Mindy. Her voice sounded as if the hurt would never go away.

"Maybe we'll see about you two having a sleepover," said Mindy's Mom.

The girl looked up, excitedly.

"We'll See," said Cassidy.

"Awww," whined Mindy. "That means 'no'."

"That means 'not today'," said Cassidy. "And we have to ask Tessy's Mom and Dad."

Liberty almost said 'sure' out loud, but some new Mom instinct told her to just quietly give a quick thumbs up, so that only Cassidy could see. Mindy's Mom smiled happily.

While Cassidy helped the inconsolable child, Liberty went over to the makeshift camp. Singh's team almost had the tents up, using pieces of wood to hold down the edges. The Librarian stopped by the Captain.

"Lumber?" she asked.

"Can't exactly drive a stake through the barge," smiled the Captain, extremely amused.

"Yeah. Cassidy would probably complain," said Liberty.

Singh smiled. "True."

Ruiz, who was standing close, twisted to add. "Giant magnets! That would be cool!"

"Oh! That's an interesting idea," said the Captain. "I'll mention it to the Admiral."

There was a clatter as a PVC pipe tried to escape in their

direction.

"I got this," Liberty told the Captain. She trotted over and scooped it up.

Farmers, Jed, and Chloe, were sitting cross-legged and arguing.

"No, we need to cut a hole in it first," insisted Chloe.

"I always started by closing up the ends," sniffed Jed, but he stopped to thank Liberty. Then he turned back to Chloe. But before he could say anything, she jumped in.

"What if a piece we cut falls back into the pipe?" said Chloe quickly.

Jed pulled up a bit of beard and chewed on it thoughtfully, and then sighed. "Okay, we'll try it your way."

"Can I help?" asked Liberty as she knelt beside them. She nodded at the PVC pipe. "So....that's our new farm?"

"Better than a farm," insisted Jed. "Don't have to till any ground with rocks in it."

"Yeah!" said Chloe excitedly. "It's actually super easy. We just cut holes in the pipes, stop up the ends, put water in and then the plant. Too easy bro!"

"Well, it's a little more complicated than that," said Jed.

Chloe rolled her eyes. "Well, Yeah! I didn't want to bore her, like you bored me."

"Please! You were on the edge of your seat," shot back Jed.

***

The second morning on the barge, Liberty jerked awake. She blinked and looked around the Gal's Tent.

'Was that...' she started.

"Shotgun," warned Uncle Danny from one of the Boy's Tents.

Scrambling up, Liberty unzipped the tent but called back.

"Up! We might have trouble," she hissed.

Ruiz started to drag herself up.

Liberty jumped out before it was even all the way open. In her left hand she carried her rifle.

There was no one around, and the makeshift fire pit, in the bottom of an old metal barrel, looked cold.

Moving carefully, she went towards the Boy's Tent but glanced at the construction area. There wasn't anyone there. The Captain came out of the Boy's Tent followed by Uncle Danny, who pointed towards the tugboat.

Liberty and Danny, watching for trouble, kept low and went as fast as they dared towards the tug.

Singh looked at Ruiz. "Secure this area Staff Sergeant."

Immediately, the Captain took off after *Dos Amigos*.

As he caught up with them, Liberty noticed that the Captain had a small turban on.

There was some serious shouting going on at the tug.

The three slowed as they reached it. No one was in the bow. The Captain pointed towards the port side of the ship where the shouting was coming from. He pointed at himself, and then with a questioning look pointed at Uncle Danny and the starboard who nodded.

Liberty was already pointing up and she disappeared with Uncle Danny.

Singh thought he was going to have to run all the way to the back when a group of five soldiers appeared in Army uniforms. They were lightly armed and led by someone with the insignia of a Full Bird Colonel.

"I told you he wouldn't fire," said the Colonel.

Behind them, Will came with his shotgun, who looked miserable.

The Colonel continued. "Let's just..."

Eyes snapping up, they found Singh waiting, M4 rifle against his hip. The barrel pointing down.

"Gentlemen," he said.

The Colonel only stopped when he realized that the guy in the turban wasn't moving.

"You're aboard this ship uninvited," said Singh. "Stop now, or I will stop you."

"Do I have to explain this all again, do I?" asked the Colonel with a long-suffering sigh, but he stopped, which meant the others did as well.

Behind them, Will called out. "Sorry, sir. I tried to stop them, but..."

"It's okay," said Singh to the man. "I got it from here."

The Colonel scowled impatiently. "You'll get it from here? Who are you even?"

"Captain Deep Singh, out of the *Teddy Roosevelt*," he

said. "I'm in charge of this operation. And you are?"

"Colonel Poughkeepsie," barked the man. "And I expect a salute CAPTAIN!"

The soldiers chuckled dutifully.

"Not until I've determined the safety of my people here," said Singh. "What's your business here?"

"I wasn't ASKING for a salute," said the Colonel.

"I figured," replied Singh calmly. "Now, what's your business here?"

"You refuse me?" asked the Colonel.

"I never met a Colonel Poughkeepsie," said Singh. "But I already had someone impersonate a major recently."

"Wait?" asked the Colonel with beady eyes. "You wouldn't be the tank people with the bus?"

"I'm still waiting to hear why you're here for a dawn raid," asked Singh.

"Who said it was a 'raid'?" demanded the Colonel. "This isn't a 'raid'."

"Then what is it?" asked Singh once more. "And I'm not going to ask again."

The Colonel scoffed. "You and whose Army."

Behind them, a shotgun chambered.

Rolling his eyes, the Colonel said, without looking back.

"Corporal. Take that weapon away from the guard."

"With force if necessary," sneered the man next to the Colonel with a major's gold oak leaf. "Just don't kill'em."

"Yes SIR," grinned Corporal Smith. Expecting to face

Will Holt, he nonchalantly turned, but then jumped back with a squeak. "Oh Shit!"

All the soldiers, including the Colonel, turned, and stiffened.

Glowering down the barrel of his shotgun, Uncle Danny's smile came without humor or mercy, and Hell followed with it.

Whipping around, the Colonel opened his mouth to yell at the Captain, but the barrel of a rifle was aimed at his sternum.

Singh had moved forward the moment everyone had looked back.

"Did you move, so your man wouldn't be in the line of fire?" asked the Colonel incredulously. "Seriously?"

"I think it's time you leave," said Singh. "Sir!"

"You wouldn't," breathed the Colonel.

Singh moved his thumb.

Gulping, the Colonel knew that Singh was on full automatic now.

"I am here on orders from the President of the United States," said the Colonel, trying to muster his courage. "We are to inspect this vessel to find out what's going on here. One of our spotters is sure that he saw a marijuana onboard."

"Isn't that legal in California?" asked Singh. "And I'm not answering any questions about what is, or isn't, aboard."

"Marijuana is still illegal on a Federal level," said the Colonel, and he saw that—even one-handed—Singh's barrel

289

had not wavered once. "And President Butterfett just reinforced that with an Executive Order this morning." He straightened defiantly. "Not allowing us on board could be seen as an admission of guilt."

"Or it could be because you came unannounced; bullying your way this far," said Singh.

The Colonel's eyes narrowed. "And what if we say 'no, we're not going away'. There are five of us."

Without looking away, Singh said. "Ms. Liberty."

The Colonel looked confused.

Above them, Liberty leaned over a rail. "Ready on your command Sir," she barked.

Freezing, the Colonel slowly glanced upwards and saw the Librarian. Looking back down at Singh, the Colonel glowered.

"I won't forget this," he growled.

"Neither will I," responded Singh with a flat voice. "Because if you'd just showed up during the day, I probably would've been happy to show you around."

"Right!" scoffed Major Brightly, partly hidden behind the Colonel. "We don't need to ask."

Coming to a decision, Singh took a step back and lowered his weapon some.

"We have zombies covering the Western seaboard," said Singh, and he motioned to Liberty and Uncle Danny to lower their weapons. As they did so, Singh continued. "And there are real freaking aliens roaming around."

"Two kinds," added Uncle Danny.

Before Singh could continue, the soldiers laughed derisively. Even the Colonel gave a little laugh.

"Wait!" chuckled Major Brightly. "They can't really be aliens. It's gotta be some Hollywood trick."

"I've seen both kinds," said Liberty.

Uncle Danny almost said that one of them lived with them but decided not to.

"And I've fought them," said Singh. "They've killed my men."

"And they might have gotten yours," said Liberty.

"But just so you know," said Uncle Danny. "Those birds are not here of their own free will. Kinda like slaves."

"What do you mean, have gotten our people?" asked the Colonel.

Liberty and Uncle Danny told of how some soldiers had been confronting a Private that they were traveling with.

"Hodgkins and Willet disappeared on patrol recently," spat Major Brightly. All the chuckles were gone.

"And you just let these things attack them?" asked the Colonel with heat.

"It happened pretty fast. Besides, they were about to shoot one of my people," said Liberty.

"And we didn't know if they were *los loco perros*," shrugged Uncle Danny. "Or regular Gravy Seals."

"Do we look like Gravy SEALS to you," snapped Brightly.

"OKAY EVERYONE!" called out Singh before anyone answered honestly. "Let's start over!" As everyone turned back, he kept talking. "My name is Deep Singh. Behind you is Danny, and above you is Liberty. I work for Rear Admiral Cirilo out of the aircraft carrier, *Teddy Roosevelt*. And I can assure you that, if they did not feel threatened, Liberty and Danny would have moved the world to protect those men."

"I really thought they were gonna shoot Frankline," said Liberty earnestly.

"*Sí*, they were looking for trouble, and did so really loudly," added Uncle Danny.

"Really, really, loudly," nodded Liberty.

"Still, I would've…," huffed Major Brightly.

"Major," said the Colonel with a quelling tone. Then he focused on Singh. "This is Major Brightly. I'm Colonel Poughkeepsie, as I said earlier. Corporals Smith and Dennings, and Private Carter. We're out of San Clemente Island under the command of the former Senator, now President Butterfett."

"I'm familiar," nodded Singh as he lowered his rifle to the deck.

The Colonel blinked and looked closer. "President Butterfett said that one of the men who got him to safety was…well, he called him a Muslim."

"I'm a Sikh," said Singh, but without any heat.

"So, *you're* really him," said the Colonel. "The President speaks really well of you, but didn't know what happened to you. He knew that you were badly injured."

"Bit of a car crash," said Singh. "But it was the only way."

"The President doesn't like the people from the *Roosevelt*," said the Colonel.

"They kicked him out," growled Major Brightly. "When he was just trying to help them! The assholes!"

No one commented immediately, so the Colonel moved on quickly. "We're working to return some semblance of order."

"I understand that" nodded Singh. He gestured towards the barge. "If you want to follow me. You can all come."

Major Brightly squinted suspiciously but followed the Colonel's lead. Once they were past, Liberty swung down to drop, almost silently next to Danny. *Dos Amigos* followed but kept an eye on the soldiers.

Singh led the soldiers onto the barge and to their camp.

"Staff Sergeant," called out Singh. "We have visitors."

Ruiz had the team spread out, with their rifles.

"Sergeant Bath took the other people to the construction site," reported Ruiz.

Liberty touched Uncle Danny's arm and nodded to the construction. They moved off, double-timing it, once they were past the camp.

Once they were far enough away, Liberty whispered. "What if there's another team?"

"¡Hijole!" said Uncle Danny. "That is true."

Closing in on the construction site, at the middle of the barge, they saw Sergeant Bath and the farmers, Jed, and Chloe, hunkered down behind some lumber.

Reaching them, Liberty asked. "Have you seen anyone

else?"

Bath blinked. "Like who?"

"*Mija* is worried that the soldiers back there might be a distraction," explained Uncle Danny.

Sergeant Bath shook her head. "All quiet here."

Liberty looked at Uncle Danny, and they had a quick conversation without words.

"We'll be back," said Liberty softly.

Going around the West side of the construction site, Liberty walked North with a methodical pace. Uncle Danny mirrored her on the East, but they soon met on the far side. It was then that they saw Captain Singh leading Colonel Poughkeepsie and Major Brightly towards them.

Walking back through the construction site, *Dos Amigos* met up with them.

"...just trying to grow vegetables," said the Colonel incredulously.

"Yeah right," scoffed Brightly, but both men ignored him.

Instead, Captain Singh chuckled. "As one of us said, it was definitely not the sexiest assignment, but it's not digging latrines, which I've done, or putting my life at risk." He looked up at the sky. "Actually, it's kind of pleasant. A nice change..."

"OTHER THERE COLONEL!" cried out Major Brightly. He bounded over and yanked a pot into the air. "Look! They do have illegal contraband."

"HEY!" cried the farmer, Jed, who ran over. "Careful with Deliah!" He tried to grab the plant, but Brightly just kept it away from him. "Seriously! She's a little girl, an' you're spilling her water all over the place."

"So, this is yours?" asked Brightly with a predatory gaze.

Liberty and Uncle Danny were suddenly there on either side of the soldier, boxing him in.

"Just give him the plant, *cabrón*," growled Uncle Danny.

"You want to impede a lawful investigation," sneered Brightly. "You WANT to be charged with impeding an investigation."

Singh turned to the Colonel expectantly, who sighed.

"MAJOR!" called out the Colonel. "Put the plant down."

"But Sir...!" responded Brightly.

"That's an order!" barked the Colonel.

Brightly's face twisted up and he let go of the plant.

"Ah!" cried Liberty as she tried to grab it, but it bounced off her fingers. Clattering to the deck of the barge, the plant fell out of its container.

Without looking back, Brightly smirked as he walked back.

The Colonel was fuming.

"Hurry, we gotta get some good water," cried Jed as Chloe went to get some.

Captain Singh turned slowly. "Colonel, we're just trying to help people, so that they don't get scurvy, and their teeth fall out. To get the farmers help, they brought along their plants, which are perfectly legal. Now, I think this tour is over."

The Colonel nodded slowly. "I understand." And he gave Brightly a searing glare.

"What?" asked the Major with genuine surprise.

"Get the men and return to the boat," said the Colonel.

"We're not done here," insisted Brightly.

"After that? We are very done," said the Colonel with exasperation.

"But they could have other stuff," said Brightly, and he said in a loud whisper. "Heroin, or cocaine, or…"

Singh interrupted the Major because he started laughing so hard. The laugh had jumped out without a chance to stop.

"Oh, thank you," said Singh. "I haven't laughed like this in ages."

"It's not funny," insisted Brightly.

"," said Singh, quickly wiping his eyes. "I…I…we wouldn't know a poppy plant if it bit us."

Brightly leaned intently. "How do you know that heroin comes from the poppy plant?"

Singh blinked at that. "Who doesn't know that? I've definitely heard about it on the news." His face grew solid. "Anyhow, let me escort you gentlemen to your boat." And he moved out his hands, as if guiding them.

"Who said that we were done?" asked Brightly defiantly.

Stopping, Singh's hand moved to his M4 Rifle.

The Colonel saw Liberty and Uncle Danny returning quickly.

"Let's go," said the Colonel.

Major Brightly whipped around to glare at him, but his eyes quickly looked down.

The Colonel moved to the makeshift camp, collecting his other troops, and headed for their boat.

"If you *yourself* ever want to return Colonel," said Singh as they walked. "I wouldn't be against that."

"I appreciate it, Captain," said the Colonel sincerely.

"We have a ton of work in front of us," said Singh.

"Still having trouble with the aliens thing," said the Colonel.

"Some are covered in tentacles," said Liberty. "And they have some type of shield to protect them."

"Really?" asked the Colonel with interest. "Any chance you got your hands on one of those shields?"

"No sir," said Liberty with a shake of her head. "They don't come out of their ships often, if at all."

They reached their boat, and the Colonel had everyone else get on board. However, he turned to Singh.

"Have you ever thought of taking down one of their ships?" asked the Colonel. "We might find something useful, like those shields."

"My concern is pissing them off too much," said Singh thoughtfully.

"In war, you kinda do have to cheese off the other side," said the Colonel, with friendly chiding.

"True," smiled Singh. "But...we don't know what else they have. They've already escalated by bringing out the birds, which are extremely deadly."

"Yeah," said Brightly from the ship. "Like Our People found out, and you didn't help them."

The Colonel raised a quelling hand and Brightly stopped.

Looking at Singh, the Colonel said. "You're worried about what else they have."

"They traveled a long way to us," said Singh. "We can't discount that they have superior firepower or know someone who does. Maybe even something that can sink an aircraft carrier from space or wipe an island clean."

The Colonel raised his white, bushy eyebrows at that. "You think they're that powerful?"

"I'm just saying that it might be best to stay under the radar for now," said Singh. "Because we don't exactly have superior forces."

"We can take some Spaghetti-Men and some birds," said Brightly loudly.

"If we work together, we'll have a better chance," said Singh. "Even if we have a smaller force, that can make all the difference."

"OOOH!" cried Liberty. "Like *300*. The Spartans stopped a whole army." She looked at Uncle Danny. "My Mom was trying to figure out if I was gay, but I saw that movie and knew that couldn't be the case." She gave a little giggle.

"¿*Mande?*" asked Danny. "Why'd you Mom think you were gay?"

Liberty shrugged. "Who knows with my Mom?"

"Anyhow," said Singh.

"Ooops, sorry!" said Liberty with an embarrassed grin. "But seriously, *300*."

"Okay," nodded Singh to her, and he looked back at the Colonel. "Maybe we can meet again soon. So, we're not stepping on each other's toes, out on the Coast."

"I'll take that back," promised the Colonel, who seemed interested. "In the meantime." And he put out his hand.

Singh gladly shook it. "Well, we have a long day of work ahead of us." He gave a little sigh. "In fact, we should probably get to work right away."

"No. Breakfast first," insisted Uncle Danny. "We'll all perform better with a good meal in us."

"After breakfast," conceded Singh.

After a little more small talk, the Colonel left with his men. The moment that they were away, Singh turned.

"Can someone check on the family?" he asked urgently.

"You read my mind," said Liberty. She swung her rifle behind her and bolted across the tugboat. But she did stop at the entrance and stand to the side of the door. "HEEEY! Is everyone okay? The bad men are gone!"

Will Holt appeared first with his shotgun, and then Cassidy followed by Mindy.

"Who the hell was that?" asked Cassidy.

Captain Singh came over and quickly explained.

"So, should we move the pot somewhere else?" asked Cassidy.

"I don't think that's what this was really about," said

299

Singh thoughtfully. "I think this was more of a power-play. They were trying to throw their weight around."

"I'm sorry I couldn't stop them," said Will, looking down.

Singh turned quickly. "What? I'm not sure what you could've done differently."

"I could've shot 'em," said Will stridently.

"And I'm glad that you didn't," said Singh. "We might get an ally out of this."

To Will, Liberty said. "And you were outnumbered."

"¡Órale!" nodded Uncle Danny. "You probably would've just gotten killed."

The little girl jumped over and wrapped her arms around Will's skinny waist.

"I'm so glad that you didn't get hurt."

Will put one arm around the girl to hug her and grinned. "Me too!"

"Actually, the shotgun blast was perfect," said Singh. "That got us moving."

"I don't think I should pull guard duty anymore," said Will. His smile faded and he looked down.

"Nonsense," said Singh. "I would like to train you with a rifle though."

"Yeah!" said Cassidy. "If they'd been raiders…"

"Oh yeah!" said Will quickly, interrupting with a wicked grin. "I wouldn't have hesitated to shoot."

"¡Fíjate! We need breakfast," said Uncle Danny as he started to herd everyone towards the barge.

300

Cassidy came to walk right next to the Captain. She leaned close, and he felt her warm breath on his cheek, which made his breath catch.

"Thank you, hot stuff," whispered Cassidy. "Poor Will was really fretting back there."

"Just told the truth," he shrugged, nervously.

"Okay, Humble Hero," smirked Cassidy and her tongue played with her upper teeth for a second.

But Singh noticed and gulped. His mind immediately went to his daughter and wife, and his chest tightened.

"CAPTAIN! CAPTAIN!" cried Private Frankline as he pounded towards him. He screeched to a halt.

Singh was absolutely utterly grateful for the distraction; he could have hugged the Private.

"Captain," continued the Private. "The Staff Sergeant let me go over to the construction site, because it seemed the worst had passed. 'Cause I wanted to make sure that we had everything, but I kept my rifle just in case." He patted his weapon. "But I just wanted to make sure..."

"Good job," said Singh. "What's you find?"

"Oh! We're gonna run out of nails. Soon," said Frankline. "I thought we had enough. I mean, they did take everything from the store, so it's not their fault."

Singh raised a hand and the Private subsided.

"It's okay," said the Captain. "Honestly, I'm shocked that we haven't had to go before this. Whenever I worked on a project, I was at the hardware store several times a day."

"They kinda took a lot," shrugged Frankline.

Behind, Liberty looked at Uncle Danny with an expectant look, and he immediately nodded.

"We'll go!" she chirped, even moving towards their small boat. But she looked down and saw that her bare legs were sticking out from underneath one of Tagg's oversized t-shirts. And then she noticed that Uncle Danny wasn't even wearing a shirt. She gave an embarrassed grin. "Mayyyyyyybe I should put on some pants first. And they're going to tell Danny, no shirt, no service."

Chapter Seventeen

"WOW!" CRIED LIBERTY as they pulled the little boat onto the sand. "We never landed on Venice beach before."

"¡Órale!" nodded Uncle Danny. "I just wish there were less zoms."

After breakfast, Captain Singh had called in their encounter to the carrier. But *Dos Amigos* couldn't head out until they had contacted Rak and asked her to scout ahead.

***

"Let's try this way," suggested Liberty later that day. "Where is this place again?"

"Rak saw it over this way," said Uncle Danny as they moved around knots of beach-going zoms.

"Oooh, that's a cute swimsuit," said Liberty as they moved around a knot of zoms. And she made a pout. "Wish I could ask her where she'd got it."

"Senior Tagg would probably like it," smirked Uncle Danny.

"Hush you," said Liberty, and she bit her lower lip with a smile.

"I guess we could take it off the zom but..." started Danny. His face twisted up.

They looked at each other and said in unison.

"Nah."

"Sí, let us leave her some dignity," nodded Uncle Danny.

"Was Rak able to give us much in the way of directions?" asked Liberty hopefully.

"Kinda yes," said Uncle Danny. "She said that we'd know it when we came across it."

"So, we're exploring," finished Liberty. She gave a smile. "Well, that's okay."

They started by walking down Venice Blvd, trying to keep a good walking pace.

"You know, I've never been to Venice Beach," said Liberty casually. "Of course, I tended to not go out."

"And now you explore at the drop of the hat," chuckled Uncle Danny. "¡Neta! That is funny."

"Actually," said Liberty, somewhat embarrassed. "I was getting bored. I'm not much of a construction person."

"You notice I didn't argue," smirked Uncle Danny. "We add 'Construction' to our list of things to Not volunteer for."

"*Sí. Grande Si!*" chuckled Liberty, but then her face grew thoughtful. "I feel bad for Rak."

"*¿Mande?* Why?"

"Seems like she's out every day, looking for her people."

"*Ay, pobrecita,*" sighed Uncle Danny. "I feel for her too. I guess they keep moving around. This is apparently normal behavior for her people when they are in an unknown place. They only nest for two nights at the most, then they move on."

"Oh yeah," said Liberty. "That makes sense. They are on an alien planet. Poor things…I mean, people."

"*MIJA!*" said Danny with a loud whisper. He pointed past her down a cross street.

"Oh no!" whispered Liberty in shock.

"Welllll," said Uncle Danny slowly. "She did say that we would know it when we saw it."

Dangling from the hardware sign was a zombie cop.

"Oh, that's just so wrong," said Liberty, but giggles spilled out of her. "Poor guy."

As they got closer, Danny pointed. "Looks like Rak used some kind of loop on the *policia* to keep him up there."

"Ur arr," grumbled the zombie cop above.

"I really feel bad for them," said Liberty as they reached the store. "Wish we could get them down safely."

Uncle Danny squinted up. "Yeah, but not today."

"Well, yeah…," agreed Liberty. She looked down to Danny but noticed him looking up. She followed his gaze.

Above the hardware store was a 2nd story in red brick. She finally asked. *"¿Mande?"*

The Big Mexican blinked, and then they both looked down.

Besides, Uncle Danny's neck was starting to hurt. "I was just noticing that all the second story windows were knocked out." He gestured at the front of the hardware store. "But none are broken here."

"Well, not yet," said Liberty. "So, what's the problem?"

Danny shrugged. "Just seemed weird."

There were zom noises behind them. "Okay, that's for another day." He brought up his shotgun and aimed the stock at the glass door.

Liberty leaned forward really quick, and the door swung open. She grinned up at him.

"Yeah, yeah, *Mija*," grumbled Danny. "So clever."

"I thought so," sing-songed Liberty.

Inside the store, they closed the door and raised their weapons immediately. All play was gone. Liberty gestured that she'd go left, and Danny nodded as he went right.

With her suppressed Glock aimed forward, Liberty stepped cautiously. Most of the aisles were in rows, so that she could see to the back of the store. That helped.

Softly, under her breath, Liberty sang. "This is the way we clean the store. Clean the store, clean the store. This is the way we clean the store of all those pesky zombies."

Sliding along the left side of the store, she suddenly heard a noise upstairs and froze. 'Was that footsteps' she wondered, but then there was only silence.

A zom turned the corner, hissed, and moved towards her.

Liberty fired once and momentum had it stumble and fall into a heap before her. She fired one more, remembering that there was some Rule about doing so, but she couldn't remember the source, which annoyed her.

Uncle Danny's shotgun went off and it made her jump. Then came a little whistle. It was actually a snippet of Football song, *Himno del Chivas de Guadalajara*, but she did not know that. She was just glad that he was safe and…

A clatter arose from the second floor and there was a frantic scramble.

Liberty spied a cardboard display in the corner near her. This was the best she had. Staying low, she ducked behind the display for Go-Man Power Tools that promised to help the man on the go.

Someone came into the hardware store, with a clacking of nails, and then stopped.

Pressed against a wall, she tried Not to think about how dirty it was. Instead, Liberty focused on the problem at hand. She contorted her body to aim her suppressed Glock through the cardboard.

The nails on the tile grew louder, and Liberty tried not to breathe too loudly. As the nails got closer, clack-clack-clack, she held her breath.

Liberty could almost hear the alien-Bird breathing. Based on those noises, she readjusted her gun, hoping to hit center mass first.

There was a soft hiss right on the other side of the thin cardboard.

Her finger went to the trigger.

"*Hojot Teal,*" cried a voice from the back of the hardware store. Another bird called out. "*Guk Fen!*"

On the other side of her cardboard, a bird replied. "*Toof?*"

'One bird was telling the other to come back', realized Liberty.

There was an annoyed screech, and the nails slowly returned to the back of the hardware store.

Liberty tapped her earpiece. "Wait."

Uncle Danny softly said. "*Sí.*"

After a long moment, no bird jumped back out. Slowly she got out from behind the sign. With no birds in sight. Uncle Danny rose on the other end of the store, and he waved.

Through the earpiece, she said. "I've seen a bird wait and jump out. Just wanted to make sure."

Above came a horrible rending scream. Liberty looked up in surprise, but then it ended. She looked back at Uncle Danny.

"Let's go fast," said the Big Mexican.

As quickly as they dared, they searched the store. A soft whistle came up and Liberty headed over to Uncle Danny. He was already putting nails into his Avengers backpack. She was about to kneel down when she glanced out the window.

"*¡Mierda!*" she hissed.

Uncle Danny did a double take when he saw the look of

308

worry on her face. He raised himself just enough so that he could see over the shelves.

Through the front windows, they saw a huge flock of the birds come closer to the windows to peer in.

Taking her arm, Uncle Danny gave Liberty a quick tug. "Slowly."

Not even daring to nod, the Librarian squatted down.

"Arriba Mija," hissed Uncle Danny. *"Arriba!"*

For the life of her, Liberty couldn't remember what 'arriba' meant, but she opened her Dora the Explorer backpack and started stuffing nails in as fast as she could.

"I'm full," she whispered.

Uncle Danny zipped up his backpack, put it on and shoveled some more boxes into a recycle bag that he had acquired.

Slowly, Liberty stood part way up. She looked over the shelves and saw one of the birds, with a Silver Tuft on its head, drawing back its big foot to smash through the glass. The bird next him, the Lime Tuft bird, pushed against the front door with her wing. It swung open.

Several birds clacked their beaks together, like laughing.

This stopped when Silver Tuft looked back and glared at them.

Then Silver ended his look at Lime Tuft.

She, for her part, raised her beak into the air and stepped away from the door.

Before Silver Tuft turned to the door, Liberty ducked back down carefully.

"We gotta go," she whispered urgently.

Not questioning, Uncle Danny put one more box of nails in his pocket. She nodded towards the back and *Dos Amigos*—keeping low—moved that way.

The door to the hardware store jingle-jangled with old-fashioned bells. Bells that had sounded so cheery to Liberty.

There was a single swinging door. Lifting her Glock, Liberty put her shoulder against it and slowly opened it up. The back room was dark, but it seemed empty.

The clacking of bird nails was spreading across the front of the store, then started to move to the back. Once Danny was through, he grabbed the door and closed it part way.

"Clear," whispered Liberty, and absently thought it was amusing that she was picking up that military-type lingo.

Dos Amigos moved towards the back door. Liberty was feeling like they were going to be able to easily duck out.

Uncle Danny put his hand out to stop them. Liberty then saw that someone was at the back door. Several someones.

They looked around quickly, and the Big Mexican pointed to some stairs going up.

Uncle Danny gave her a questioning look.

Liberty scrunched up her face in reply, 'What choice do we have?'.

'I reluctantly agree,' came Uncle Danny's look.

Cautiously, *Dos Amigos* moved up the dark stairs.

They were nearly at the landing when someone began to

open the door to the back room. Swiftly, they moved across the landing and hid.

At the top of the stairs was a corridor. There were several rooms on the left with open doors and four windows on the right with no glass in them.

Reaching the top of the stairs, they listened carefully, but did not hear anything.

As Liberty was about to step forward, Uncle Danny reached out in front of her, and she stopped. He pointed down to the glass all over the floor.

Uncle Danny mouthed the word, 'Noise'.

Nodding that she understood, Liberty stepped forward slowly, in and around the glass. They came up to the first open door but stopped. Liberty looked back.

'Ready', mouthed Uncle Danny, thinking of Tessy and Colin and Rak.

Steeling herself, Liberty moved through the door sweeping left like always. Danny through to the right.

But there were no birds in the room. Outside the window, they could see the poor zom hanging on the sign.

"*Veet Hie!*" cried a bird from downstairs.

There was a scramble in the next room. Birds were coming out.

Hiding, Liberty leapt against the wall, while Uncle Danny slipped behind the door.

Two birds ran past in a hurry and scurried down the steps. Outside, they heard more birds moving away. Both of them peeked out, but it was clear.

311

Down in the hardware store, it sounded like something was going on.

Liberty looked at Danny.

'Go?' she mouthed, pointing down the hall.

Nodding emphatically, Uncle Danny followed her.

They moved down the corridor as fast as they dared but there was no way down.

Below, the door to the backroom slammed open. Someone was stomping in fury and muttering to themselves, but they couldn't make out the words. Uncle Danny moved to a window and peeked out.

No birds.

The large bird stomped up the steps and down the empty corridor. Resigned, they turned into the second room, but did make a cheerful noise.

Liberty was able to lower herself from the open window onto an air conditioning unit. And from there, she quietly slid to the ground. Looking up, she saw that there was nothing below Danny.

After quickly searching the alley for anything soft, Liberty grimaced and ran under him. He looked at her incredulously.

'HURRY', she shouted noiselessly.

With no other choice, Danny dropped. Liberty did not quite catch him, but she let him partially fall against her.

"Oof," she exclaimed.

But Danny hadn't hurt himself.

Liberty pointed down the alley behind the hardware

store and they went as quickly as they dared. Out on Venice Blvd again, they kept near the storefronts, trying not to go too fast.

They were almost to the beach when they saw a couple of birds come out ahead. Both of them slowed down, but that meant that the zoms were able to get close for comfort. *Dos Amigos* tried to keep moving, not daring to shoot.

The birds were looking at the beach, searching.

Uncle Danny's eyes went wide. He reached into his coat and tossed the contents across the street.

The box of nails hit the top of a cop car and exploded. While the nails weren't fast enough to hurt anything, they sure did make a good clatter.

The birds in front shot towards the noise.

Dos Amigos soon reached the beach, went past the woman with the cool bikini, and carefully pushed their boat out onto the water.

They looked at each other and both grabbed for the paddles at the same time. Hands collided together.

'OW!' mouthed Uncle Danny with mock hurt. Rowing hard, *Dos Amigos* were finally a good distance away.

"I think we can stop rowing and use the engine" suggested Uncle Danny.

Liberty looked up with tears in her eyes.

"That...that was *way* too close," she said. "When I thought of the kids..."

"*Neta, No Manches!* You're not kidding *Mija*," said Uncle Danny and he put out one big arm. "If you don't need a hug, I do."

Chuckling sadly, Liberty leaned over and gave him a hug. He wrapped one arm around her shoulders.

"I...I really need to see the kids," she whispered.

Uncle Danny straightened up and they detached.

"¡Fíjate! Here's the plan *Mija*," he said. "We drop off the nails, an' then we race over to the *Wolf Pack*, hug everyone... okay, I'm not hugging Smalls..."

Liberty snorted with laughter. "Sorry, I snorted. And that's okay. I think he'll manage."

"¡Órale!" nodded Uncle Danny solemnly as he went to the outboard motor. "An' Tagg, he's on his own."

"I'll give him hugs enough for both of us," agreed Liberty with playful solemnity.

"Whatever," said Uncle Danny. "As long as I get No Details. I must *insist* upon this."

Liberty let out a joyful little laugh as the Big Mexican started the engine.

Chapter Eighteen

"THE *WOLF!*" CRIED Liberty as she scrambled up to the front of their little boat. "The *Wolf Pack* is HERE!" She looked back with a grin that went ear to ear.

"See!" called out Danny over the engine. "You needed to see the kids, and He answered." Danny pointed up, but then his brow furrowed. He shrugged. "Or it was *Mi Abuela*. She likes a happy ending."

"Whoever it was," said Liberty. "I'm grateful." She looked up and called out. "Thank you!" Then, she turned back to him. "We should still stick to your plan. Drop off nails first, and then find the kids."

"*¡ÓRALE!*" grinned the Big Mexican. "If those lil troublemakers don't find us first."

After docking to the tugboat, *Dos Amigos* scrambled through the ship and up to the barge.

"MOM!!!" cried Tessy. "UNCLE!!!"

Danny grinned. "I called it. They found us first."

Streaking across the barge, the little girl almost hugged Liberty first, but stopped.

"No, you got First Hug last time," said Tessy, very seriously. "Sorry."

"I'll live," chuckled Liberty.

With that settled, Tessy threw herself at Uncle Danny for hugs.

"Ooof," he cried with exaggeration. "I felt that. You are getting bigger and bigger. Soon, I won't be able to do THIS!!"

Uncle Danny picked up the little girl and swung her around. Tessy laughed so hard.

Colin reached Liberty.

"Hey," said the boy.

Unable to help herself, she drew him into a tight hug.

"Tough trip?" asked a muffled voice against her stomach.

Leaning back, Liberty looked puzzled. "Why do you say that?"

"You often need hugs after things are tough," he said, a little embarrassed. "I'm glad you're okay."

Pulling him all the way back into the hug, Liberty kissed the top of his head.

Tessy suddenly plowed into them.

"Hey!" cried Colin indignantly. He stepped back and

tried to look dignified and tough. Except that Uncle Danny came over and hugged him fiercely.

'Wow,' thought Colin. 'It was a *really* close call.'

Thrilled that they were okay, Colin even hugged him back.

Shortly, Uncle Danny detached and looked down on the boy proudly.

"Someday, you will be a great *hombre*," said the Big Mexican.

Captain Singh cleared his throat. "Um, did you get the nails?"

Liberty and Uncle Danny looked at each other.

"Nails? I thought we were supposed to get sushi?"

Dos Amigos laughed as they handed off their full backpacks.

"We need those backpacks returned," called out Liberty, and the Captain waved.

"What about me?" cried out little Mindy. "Don't I get a hug?"

Her Mom, Cassidy, chuckled and gave her a big hug.

The Navy Engineer, Smalls, bounced up next. "Hey! I hope you don't mind that I brought the kids here. But they needed help on the water pumps, and they called me in. I figured I could get them settled and on the right track and then we'll go soon enough. Because..."

"It's okay," said Liberty quickly, jumping in. "I'm glad to see you all."

"We should be safe enough right now," added Uncle

Danny and he gave the Engineer a light punch on the arm.

"Whew!" said Smalls as he deflated. "Well, I better get back."

"Hey, did Tagg come with you?" asked Liberty.

Smalls looked around. "Yeah. He's been working at the North end of the..."

"There he is!" cried Liberty happily with one arm still around Tessy.

As Smalls left, Dr. Tagg arrived.

"Sorry!" called out Tagg as he drew close. "I was all the way on the other side..."

Liberty pulled him down for a deep kiss.

When she let him go, Tagg looked at her and Uncle Danny.

"So, it was a *really* close call," suggested Tagg.

"That's what I said," cried out Colin.

***

"Mooooooom," wailed Tessy. "I'm hungry!"

Liberty looked at her watch. She and Tessy, Colin and Mindy had been helping put together the PVC pipes for the hydroponics garden. The Librarian looked questioningly at Colin.

"I'm kinda hungry too," he admitted.

"Can I get some food too?" asked Mindy sweetly.

"Of course," agreed Liberty immediately.

Turning to Jed, Liberty was about to ask, when the Farmer said. "Feed the young'uns. We'll be fine."

Liberty looked at all they had still to do, but she took the kids to clear it with Mindy's Mom.

Cassidy was seated with Smalls, Frankline, and Ruiz. The poor Staff Sergeant had to sit awkwardly, because of her hurt derrière. But, it had thankfully not required stitches.

Smalls was saying. "...these pieces are just not going to work."

"If only they were a little smaller," muttered Ruiz thoughtfully.

Frankline saw Liberty and waved.

"Hey!" he said half-jokingly. "Maybe Liberty and Uncle Danny want to do another hardware store run."

Liberty went stiff as a board. She had to stop herself from crushing Tessy and Mindy's hands, which she was holding.

Ruiz saw this, and jumped in. "I think we need another solution." She took a second to whap Frankline on the arm.

"What?" he asked softly.

Smalls turned to the Librarian and saw a haunted look on her face. He whipped back around to Ruiz.

"I know!" he cried. "I can grind them down."

Frankline's face twisted. "It's probably not going to be quick."

"That's okay," said Smalls blithely. "I've been out in the sun long enough. I could use the cool air of my workroom."

"That works for me," nodded Ruiz.

"We have plenty to do in the meantime," chuckled Cassidy.

Collecting all the pieces that needed to be ground down, Smalls hopped up with a box and turned to Liberty.

"I need to go back to the *Wolf,*" said Smalls. "But did you need anything first?"

"Oh!" said Liberty, coming out of her nightmare of poor Rak finding what was left of them. She focused on hungry little beasties instead. "The Wild Things are hungry."

"Would you like me to take them to the ship?" asked Smalls helpfully.

"I only came over to ask if Mindy could go with the kids," said Liberty quickly.

"Pleeeeeaaaase Mom," asked Mindy.

Liberty was still talking. "I wasn't trying to dump the kids on you, or Anyone! I can make the kids lunch."

"Actually," piped up Colin next to her. He worked to make his voice very diplomatic. "Actually, Mr. Smalls does make really good sandwiches."

Smalls stood a little straighter. "Oh. Thank you."

"Yeah," added Tessy. "Really, really good." But then she looked up. "Not that you're a bad cook, or anything…"

Hearing the longing in their voices, Liberty gave her a side hug. "It's okay sweetie." She looked down at Mindy's Mom and got permission for the little girl.

Tessy and Mindy immediately made loud, happy noises,

which gave Colin a worried look. Liberty went to him.

"You guys have fun," she said.

Colin forced a smile. "It's okay."

"I know that means 'terrible'," said Liberty softly. "Thank you for being a great big brother."

The boy straightened a little.

"I won't embarrass you with a gigantic hug," she smiled.

However, she did go over to Smalls.

Speaking quietly, she said. "You can always say 'No'."

The Navy Engineer looked at her in confusion.

"You don't *have* to take care of the kids," she continued. "Except every now and then. Really. It's Not one of your jobs."

Smalls gave a warm smile.

"It's okay," he replied quickly. "Even if I'm not... whatever. I don't mind helping. There're really great kids."

Liberty looked up, and she came to a quick decision.

"Okay kids," she said. "Uncle Smalls is going to get you food."

The Navy Engineer looked up in surprise. "Oh! I wasn't..."

Liberty smiled at him. "I know. Now get the kids fed Uncle Smalls."

As the Engineer smiled happily, Tessy bounced over. "Oh yes! Uncle Smalls. I like that."

Captain Singh came over to Frankline at that moment. "Private. You got guard duty at the North end."

Standing with a stretch, the Private smiled. "I could use a break." Then he looked at Ruiz. "I'll be back."

Not sure what to say, Ruiz clammed up. Part of her wanted him to stay by her side, but then she felt guilty about that.

"Sure, no prob," she said quickly.

Frankline grabbed his rifle and did an easy jog to the North end.

As Smalls left with the kids, Liberty took a route by Uncle Danny and gave him an update, including Smalls 'Uncle' promotion.

"You trying to keep me competitive, *Mija?*" asked Uncle Danny with mock annoyance. "So, I don't rest on my Uncle laurels?"

"A little competition is good," smirked Liberty. "Unless you're scaaaaaared."

Danny made a dismissive noise. "*Pollas en vinagre.* You are so mean to an old man."

"Pfft. Please!!" scoffed Liberty. "As if you're some poor old man." She started to step away.

"Now," she continued. "I want to find Tagg and pinch his butt."

Uncle Danny let out a mock mournful noise. "Ahhh! No Details. I don't want to know!"

Feeling better after the nail run, Liberty walked around. But Operation Butt Pinch was a failure. Unable to find her target, she headed back to the Farmers and their PVC pipes.

Not long after she sat, Liberty spotted Tagg at the far North end of the barge near Frankline. He was building the jellyfish structures. She couldn't tell if he was happy or not. Liberty almost went over, but she knew the sooner she got this done, the better off they'd be.

***

Almost an hour had passed when Liberty heard a shout. She looked up and saw Frankline waving down the length of the barge.

The Private said over the earpieces. "We got boats coming in fast."

"Identity?" asked Singh.

"I don't know," said the Private, trying to keep the worry out of his voice.

Liberty looked at Uncle Danny as they both rose.

Turning, the Librarian called out to their ship. But there was no reply.

Scooping up her rifle, she fired off a shot over the boat.

In no time, Smalls ran up onto the deck with his M4 rifle.

"Over there!" she cried, and the Navy Engineer followed her point. He immediately looked back at her. "THE CARRIER! GO! NOW!"

For half a second, Smalls hesitated, his face pained. But then he gave a thumbs up and disappeared.

Captain Singh was calling out. "All civilians into the tug!"

"Get into the engine room!" called out Ruiz.

The Captain looked at her and nodded encouragingly.

Liberty, who didn't consider herself a civilian, urged the Farmers towards the tug as the *Wolf Pack* started up. Her stomach unclenched a bit as the big ship started to pull away.

'TAGG', she thought. Spinning around, she looked for him, but didn't see him.

In her ear, Liberty heard Frankline calling out.

"Captain," said the Private. "It's a bunch of boats, and they're pretty much in formation."

"Armed?" asked the Captain.

"Nothing big in view," said the Private.

Uncle Danny grunted. "Like Mad Max on Cape Cod."

Liberty jumped in where there was a little lull. "Private? Sorry to interrupt," said Liberty. "But do you see Dr. Tagg?"

"Umm," started Frankline. "Not immediately. I think he had some headphones on."

"We found him a portable CD player recently," said Liberty worriedly.

"Private," said Singh. "How are the boats?"

Frankline turned and looked. His stomach clenched.

"The first ones will be here any moment," said the Private as he shouldered his M4 Rifle. "They look military, but who knows. Ord...?"

A bullet pinged off the barge near him.

"Yipe," cried Frankline. "They're shooting."

The Private heard several boats come to a stop and boarding hooks clanked near his head.

"They're boarding," said Frankline, trying to keep his cool.

"Back up," ordered Singh.

Moving backwards, Frankline stood partially up. There were several more boats arriving, but one peeled off.

"Shi...I mean...anyhow," said Frankline. "There's a boat following the *Wolf Pack*! I repeat, one of them is after the *Wolf Pack*."

Turning, Frankline started to move quickly towards his team.

Over the earpieces, Singh called. "Liberty?"

There was a sniper shot.

"I'm...dammit," she growled. "I was trying for the engine. SHIT. They better not hurt them."

"¡Órale!" agreed Uncle Danny with a dark voice. "Or we will rain sulfur down from the sky and burn them to the ground."

"Amen," growled Liberty with a You-Cheesed-Off-The-Librarian voice.

Frankline was getting closer to them, running along the edge of the ship. He glanced back. One of the boats had gone around the North end of the barge. In that instant, the Private knew that they were trying to flank them, to get to the tug. And they could easily dig in before he ran that far.

The boat was almost next to him. Two military men in the back of the boat and two more in chairs.

"Shit!" he exclaimed.

"What?" asked Singh immediately over the earpiece.

But the Private did not have time to answer, or really, even think.

Frankline sprinted to the edge of the barge and jumped.

"Wha...?" came Ruiz's voice.

The Private plummeted towards the water, but then the boat came under him. Holding his rifle out in front and tucking his chin to his chest, Frankline slammed into one of the soldiers in back. That gave him a good cushion, though momentum slammed him into the rear bucket seat.

Frankline scrambled forward to the other soldier in back who was trying to draw his gun. The Private slammed his rifle stock into the man's face. The military man slumped back.

Pushing that soldier off the seat, Frankline dropped his butt down and aimed his rifle.

"Don't do it!!" he called out.

The passenger had started to bring his rifle around.

Frankline fired twice past him into the dashboard and the Private aimed it right at the passenger.

"Put it down, or I shoot!" he cried.

The passenger stilled, but then put down his rifle.

"Now!" said Frankline, and for a second, he didn't know what he could do. He realized that he couldn't just throw them into the water. Swearing inwardly, he came up with a solution.

"Head to the Coast! Right Now!" he ordered.

The Pilot looked at the Passenger.

Frankline barked. "Don't look at him! I could shoot you all dead. That would be easier for me." He aimed his rifle at the Passenger's head. "Your choice."

The Passenger ground their teeth but said. "Get to the Coast."

"And make it snappy," grinned Frankline. "I haven't got all day."

***

"He JUMPED???" cried Ruiz as she ran over to Liberty. They saw the boat go around the end of the tug and head for the Coast. "Where is he going?"

"Nevermind!" called out Singh. "They're boarding now." He waved them down behind a pile of wood for the Jellyfish.

Liberty dropped down on her side, and then she carefully leaned around the edge of the pile—sideways—with her rifle.

Looking through her scope, she reported. "It's that major guy."

"The colonel?" asked Singh as he peeked over the edge. The soldiers were moving in precise military fashion.

"I don't see him," said Liberty.

"Maybe he got voted off the island," suggested Uncle Danny.

Staff Sergeant Ruiz glanced. "These are not Gravy

Seals."

"Nope," agreed Singh. He ducked and glanced back. "Civilians have disappeared." But then he remembered something. "And wait! What did Frankline do?"

Liberty explained what she saw.

"That boat was trying to flank us," said Ruiz.

Singh nodded.

"Has anyone seen Tagg?" asked Liberty worriedly.

***

On the North side of the barge, 'Coldplay' rocked in Tagg's earphones as his nail-gun secured two more boards together. After months in the lab, this was just the break he needed. He gave a little dance as he went to nail two more boards together, but the gun was empty.

Whistling along now, Tagg knelt to reload the gun.

There was an odd movement on the other end of the barge, and he froze.

"What?" he whispered out-loud. There were creeping soldiers in black there, starting to spread out. "¿Mande?"

Tagg suddenly realized that they were spreading in his direction.

***

"CrapCrapCrapCrap!" muttered Smalls as he pulled away

from the barge. He could see the boats getting closer on his radar. "I really hate this."

Little voices came up behind him.

"What's wrong?" asked Colin.

"Why are we going?" asked Tessy.

"Where's my Mommy?" asked Mindy.

Smalls said calmly. "Give me a moment."

"Are we leaving my Mom and Uncle Will?" asked Mindy in horror. "Where're we going?

Colin jumped forward pointing at the radar. "Wait! Those boats are coming in real fast. Who's that?"

For a second, Smalls was tempted to lie to the kids. Tell them that everything was okay.

"We don't know," said the Navy Engineer. "So, your Mom...I mean Liberty-Mom told me to head for the carrier."

"And leave them?" cried Tessy.

"Not my choice...," started Smalls, but then he stopped. "No, actually, I think this is best. Then everyone else back on the barge can deal with...well, whatever it is."

"Raiders?" asked Mindy with a small, terrified voice.

"I don't know," admitted Smalls. He glanced back and saw how scared Mindy was. "But Liberty and Uncle Danny are back there. The people in the boats better be nice."

"Mr. Smalls!" called out Colin as he pointed to the radar.

"Shoot," said Smalls. "One of them is following us."

"Um. I think they're a little faster than us," said Colin.

"Let me see," said Tessy as she crowded in.

Without complaint, Colin turned to let her look too.

"Okay," said Smalls, coming to a decision. "Colin! You drive towards the Carrier, and straight there. I already set in a course; you just have to make sure we don't run into anything big along the way. Tessy! I need you to call ahead to the *Teddy Roosevelt*. Use the…"

"Emergency channel, right?" asked Tessy.

Smiling, Smalls nodded. "Tell them…" But he corrected himself. "Ask them for help with a please and thank you"

"What're you going to do?" asked Colin as the boy climbed into the Captain's chair.

"I'm going to see what they want," said Smalls blithely, trying not to sound worried. "Now, regardless of what you hear, I need you to stay here. Lock the doors. Just…get to the carrier as quickly as possible."

Before there could be any more complaints or questions, Smalls took his M4 rifle and booked it down through the ship. He reached the stern of the boat where people normally disembarked.

The white boat was almost upon them. They looked like a bunch of military men crammed in there.

Letting only part of himself lean out, Smalls held up one hand to stop.

Suddenly there was a gunshot and then two from the chasing boat.

Whipping back, Smalls gave a rather naughty swear, and he was happy the kids weren't there. He could hear the white boat getting really close.

330

Twisting so that only a small part of himself was visible, Smalls aimed his M4 rifle towards the waterline of the boat and fired as a warning.

Immediately it was answered by a huge volley of gunfire as the Navy Engineer pulled back. Next time, he leaned out and fired most of the magazine. But the soldiers in the boat just ducked and laughed.

They were getting too close.

Smalls' stomach twisted. He only had one more magazine.

More bullets hit the back of the boat.

Suddenly, Smalls was reminded of the ending *Butch Cassidy and the Sundance Kid*, which they had watched last week. And just as suddenly, he wished that he hadn't.

It had not gone well for Butch and Sundance either.

***

Moving across the North side of the barge, Major Brightly moved his men—and he only brought men on his team— across the North side of the barge towards the wooden structures.

"I don't see any drugs," commented one of the soldiers, Private Carroll.

"Quiet!" hissed Major Brightly.

They went through the Jellyfish that had been built so far.

"What's with these structures?" asked another soldier,

331

Private Routtah.

"This is where they're going to grow the drugs," said Major Brightly with a harsh whisper. "Now shut it."

"Hey!" called out Private Carroll softly. "I got a bunch of seed packets over here."

"Like for Poppy plants?" asked Private Routtah.

"Naw," said Carroll with a shake of his head. "It's like… spinach and kale and shit."

"You're kidding," said Routtah with disgust.

Carroll just picked up one of the seed packets and tried to throw it. But it spun wildly and smacked gently into Brightly's chest. The Major squinted down at the fallen packet and then over at Carroll.

"Sorry sir," moaned Carroll.

"Stop messing about," growled Brightly. "And we're going to need those too."

"The seed packs?" asked Carroll in surprise.

"That's part of our mission," said Brightly. "To secure the vegetables as well."

"Um. Maybe we should have waited for them to grow first," muttered Routtah.

"What was that?" asked Brightly.

"Nothing Sir," said Routtah quickly.

"Besides," said Brightly. "Once they're done building, they'll probably go near the carrier. And we'll never be able to lay a finger on them then."

"But…vegetables?" moaned Carroll in horror. "Really?"

"A little green won't kill you, you wusses," said Brightly. "Now first, let's secure the tugboat. Oh! And I almost forgot! SHUT UP!"

As they went past, Tagg pulled himself from where he had been hanging over the edge of the barge. He kept low. Not sure what he could even do, he hid behind some half-built Jellyfish and gripped his nail-gun tightly, wondering where his kids were, and worried about Liberty and everyone else.

***

As the boat got closer and closer to the *Wolf Pack*, Smalls peeked out. Someone was draped across the bow of the ship with a steady rope. They were readying to board. And there were two soldiers on either side ready to shoot if he stuck his head out.

Deciding not to shoot now, and waste ammo, Smalls thought through the map of the ship in his head. He just needed to slow them down until help came from the carrier. The Navy Engineer had no illusions that he would John McClane his way out of this one. The men in the boat would 'Ho-Ho-Ho', now they had his machine gun in no time.

"Stop it!" he told himself. "This isn't helping."

Readying his rifle for his last stand—Stop That!—and thought furiously about what he could do. The Navy Engineer wiped the sweat from his brow.

A rope flew into view, but didn't catch.

333

Smalls put his finger on the trigger.

A Huge Noise came from above.

***

"Pot plants!" cried Private Carroll. "Sir! Over there!"

"And how do you know what pot plants look like?" asked Private Routtah with an oily voice.

"SHUT IT," growled Major Brightly. "This way."

On the other side of their stack of wood, Captain Deep Singh raised himself part way into view. He rolled through a bunch of things to say.

"Hey Guys," said Singh with a neutral voice. "We're not quite ready for visitors yet."

The Captain saw that there was another construction pile with wood near them. He didn't want to trigger a fight. Not if they had a place to hide.

'Damn, should have had everyone hide behind that one,' he thought.

Major Brightly did not respond but pointed.

"Private Carroll!" he barked. "Secure those plants."

With a loud 'Yes Sir', the soldier moved quickly toward the plants, which were right before Singh.

"Don't come any closer, soldier!" ordered Singh and he identified himself.

Carroll stumbled to a halt and looked back.

"You have your orders," shouted the Major. "I outrank

334

him."

"And I'm in charge of this mission," replied Singh. He whispered down to everyone. "Be ready."

"If they just want the plants...," started Ruiz thoughtfully. But she swiftly stopped herself with a grimace. "They're not going to stop at just the plants. Never mind."

Private Carroll looked at Singh's steely, unyielding look, and then back to the Major's annoyed expression.

"MOVE!" snapped Brightly.

Unhappily, Carroll took a tentative step towards the plants.

Singh brought up his Beretta with his good arm. "Stop. Now!"

"Watch IT!" cried out Private Routtah and he started firing his AR-15.

Carroll let out a scream and scrambled back.

Singh fired a little high, mostly as a warning. Dropping down, he went behind the wood.

"How dare you shoot at us?" cried Major Brightly.

"Hey! Your boy fired first," retorted Singh, unbelieving.

"That's it!" bellowed the Major. "You're all under arrest. Come out with your hands up."

"Tsk," muttered Liberty. "As if that's going to happen."

"*Pendejo*," snorted Uncle Danny.

"I heard that!" screeched the Major. His voice managed to get louder, which seemed impossible. "Don't you ignore me! You Will Come Out! Or Else."

Singh glanced over the wood. "You are formally asked to leave this ship, tug, and barge, and Not to come back. Ever."

"Who do you think you are?" demanded the Major.

"We don't want any trouble," said Singh. "But you came aboard our boat without permission."

"We don't need permission from lawbreakers," said the Major. "That's it! We are seizing this vessel and all it holds. Once you have been relieved of your weapons, you will be dropped on the Coast."

Liberty snorted with laughter. "Sorry, I snorted."

"Is...is someone laughing back there?" asked the Major incredulously.

While laying on her side, Liberty raised her hand and waved it.

"That was me," she said and returned to gripping her rifle.

"That's it!" screeched the Major. "Fire!"

The soldiers gleefully opened fire.

"Wasn't trying to get them to start shooting," called out Liberty over the din.

"*¡Neta, no manches!* He was just looking for an excuse," said Uncle Danny.

"Agreed," said Singh. "Well, if they want a fight..."

***

At the stern of the *Wolf Pack*, Smalls jumped from the large sound.

The soldiers in the boat were crying out in surprise and anger.

The Navy Engineer did not even look. He ran, as fast as he could, up to the helicopter pad where the big gun was mounted. Standing on a chair, Colin tried to aim the .50 cal machine gun, firing in bursts at the retreating ship. Beside the boy, Tessy was shouting at the soldiers in Spanish.

The Navy Engineer came up, past a scared Mindy, to stand behind the kids.

Unable to help himself, Smalls said. "Language."

Tessy whipped around in surprise. She immediately clammed up, embarrassed.

The .50 caliber went empty, and Smalls realized that the boy had been talking the whole time with a worried mumble.

"...didn't mean to," said Colin. "I was trying to hit the side of the boat, so it started leaking, but the gun was kinda hard to aim. An' I hit the boat, but I was worried about hitting anyone. I jus' wanted to scare 'em."

"It's okay," said Smalls as the boy climbed quickly off the chair and stepped over the spare ammo.

"I know that you said to stay in," said Colin quickly. Tears brimming at his eyes. "I just..."

Smalls gave a smile and reached out to pat the boy on the shoulder. But Colin jumped in and hugged the Engineer hard.

"Sorry Uncle Smalls," came a muffled voice.

337

"It's cool," said Smalls as he hugged the boy back. "You're cool." But then he pulled the boy back to give him a mock grouchy look. "But next time yah don' follow me orders, Imma gonna keelhaul you."

Colin gave a grateful and relieved laugh as he stepped back. Tessy was immediately at his side and hugged the boy's arm with a hard grip.

"But it wasn't just him," she said bravely with a little voice.

"You're cool too," said Smalls immediately and then he turned to Mindy to let her know that No One was in trouble. "Except for those ass...idiots in the boat." He glanced again and gave a huff of annoyance. "Oh, for fu..." He paused.

"They're coming back?" asked Colin.

"I kinda thought that might get them to leave us alone," commented Smalls, mostly to himself.

"We gotta reload!" said Tessy, letting go of Colin.

"Yeah, we probably...," started Smalls, but then he stopped. "Actually..." He went over the .50 cal and gestured angrily at it. He said in a loud voice. "I'm talking loudly to make the soldiers think I'm mad at you."

"Which you're Not, right?" asked Tessy.

Continuing in a loud voice, Smalls said. "No! Not at all." He dropped his voice. "They getting close?"

"Too close," said Colin.

"Okay," smiled Smalls.

Chapter Nineteen

"THIS PISSES ME off!" cried out Liberty.

"What?" asked Ruiz next to her, after she fired a few shots.

"They're hitting all the wood," said Liberty.

"Better the wood than us *Mija*," smirked Uncle Danny, joining in as the soldiers were reloading. A little moment of quiet.

"No, it's just...," said Liberty, and she stopped to fire in front of a soldier, who was trying to sneak around them. The soldier scrambled back—almost comically—to Brightly's squad of men. Liberty looked back at her friends. "They're mangling all this wood that we got."

Singh opened his mouth, but then closed it. "Shoot. We've got to end this fast." The shooting was starting again. "Honestly, what's pissing me off more is the lack of trigger discipline."

Uncle Danny stopped and a goofy grin came over his face.

Liberty squinted hard at him. "Whatever you're thinking…"

***

Pursuing the yacht, the soldiers were seriously wondering if they were going to go back to the island.

"I'm just sayin'," suggested one of the soldiers. "With that thing, we can go anywhere we want."

"Until we run out of gas, or fuel, or whatever it takes," said another thoughtfully.

"Well! Then we need to find fuel first," said the first soldier.

The Driver barked. "You all shut up! Something's happening up there."

"Jeez, he's really laying into the kids," said a third soldier.

A Fourth gave a shiver. "Reminds me of my dad."

The Guy in the Blue Jumpsuit suddenly picked up a metal box, waving it at the kids.

"That looks like a canister for carrying ammo," suggested the First Soldier.

The Guy in the Blue Jumpsuit suddenly threw it overboard and glared at the soldiers. Then he shooed the kids away and disappeared himself.

"Hurry in," said the Second Soldier.

The Driver waited though.

"There!" cried the First Soldier, pointing like a dog, the Driver thought.

"The guy was back to where he was," said the Second Soldier. "He's gonna try and hold us off."

"We got 'em now!" sneered the Fourth Soldier.

The Driver didn't say anything. Their boat picked up speed. Back down where passengers disembarked, Blue Jumpsuit peek out with his little rifle.

The First Soldier scrambled back up to the front to throw the rope. Two other soldiers flanked him with their AR-15's.

"Remember!" called out the Driver. "Go Slow. Check corners. No looking for rooms. We need to make sure there aren't any surprises. IS THAT CLEAR!?!?"

"Yes Sir!" cried every man with feeling. They weren't going to cross him…yet.

Their boat closed in on the yacht with a predatory gait.

The First Soldier glanced quickly at the soldiers on either side of him.

"Don't hesitate to shoot," he said, nodding to where they last saw the Blue Jumpsuit guy.

"Don't worry and hurry up!" grumbled one of the soldiers not taking his eyes off the lower half of the boat.

Their boat was almost there.

Someone strung up on top of the ship.

The Driver began to look up as Blue Jumpsuit shot the bolt forward on the .50 cal Browning.

Beside him, the Little Latina girl hopped up, though struggling with a fresh belt of ammo.

"Shit," whispered the Driver.

Blue Jumpsuit loaded and aimed in a moment.

The Little Latina girl stuck her fingers in her ears.

The .50 cal roared.

Unlike the boy, Blue Jumpsuit had excellent control of the mounted gun.

The Driver was already yanking their boat right as the bullets tore into the boat.

The other soldiers were thrown left and then back as the Driver tried to get away. Behind him, the Browning went empty, and the Driver glanced around. Everyone was still alive. HE was alive. The soldiers were bitching up a storm, but They Were Alive.

Swinging around, the Driver grinned. They weren't going to be caught by that trick again. He started to follow the yacht.

"That's it," growled the Driver. "No more fu..." His voice trailed off. Were they listing to the port?

"Hey Cap'n?" asked one of the soldiers with rising panic. "Should there be water in the boat?"

***

"You didn't kill them?" asked Tessy wonderingly.

"Didn't have to," said Smalls with utter relief. "Just used Colin's idea and hit the boat right above the water line." And because he was also part of the kid's education team, he added. "Despite how fast bullets go through the air, which is a form of liquid—but more on that later—bullets slow down pretty much immediately when they hit water."

"So, that's why you had to shoot above the water?" asked Tessy carefully.

"Exactly," said Smalls. "And now…"

The Navy Engineer gestured happily as the soldier's boat started to sink in earnest.

"Now, let's get back to Pilot's House," he said.

"Aren't we going to go back?": asked Tessy.

"Not without half the Navy," said Smalls. "My job is to keep you safe."

"BUT! We gotta go back!" insisted Tessy.

"And we will," said Smalls. "I promise."

***

A piece of wood meant to hold up the wall in the Jellyfish broke in half as a bullet smashed into it.

"Damn it!" cried Singh. He leaned up swiftly and fired two quick shots. "We're going to have to start killing them in a second. 'Cause sooner or later, they're going to get lucky."

Liberty though was watching Uncle Danny's face. The

343

mischievous smile was growing across the Big Mexican's face.

The noise lessened as soldiers started to reload again.

"Don't you dare," said Liberty, even though she wasn't sure what his exact plan was.

"*Sorry, not sorry*," grinned Danny.

Singh was looking between them; about to ask.

Uncle Danny jumped up waving his arms.

"*Aye pendejos! Malgastes munición, por favor.*" And he ran swiftly to a jellyfish that was partially built.

"Get 'em!" cried Major Brightly. "Don't let him..." The rest of the words were drowned out.

Uncle Danny made a rude gesture and jumped behind a small pile of wood that barely gave him cover.

The soldiers unloaded on Uncle Danny's position.

Several tried to go towards him, but Liberty fired in front of them, so they were forced to scramble back to cover. But still they kept firing.

However, the machine guns soon began to empty.

"Out of am...," began Private Carroll, but his voice was lost in the din.

The noise swiftly turned to handguns.

A shout of 'Wait' came up from the soldiers. It might have been the Major.

***

Liberty looked over where Uncle Danny had hid. From her angle, she could see most of him. He looked back and saw her. Without breaking cover, the Big Mexican gave a big thumbs up. The Librarian responded with a different finger.

Uncle Danny shook with laughter.

***

"I'm out!" came Private Routtah's voice out of the gunfire.

Private Carroll caught Routtah's eye, and both, as one, looked back to the boats.

Major Brightly bellowed. "Wait! Where're you going? Stop Running Away!"

***

Captain Singh tugged on Ruiz's uniform.

"Be ready," he whispered.

***

Trying to keep low, Carroll and Routtah ran full tilt back to the boats.

"If he's mad," said Routtah. "We tell him that we were getting more ammo."

"That's true," said Carroll.

They were so focused that they didn't even see Tagg, crouched down, as they went by.

Stopping at the edge of the barge, they looked down at their boats. The soldier left to guard them, Thompson, looked up.

"Is it over?"

"Do we have any ammo down there?" asked Routtah.

Carroll looked at him.

Routtah replied to the look. "That way we can say we asked."

"Oh," said Carroll. "That makes..." He stopped and looked around. "Do you hear..."

One of their boats came around the edge of the barge, but it wasn't one of their soldiers.

Frankline slowed long enough to throw something into one of the boats.

"FIRE IN THE HOLE!" he cried.

***

Several soldiers were having too much fun firing their handguns.

Jumping forward, Major Brightly slapped down a soldier's gun, and then pushed down another.

"STOP! CEASE FUC..." A handgun went off. "...NG FIRE!!" screeched the Major. "EVERYONE STOP. JUST STOP!"

There was a large explosion from the end of the barge, followed by two others.

That distracted the soldiers enough that Brightly was able to pull them down behind the wood pile.

"Goddamn it!" snarled the Major. "When I tell you to STOP, you…"

"Stop," said Captain Singh.

The Major froze. Several soldiers started to put up their hands. But one was thinking of chancing it.

"Don't even think about it," said Ruiz, as she came around the other side of the pile.

Face twisting with anger, the Major glared at the Captain.

"How Dare You?" demanded Brightly as he started to rise.

Singh shot forward, but the barrel of his Beretta was utterly steady.

The Major froze at the gun in his face.

"We dare just fine," he smiled.

***

Carroll and Routtah had thrown themselves down when the boats had exploded.

"What the heck?" snarled Routtah.

They quickly started to stand when they found a big man with a storm cloud in his face and a nail gun trained

347

on them.

"You guys chased my kids away," said Tagg with a harsh growl that mostly just surprised him.

"Hey," said Carroll quickly. "They weren't supposed to do that. They were supposed to help us. We don't know what's up with them."

"For your sake, you better hope they're all right," said Tagg. "Now lay down and don't move."

"Heh," sneered Routtah. "That nail-gun won't kill me."

Tagg suddenly dropped the business end of the nail gun to right below Routtah's belt.

"True," said Tagg. "But how many shots until I puncture something important."

***

Below, Frankline brought his purloined boat around. He didn't see the two up above, but there was still one in the drink. The Private was relieved that the soldier had jumped clear. He didn't want to have to kill anyone, not if he didn't need to.

"Help...I can't swim too good," cried the soldier. He was floundering a little, but Frankline didn't want to take him on board, not until he was sure that everyone else was safe.

After a second of thought, Frankline used his purloined boat to push some debris towards the soldier. They immediately clung on to it.

Knowing that the water wasn't Titanic temperature, Frankline was trying to figure out where to go next.

Suddenly, a Librarian with a furious expression appeared at the edge of the barge with rifle pointed.

Frankline put up his hands. "Hey! It's me!"

"You have a boat," she said, mostly to herself. "Come around to the tug."

Turning, Liberty looked back, and part of her heart was thrilled that Tagg was okay. But she was still too worried.

"The kids?" asked Tagg.

While Frankline drove the boat around to the tug, Liberty gave a little kick to one of the soldiers laying down.

"Ow," muttered Carroll, mostly on reflex. He barely felt it.

"Up! Up! Up!" ordered the Librarian as she stepped back. "And hurry!"

They saw the fury in Liberty's eyes and scrambled up.

"Slowly!" said Liberty at the fast movement.

"But...you said to hurry," whined Carroll in confusion.

Now that they were up, Liberty did not answer. "Move!" She pointed her rifle towards the rest of the soldiers.

Carroll and Routtah moved as fast as they dared.

Tagg fell in beside Liberty.

"It's going to be okay," he whispered to her.

Liberty bit her lower lip, but her rifle did not waver. They soon reached the rest of the soldiers.

"Here are two more," said Liberty. "And there's one in the water hanging onto some debris."

"Is it safe?" called out Cassidy's tenuous voice.

"We're good," replied Singh loudly, without turning from his prisoners. "Best to keep everyone there. And Cassidy? Can you start taking us towards the carrier?"

They didn't hear a reply as Cassidy disappeared.

Uncle Danny walked up with a smug expression, but there was worry there too.

"I'll hit you later," she said.

"Any word from *los niños?*" he asked.

"Frankline has a boat," said Liberty.

"Oh, that's right!" growled Ruiz. "I need to kill him later for that damn fool stunt." She looked at Liberty, half-joking. "Don't let me forget."

"I'll hold him down," nodded Liberty, mostly joking.

"What's this?" asked the Captain.

They felt the tug's engines starting up and Cassidy was running up with the shotgun. She immediately stopped next to Singh and pointed her shotgun at the men on the ground.

"Glad to see you alive Tall, Dark, and Handsome," murmured Cassidy with relief.

Singh tried to speak, but he was tongue-tied once again.

Liberty jumped in.

"Captain Singh?" she called. "Do you have the prisoners?"

"Prisoners?" squawked Major Brightly.

The Captain ignored him. "The kids?"

Not trusting herself to speak, Liberty nodded.

"Go!" said the Captain. "We got this."

"Are you going after the kids?" asked Cassidy.

"You can come with," said Liberty.

With Will Holt driving the tug, Liberty led Uncle Danny, Tagg, and Cassidy into the waiting boat.

"We're In!" cried Liberty.

Frankline gunned the engine, and they flew forward before they had all gotten settled. Uncle Danny's arms pinwheeled and he fell into a heap on the bucket-seat across the back.

"Darn kid drivers," he smirked.

Trying to untwist himself, Uncle Danny had to flop around a bit to get himself seated properly. As he was doing so, he glanced at the Coast, but then did a double take.

"¡Mierda!" he breathed out.

There were birds above the City of Angels, and they were chasing someone through the air.

Climbing onto the back of the boat, Uncle Danny squinted, as if that could help him see better. Rak dove out of sight and the birds followed.

The Big Mexican's heart clenched with worry.

However, he couldn't ask them to turn around. Would Rakduson really want him to help her when the kids may be in danger? Still....it hurt.

351

Soon, Frankline called out and pointed. "We got people in the water!"

The Private slowed enough to properly see the men.

"Hey! Help us!" cried the First Soldier.

"Were you in a white boat behind a yacht?" asked Liberty.

"Um, yeah," admitted the First Soldier, and the Driver winced as he tread water.

Frankline gunned the engine, speeding around them. Nervously, he glanced at Liberty.

"I...I hope that was all right," said Frankline. "I just..."

"You don't hear me complaining," said Liberty with a cold voice.

Tagg had moved forward to be beside her. He gently rubbed her back.

"That's a good sign," said the Scientist.

Liberty could only nod.

Speeding towards the Fleet, they saw the Destroyer first.

"Is that...one of ours?" asked Tagg over the wind. He too was trying the squinting method of seeing far.

"I...I think," called back Frankline. 'I hope,' he added.

Glancing down, the Private tried again to find a radio, but didn't see one.

'Cheap-ass soldiers,' he grumbled to himself.

As they got close, the Destroyer set off their horn and Frankline slowed down next to it.

"Hey! Are you with the yacht?" asked one of the sailors.

"Yes! Are they okay??" asked Liberty.

"Sweet ride," grinned the sailor

Liberty ground her teeth and managed not to yell. "Are. They. Okay?"

"Who?" asked the sailor. "Oh! You mean the kids."

"I GOT THIS," said the voice and the sailor straightened immediately. A woman appeared and said to Liberty. "Your kids are okay, and the guy with them."

Immediately, everyone in the boat relaxed a bit.

"Sweet Jesus, thank ya!" cried Cassidy with relief.

"They should be close to the Carrier now, being escorted by two Coast Guard ships," reported the woman.

"Thank you," said Liberty. "Are you the captain?"

"Yes ma'am," replied the woman. "Captain Shannon Jones. And Captain Singh and the barge?"

Liberty told the Captain about the prisoners.

"We should get there sooner rather than later," said Captain Jones. "We don't want to push our luck."

Frankline whispered loudly to Liberty, who nodded.

"Oh! And there're some bad guys back there treading water. They were trying to steal our boat, with the kids," said Liberty.

"So, enemy combatants. We'll fish them out too," said Captain Jones, without pleasure. "I don't want to hold you up, if you want to head after the kids..."

"NO!" said Uncle Danny suddenly.

Without even slowing, the small boat flew past the men in the water. Liberty almost felt bad about that, but only 'almost'. Then she remembered something. Pulling away from Tagg, she went to Frankline.

"I'm sorry for being so order-y earlier," she said.

Frankline looked at her with confusion. "Wait. When?"

"When I ask...well, ordered you to go over to the tugboat," said Liberty.

"I don't remember," smiled Frankline. "And you were worried about your kids."

Liberty returned to the front where Uncle Danny was as well.

As they got closer to the Coast, they had to pass by the tug/barge which was slow going.

There was nothing happening above the city now, so they took a moment to drop off Cassidy to tell the rest about the Destroyer. As soon as she was off, Frankline raced towards Malibu Beach.

Liberty turned to Tagg.

"Are you sure you didn't want to stay?" she asked him.

The Scientist smirked. "I don't feel like working anymore today."

"Hey!" called Frankline over the wind. "She might be hiding."

Uncle Danny turned to him.

"She might be laying low right now," continued

Frankline. "Maybe if we could, I don't know…we can't call her…" He looked down. "Sorry."

"No Sorry Needed," said Uncle Danny, and he took a flare gun from one of his many pockets. It was designed to be lighter and easier to carry.

Readying the flare, Danny stopped to look at Liberty once more. She nodded in agreement.

As they got closer to the beach, the Big Mexican set off a flare. Excited, he watched the flare go up. It was a bright red in the blue sky.

"It's pretty," smiled Liberty.

Uncle Danny suddenly pointed. "I…I thought I saw…"

A bird roared up from between some buildings and then immediately dove again.

"There she is," cried Danny.

Reluctantly pulling a little away from Tagg and his warmth, Liberty took her rifle and looked through her scope.

"It's not Rak," said Liberty. "Holy Crap! That's the Lime bird that tried to get me in the hardware store."

"What?" asked Uncle Danny in surprise, looking more closely. They were closing in on the beach now. He squinted as hard as he could, but as the bird bobbed up and down, he could only catch a glimpse. "¡Neta! What's going on?"

The bird flew upwards, closer now.

"That is definitely not her," said Uncle Danny.

Running out of buildings, the bird with the Lime tuft

355

raced over the beach towards them. The birds chasing behind were getting closer.

"After she attacked me…," said Liberty slowly. She looked at Uncle Danny.

"Was she buzzing?" he asked, gesturing at the back of his head.

"Actually…," said Liberty, but then she nodded. "So, she wasn't in charge of her decisions."

"*Sí*," agreed Danny.

Lifting her rifle, the Librarian said.

"I'm going to fire and try to give that bird some room."

"*Por favor*," said Uncle Danny.

Liberty fired before the lead chaser, but that did not dissuade them.

Using a pincer move, the birds snapped down on Lime, grabbing her in mid-air. Four birds grabbed Lime in mid-air, but they kept flapping their wings to keep her aloft. The birds yanked her around viciously.

While they did that, other birds dropped, pulling in their wings. They shot right between the birds holding Lime aloft. When they were in striking distance, these birds lashed out with beak and claws to score hits.

Lime's beak was free, so she tried to get at them, but she was also getting yanked to and fro.

"*Du, Tass Ree*," cried Lime.

Hearing that cry, Liberty looked at Uncle Danny plaintively.

'What can we do?' her Look asked.

The Big Mexican shrugged. 'There is only one thing,' his reply came.

As one, *Dos Amigos* raised their weapons, ready to fire. Liberty aimed at one of the birds holding Lime's left leg. One leg would give her another weapon. Breathing out, she began to squeeze the trigger.

"Over there!" cried Tagg.

Liberty let up on the trigger and looked.

Swooping down, out of the glare of the sun, someone dove swiftly.

"RAK!" cried Uncle Danny with joy.

Smashing into one of the birds holding Lime, she knocked that one away. Rakduson spun around and managed to slash at another. As the two birds spun away, Rak snapped open her wings and flapped up.

One of the birds waiting to attack Lime came after her instead. But, as she was about to reach her, Rak pulled in her wings at the last moment and spun.

"*¡Hijole!*" breathed Uncle Danny.

Rakduson was suddenly above the other bird and pushed down hard on her back. Using that bird as a springboard, Rak shot up and attacked the last two birds holding Lime.

One bird let go of Lime's left leg to defend itself. The moment it did, Lime threw her feet upward and slashed with her claws at the last bird. They started to spin out of control.

As the last bird let go, Lime opened her wings and tried to stop her descent. But one wing was not quite working.

357

WALTER G. ESSELMAN

One of his former captors dropped towards Lime when a bullet went right in front of his beak. Frightened, the bird veered momentarily. But his purpose kept him on the hunt.

However, Liberty's shot did slow the bird long enough for Rak to catch up.

Using her claws, Rak slashed at the other bird's back. Not too deep, but the bird got the message and dove away.

Unable to stay aloft, Lime fell into the water. But she had managed to slow herself enough that it wasn't that bad.

More birds were starting in to finish the job. Rak veered towards them, gaining altitude.

Dos Amigos saw Lime struggling in the water, a mile from shore, and then at each other. There was the faintest nod of agreement.

Liberty whipped around. "Private Frankline, can you take us to that bird?"

"What? Seriously?" he asked. But he got the boat going.

Turning to Tagg, Liberty grimaced as she tried to smile. "Um, can you...?"

However, Dr. Tagg was already standing up. "Certainly...but I'm a human doctor..."

"It'll be enough," assured Liberty.

"Come on *mi hermano!*" smiled Uncle Danny. "We got this."

Frankline brought the boat in as close as he dared to the thrashing bird.

Uncle Danny and Tagg went to the very stern of the boat.

358

Dr. Tagg talked quickly, nervously. "They taught me in summer camp to never get near a person drowning. They can take you down with them. We need to throw something out to her."

"*Estoy de acuerdo.* Especially a drowning person with razor sharp claws. But what?" said Uncle Danny going back into the boat and looking in all the compartments.

"Maybe a rope," suggested Tagg worriedly as he heard shots from the bow.

A bird tried to dive in on them, but Liberty fired and got one of the pinions in his wing. Like the last six, the bird quickly flew away.

"I winged him," muttered Liberty, but then her eyes grew wide with delight. "Ha! I Winged him!" But there was no one around to share. Feeling a little cheated, she fired at another bird who had gotten a little too curious. The bird immediately flapped away.

Glancing up, she saw Rak above.

Rakduson was trying to dive in and around the other birds, but the Librarian knew that she could not keep that up forever.

Towards the stern, she heard Uncle Danny growl.

"*¡Pollas en vinagre!*" He could hear Lime's movements getting slower. Suddenly, he straightened. "I got it!"

Running back, Danny stopped at the stern while tying two life jackets together.

"I got some rope," announced Tagg.

They threw the life jackets near Lime, but it fell short. Her struggles were getting weaker. Reeling the jackets back in, Uncle Danny really heaved it.

The jackets nearly clonked Lime on the head. However, she put her left wing through the nearest life jacket and tugged.

Uncle Danny nearly pitched forward into the water. Tagg grabbed him, arms trying to go around the Big Mexican's barrel chest. Dr. Tagg pulled back with all his might and held Danny steady.

Hauling the rope in, Lime got closer.

A bird dove in skimming the water, Lime just managed to dodge fierce talons.

"Oh shit!" exclaimed Tagg. "That was too close."

As the Scientist held him steady, Uncle Danny poured on more strength to get the bird to the back of the boat.

"That bird. It's coming back!" cried Tagg too loudly, right in Danny's ear.

Wincing, Uncle Danny did not dare let go to get his shotgun.

This time, it was coming in slower, to assure a strike. Lime turned her head, ready to defend herself.

A machine gun roared beside the men, strafing the air in front of the attacker. The oncoming bird veered hastily and nearly went into the drink himself.

Frankline fired a few more rounds as it started to fly away, but purposely missing.

"Yay! You better run!" shouted the Private with glee.

Lime reached the back of the boat.

Letting go, Tagg went to drop the ladder.

360

"Not sure how this is going to work," said Tagg with an embarrassed and nervous smile.

As Lime pulled her wing out of the lift jacket, she clung to the back of the boat. Throwing the jackets and rope haphazardly back into the boat, Danny leaned over the stern towards the bird.

"Will you let us help you?" asked the Big Mexican, putting out one hand, but not too close.

Lime's brow furrowed, but then she started to lift her right wing. Her eyes shot open in pain.

"It's okay," said Uncle Danny soothingly. "We'll help you."

Between the three of them, they managed to get Lime into the back of the boat.

The moment she was down. Everyone jumped back.

Uncle Danny looked at the Private.

"Get us out of here!" said Danny, breathing heavily from the exertion.

Frankline didn't even answer.

Jumping into the helm chair, he shouted. "Hold on to your butts!"

Gunning the engine, Liberty had to dive into one of the bucket seats in front, or crash back down the length of the boat. She was a little annoyed at the lack of notice, but she twisted around and saw Lime.

The bird was huddled in front of the bucket seat in back, Uncle Danny and Tagg were on either side, having been thrown back.

361

The Big Mexican scrambled up and turned, waving his arm.

"RAK!" he shouted. "WE GOT HER! RUN! *ARRIBA!*"

Worriedly, Danny wasn't sure she could even hear him. Then he knew she couldn't, but he kept waving his arms.

Just as he was about to tell Frankline to go back, Danny saw a bird drop out of the air. His stomach dropped.

Wings snapping open, Rak gracefully skimmed the water and began to follow.

"*¡ÓRALE!*" cried the Big Mexican.

Coming back to the middle of the boat, Liberty gave a weary smile.

"Nooooooooooow, can we go see the kids?" she asked, half-jokingly. "I just need to see that they are okay."

Chapter Twenty

COLIN RAN AS if his life depended on it. He had almost gotten away too when strong arms snagged him, pulling him into their embrace.

Liberty hugged him fiercely.

"No running on the carrier," she whispered into his ear.

Pulling himself away, he tried to maintain his 11-year-old dignity. Colin looked up at her.

"They're doing it again," he said darkly.

"Doing what dear?" asked Liberty.

"The girls," he replied, imbuing 'Girls' with the same tone as one would speak of aliens, zoms, or other dangerous creatures.

"COLIN!" cried a voice somewhere near.

Liberty grabbed Colin and tugged him into a room, then shut the door behind.

"Have you seen Colin?" asked Tessy with an aggrieved voice. "Me and Mindy were just..."

"'Mindy and I' dear," corrected Liberty.

Making an unhappy noise, Tessy fixed it. "MINDY AND I were going to play an' we needed Colin, but he ran off. Didja see him?"

"Why don't you and Mindy play by yourselves right now," suggested Liberty.

Relaxing, Colin turned into the room and saw Uncle Danny, Aunt Rak, and what looked like doctors and patients.

Danny waved the boy over.

"...is stabilized," said Doctor Candleross, the Senior Medical Officer. "First time I've helped a bird."

"¡Neta, no manches!" commented Uncle Danny. "I understand."

"Routra dua?" asked Rak, but then she swiftly amended. "How hurt is she?"

Doctor Candleross, who looked like he was still getting used to a bird talking, nonetheless managed to answer smoothly. He had worked in too many ER's not to do otherwise.

"Multiple lacerations," he started, but could see Rak's brow furrowing. "Lots of cuts. Some deep. Is she going to be okay? When she wakes up? I'm not sure. We have locked her in one of the rooms for right now, just in case..."

"I will stay," said Rak. She tried to say, 'help' but it came out as 'helt', but she kept going. "I will assist. Make sure."

"Good," said Doctor Candleross, though he looked a little worried.

Colin jumped in and asked Rak. "Did you REALLY fight a whole bunch of birds?"

Getting out of the doctor's way, Rak, in her native tongue, English, and Spanish, explained. The rest of the birds had found out that the Lime Tuft bird was pregnant and came after her.

"Why should that matter?" asked Colin before Danny could.

"My people," started Rak, though it came out as 'heaple'. "They don't want anyone to be born to this life. Captive. Not free. So..."

"They tried to kill her?" asked Colin, completely horrified.

"¡Hijole!" muttered Uncle Danny. "Wait. If she still has the..." He gestured to the back of his head. "Then if the aliens set it off."

Rak nodded. "She will hunt. Why I need to stay."

"That's sad," said Colin.

"Only be little time," said Rak, consoling.

"Oh, I know you'll be back," said Colon. "But about trying to hurt the baby."

Rak gave a little noise. "When baby old enough, taken from mom and has device in back of head too. No life for child. No life for anyone."

Colin's eyes grew wide and blazed with anger. "What

the hell."

Uncle Danny put his hand on the boy's upper back, to comfort him.

Almost out of earshot, one of the doctors leaned toward another. "We would've been better off just dissecting the bird than saving it."

Rak stiffened and looked at Uncle Danny. She asked in a low voice.

"What is die-sect?"

"*¿Mande?*" he asked in confusion.

Colin chimed in, who had been working with Dr. Tagg. "It's like when you examine an animal after it's dead. Wh…?"

The boy didn't even get a chance to finish.

Rakduson let out a terrible noise and ran. Throwing out her wings, she bolted to the door leading to were Lime Tuft lay.

Whipping around, the bird went into a battle pose and shrieked hard.

The doctors and nurses scrambled away. Even a few patients jumped out of their beds.

Uncle Danny gripped Colin's shoulder.

"Colin," said the Big Mexican in a low voice. "I need you to go play with your sister."

"But…," started the boy.

"*¡Fíjate!* Please."

"*Sí*," nodded the boy. He turned to run, but Danny held him tightly.

"Slowly," said the Big Mexican.

Carefully, Colin went towards the door. He didn't think Aunt Rak would hurt him, but still, he reluctantly left.

Liberty was just coming in. "Wha…?"

"¡*Aguas!*" said Colin. "Something made Aunt Rak really, really mad. Like *Chancla*-mad. Uncle Danny wants me to go play with Tessy." The boy looked up hopefully.

However, Liberty helped move Colin out the door.

Uncle Danny took a few steps towards Rak who hissed mightily. Even he was a little nervous right now, not that he'd admit it.

"Hey Rak," he said.

The bird snapped at him.

"What's wrong with that bird?" demanded Doctor Candleross. "We might want to call for help."

Liberty turned to the doctors, nurses, and patients. "Shush and give him a minute," she said in her You-Cheesed-Off-The-Librarian Voice. She tried to remember the doctor's name but couldn't.

Gratefully, they all quieted down, at least for the moment.

Carefully, Uncle Danny took off his great yellow coat.

Rak eyed him.

Laying that on a bed, Danny sat down on the floor.

"What's wrong *mi amiga?*" he asked softly.

"Danger!" said Rak with a dark voice. Her eyes glanced at the doctor.

"What kind of danger?" he asked.

Rak was still glaring at the people.

"*Oye*, they're not going to hurt you," he said. "I won't let them."

Looking at the Big Mexican, Rak shook her head. "Not me."

"Then...¡*Hijole!* You asked what 'dissect' was?" he rose quickly so that Rak tensed. But the Big Mexican turned towards the doctors, nurses, and patients. Now, they faced an angry Uncle Danny as well. "My friend here mentioned the word 'dissect' before she got so angry."

One of the doctors tried to grab an unused IV stand but knocked it over in their haste.

"Shit," cried the doctor. "Sorry! Sorry!"

Doctor Candleross stepped a little forward. "WHAT? We would never do that. We just spent hours patching her up."

"And she's an expectant Mom," added one of the nurses.

Uncle Danny just glared menacingly.

Doctor Candleross turned to his people. "Well?"

One of the doctors, in a wretched voice, said. "It was just a joke."

"Just a joke?" asked Doctor Candleross who moved up to him and said in a low voice. "Go to your quarters. Do NOT leave until I tell you."

The doctor started to move quickly for the door, but Rak made an angry noise.

"I'd go real slow *cabrón*," growled Danny. "If you know

what's good for you."

Knowing what was good for him, the doctor went slowly to the door. Liberty scowled but moved out of the way.

Doctor Candleross also moved slowly to Uncle Danny and Rak and assured them.

"We're not going to hurt our new patient."

After a moment, Uncle Danny turned to Rak.

"What do you say?" he asked the bird.

Rak pulled in her wings, but she settled down in front of the door. "I will stay until she is better."

"It may take a week or so," said Doctor Candleross.

Settling in, Rak waited patiently.

Uncle Danny looked over at Liberty and went to her.

"I think she means it," he said softly.

"I Do," called out Rak.

Smiling, Uncle Danny looked over at her. "Will you at least accept some help?"

After a moment, Rak nodded. "As long as I know them. Trust them like Du."

"'Due'," asked Doctor Candleross.

"That's their God," explained Liberty. She looked between Rak and Danny. "I'm going to see if I can get some help."

Before Danny could say anything, Rak said, "*Muchos Gracias*."

The Big Mexican chuckled. "What she said *Mija*."

As Liberty headed out, she heard Dr Candleross telling a patient to get back in bed.

Out the door, Liberty first went to let the kids know where Uncle Danny and Rak were, but NOT to go in. She saw the barest flicker of a Look between Colin and Tessy. Realizing that she had just encouraged them to go check it out, she silently chastised herself, but she needed to go.

***

"Yi Fon."

Candleross jumped as he heard what sounded like another bird, abet a small one. He whipped around to see a little girl in the doorway.

"Tut oo Du?" asked Tessy of Rak.

***

A moment before, Liberty knew that she couldn't have them wandering around.

"Okay," she said to them. "Come on."

Colin and Tessy went wide-eyed.

"Mierda!" hissed the boy. "I think she reads minds."

"I know what that word means," said Liberty, giving Colin a sharp look who winced. "Come on! I still gotta go."

The kids got up and she took them back to the room.

"Now, I really do need you to stand out here," said Liberty firmly. "But actually, you could do something really important."

"What?" asked Tessy.

***

Now, Tessy spoke as fast as she dared.

"*Du foe,*" replied the bird indulgently. "*Hans som tut. Unteel cull tata.*"

Uncle Danny saw Liberty out in the hall.

'Can you...?' she mouthed silently.

The Big Mexican nodded.

"*Mah rust tutil,*" continued Tessy with a bright smile, still talking to Rak. And the little girl turned to Uncle Danny. "Right?"

Resisting the urge to fib, Danny shrugged. "Not sure I got all that, *mi mariposa unicornio.*"

"She said going to be good," translated Rak.

Uncle Danny turned back to the bird and smiled. "I agree." Returning to Tessy, he said. "And just so you know, the bird they brought in is pregnant."

Tessy let out an ear-splitting shriek of joy.

"Great," grumbled Colin loudly. "Now I'm deaf."

***

There was a rapid knock on the door, and everyone looked up in surprise.

"It's Liberty! We need help down in the medical place, or whatever it is."

Frankline jumped off the side of his bed and ran to the door. Singh almost beat him there.

"What's wrong?" they asked together when the door was open.

Liberty went into a rapid-fire explanation, which didn't quite make enough sense.

However, Singh just nodded. "Let us come with you." He turned to his men. "Let's check this out. Just sidearms."

"Umm," started Liberty.

Singh looked at her. "Orrrrr do you think a bigger show of force?"

"Yes please," squeaked Liberty.

"We'll get the Staff Sergeant as w...," started Singh.

"I'll get her!" offered Frankline and he squeezed out past Liberty, without touching her.

Shortly, Liberty guided them to the carrier's Hospital. Excitedly, Frankline moved to the front and reached the stairs. Not rushing, he was halfway down when he heard a wet pop in his left knee.

Stopping instantly, the Private's eyes widened a bit. Reaching out, he grabbed the handrail.

"Hurry up Private," snapped Staff Sergeant Ruiz.

"Um," said Frankline. "Can you all go on ahead? I think I need a moment."

Singh moved everyone past him but pulled in front of Frankline on the stairs.

"What's wrong?" asked the Captain as Dr. Washington stopped as well.

"Ummm, I think I hurt my knee," said Frankline, embarrassed.

"What?" demanded Ruiz loudly. "You're not serious."

"I...I don't know what happened," said Frankline. The words tumbled over one another. "I was just walking normally. I wasn't even going fast. At least, I don't think I was going fast."

"You *literally* just jumped off a barge onto a speeding boat," said Ruiz.

Without looking back, Singh said with a calm voice. "Staff Sergeant, you and I are going to accompany Ms. Liberty. Dr. Washington if you can help him along?"

As they kept going, Liberty had thought Ruiz had sounded harsh, but a quick glance showed a different story. The Staff Sergeant looked worried.

Unsure if she should say anything, Liberty led the two.

In the doorway, Tessy and Colin were trying to teach Mindy some of Rak's language.

Liberty stopped and had them move to one side but whispered.

"Thank you for staying in the doorway," she whispered, but sadly did not have time for a hug. She walked into the room looking at Danny. "I did manage to find them."

"¡*Órale!* That's Big," he said proudly.

"Right!" grinned Liberty.

Singh stopped a ways from Rak with the Staff Sergeant and nodded to the bird.

"Ms. Rakduson," he said. "I hear that there was an incident."

"One of my people, I'm afraid," said Candleross, who explained what happened. "They are now confined to quarters. But the rest of us do need to return to work. There are more patients."

Singh thought that 'patience' is exactly what the doctor was running out of.

"Okay," said the Captain, and he looked at Rak. "Would it be okay if we helped you?"

Rak tilted her head in thought, but then she shook her wings a little. "Okay."

Singh looked back at the Candleross. "How long will the other bird…"

"Tanidos," said Rak. "Tani."

"That Ms. Tani needs to recover?" asked Singh.

"And she's still susceptible to the device in her *cabeza*," said Uncle Danny.

"A secure room maybe?" suggested Liberty.

Rak started to open her beak.

"But *Not* a cell," insisted Uncle Danny. "That is *muy importante*."

The bird closed her beak.

"Of course," said Singh.

"We got your back," called out Frankline from the passageway. The Private was leaning a little heavily on Dr. Washington as they maneuvered into the room. Seeing a chair next to a bed, Frankline let go of Washington and hopped on one leg. He flopped down into the chair because the bed was up high. Straightening up, he could just look over the high bed. "Rak helped us, so we should help her."

"True," said Singh. "In part." As people started to look at him, the Captain continued, speaking to Frankline. "We're going to help Ms. Rak without question. But before that, we need to see what's up with your knee."

"It's nothing," shrugged Frankline, unconcerned.

Ruiz was suddenly standing over him. "No, it's not. You don't admit when you're in pain. So, for you to do so..."

Amused, Singh let those two bicker and turned back to Uncle Danny as Liberty walked over. "My team is also helping to still build the Jellyfish...but now that the barge is near the Carrier, we're not too worried about security." He smiled at that.

"If you can help a little," said Liberty.

"And we're going to help too," said Uncle Danny. Then he stopped to check. *"Perdón Mija.* If that's all right."

"Yeah, *Absoluto!"* said Liberty.

"We do need to clear it with the Admiral," said Singh thoughtfully.

"Of course," said Liberty, and her mind started to move swiftly. "I mean, maybe we would've been okay on our own. Actually, we should have looked at where we were

375

before bothering you." Feeling a little panicked, she looked at Singh. "Shoot. Maybe I overreacted. It's just that it might be a few weeks. An' I was just worried and trying to help Rak. And I'm sorry…"

"It's okay," said Singh quickly when Liberty took a breath. "Really. I'm just trying to take everything in, between Ms. Rak and my Private. But Ms. Rak has become a friend, so I want to help her too." He looked at *Dos Amigos*. "Doesn't she help you guard your boat as well?"

"*Sí*," nodded Uncle Danny. "She helps guard at night."

"That's important too," said Singh. "Especially…" But he stopped, not wanting to mention the two times that they had been boarded. "We'll have to look at that. And we won't be able to help on the Jellyfish as much." Unconsciously, he gave a sad, little sigh.

Liberty looked more carefully at Singh.

"You okay?" she asked.

The Captain immediately looked up with a chipper smile. "I'm fine. Wish we had coffee. First, let's sort this all out first, so I even know What to tell the Admiral."

***

"There's already a rumor that the bird, Rakduson, tore off someone's arm," said the Rear Admiral Antony Cirilo, with a mock seriousness. "Hopefully no one we liked."

"No one's arm got ripped off," said Captain Deep Singh quickly.

"Maybe a light disfiguring?" asked the Rear Admiral.

"Of course not," said the Captain.

"I was just joking with you," smiled the Rear Admiral.

The Captain's shoulders softened a bit. "Sorry sir...I just..." But he was at a loss for words.

"Why don't you start at the beginning," said the Rear Admiral

They sat in a small unused room.

Straightening, the Captain gave a precise account of what had happened.

"So, you wouldn't be able to help as much on the Jellyfish," said the Rear Admiral at last.

"Unfortunately," replied the Captain too quickly.

But Antony looked carefully at his friend. "But that's not what's really bothering, is it."

Singh looked up at him questioningly.

Antony gave a little smile, which felt like a rare sight.

"Are you worried about finishing the Jellyfish, or about disappointing someone on the tugboat?" he asked.

"What?" asked Singh swiftly with a frown.

"Did I tell you that I met Ms. Cassidy the other day," said Antony. "She and her nice daughter got the nickel tour. The little girl spoke Very highly of you. And as for Ms. Cassidy..."

"So?" asked Singh with a guarded voice.

"Just spit balling. I mean, if you were—hypothetically—interested in someone, you wouldn't be doing anything wrong," said Antony gently.

Singh's back stiffened and his eyes grew dark. "I don't know what you're talking about."

Antony put his hands up in supplication. "I'm just saying this as a friend. From what you told me, you were a great father, and the best..."

There came a pounding of footsteps, which distracted them. They looked up to see Liberty zoom by.

"Wait!" she cried.

They heard her come to an abrupt halt and then scramble back.

Red-faced and wide-eyed, Liberty appeared in the door.

"Oh. I almost forgot...," she cried. "They had asked about our boat, but I might have a better idea."

Chapter Twenty-one

RUNNING FOR DEAR life once again, Colin shot across the barge and rounded one of the wooden Jellyfish.

An arm swiped out and snatched him about waist.

"Hey!" cried Colin as he was pulled closer.

Worst of all, Liberty bent down and kissed him on the top of the head, *in front of all these people*.

"Not so fast," she murmured, enjoying a quick hug.

Regretfully, Liberty let the boy go.

Colin jumped a little away and quickly straightened his clothes.

"I didn't have a choice," said the boy defensively. "TessyMindy were whispering."

The adults around started chuckling.

"Oh No," said Private Frankline. "Not that."

Colin whipped around. "You don't know! Whenever *They* start whispering, they are Plotting."

"Now plotting!" said Dr. Candleross.

"Yes, Plotting," said Colin, getting upset. "An' it never goes well for me when they do."

Liberty stepped closer. "It's okay. Go find a safe place, if they come by, we'll distract them. I'll give 'em hugs."

Colin grinned and turned to go.

"And stay away from the wedding cake," she called as the boy disappeared into the crowd.

All the nearby Jellyfish were lit with anything Liberty and Uncle Danny could scrounge from the Coast on short notice. But, it had turned out really nice. Especially in the late evening when the sun had almost set.

Liberty pirouetted back to the people that she had been talking to.

Dr. Candleross turned to Frankline, who was leaning heavily on a crutch. The doctor smiled. "I heard you fought tooth and nail for this barge."

"I don't know about that," shrugged the Private. "It wasn't that bad."

"Is that where you hurt your knee?" asked the *Roosevelt's* officers, Rando.

"Oh!" said the Private, embarrassed. "Um..."

"¡Oye!" cried Uncle Danny suddenly appearing. He looked at Dr. Candleross. "Didja hear what happened to the guys who attacked us?"

Dr. Candleross looked curious. "I heard that they were dropped off by their island."

Uncle Danny gave a hearty laugh. "But how they were! There was only the boat that Frankline had taken, with Great Courage."

"And could have gotten himself killed," grumbled Ruiz, coming up beside Frankline.

"What is life without a little danger?" asked Uncle Danny.

"Have you been drinking?" asked Liberty, but she tried to keep the disapproval out of her voice.

"Dr. Tagg let me have one," said Uncle Danny. "But I haven't had anything in a while, sooooo whatever that fruit juice was, *might* have been stronger than I thought." He grinned sloppily.

Despite herself, Liberty matched his grin.

Turning with a flourish, Uncle Danny said. "And Liberty...she is vicious when she's mad."

"¡Aguas! She gets scary," agreed Colin, who had suddenly returned, figuring he was safest by her.

Liberty looked down at him. "Hey!"

Colin craned his head to look up and replied plaintively. "What? You do."

"And do you know what she is capable of?" asked Uncle Danny melodramatically, pulling everyone back into his story.

"They threatened my kids," grumped Liberty, a little embarrassed.

"They Did! And we had all these soldier-wannabees... Gravy Seals! An' we were trying to decide what to do with them," said Uncle Danny, enjoying himself. And he was enjoying himself so much that Liberty did not protest any further.

"Drop them on the Coast?" asked Colin with rapt attention.

"We thought about that," smirked Frankline.

"But The Liberty!" grinned Uncle Danny. "She declares, in a voice as cold as the depths of Hell, that we should tie them up and send them back in one of their boats." He gave a dramatic pause. "Piled on top of one another like firewood." He gave a final pause. "But Without Their Pants!"

Everyone started laughing, except Liberty who blushed a little.

Thoroughly amused, Colin looked up. "You didn't?"

Liberty responded by giving him a little hug.

"That was Dope!" crowed Frankline.

"Remind me not to piss you off," laughed the Rear Admiral.

"I was just so mad," mumbled Liberty, though no one quite heard.

"¡Chido! What do they say...," asked Uncle Danny. "Hell hath no fury."

There was a shout from further down on the barge, opposite the tug.

Captain Singh called out.

"WE GOT TROUBLE! TEAM! TO ME!"

***

Shortly before, Captain Singh had been sitting on the edge of the barge.

A little aways from the crowd, he looked over the edge. The water lapping at the side was comforting.

"Um...," started a voice.

Singh looked right up, pulled from his blues. His heart skipped and he was momentarily at a loss for words.

Cassidy was standing there.

"Um," she started. She had an old dress, but it had been scrubbed clean for today. Then her words tumbled out. "Did you want to be alone? Or are you avoiding me? That's Okay if you are! I can give you your space. I'm sorry. I just get over-excited, an' I'm going to stop bugging you."

Cassidy began to turn away.

Singh's heart jumped, but this time in fear.

"No," he said quickly, almost desperately.

Turning in surprise, Cassidy looked at him, a little cautiously.

Unsure of how to even begin, Singh went with easy.

"I...maybe I need some 'over-excited'," he said.

Cassidy's eyes shot up in surprise. "Really?"

Shrugging, Singh said. "Honestly, I was kinda moping a bit."

"You? Moping? Never," smirked Cassidy.

Gesturing that she could sit beside him, Singh was about to say more, but then he noticed her clean dress.

"WAIT!" he said.

Cassidy froze. "What?"

Singh scrambled up and she almost took a step back.

"You need something to sit on," he said quickly. He was soon back with a mostly-clean piece of cardboard, but he was still brushing it off more.

Setting down the cardboard, Singh sat next to it.

Thanking him, Cassidy sat down and looked out at the water.

"Beautiful," she murmured.

Singh agreed, though he was not looking at the water. Suddenly, he remembered himself and hastily looked forward.

"Um...," he tried. He was not even sure what to say. Again, he decided to go for Easy. "I lost my daughter...and my...wife I guess, in a car accident."

Turning, Cassidy looked at him with wide concerned eyes. "Were they fleeing the zoms?"

"Oh No!" said Singh. "It was before." His eyebrows knitted. "It's been three years now."

"You must miss them," said Cassidy softly.

A smile hit his eyes with some sadness. "You know what my favorite memory of my daughter is?"

"Please," she replied.

"So, my wife was out of town...," he started. "She was out of town a lot in our last few years together. So, one Saturday morning, Harita—my daughter—declared that we needed to see all the Transformers films."

"You're kidding?" she asked.

"I know," chuckled Singh. "I have no idea where that came from. The thing was, her mother had a house rule that Harita, and really anyone, was not allowed to watch movies until after dinner."

"Butttttt," smirked Cassidy.

"A solemn oath was given," said Singh with a booming voice. "If she didn't tell, I wouldn't."

"Oh my," she said, leaning towards him. "And did you watch them all?"

"Well, there are a lot," said Singh. "But we watched a bunch. Ordered pizza as soon as the place was open and ate that all day."

"Sounds like fun."

"It was. It was so worth it. Even when my wife found out."

"She didn't? How?"

"I...," began Singh. "I don't even remember. But it wasn't because either of us blabbed."

Cassidy laughed.

"Harita was gone, not too long after," said Singh softly. "Sometimes...sometimes I think about how I would feel if I had said 'no'. If I..."

"But you said 'yes'," said Cassidy earnestly. Her

385

expression grew serious. "You and...Harita, right? You had a marvelous day."

Singh's shoulders relaxed. "I guess..." His eyes snapped out to the sea. In a second, he was on his feet.

"What?" asked Cassidy.

"Can you go back to the rest?" asked Singh. "We got trouble and I...I really need to see you safe."

Cassidy looked at him for a moment, but then she nodded. "I'll get Mindy."

"Thank you. And Tessy if they're together," said Singh as they moved quickly back to the crowd. Shortly, the Captain called out. "WE GOT TROUBLE! TEAM! TO ME!"

There was an immediate response. A small part of the crowd surged towards him.

Liberty and Colin reached them first. She was about to say something when she noticed Colin right by her side.

Eyebrows furrowing at him, Liberty asked. "Where do you think you're going?"

"Um....," began the boy.

Liberty looked at Cassidy and asked. "Can you do me a huge favor?"

Cassidy was already reaching out. "I got'em. And your weapons are still on the tug in their usual place."

"ThankYouThankYou," said Liberty.

"¡Órale! I second that," said Uncle Danny as he arrived. He looked at Colin. "Take care of your sister."

"Do I have to?" asked Colin.

"Do what your Uncle Danny says," insisted Tagg as he ran up.

Liberty looked up at him. "Can you...??"

"You...you just be safe," replied Tagg. They wanted to embrace, but there was no time. Looking down at the boy, he surged. "Come on Buddy."

Tagg took Colin and followed Cassidy to find the girls.

The Rear Admiral arrived, walking more slowly, with Frankline on his crutches and Ruiz, who wouldn't leave him.

"Thank you, Captain Crozier," said the Rear Admiral on a walkie-talkie. "Let's see what they want first."

"I got our rifles," called out Dr. Washington. He stumbled up leaden with M4 rifles and his medical, Unit One Pack. "Please take them!"

Ruiz stepped forward immediately to ease his burden.

"Thank you," said Singh as he was handed a rifle. He held it in his good hand, more for a show of force, than anything else.

Dr. Washington looked at Liberty and Uncle Danny.

"Sorry," he said. "I didn't see your weapons."

"No worries," said Liberty. "They just got put in another spot."

"Okay," said Captain Singh.

"Oh! He's using his 'Authority' voice," smirked Liberty. "We better pay attention."

Captain Singh gave her a look of mock annoyance and continued on. "Right, as I was saying...Frankline, I want you by the wedding guests near the other side of the barge."

"Sir?" asked Frankline, but then he quickly recovered. "I mean, Yes Sir!"

"Just in case someone tries to surprise us by sneaking through the boats there," said Ruiz to Frankline in a hurried whisper.

"Oh. Yeah, that makes sense," he nodded.

Frankline slung his rifle and moved off quickly on his crutches.

"Everyone else, with me," said Singh, but then he noticed his audience. He looked at the Rear Admiral. "If you please sir." And to Liberty and Uncle Danny. "Please?"

They quickly returned to where Singh and Cassidy had been sitting.

"We better not bunch up," suggested Ruiz, and they settled with her on one side and Dr. Washington on the other with their rifles.

Singh whispered to the Rear Admiral beside him. "Do you want to speak, or...?"

"Let's have you start," replied Cirilo. "Then we can escalate. Continue as you see fit Captain."

The Rear Admiral lifted his walkie-talkie. "Mr. Crozier. We have six smaller boats flanking a bigger boat, maybe for fishing, that's seen better days."

"Much better days," commented Singh.

"We see them," replied the captain of the *Roosevelt*, Crozier, over the walkie-talkie. "And we don't see any others."

The small group of boats had started to slow down.

"Show of force," said the Rear Admiral. "Or, at least they're trying." He shook his head sadly. "Senator Butterfett is in front of the bigger fishing boat." He continued sadly. "And he's got a megaphone, just in case."

"Let us know about the Contingency," replied Captain Crozier.

Singh wondered what the Contingency was but didn't have time.

The Senator's fishing boat was just now in shouting distance.

"This is a Private Event," called out Singh. "Only those with an invitation can attend."

A small '*snerk*' of laughter came from the Rear Admiral, but his face did not change. He held the walkie-talkie close to his chest.

Immediately, Senator Butterfett began to sputter, and speak, but the ocean ate up his words right away.

The Rear Admiral said, trying hard not to reproach. "That might antagonize him more."

"He's already antagonized me," grumbled Singh.

Butterfett finally remembered that he had a megaphone.

"Who are you?" cried the Senator.

Singh spoke loudly, not needing a microphone. "This is not a good time to talk. If you want to set up a better time, at a mutually agreed-upon, And Neutral, location. I'd be happy to listen."

"We don't have time for pussyfooting around," cried the Senator. "Do you know who I am?"

"Isn't that the guy that the Captain got injured while saving?" asked Liberty from behind.

Singh didn't answer and continued. "Or you can send us a message by paper or radio," continued Singh.

"I think so," said Uncle Danny. "An' that *pendejo* doesn't even recognize him."

Butterfett sputtered. "NO! No. No. This isn't some sissy diplomatic mission. I'm here..."

And in the overly dramatic pause Liberty whispered. "Is he posing?"

Butterfett finished. "...To Save The People Of This Fleet."

Several of the soldiers in black, who flanked Butterfett, nodded enthusiastically. This went double for the big muscle-bound man at the Senator's right hand. Butterfett's fishing boat had started to drift closer to the barge, and it was easier to hear them.

Singh's brow furrowed. "From what?"

With a condescending tone, Butterfett laughed. "Oh, you poor sap. From all this." He made an expansive wave with one arm and almost hit the muscly guy next to him. "From this decadence. From this waste, as people eat avocado toast and smoke dope all day."

"I'm not sure what you're talking about," said Singh. "We don't have any avocados. We're growing Kale here."

"Whatever Kale is," said Butterfett dismissively.

"That's what I've been trying to get you to try," said the

muscly guy earnestly.

"Not Now Bartholomew," said Butterfett, a little too loudly. He turned back to his megaphone. "We need to reclaim America! Now! So, we are here to bring these poor people home."

"By home...?" asked Singh.

"We have a great plan to take back Our America, starting with the City of Angels," said Butterfett. "I am here to help this motley group of ships and lead them to something greater."

"Help how?" asked Singh.

"I'm going to show them that we don't have to take this, living on avocados and weed," cried Butterfett, even though he didn't need the megaphone anymore. "We can be the vanguard to take back our great nation."

"Wait?" asked Singh. "Are you talking about using the people in the Fleet as soldiers?"

Butterfett rolled his eyes. "Haven't you been listening? Lift up that turban so you can hear properly. This is America."

"*Hay días tontos y tontos todos los días,*" growled Uncle Danny.

Singh whispered. "I got this." To Butterfett, he said. "Only a few of these people have ever really fought. Most just did what they could to survive and get here to safety. Some were lucky enough not to pick up a weapon at all."

"We would give them training," said the Senator defensively.

"Am I the only one getting *reaaaal* tired of that

391

megaphone?" asked Liberty tartly.

"*Sí Mija*," growled Uncle Danny.

"Throwing these people out onto the Coast will have a high cost," replied Singh.

"Which is regrettable," said Butterfett solemnly. "But the more people we have, the more territory we will gain. And this is preferable to wasting their life here."

"I assume you'll be on the Carrier, safe and sound," said Singh.

"Monitoring and Coordinating!" corrected Butterfett quickly. "And I won't rest until we have achieved our mission."

"While people die on the Coast," said Singh.

"You can't make an omelet...," smirked Butterfett. "Now, the admiral should send out word of our new mission. And that I am here to take control." He looked directly at Cirilo. "Your Country appreciates the work that you have done. So, let's get to the *Roosevelt* and make this happen."

The Rear Admiral stared at the Senator.

Butterfett scowled. "We need to go. Time is wasting."

The Rear Admiral gave a little smile and said. "No."

The Senator blinked and leaned a little forward. "What was that? You need to speak up."

"He said 'No!'," supplied Singh.

"Wha...what?" sputtered the Senator.

Uncle Danny blinked. "¡Neta! He seems genuinely surprised by the answer."

"How curious," continued Liberty.

"WHO DO YOU THINK YOU ARE?" screeched the Senator, still using his megaphone. "YOU WORK FOR ME! NOT THE OTHER WAY AROUND! AND NOW YOU ARE HAMPERING A VITAL AMERICAN MISSION!"

"I wish I could've voted against him," said Liberty with a dark voice. "But he wasn't on my ballot."

"Agreed," smiled Singh.

"THAT'S IT!" cried the Senator. "ADMIRAL CIRILO, YOU ARE RELIEVED OF YOUR COMMAND. AS OF THIS MOMENT, YOU ARE CONFINED TO YOUR QUARTERS UNTIL FURTHER NOTICE." Butterfett pointed towards the carrier.

The Rear Admiral did not move, but he gave those near a quick warning.

The Senator's eyes bulged. "DO YOU HEAR ME!! RIGHT NOW!!!"

Lifting up the walkie-talkie, the Rear Admiral said. "Now Mr. Crozier."

While the Senator took a deep breath to keep it up, there was a loud boom from the carrier.

The muscly guy, Bartholomew, grabbed the Senator.

"INCOMING!" cried Butterfett's soldier as he shoved the politician to the deck, forever infused with a fishy smell.

However, the shell went way behind them.

The Senator looked up and saw everyone staring at him.

Smirking, Liberty gave a little wave.

Eyes wide with fear, the Senator realized that the muscly

393

guy was still on top of him.

"GetOFF! Get Off!" growled Butterfett, and he scrambled out from under the muscly guy, still clutching his megaphone.

To the Rear Admiral, the Senator began to laugh melodramatically.

"HA! HA! HA!" he cried without his megaphone. "You Missed!"

"Um...Sir," said one of the Senator's soldiers, pointing behind them.

Ignoring his soldier, Butterfett screeched. "That's why YOU are NO LONGER IN COMMAND OF..."

A large wave, born out of the Navy shell, slammed into the smaller boats.

This mini-tsunami bounced little boats around, some crashing into one another. One was immediately flipped, jettisoning its people.

The Senator's fishing boat shot forward and collided with the bigger barge, which barely seemed to notice.

Butterfett was thrown forward across the deck. His megaphone fell from his hand and bounced to the edge of the boat.

"Yes! Yes!" said Liberty excitedly as she took a step forward. "Fall over!"

The megaphone stopped right at the edge, teetered for a second, but stayed aboard.

Liberty let out a curse.

Uncle Danny looked at her in surprise.

Giving him the side-eye, Liberty said, a little defensively. "What? I'm allowed a naughty word now and then."

Raising his hands in supplication, Uncle Danny said. "Just surprised me, Mija."

"Sorry, that megaphone-thing was just really bugging me," said Liberty.

"It's a power move," said the Rear Admiral. "Though, not a really strong one."

Captain Singh chuckled. "Not like a makeshift tsunami."

Despite himself, a little smile escaped the Rear Admiral, but then he quickly shoved it back into place.

The Senator lifted his megaphone triumphantly and brought it to his moist lips.

"AH-HAH," cried Butterfett with a sneer. "NICE TRY. BUT THIS OLD WARHORSE IS NOT GOING ANYWHERE."

"I thought you never Served," called out Singh with a look of faux confusion. "Because of a spastic colon."

The Rear Admiral looked at the Captain questioningly who shrugged.

"That's what I remember."

"IT'S IRRITABLE BOWEL SYNDROME. AND IT'S A REAL PROBLEM!"

Rear Admiral. "I'm not sure that's better."

"He might've still been able to join," mused Singh. "And that's the only time I've ever heard of him having it."

"I don't know that I'd talk about it much," suggested the

Rear Admiral.

"True," admitted Singh.

"PAY ATTENTION WHEN I'M TALKING!" screeched the Senator.

Singh looked up. "You know, you don't have to use the megaphone. We can hear you well enough."

"OKAY!" cried the Senator. "OKAY! I WAS GOING WAIT UNTIL WE WERE INSIDE—PRIVATE—SO AS NOT TO HUMILIATE THE ADMIRAL, BUT YOU'VE LEFT ME NO CHOICE."

"Did we really leave him no choice?" asked Singh.

"Apparently," said the Rear Admiral.

Singh pointed. "Um, you still have men in the water."

"THEY'LL BE FINE," sniffed Butterfett. He pulled a bunch of papers from his pocket.

"Oh-oh," murmured Singh.

"Maybe he'll tire out sooner, rather than later," said the. Rear Admiral.

"No," said Liberty with a cold, flat voice. "He's having too much fun."

The Rear Admiral looked towards her, but she was suddenly gone.

Uncle Danny just appeared to notice. "*¿Mande?*"

"THESE POLICIES ARE HEREBY INSTITUTED FOR THIS COLLECTIVE OF NAVAL AND CIVILIAN BOATS, HENCEFORTH KNOWN AS THE FLEET...," cried Butterfett.

"And Army, Marines, Air Force and Coast Guard!" called

out Singh.

"WHAT?" asked Butterfett in confusion.

This pulled the Rear Admiral's attention away, so he didn't see Uncle Danny melt away into the background.

"It's not just the Navy," explained Singh with an earnest expression, as if he were trying to help.

"SHUT IT!" snapped Butterfett. "NOW WHERE WAS I?"

Bartholomew piped up. "Henceforth the Fleet."

The Senator lowered the megaphone long enough to shush the muscly man. Then he raised it again.

"...THE FLEET WILL HENCEFORTH BE UNDER THE UNDER THE COMMAND OF THE CURRENT PRESIDENT OF THE UNITED STATES OF AMERICA, WILBERFORTH FRANCIS BUTTERFETT."

"Wilberforth," began Singh.

"Francis?" finished the Rear Admiral.

"FIRST POLICY!!!"

***

"THIRTEENTH POLICY!" called out Butterfett.

"How many are there?" moaned Captain Singh in misery.

Elsewhere, Liberty took a little breath and exhaled it.

"THERE'S WAY TO...," began the Rear Admiral.

The megaphone in Butterfett's hand exploded, due to a .

397

308 bullet passing through the main body of it.

Before the Senator could react further, he was once again thrown to the ground.

"Get Us Out Of Here!" cried Bartholomew, who was atop the Senator.

The pilot didn't need to be told twice.

"What're you doing?" screeched the Senator. "I wasn't done..."

The rest of his tirade was cut off by the roar of the fishing boat as it backed away. One of the flanking boats was still capsized, but they left it. As the smaller boats turned, the Rear Admiral had a chance to look at them.

"That wave really did a number on those boats," he commented drily. "I'm surprised that that one over there is still afloat."

Not a moment later, the pathetic fleet stopped so that the soldiers could abandon that very same boat. The boats surrounding it huddled, as if embarrassed.

"Anything interesting happen while I was away?" asked Liberty casually from behind.

With a smile of pure mischief, Librarian sauntered up with Uncle Danny. Slung across the back of her nice dress was her sniper rifle.

"The Senator's megaphone exploded," commented the Rear Admiral with a casual tone.

"What?" asked Liberty with mock surprise. "However, could that have happened?"

The Rear Admiral gave a dry laugh. "We may never know."

"Oh poop," said Liberty. "I hate a mystery."

"I don't know *Mija*," smiled Uncle Danny. "Where would we be without a good mystery now and then."

"ADMIRAL! ADMIRAL!" cried a voice behind them.

Everyone swung around, ready for trouble.

But it was the HairArtiste, Renoir, bounding up with his beautiful bride, Dr. Milton, close behind.

Renoir clapped a hand on each of the Rear Admiral's arms and beamed.

"You have not only given us fireworks for our wedding," cried Renoir joyfully. "But a show to remember."

"We aim to please," shrugged the Rear Admiral, who did step away from Renoir's near embrace.

The HairArtiste immediately turned to his new wife.

"Oh! But your feet must be hurting. With all this walking around," he exclaimed. "Let me find you a seat."

Bouncing off, Dr. Milton just smiled. "Not the wedding I envisioned as a little girl...but I wouldn't trade it for all the scientific equipment in the world."

***

Uncle Danny was carrying Colin, who was almost asleep, back onto the boat while Tagg had Tessy.

"I can carry someone," insisted Liberty.

"*¡Órale!*" was all that Uncle Danny said.

"I'm enjoying this," smiled Tagg.

Liberty huffed, but did not argue any further.

Chapter Twenty-two

A VERY DISGRUNTLED Private watched the small boat approaching. He was not amused by his current posting. Despite having a .50 cal Browning machine gun at his fingertips, he did not even go near it. Some things were not even to be joked about.

The Private's heart skipped a beat when he saw the Staff Sergeant in the boat. But he restrained himself.

Below, he heard Liberty giving an exclamation of joy.

The Private assumed that there were hugs involved. Possibly even bear hugs.

After a few moments, Captain Singh and Staff Sergeant Ruiz appeared. On the helicopter pad, a Private was sitting on a rather comfortable chair, which he felt vaguely guilty about.

Immediately, the Private stood up, a little awkwardly with his crutches. Leaning on one crutch, he managed a salute.

"At ease Private," barked Captain Singh. "Sit down and rest that knee."

Frankline hesitated.

"That's An Order!" continued Captain Singh.

Practically dropping, Frankline sat back down.

"How's the knee," asked the Captain.

"It's better," replied Frankline with immediate enthusiasm. "I'm ready to come back."

"Lying to a superior officer?" tsk-tsked Staff Sergeant Ruiz.

Frankline gave her a disapproving Look.

"Don't you give me that," said Ruiz with authority, but there was a smirk there. "You're no good to us broken."

"I'm Not Broken," replied Frankline hotly.

Liberty squinched her face. "You're a little bit broken, sweetie." However, she quickly added. "But you'll be better soon."

Frankline's face grew pinched. "Not soon enough. Besides, the Captain did jungle warfare with a fractured arm."

"Ah," said Singh. "The difference is that none of you outranked me."

"I wish I had," grumbled Ruiz with a pointed look at him.

"Fair enough," chuckled Singh. "It might not have been

one of my best moves, but it all turned out okay."

"Not for me," said Frankline with almost a whine.

"Well, we really appreciate you being here," said Liberty earnestly.

"Actually, the Rear Admiral and I are really happy to have you here," said Captain Singh.

Liberty looked at him in surprise, but the Captain kept looking forward, almost embarrassed.

"Because of the invaluable assistance of Ms. Liberty and Unc...," began Singh, but then he scowled. "MR. Danny! It is important that they receive a higher level of security."

Frankline gave a little sigh. "Which is me?"

"Of course," sniffed Singh, and he glanced at Ruiz. "I mean, it's not the kind of job that you can leave to just some private."

"Oh No," agreed Ruiz swiftly. "Privates can barely tie their own shoes."

Liberty spine straightened. "Excuse me." Her eyes narrowed at the Captain and the Staff Sergeant.

Singh saw the look and a little smile escaped for a second, which made Liberty pause.

Despite his best efforts, Frankline's face had gone red with embarrassment and growing anger.,

Turning to the Staff Sergeant, the Captain said. "Thankfully Corporal Frankline will be able to help *The Wolf Pack* out."

"I agree completely," nodded the Staff Sergeant with mock seriousness. "As I stated earlier to the Rear Admiral,

Corporal Frankline is the best man for the job."

Liberty was grinning ear to ear now.

"Wait. What?" asked Frankline, confused.

Ruiz leaned towards him, unable to hide her grin any longer.

"You got a promotion dummy," she cried.

"Wha…What?" stammered Frankline.

"I'm so happy for you!" burst out Liberty and she jumped forward to hug the Former Private, now Corporal. Jumping back, Liberty continued. "I gotta tell Danny!"

Leaving them at a run, Liberty started to go down into the ship but screeched to a halt.

Turning the Librarian called back. "OH! And you're all invited to dinner! Now a celebration!"

With a joyful whoop, Liberty spun around and dove into the ship. Her mind ablaze, several threads going at once.

Deep in the ship though, she heard voices and realized that Uncle Danny was in trouble!

The Big Mexican was conducting a Bible class with the kids. Despite her near-explosive joy, Liberty made herself slow down, curious to be a fly on the wall. Not that didn't trust Danny, but she usually didn't have time to sit in on his lessons.

"…that's weird right?" asked Colin.

Liberty could imagine the cute little frown on his 11-year-old face, an image which he wouldn't appreciate, but tough beans kid. He was adorable to her.

"Well…I…," started Uncle Danny.

"I mean, in the Gospel of Luke, Jesus and his family stay in Bethlehem for 40 days, but in Matthew, they go run off to Egypt, an' then stay there a couple years."

"Ah...um...," continued Uncle Danny. The great warrior was unsure of what to do.

Liberty heard her friend's rising panic and leapt into the room. She dove behind Colin.

"Cuddle Attack!" she cried.

Wrapping her arm around the boy from behind, he cried out.

"Mom! Stop!"

But he didn't struggle too hard.

"Annnnd," said Liberty to the boy. "It's, 'they HAD to run off to Egypt AND stay there a couple OF years."

"MOM," whined Colin.

Liberty suddenly let him go and grabbed Tessy, bearing her to the ground.

"You thought you could get away from me, did you?" asked Liberty like a proper villain. "I got you now."

The little girl squealed with delight.

"¡Aguas! There's no hugging in my classroom *Mija*," said Uncle Danny, who had recovered. Now had a great big mock frown on his face.

Liberty looked up from Tessy, but she didn't bother to get up. And the Little Girl seemed content.

"I got...," started Liberty, but then she glanced at Colin. "I HAVE a good reason." And she told them about Frankline's promotion.

Suddenly, the Librarian sat bolt upright.

"Smalls," she said.

"*Mande?*" asked Uncle Danny.

Liberty got on her hands and knees and crawled over to Uncle Danny to whisper urgently. Though she did stop before she was tooooo close.

"*Sí, SÍ*," nodded the Big Mexican after a quick exchange.

"We can ask for that for our next job," suggested Liberty.

"No," said Uncle Danny, shaking his head, face serious and scowly. "We go over there soon. Maybe even today."

Liberty grinned.

"What're you guys talking about?" asked Tessy.

The Librarian looked back at them. "A surprise for Mr. Smalls."

"You mean a promotion?" asked Tessy.

"Duh!!" grumbled Colin.

Turing to sit on the floor near Uncle Danny, Liberty looked at her son. But the Big Mexican got there first.

"Don't say 'Duh' to your sister," said Uncle Danny.

"Why Not?" barked back Colin.

"Because a real *Hombre* doesn't need to belittle those around him," said Danny. "It shows that he is insecure and weak."

"I was just saying…," grumbled Colin.

Tessy looked at her Uncle and Mom.

"It's okay," said the Little Girl meekly.

Liberty looked at her. "No. You are not a doormat, and you deserve to be treated with respect."

"Look at Captain Singh," said Uncle Danny. "A real *Hombre* if there ever was one…except for me, of course. But he never belittles others…"

The Librarian nodded. "Yeah…and he doesn't let people be mean to him."

"Or" continued Danny. "He calls them out for their meanness."

The kids looked away from Liberty and Danny, thinking about what they had said.

Leaning towards the Big Mexican, the Librarian whispered.

"One of these days, we might Not be able to use Captain Singh as a shining example," she said. "Not that he's going to do anything bad, but that kind of thing only works for so long."

"That's okay, *Mija*," smiled the Big Mexican. "We'll think of something."

Which made Liberty smile again.

Epilogue

"RAK! RAK! RAK!" cried Smalls as he burst into the Hospital on the Carrier.

The large bird was suddenly on her feet, wings spread and ready for danger.

"Danger?" asked the alien-bird.

Smalls immediately skidded to a halt. "Oh No! No! No danger. Everything's cool."

Rakduson relaxed a bit. She was still parked in front of the door, guarding the alien-bird behind it.

"I'm sorry," said Smalls quickly. "No, it was good news."

"Good?" asked Rak.

"Well, for me," said Smalls. "I got a promotion. Liberty and Uncle Danny went and talked to the Rear Admiral

Himself!!"

"That's good," nodded Rak, a little sluggishly.

Smalls was about to say something when Dr. Washington appeared at his side.

"Did I hear something about a promotion?" asked Aaron.

"Oh yeah," grinned Smalls. "For saving the kids...not that I expected anything for that...I mean..." He faltered.

"If you expected something for saving the kids," said Washington. "Than you would not have been the right person for the job in the first place."

"I guess," said Smalls. "Still, it's good to be acknowledged. I mean, Liberty gave me a hug that nearly broke my back, and I think Uncle Danny did crack a few bones when he shook my hand..."

"It's well-deserved," nodded Aaron. "Now, what're you doing here? You're not here to do guard duty for Rak, because I'm supposed to have this shift. But since she's still there, I'm helping out with patients."

Smalls looked from the doctor to the alien-bird.

To Rak, he asked. "When was the last time you had a break?"

The alien-bird looked away.

"I don't think she's had a break, at all," said Washington with reproach. He looked at her. "And since I've bound your wounds in the past, that technically means I'm your doctor."

Rak turned her head, on her long neck, to glare at him.

"You can look at me All Day Long," huffed Washington. "Doesn't make it not true. Or do you got another doctor out there."

Huffing at this, Rak still wouldn't look up.

"And you look tired," continued Washington, and he glanced at Smalls. "We tried to get her some food."

"What?" exclaimed the Navy Engineer, and he looked back at the bird with annoyance and concern. "What're you doing?"

The alien-bird looked away again. "Must pro-tect."

"And Aaron can't do that?" asked Smalls, gesturing at Washington. "I mean, Really?"

Rak did not reply.

"OKAY!" said Smalls. "We Are Having An Intervention."

The alien-bird looked at him in confusion.

"An Intervention is when you step in because your friend needs help," explained Smalls.

"And sometimes people can't see what they are doing to themselves," added Washington.

"Let us help you Rak," said Smalls earnestly.

"As your doctor, I recommend some food and a little shut eye," said Washington.

"Shut...?" began Rak.

"Sleep," amended Washington smoothly. "You can sleep here in the hospital, after you eat of course, but you have to sleep."

"But...that man," said Rak. "He might harm them."

411

Then she looked around wearily at the medical staff and patients. "Or...."

A little hitch of breath and Smalls smiled. "No one's told you." Turning away from Rak, he looked at the doctor.

"She didn't want to talk to me," said Washington, a little defensively.

"No, no!" said Smalls as he put up his hands. "I'm not blaming anyone."

"Uncle Danny has next shift, so if all else failed...," began Washington. "Heck, if I'd known that he was here..."

"I know," said Smalls. "And they're probably on their way back."

Rak stuck her head forward. "What? What is going on? Baby safe?"

Smalls straightened up and turned to the alien-bird. "Do you know what a Baby Pool is?"

The alien-bird just frowned and waited.

"There is an Earth tradition that when a baby is about to be born," said Smalls. "People pick, first the day the baby is going to be born, and then the time of day."

"How do they know?" asked Rak, curious.

"They don't," added Washington. "I picked next Tuesday at 5am, because my Mama had me at 5am."

Rak reared back a little in surprise.

Smalls put down his cardboard box on an empty bed and ran over to a doctor.

"Excuse me?" he asked. "Are you in the Baby Pool?"

Dr. Patel glanced past Smalls to the alien-bird.

"I'm just trying to help," said the Navy Engineer earnestly.

"I took this Friday at 6:04pm," said Dr. Patel.

Thanking her, he went to a patient. Soon, everyone was calling out their guesses. Turning, Smalls saw that Rak's eyes were as big as saucers. He walked over.

"And I picked two weeks from today, at 1pm," said Smalls.

Before the alien-bird could reply, one of the doctors called out. "Rakduson should give a guess too."

"I don't know," said a patient. "She might know exactly how long till the baby is born, since she's the same species."

"Who cares?" called out another patient. "It's just for fun."

"I wonder if we can get a Baby Cam," suggested a nurse.

As they all spoke animatedly with one another, Smalls turned Rak.

"Noooooow, will you let Dr. Washington cover," said the Navy Engineer. "An' I'm going to take you to the Mess and get you some food."

Rak thrust out her abdomen in surrender. "Am kinda hungry."

"Well, we only got Navy food, but thankfully, there's plenty of it," said Smalls. "An' I'll join you, 'cause I oddly miss the food here."

Dr. Washington put his hand to Small's forehead, as if to check for a fever.

"You feeling okay?" asked the doctor.

Smalls laughed and ducked away. "I'm fine." He reached out, slowly, to guide the bird to the door.

As soon as she was away, Washington was back with his M4 rifle. Rak hesitated a moment.

The doctor looked her square in the eye. "I will guard her with my life."

"Thank you," said Rak.

"We take care of our own," nodded Washington seriously.

Smalls kept guiding her out the door. He was talking quickly.

"I have some ideas for blocking the device in the back of head," he said. "But I got a few more questions on alien... well, your physiology."

"Fizz-E-Ol...," started Rak,

"Your body."

Their voices faded.

Doctor Patel pumped her arm in the air in triumph. 'Good Job,' she mouthed with lovely lips.

Washington smiled.

On one hand, he was thrilled that Rak was going to finally get some food. On the other hand, they'd gotten her out so quickly, he forgot to ask to hit the bathroom first. Especially with Dr. Patel in the room.

'Luckily', he thought. 'I got a bladder like a camel. But I hope they're not gone too long'.

FIN...
For Now!

Easter Eggs

Dr. Patel won the baby pool, and the Crew was delighted to get a baby cam.

Mother and little fuzzy baby are doing great.

Dr. Milton, on other hand, flat out refused a baby cam.

Creator - Type - Person

CIRCA. 1994

NOT THE COOL BLACK DUDE

Walter G. Esselman

THE AUTHOR

NOW LEVEL 53

ADHD LEVEL: HIGH

MISSES: TRAVELING
WITH CAIT IN FALLOUT 4

WALTERGESSELMAN.COM

After winning the Open Contract Challenge in 2021, Walter G. Esselman had his first book, "SuperhorrorMax", published. Since then, "Liberty's Run" 1 and 2, have come out. He also has an art project , "Catmandu", about a CatGod coming to Earth. You can see more on Instagram,

Walter G. Esselman

Catmanduforyou. Walter's favorite game is probably "Fallout 4", especially if he is with Cait; and he wouldn't say 'No' to a banana daiquiri.

www.ingramcontent.com/pod-product-compliance
Lightning Source LLC
Chambersburg PA
CBHW051436260626
47162CB00001B/117